FINDING THE FIELD

An adventure of body, mind and spirit

Michael Brown

Other books by Michael Brown:
The Weaver and the Abbey
The Weaver's Apprentice
The Idiot Played Rachmaninov
Taming of the Crew
Speaking Easy
Media Easy

To my family

This is a work of fiction. No character is intended to represent any living person.

PART ONE

PROLOGUE

As he stumbles, the rifle smacks against a jutting rock. He resumes his pace immediately, without inspecting the butt or the telescopic sight for damage. A ravine cuts across his path, its sides too steep to scramble, and he turns instantly along the bank. His boots continue to lift and drop, the earth keeps rolling under his feet. He cannot stop; if he stops, he will think.

His breath is ragged, his jaw slack, his thighs trembling even as they tighten and thrust him forward. He has not eaten for two days, because he gave his supplies away to a party of hikers caught out in rough weather. He could just as easily have shot them. But he can barely remember it now, let alone make sense of it.

His mouth is dry, the back of his tongue sticky with mucous. Since dawn, he has scooped water from niggardly melt streams or snapped icicles off overhanging rocks. He's vaguely aware that he is moving west. Which is not important, but perhaps, when the time comes, when he arrives at the required state, he will sneer into the face of the setting sun.

The wind ceases whining, slowing to a fitful breeze that fumbles around his ears. Gravity strokes his bones.

The last time he stopped was the evening before, high on a mountainside, far above the affairs of humans. It was only then that he knew his real purpose. But he decided it could wait until the morning, and passed the night wide-eyed but unseeing, on his back, in a cave too mean to allow him to roll over. As first light cribbled onto the ledge, a chamois sprang down beside him, then doubled away in panic. When the rattle of hooves faded, he unwound his limbs and stood up, with his rifle and his rage. He peered down to the blackness of the valley floor and imagined men walking there, hunting him like an animal. Saw himself firing on them. Saw their bodies, mouths agape, rolling slow in the floodwaters, down to the sea. Saw sharks ripping at them in such frenzy that only a few pieces reached the bottom to make slow-motion explosions in the silt.

Then his rage returned him to the mountain ledge and to his original purpose. He shut his eyes and imagined it over and over, but his muscles would not yet perform the simple action involved. So just before sunrise, he strapped rifle to pack and resumed his journey.

Now, he knows what he must do; he must push himself beyond mere fatigue, even beyond exhaustion, until he reaches the necessary state of detachment. Then it will be easy. And with the sun lowering in the sky, that state is close.

He stumbles out across a steep scree slope, boots shifting in the sly stones, rifle in the downhill hand.

ONE

I scowl through the north window, at the storm front strutting through the mountain peaks. It mounts the closest ridge, straightens its grey-blue cape, then topples forward, hollow-bellied over my valley, closing down the far places first: the sunset over the Tasman Sea, the hair-thin surf line, the coastal plain and the distant, salt-and-pepper houses of Hokitika. When only my hanging valley is left in the world, the first snowflakes come casting about, scouts before the invasion.

Then the fall begins in earnest. Early twilight turns the farm into a grey and white snapshot stuck to the outside of the window. There's a moment of vertigo; if I close my eyes, I will fall forward and become part of the image.

Across the pasture, the alpacas look about them with lofty disdain.

Above me, claws scrape on iron roofing. There's a flash of orange and olive green past the eaves, and a thudding of wings. The keas are back, Rangi and Papa. These puffed up mountain parrots think my roof is an amusement park. In the evenings they launch themselves sideways down the corrugated iron, fall off the end, recover in squawk and flurry, then swagger along the ridgeline to take the ride again. Soon they discharge ululating blares of pleasure and flap away, shrinking to micro-dots in my window, then vanishing altogether. Tonight, they will drop to the flats to look for newborn lambs, some of which will lose their eyes before dawn.

I cross to the opposite window, on floorboards that complain to the silence even though they are made of heart *rimu*. Visibility to the south is down to a few miserly paces, begrudging me a glimpse of even the closest trees. No clues there. On the outside of the glass, fat snowflakes hang in a cobweb. The spider is a compact black star, motionless between silk and glass, patient beyond time and desire.

Something is going to happen. I know it. I have known it for days.

I flick the light switch. No power. Which is not a surprise; the power line didn't wait for the snow, it capitulated in a blow two days ago, and is probably still hissing under a fallen tree on the road through the bush. And now the snow will make the road impassable—a gratuitous act of nature because my ute lies in pieces in a repair shop down in Hokitika. It snapped its drive shaft negotiating potholes on the very same road.

A run of mishaps like this is unusual.

I lift the phone; there's still a dial tone.

You can call me Jack. It's less complicated that way. I have seen seventy winters, half of them here in the Southern Alps. No doubt you think that is old, but apart from minor irritations, such as a bladder the size of a walnut, my health has never been better. And except for the vagaries of weather and transport, my control of my own universe is comprehensive.

My head is a shiny brown dome, on which you can see from almost any angle whether the electric light is on or off. It is off. My only head hair is my eyebrows, which stand so far out that neighbours in the next valley suggested I avoid taking them outside in a strong breeze. Just behind my right ear I have a scar, from the accident: a depression the size of a fifty cent coin and deeper than the width of my little finger. An old crater, preserved on the surface of the moon.

You might think that my bone-and-gristle body could use a good meal; but you would be wrong. I eat well. And besides, in these ranges I can still out-walk men half my age. My back is like a cricket bat of best willow, my stomach is flat, my thighs lean and calves taut. There's still fire within this leathery sack that passes for skin.

Yes, I know. I'm boasting. If I stop and listen carefully, I am sure to hear Siobhan laughing.

Manuka logs crackle in the fireplace and their sweet fragrance fills the room. I have noticed, this winter, that when I burn manuka, field mice run in the ceiling. When I am still, the sounds of tiny paws nudge the threshold of hearing. Only for manuka. Why? Do they run towards the fragrance or hide from it? Perhaps it sends them into some ecstatic, excuse-me rodent dance in the attic. But not now; in this deep cold they will be huddled in a squirming lump, one body with many ears and eyes and inquiring noses. Like the mass of humankind.

When I stop tenanting this body—if all goes well, that will be in a few months—I will leave it on the flat rock that juts out into the farm reservoir. I can only just see it now, through the murk, covered in white. The blarney rock, Siobhan called it. Instead of leaving my atoms to work their way up the food chain, the birds and mammals of the forest will use my form to directly sustain their own. Tibetan monks had such a relationship with vultures; in their case, it was to make sure there was nothing left to bind the soul to earth. I plan to leave my flesh on its back, with arms and legs spread, like Da Vinci's Vitruvian man. A whimsical vanity.

So, you see? Not only boastful but also vain. You may even think me arrogant, but while I would enjoy your good opinion, I don't need it. I have my music, my alpacas, and the mountains and bush.

Boadicea glides out of her basket by the fridge; that location is her joy and her torment, a hint that heaven and hell might have the same address. She stretches, a slow wave passing down her orange and white feline spine. I reach down to stroke her back, and when I stop, she punishes the withdrawal of love by hissing at me and lunging at my ankle. I return the sentiment and we hiss and lunge at each other until honour is satisfied, then she lies on the sheepskin near the hearth and watches me, chin on paw.

She is a three-scar Amazon: she has one down her side and front right leg, another across the top of her head, and the third diagonally across her face, leaving her nose askew and her lip with a permanent sneer. I found her over in the Hooker Valley, a feral kitten trying to chew sustenance out of *kanuka* bark. When I picked her up she became a skinning machine, so I peeled her off my hand and dropped her into my pack. As I walked the track, I was impressed by how much thumping, ripping and squealing can come out of one half-grown kitten. The pack lining was destroyed, so I named her after the first century Icenian noblewoman who fitted scythes to her war chariots and laid waste an entire Roman legion. Even the powerful keas keep watch for Boadicea; I have seen her flow into a kea committee of ten and register a point of order with deadly effect.

"Hey, Boa."

I pick a scrap of paper off the table and throw it at her. It misses, bouncing into the fire, and her sneer deepens. Her eyes twitch restlessly.

Why this feeling of apprehension? Or is it anticipation? It can't be the weather; my heart does not beat faster for a snow shower. I dislike the not knowing. I dislike the lack of control. I have sent the obvious question, but the field has not yet answered.

The falling light has stolen another shade of white from the walls. But when I turn back to the window, the light stands spare, pretending innocence and waiting for my attention to wander. I like this limbo between day and night, so I will delay switching on the generator. I like the sounds that seed the silence: the creak of the house, the crackle in the hearth, the clunking, measured authority of the grandfather clock.

The clock is hand-crafted in solid mahogany, with carved

wooden horns that give the machine a devilish aspect. The mechanism rested for many years, but that changed the morning I carried Siobhan out of the house for the last time. At her insistence, I held her in a standing position while she inserted the key, willed strength into her wrists, wound the main spring and swung the pendulum into motion. Then I carried her to the waiting station wagon, with its rear seats down, mattress and pillows ready. Now, every seven days, I wind the clock for her and the pendulum marches on, doling out time. The tick asks, the tock answers.

I have become a time-serving anachronism in my own house.

I do still see myself in the stuff of wealth—in the Renoir and the Rubens, the antiques, the Italian leather suite and marble fireplace—but I'm also detached from it all, perhaps like Nero contemplating the seeds of decay.

Many of the luxuries are gone. They gave us pleasure in their time, until we found greater pleasure in riches that cost little or nothing. Even so, I have kept the *kauri* colonial furniture, the oil-fired oven, and the first edition novels from three centuries, pages yellowed and rag-edged and smelling of old glue. The ceiling-high bookshelves were never big enough and books lie about in crooked, hopeful stacks. On the mantel, dusty chess pieces await new orders to attack, the Indian hourglass aches to be turned, and a globule of ancient kauri gum holds a hornet, sting extended, imprisoned forever in its present moment. Above the mantel is the oil painting Siobhan brought home from Devon: a clipper ship skippered by her great, great grandfather. It soars, every stitch of its exuberant canvas spread for the pleasure of the trade winds. But what the frame really holds is Siobhan's love of the ocean. When she was with me in the flesh, she would only live in a house which looked out to open sea.

I have a fantasy that when I exit, the farm, the house and

contents will all somehow dissolve away, leaving the valley as it was before man arrived in this land.

Now there's a thought. If it all dissolved away right now, what would I truly miss?

Not much. The alpacas, of course, and Boa, and Sheba and the hens. I would miss the clipper ship, the brass sextant, the globe of the earth, and Siobhan's pear wood spinning wheel. And I am attached to the grand piano: an original J. J. Hopkinson, half a world and half a century from its birthplace, lifted up here by helicopter. I polish the black lacquer every morning, so I can see Siobhan's photograph reflected in the surface. Sometimes I turn the frame upside down so that it is her reflection that looks at me right side up.

TWO

When I woke from the coma, thirty-seven years ago, I was suspended in a warm sea, an ether, a vast force field so subtle, so penetrating and pervasive, it did not stop where my flesh started, but went through my atoms like mist through the stars. Nor was the force field passive; rather it was keenly aware, rich with intent, and brimming with powerful, limitless possibility.

I know... you think I was addled by the post-anaesthetic honeymoon, or by the chemicals dripping into my forearm. Or by the hole in my head and the brain damage. But I was not. Unlike the drugs, my field would not fade away.

The field is my first memory, since waking. It's my first memory of anything.

Yes, do the arithmetic.

I was in a hospital, that much was obvious from the clinical aromas. Staff walked in and out of my room, careless with their words and sounds, with their small collisions with the bed, even with my body. Lift wrist, measure pulse, drop wrist, perform ritual duty to the empty shell. No one home. No one expected.

But I'm here.

Yet I held my tongue, because they were all doing something that puzzled me. Even with my eyes closed I could tell that although they were walking around in the intelligent field, they were somehow unaware of its existence. I mulled on the meaning and got nowhere. Why was the field not obvious to them? Is a fish aware of the sea it swims in? Perhaps not. I opened my eyes, saw a crack in the plaster between wall and ceiling, then the door, the bed curtain, the back of a nurse writing on a clipboard, the sage green linoleum, all suspended in and penetrated by the field. An impressionist watercolour leaned out from the wall above the nurse: a punt, gliding, poled by a straw hat and striped white shirt and the merest suggestion of a man—hardly more than the simple brush strokes of a child.

Simple. I said the word aloud.

The nurse spun around and gasped, "You're awake." Which I knew. And she rushed away with the walk of one forbidden to run. The matron and ward sister arrived at equal speed, and the matron also informed me that I was awake. She felt for my pulse, took my temperature, shone a light at my pupils, looking for more convincing evidence of my arrival.

"You've been asleep for a long time, young man. Can you hear me?"

I said yes, and asked if there was a river nearby. But she recoiled, put one hand on a hip and shook her head at me slowly.

"I can't understand a word you're saying. Try again."

I did.

"Well, never you mind. You just rest now and you'll be talking like a pro in no time."

So, I was fluent in gibberish—I was a working mind with a wastrel tongue. I deposited that lucid thought in what turned out to be a remarkably small bank of personal memories.

A nurse checked the wound on my head and rewound the bandages. My right ear hurt, my left shoulder, arm and leg tingled. All day, people in uniforms stopped at the door to gape and when the curtains were drawn, peered round them. When they saw me looking back they nodded uncomfortably and moved on, talking in tones of incredulity.

A uniformed policeman appeared, stared as if I had green skin and pointed ears, then sat in the corridor where he could keep an eye on me. He removed his helmet, read magazines, paced, and attempted conversation with every nurse younger than his mother—which amused the nurses and wound up the matron, who was not younger than his mother. As she swept past, she snapped, "He's not going anywhere, you know; it'll be weeks before he can even get out of bed."

"Orders," the constable shrugged. But at the end of his shift, he was not replaced.

The day after that—around the time a thrush landed on the window sill to preen and poop—my synapses fired the correct volley in the correct sequence. Thoughts and tongue became family, though my tongue was, at first, the country cousin. My first clear words were, "Good morning." Hardly profound, but the effect on the attending nurse was gratifying. Within moments, staff were around me again, with mobile patients peering at the door, warily, as if I might leap out of bed and frighten them.

And not one person showed any awareness of the field. What was wrong with them all?

Two senior policemen came to question me, only to be warned by the ward sister to keep it brief. Their manner was a curious mixture of approval and disapproval; but the approval vanished swiftly when I didn't know what they were talking about. And they kept calling me by an unfamiliar name: Fleming. It meant nothing. So they opened the top drawer of my cabinet and helped themselves to a wallet, which contained a driver's licence with the same name. Conrad Fleming, d.o.b. 20th of August, 1941. One of them thrust that in front of my face and said that if I wasn't Conrad Fleming, then what was I doing with his wallet? So could I just drop the act, then we could all get on with the business in hand? But the name was an empty web, catching nothing but the breeze. The police glanced at each other, then informed me that this little charade would just make the court go harder on me.

A headache began to grind forward from the back of my skull. The sister reappeared with her jaw prominent and the police departed, talking about security and locked doors, leaving the air heavy with unfinished business.

A surgeon came, trailing matron, sister, staff nurse, student nurses and a committee of the curious. He was openly admiring. "You, my friend, must have a special arrangement with the Almighty. You do you realize that you have a bullet in your head?"

A bullet? Immediately, the wound behind my right ear ached, calling for my hand, which rose from the sheet and moved vaguely upwards. Surgeon and matron exchanged glances.

"Obviously you don't." He held up an x-ray, which featured a white deformed shape like a twisted *huhu* grub. "Here it is. I really don't know why you're alive, except that it had to be a ricochet. The bullet was on its last legs. What happened?"

My head seemed so heavy it might fall off my shoulders, and my body flushed hot and cold at the same time. Someone had shot me? Why? But no answering images came. When? Where thoughts and memory should be was only grey fog. I found my voice and asked about removing the bullet.

"Forget it," he said. "We've taken out a few bone fragments, but that bullet is way beyond reach and if you get an infection from it you'll die." He didn't notice the matron wince. "If you don't get an infection, well, we don't know what will happen because this is new territory. You're an interesting case, young fella."

The police returned, glanced in at me, talked at length to the matron, then went away.

The medical school neurology professor who came next could barely contain his excitement. For my benefit he had persuaded someone in the hospital's medical illustrations department to make a drawing of the deformed bullet pushing up against two brain organs, one shaped like an almond, the other like a croissant.

"To the best of our knowledge this is a world first," he gushed. "Look here. The bullet is touching the amygdala, which is the source of your emotions, and the hippocampus, which is the key to your memories. We don't know what will happen with your emotions, but damage to the amygdala is associated with borderline personality disorder, which... well... you already... I mean... I'm not really qualified in the mental health arena..." He broke off, embarrassed, then brightened. "Anyway, one of the possibilities is retrograde amnesia."

"Ah," I said.

"And you can't remember anything? What's the last thing you remember?"

"Uh..." I said.

"Fascinating," he responded.

I didn't tell him about the field.

Nor did I tell the clinical psychologist, an elderly man with a kindly face and a body rounded by the pleasures of food and drink. He was armed with word association devices, deceptively simple questions, and a sibilant stutter. From his first question he showed he was smarter than most.

"Do you *want* to recover your memory?" he asked, watching me carefully.

"Yes. I suppose so. I want to get out of here."

"Why do you want to get out of here?"

"I... I don't know."

He wrote a note, then looked up. "I'm interested in anything you can remember about your s... self before you were shot. Even a s... single fragment could be useful."

I gave it serious attention, though it hurt to concentrate. All I could see was a grey, fuzzy wall.

"No," I said. "I can't remember anything."

"All right. What's s... six times four?"

"Twenty-four."

"Where were you born?"

Blank. "No, nothing."

"When did Neil Armstrong walk on the moon?"

"Nineteen sixty-nine."

"Where were you on that day?"

Blank.

"What does it cost to post an ordinary letter?"

"Eight cents if it's a health stamp."

"When you were a child, did your mother ever catch you raiding the biscuit tin?"

Blank.

"What's the most exciting thing you ever did with a friend?"

Blank. "There's nothing there," I protest. "I can't remember."

After a barrage of such questions I told him I knew what he was doing. He smiled, not at all put out. "S... say the first thing that s... springs to mind for these words: Happy?"

"Smiling."

"S... sad?"

"Crying."

"Angry?"

"A bear in a dentist's chair, having a wisdom tooth removed."

"Girlfriend?"

"Yes please."

"What do you think of Valentine's day? Do you ever buy the cards? Or do you ignore it as a commercial enterprise?"

That was cunning of him, but it was another blank.

"S... sex?"

"Yes please," I said sourly. "But not with you."

He grinned. "I can live with the disappointment."

"You're trying to manipulate me through my emotions," I accused him. "So I'll either remember or reveal myself as a fraud."

"Are you a fraud?"

"No. I'm just fed up with your questions."

More notes. Turn the page.

"All right, can you tie a bow knot?"

Well, that was different. I looked at my hands, raised them slowly and demonstrated on my pyjama cord. He asked if I could describe making a cup of tea. No problem; I even twirled a finger to mime turning the pot three times clockwise. He was becoming seriously thoughtful.

"So, if I can remember that sort of thing, does that make me a fraud?" I demanded.

"No," he said. "But it's too early for a judgement."

On the third session, he ambushed me, starting with photographs.

"Who is this?"

"The Prime Minister, Norman Kirk."

"And this?"

"Dame Te Ata, the Maori Queen."

"This?"

"Andy Leslie. Captain of the All Blacks."

"These?" He showed me a middle-aged couple. Well dressed, conservative, the usual say-cheese smiles. I had no idea who they were and said so. He pushed the photo closer to me and said, "Pretend that you do. What sort of people might they be?"

Blank.

"Would they be the sort of people who would love you or hurt you?"

Blank. "Why are you showing me these people? Who are they?"

"They were your parents."

"What are you playing at?" I would have laughed, but feared a bolt of pain.

"How do you feel about your parents, Conrad?"

"I just... I just need to think. Hard to think... I'm a bit tired..." He watched me closely, as I tried to pull a memory of my parents out of the fuzzy, grey wall. After a while I stopped trying and stared ahead.

Then, Sister was in the doorway. "Mr Filer, *please.*" It was a command.

"Of course." He made a final note, slipping the paper into a manila folder, which had the same empty name, Conrad Fleming, on the front. He nodded warmly to me, shook my feeble hand, wished me well, and left. Small beads of sweat broke out on my forehead. Sister frowned at my pupils and checked my pulse.

"Right. That's it for you. No visitors for three days, except immediate family."

The reference to family turned out to be an academic clause. Not that I could have responded anyway for the next twenty-four hours: headaches tried to squeeze the brains out of my eyes like toothpaste out of twin tubes.

***

A forensic psychiatrist bustled in, navy suit, white blouse with pearl buttons, and square-rimmed glasses. As she sat, her cheerful smile seemed genuine. Another manila folder lay neatly in her lap, determining the future liberty of the person with the eggshell name. *Hello, is there anyone in there?*

She asked even more questions than the psychologist and with each visit, her folder fattened.

On the third visit, she produced a mirror from her purse. Would I like to see what I looked like?

I thought about that. I felt puffy around the eyes and the nurses had told me I was still severely bruised; so I knew the sight was not going to enhance my recovery. That settled it. I averted my eyes.

She nodded, then put the mirror away, in her briefcase.

"Would I have cracked the mirror?" I croaked. "Or am I the fairest of them all?"

"Ask the mirror," she grinned. Then, lightly, "Did you have that story read to you as a child?"

Blank. There was only the fog in which nothing moved.

The detectives returned, and she took them out into the corridor and whispered intensely to them, a sure way to make me hear every word.

"If he's faking it, then he's Oscar material. His intellectual function is unimpaired, speech and language functions unimpaired, social function unimpaired, humour somewhat juvenile but unimpaired. *However,* he has complete, global, retrograde amnesia on anything relating to self identity. Utterly fascinating, medically very exciting. It's new ground. It's going to make a priceless contribution to our understanding of the nature of ego."

There was a shuffling of regulation police shoes and a voice asked her to please restrict herself to the Queen's English.

"Yes, of course. I mean it will help us understand what we mean when we say 'I'. It will break new ground, there's going to be a flood of international interest. We're already getting calls from-"

"Doctor. Please-"

"All right. Look, he is essentially a new individual in his own right, developing new memories. Don't you get it? The personality growing on that bed didn't exist at the time of the crime. He's innocent."

For some reason the police still seemed reluctant to order champagne. Is that what she would say in court? Yes, she certainly would. Was I safe to be let out on the street? No evidence otherwise, and it was going to be months before I saw the street anyway. As for memory returning, well there was nothing in the literature to help her with a prediction.

"Anyway," she added, dropping her voice even further but still not enough, "if the bullet decides to go walkabout in his brain, he could be dead in minutes."

The police conferred, then departed, and she returned to my bedside with a grin of satisfaction.

"All without a word of a lie. How much did you hear?"

"Enough."

"Good." She beamed. "So, you understand the significance of what's happened to you."

"I'm getting the picture."

"Are you tired? Can we keep going for a moment?"

"Keep going."

She declared that she had begun writing a research paper that would make medical history. It would make me as famous as Phineas Gage. Gage, she enthused, was a much admired, railway construction gang foreman in America. On the 13th of September, 1848, in a moment of uncharacteristic carelessness, he set off an explosion. A three-and-a-half foot, fifteen pound tamping iron passed through his head collecting his pre-frontal cortex on the way. Somehow, though measured for a coffin, he survived; but his personality was utterly changed, his self-control left to the scant mercy of whatever primitive feeling was running through him at the time. That led to understanding the link between the pre-frontal cortex, the seat of conscious will, and the amygdala, the seat of feeling. She reminded me that my own amygdala was, at this moment, up close and personal with a bullet—her tone suggesting a new type of erotic activity.

I shook my head. "No thank you."

"No?" She was confused.

"No, I won't contribute to your paper."

She was shocked. "Isn't that a little...?" She gold-fished, unable to find the correct word.

"I need to recover in my own way."

Now she was puzzled. "Are you worried about privacy? This will just be for clinicians. I can guarantee anonymity. I'll change your name."

"I guess you mean that name?" I pointed to the manila folder. There it was, Conrad Fleming, like a bubble around cold breath.

She understood immediately, and in desperation dealt her last card. "Understanding you could help many people." A low blow, that was... one small step from emotional blackmail.

But I wasn't angry. I shut my eyes and thought about it. As I thought, I felt the presence of the field and realized that here might be a source of help. So I formed the question in my mind and sent it.

What do I do?

Nothing came back.

Answer me. I need you to speak to me!

I wasn't sure how the field might go about answering—a sign? A voice? A thought? But it gave me nothing at all. I would have to deal with this myself.

I opened my eyes to answer the psychiatrist, but was astonished to find her expression tight with shame and embarrassment, a tide of red rising up her neck.

"I'm sorry. I shouldn't have said that," she said in a small voice. She drew herself up to a more formal position to restore dignity. "I let my professional interests get ahead of yours. I crossed the boundary. I'm so sorry."

"Forget it," I answered, wondering where psychiatrists go when they need therapy.

She gathered her things hurriedly, standing. As she did so, I felt a strong impulse to call her back. Was this the field's answer? A critical moment. But she was in such a welter of confusion at having breached her own standards, that she exited swiftly. I wonder now, if I had called her back, how my path might have been different.

As she departed, she wished me well.

Later that afternoon, when a nurse was removing my bedpan, a shiny-faced, freshly minted registrar entered. He stared without greeting, then, feeling the weight of his own silence, asked the nurse—in front of me—if my motions were regular. I answered for her; alas the full-frontal lobotomy had put my bowel motions way behind schedule. The nurse peeled away from his side, trying to hide her grin behind his back.

As he departed, he did not wish me well.

The nurse returned with a thermometer. She told me I was a little on the hot side, so I told her she was only saying that. You wish, she replied. She may have heard that one before.

Later, I tried again to make the field talk to me.

Even when people tell me my past, I still can't remember. Why is that?

No reply.

What use are you then, if you don't speak to me?

Nothing came back.

Are you something in my subconscious? Are you my subconscious?

No reply. It was as if the wisest, most powerful person in the world was right there, closer than touching distance, listening, nodding, supporting, yet staying utterly silent. Baffling.

My room was a railway terminal. Clinicians visited from other wards, other departments, even other hospitals until Sister put a stop to it.

Reporters were rebuffed by the ward office, those being the days when most reporters phoned politely first. But one, perhaps the first of the nation's conscience-free paparazzi, came in person. He must have waited until the corridor was clear of white dresses and red epaulettes, then walked briskly along and straight into my room. He snapped three shots in quick succession, then pulled a notebook. He got out two questions: Why did you do it, Conrad? And, How does it feel to be a freak, then? When Sister arrived, he grinned at her, showing yellow-brown smoker's teeth. His ejection was truly emphatic, heard throughout the ward, and generating applause from staff and patients.

Sister also called the police station, and within the hour I had the original uniformed policeman back at my door, this time with a different purpose. And this time he was forbidden to talk to the nurses. Instead he used his eyes to remove their clothes as they passed. They referred to him as the stripper and cut a wide path around him.

But they couldn't avoid me. Most entered with starched smiles, freshly arranged for the dangerous but fascinating head case in room seven. A cleaner told me that I was known around the hospital as The Bullet, or as Superman: stops speeding bullets with his head.

* * *

I was allocated an overworked social worker.

She was well into her sixties, with stick-like limbs and arthritic joints. Even so, she travelled the corridor at such speed that anyone coming the other way would automatically step aside. Until she neared my room. There, her harried steps would slow, stop for a few moments, then resume at a deliberately casual pace to enter. Some mental process there. Perhaps a clearing of the mind. She always entered relaxed, warm and focused.

I recall her name even now. Janet, though I thought of her as Twiggy's grandma.

She had fierce, uncompromising standards of behaviour. It was obvious from the beginning that if I had anything personal to tell her, not even the rack would induce her to repeat a word.

She understood that behind my wit and my tongue, I was in many ways a newborn. Worse, the list of people I knew personally could be comfortably written inside a zero, so I had no one to ease me back into the waiting world. She gave up trying to probe my faulty circuitry for clues and asked if I would like her to play detective elsewhere, to try to find a relative who might help me. And if she succeeded, did she have my permission to call them?

Yes, I said, and immediately felt queasy.

She returned three days later, crestfallen. She had found four leads, to relatives on both sides of the family. Two had not returned repeated calls, the third had denied that I was family, and the last was a great-uncle in Australia, a private school headmaster, who told her that he had his reputation to consider.

"I'm very sorry," she said. "There's been so much publicity." She sat there in silence for a moment, then stood, telling me that she would keep trying. But she added with an inquiring eyebrow, "Perhaps I will just report back to you when I find someone helpful?"

In the corridor her steps reached full speed in less than five seconds.

***

I got to know the cleaners better than the nurses, because they were willing to risk stopping to chat. Moana, for example, with arms that could have punished Mohammad Ali. She said things like, "Hey, danger man, you found a pretty nurse yet? That'll wake you up proper, eh boy?" Her flesh heaved with laughter. "Heh, heh, if you wasn't just a kid, I'd wake you up myself." And there was red-head Marjory, who wore rescue-orange clothes of such violent hue that she destroyed any restful visual qualities the hospital might have. One morning, while using the mop to batter the bed legs, she said, "I don't care what you did. You're all right."

A student nurse brought in a tiny suitcase. "This is for you.

Someone left it at the main entrance."

"Who?"

"Don't know. Didn't leave a name."

It was so small—hardly bigger than a school lunch box—it had no business being a suitcase. But it was expensive, with embossed leather and reinforced corners. That same name was on the label: Conrad Fleming. *Nobody lives in that name. Vacancy. Apply within.* I had a headache at the time, so the nurse put the case down beside the cabinet and departed. After a while someone must have parked it behind the cabinet, so I forgot about it.

Yet another medical visitor came. Gravitas preceded this one along the corridor: the deft tread of a man of consequence. He entered breathing through his nose and announcing himself as a medical professor and a specialist in psycho-neurology, his tone suggesting that I should take his words as a suitably modest understatement. Very dark charcoal suit, very thin pin stripe, vein-red tie, and rest assured you're in competent hands. He optimised the efficiency of his valuable time by not asking me anything at all.

He had heard of my case, he said, nodding gravely, and he would consider taking me on. Then his groomed eyebrows rose by the thickness of one of his lashes, indicating that this was in fact a question.

No, thank you.

His brows jumped and fidgeted up there, unused to such heights. Did I not want to recover?

I did, but I wanted to do it my way.

"You're very confident," he observed, finding the concept truly challenging. He tried another tack. "If the cost concerns you, I'll see that it's done on the state tab."

"Thank you, but no."

"In the strictest confidence, of course. No one would know who you are."

"No kidding?" I chuckled. The chuckle cost me a thunderbolt, but it was well worth the price. His jaw tightened. He disliked making mistakes, because they did not reflect the abilities of one with his standing.

"You're sure?"

"I am," I said.

Dismissed. Arguing was beneath him, so he rose stiffly, inclining his head in old world courtesy. "Very well, I must respect your decision, thank you for your time." He went, his brows promising an overhaul of the medical ethics guidelines allowing brain injuries to make their own decisions.

Sister told me I was international news. She had so far refused reporters from three continents, an action that gave her untold pleasure. However, there were also calls coming in to the Clinical Director, from clinicians as far away as New York, Paris and Berlin. It was a protocol hot potato the Director passed swiftly to the Board, who passed it to the lawyer, who now passed it to me via Sister. What were my wishes?

"Is anyone out there claiming to be able to remove the bullet?"

"No, they just want to be in the loop. Our treatment and your response. Access to your encephalography readouts and psychological reports."

In other words, I would be a lab rat, living under a global microscope. So I made my wishes *very* clear. And she departed with an unmistakable gleam, which I suspect had to do with saying no to male clinicians so high up the medical ladder as to be hearing harps.

***

The headaches eased.

Especially at night. That's when I found a measure of peace, not just in the patches of quiet, but also in the sounds which hunted in barren corridors: the clack and sigh of a ventilator, the rattle of stainless steel on formica, the swish of curtains on rails, the tick of a water heater, the squelch of soft-sole shoes telling tales to waxed linoleum. Often, two such pairs would begin their tales separately, rising or falling in volume until they became the same tale, punctuated by the exchange of human words, then separating again. Once, while I was lying in the near dark, an orderly and a student nurse passed by the door, with expressions that suggested they were both about to hear good news. They went into the next room and closed the door, so all I heard of their news was a couple of squeaks and muffled thumps against the other side my wall.

It was in the small dark hours that the field began to hint at what was to come. The hints were experiences—so subtle, that I was often not aware of their significance until they had passed by. They were also lessons, delivered in a language whose vocabulary was not words, but feelings and understandings.

It's one thing, for example, to read that all things are connected; it's quite another to experience it.

Once, when the midnight orderly passed by, I found myself thrust forward. I became the trolley, it's over-oiled wheels, its cloths and bloody swabs, its restless instruments jiggling on the trays. I became the man, corkscrewing through the night corridors with lurching gait and inner bitterness, permanently deformed in a place of healing. I knew these things the way the earth, in all its tides and rhythms, knows the moon. I remember that the orderly looked around, startled, convinced that someone had brushed by him. Such events were both real and illusory, like plays of such quality that the actors forget they are acting.

But still, no words came out of the etheric field. Sometimes I imagined my field as an attentive Nubian bodyguard with tongue removed.

"What's the matter?" asked a night nurse, when she found

me with a thousand yard stare. But I could not explain, so I answered a different question, in genuine wonder.

"I'm not afraid."

She lifted my wrist and looked at her watch and said, "That's the ticket, love."

At three o'clock one morning, a demented patient stumbled in, gaunt, staring, teeth missing, his pyjama top undone, his genitals showing below. He held his colostomy bag in one hand and grasped my arm with the other. His bony fingers dug into the flesh around my elbow.

"It's here," he rasped.

"What's here?"

"It's here," he said urgently.

"Yes, it is," I agreed, "It's right here."

"It's here," he insisted in an awed voice.

***

A large clutch of spring daffodils arrived, wrapped in wax paper, with a get well card attached. Alternating 'X's and 'O's, signed with a name I couldn't pronounce... I guessed at *Siobhan*.

My whole body flushed as some kind of wave surged through. I struggled more upright in the bed and interrogated the orderly who brought the flowers. And he told me they had been handed over by a young woman who was refused permission to visit.

"What young woman? What did she look like?"

"Don't know, mate. Didn't see her. She got turned away at reception and I got told to deliver the flowers."

"Turned away? Why was she turned away?"

"Orders," the orderly shrugged. "Only immediate family."

Within minutes, Sister amended the order. She was furious that she had not anticipated something like this, and for the next hour nurses in her presence walked straighter and faster.

Within the hour, Janet was back. But her excitement at the possibility of a breakthrough quickly faded. No, the card and flowers had not jogged my memory. No, I could not picture what the sender might look like. If Janet could have extracted more information by taking the flowers and the card apart under a microscope, she would have.

Before the afternoon was over, the entire hospital knew that someone anonymous had sent flowers to the bullet man. The news leaked and Sister reported another barrage of calls from reporters. She sent instructions to the switchboard and no more calls reached the ward.

XOXOX. Siobhan.

I wanted to know how to say that name, so I asked the technician who was bothering a machine by my bed. He asked a nurse passing with a smelly pan, who asked a cleaner wielding a duster, who said it's pronounced *Shivaughn*. The sound was strong and resonant and fitted the contours of my tongue. I said it quietly when no one was in the room. *Siobhan.*

***

The physiotherapy team took gleeful, proprietorial interest. They forced every muscle to justify its continued existence, working backwards to re-build its associated brain map—a torment that began long before I was allowed out of bed. The torturers told me the name of every body part they touched and were delighted that I remembered every one. They measured, they tested, they entered the results in yet another manila folder which also fattened by the day.

Half a dozen folders and counting, all with the hollow name. No doubt they are still lying somewhere in that hospital, in obscure boxes in remote basements, suffocated by dust.

When a new x-ray showed that the bullet had not moved,

they took me off the danger list.

The scar behind my ear healed, and the bandages came off.

A nurse aid washed and dried my hair, which had been stealthily making up for lost time. The hospital's only male nurse, Chris, had once been a Harley Street hairdresser, and he said I resembled something that wandered out of the jungles of Borneo. So he set about hacking through the jungle while nurses watched, poised for flight in case Sister appeared. So much hair fell to the floor that jokes were made about Samson and Delilah.

When Chris finished, he said quietly, "I'm really sorry, you know, for all this that's happened to you." The other nurses quickly nodded their agreement. I felt a hot prickling behind my eyelids, and distracted myself by thanking him.

He handed me the wall mirror, so I made a pantomime production of covering my eyes and thrusting it away in terror.

"Oh," said Chris, hand to chest. "You've hurt my feelings."

"What do you want us to call you?" asked one student nurse, knowing that I never responded to the name at the end of the bed.

"Jack," I said, and wondered where the name came from.

"But I'm not changing it on your card," she said. "Sister will have my head in a pan."

Right then we heard the sound of Sister's approach. Her stride was distinctive for its speed and authority, powered as it was all the way from her jaw. The nurses scattered like a flock of starlings, because it did not pay to be caught in the act of being idle; new student nurses were told that Sister's gaze was the reason flies were only ever found with their feet pointing upwards.

One student nurse who had watched the haircutting in silence came back when I was alone, supposedly to check that my pillows were comfortable. Before she departed, she bent over close and whispered.

"If it was me, I would have used the match the way it was intended."

She assumed I would understand this and turned away. She had a sour countenance and bloodless lips. She was always in trouble with Sister and hospital rumour said she wasn't going to make it to registration.

***

As I surfaced from an afternoon sleep, someone was holding my hand. It wasn't a professional hand. It wasn't seeking a pulse, dressing the wound, or working a muscle. The feeling was so sublime I pretended I was still asleep. All of me wanted to sink into that hand with its slender fingers and warmly cupped palm. Was it a nurse? It had to be a nurse. After hours. Heaven help her if Sister found her hand in mine. *Please don't take it away.*

It wasn't a nurse. First I saw a wrist, then raven-black hair framed by window and bright sky, then a gold locket on a black skivvy, and finally, the greenest eyes and warmest gaze ever to alight on a human being.

"Well here you are then," she smiled. "Hello, you."

"Hello, you," I offered in scintillating response. There was another bunch of daffodils on the cabinet.

"Brought you a touch of spring, didn't I," she said.

I was about to ask if she was Siobhan, when something streamed out of her eyes, across the gap, and poured into me. I felt my free hand came over to join the other, trapping hers, and my body curled up around that hand as if it would cost my life to lose it. *Please don't take it away.* Even more astonishing was that my eyes flooded, my shoulders trembled, and my whole body started to shake. I heard someone cry out in alarm and realized it was me. Then great, heaving sobs burst out of me, sharpened by my own fright at what was happening. I tried to strangle them with my throat, without success, so I turned my face into the pillow to stifle them, but they went on and on, forcing their way out. Shoulder and arm muscles tightened to the point of tearing and sweat poured from my body. My teeth began to grind. The woman's hand changed angle briefly; she must have pressed the help button, but the hand remained crushed in mine. *Don't take it away.*

Several times I heard footsteps, moving quickly, voices murmuring, brisk and low-toned. Some rational thread of me could hear it all. Once, twice, my chart clattered off the hook and clattered back.

"Here now, open your mouth, Mr Fleming." It was Sister's voice. When nothing happened, she repeated it, using the same name. "I need you to open your mouth."

"Try calling him Jack, Sister. He likes that." A nurse's voice.

"Jack! Open your mouth, there's a good lad."

I tried, nostrils snorting. My jaw was locked.

Then another voice, this time belonging to the hand.

"Jack, listen to me, boyo. Let your teeth open a little so they can put something soft in there to stop you breaking them." I tried so hard, I squealed like a pig and the teeth opened just enough for a hand towel to be slipped in sideways.

"Valium?" A nurse's voice.

"No." Sister snapped. "Just get a damp facecloth, not too hot." Then her voice redirected and softened. "Want us to rescue your hand?"

"No, it's all right. I think he wants it there."

Sister's reply was drier than the Sahara. "*That* seems to be an understatement."

The cloth caressed my face, the warmth rushing into the welcoming skin. Gradually the sobs softened, the shaking eased and, all at once, the tension sighed out of my muscles. Then I fell through cotton clouds and never reached the earth.

When I woke the second time, the woman was still there.

This time her hands were in her lap. When she saw me looking at her, a smile blossomed and a wicked glint grew. She shook her head reprovingly.

"All this sleeping in. You're a lazy devil, you are."

"Siobhan?" I whispered. "Flowers?"

She leaned forward, hair touching feather-light on my shoulder, and gazed at me intently, searching. "It's true, then. You really don't remember?"

I shook my head, which took an effort.

"Well, that's all right then," she said firmly.

I whispered again, "Why?"

"Because there'll be time enough for rememberin'."

At that moment, I was distracted by a movement at the door, and there was Janet, professional Janet, with moist eyes, turning away swiftly and quietly so as not to disturb us. That's why I never forgot her name.

Siobhan came the next day. Sister hovered ready to pounce, but nothing alarming happened. Then Siobhan came every day.

Soon I was on my feet, walking further every time. The surgeon deemed it safe to move me into an open ward. I moved around easily, talking to patients, nurses and doctors, all gradually relaxing in my presence, in spite of what they had heard. I liked to roam at night, so other patients would greet me with, "Ahah, it's the Bullet that Walks in the Night."

No, call me by my name. Call me Jack.

All medication ceased, except for pain relief. But when I went to the bathroom, I held my hand between eyes and mirror. When a nurse saw me do it, she joked that if I saw myself, I might turn to stone. I shouted at her that I didn't think much of her sense of humour, but was shamed by her stricken expression. We both apologized simultaneously.

Then they let me go.

Sister kept the departure date on a need-to-know basis, so as to outwit the media.

I dressed in clothes Siobhan bought from an op shop. My originals couldn't be found and the staff nurse said they were in such a state of blood and filth when I came in that the laundry probably re-directed them to the incinerator and forgot to inform anyone. To solve the size questions, Siobhan ran a tape measure over me, stood me on a piece of cardboard and drew around my feet, an activity that so fascinated the other patients she might have been Rembrandt. The result of her shopping trip was socks and tennis shoes, underwear, jeans, jeans jacket, and a tee shirt featuring Jimi Hendrix in full cry at Woodstock.

I stared at the tee shirt, wondering how to react to it.

"I'm still in mourning," Siobhan said by way of explanation.

When it came time to shed the pyjamas, we both hesitated, eyes locked on each other, grinning. Her hand came up and pulled the curtain between us.

Swish. Hasty action. Unswish.

"Tasty," she announced, to supportive applause from nearby beds.

I could have walked, but Janet and two nurses turned up with a wheelchair and insisted on pushing me through the ward in ceremonial farewell. Then I was trundled down the corridor for the last time, wheels squidging on polish.

"Wait! You left this behind."

An orderly was hurrying after us, holding the tiny suitcase the student nurse had left beside my cabinet weeks ago. I had forgotten all about it. The name on the label still irritated me and I wanted to leave the case behind, but Siobhan took it and the cavalcade rolled into the lift and then through more corridors to the entrance. One of the nurses winked at Siobhan, puckered up and applied her lipstick to my right cheek, then demanded that the other nurse not inform Sister. No worries, said the other nurse, who promptly applied the same therapy to my left cheek—because, she said, it would not be wise to let me go out there unless I had a well balanced head.

My head agreed.

Siobhan agreed.

The doors disagreed, whingeing and wheezing across the mat, then banging shut emphatically. You're gone, you're out of here.

The secrecy worked. There was not a single reporter to be seen.

I stood shakily, arm-in-arm with Siobhan, taking a very deep breath of crisp spring air. Then, on October the sixth, 1974, I walked out into the world, as Jack, for the first time. I walked out with a head containing a brain, a bullet and a priceless gift.

THREE

Boa's head lifts abruptly. In a few seconds, it sinks again, her eyes watchful slits. There's nothing to see, of course, just the snow streaming down beyond the window. The fall has become one of those sky dumps that makes you feel short of oxygen. I remember now—the last time it fell like this, half of the glasshouse roof gave way, wiping out most of Siobhan's exotic nursery.

I remember. Yes... well... my memory holds only the second half of my life. And yet that half has contained more daytime magic than a whole lifetime of dreams. I have been blessed almost beyond reason. I have no complaints, just a single regret, that the magic of the field will die with me. Many have looked at my wealth, and asked how I did it, how was I always successful whatever the risk, but their obvious envy has always kept me mute.

I lift the phone, and this time the line is dead. Phone and power both gone. Now I am completely isolated. And I have no idea what I am waiting for. I have commanded the field to tell me, and it will not, in any form.

Another night of semi-sleep lies ahead, with dreams that roil through me. In one, I am beset by people who point urgently to their leprous ears. I am besotted with a mysterious gunny sack which, when opened, reveals disembodied mouths chattering about the valley of death. I am loping up a mountain track behind a friend whose face I cannot see, but the long-limbed gibbon riding on his shoulder peers back at me constantly, eyes and mouth roundly astonished by my every word. If there is meaning in the dreams, I cannot fathom it.

Time to prepare dinner. Tonight, spinach and cottage cheese cannelloni, accompanied by a well rested '96 Cabernet. For the music, I think something in a minor key to complement my mood. Vivaldi? Rachmaninov? No, I will have Mozart entertain me; Symphony number 40, music that reaches through the centuries to play the musician, making him as much an instrument as the instrument he plays.

Time to start the generator.

At that moment, Boa jerks to her feet, uttering a short guttural sound. Her eyes are wide, ears straining. I hold my breath and listen with her.

Boots clomp on the porch, south side. In my noise-deadened world, the reverberating sound is shocking. Boa lowers her head, spine erect, ears flat, eyes riveted to the back door passage.

But the boots turn away from the back door and around onto the east side. Whoever it is has a limp. He favours a leg along the east side porch and around onto the north side. Boa's body rotates like a needle in a compass until she faces the front door. She draws her back into a staple, teeth bared, eyes a cinder warning.

It's probably some hiker who didn't listen to the forecast. And he'll be wanting a bed for the night. It's just a matter of time before some idiot has a short incarnation up here. Last spring I found two tourists swimming in my reservoir, naked, frozen and trying to convince themselves they were having a good experience. *Cool*, they chattered through their teeth. Heart-stopping, more like. If they were intending mountain sex, it wasn't likely to happen, considering the co-lateral shrinkage. On the bank, they had little more than jeans, tee shirts and soft shoes. No idea. Up here the weather can turn in half an hour and hustle you off the planet before breakfast.

The boots stop at the front door, a fist knocks and Boa bares her teeth. Surprised by my own reluctance, I open the door.

He's standing there with snow swirling behind him in the last of the light. There's a snow-covered hood over his head and I can't see a face. Rifle in hand, held low. Pack on his back. A hunter, no doubt, stinking from too many days in the tops.

"I'm bleeding. Need something to stop it." The resentment is palpable, more a slap in the face than a plea for help. His rifle points too close to me, just past my left knee.

"Then you'll be wanting to point that thing further away from me."

The hooded shape doesn't move as it considers my demand. The eyes are no more than twin red glimmers reflected from flames licking in the hearth behind me. I want him to change his mind and go away.

"Can't see you in this light," the voice says.

"And I can't see you. You can come in, but the rifle stays outside."

Another hesitation. Without shifting his head he swings the rifle insolently across my chest, provoking, mocking, daring me to change my mind, then using his left hand to prop the weapon against the outside wall.

"And the pack," I insist.

With an effortless drop and swing, he places it down, then adjusts it so that the frame is exactly parallel to the wall. He turns and gazes behind him, as if expecting someone to materialize out of the snow. I should shut the door on him, but it might be safer to help him quickly and see him on his way. I look down at his leg for evidence of an injury, but it's too dark to see.

"Come in. Stand there." I point him away from the carpet, in case he's bleeding heavily.

Boa slips out, ears low, slick orange grease around the door frame.

A clump of wet snow slides off his oil-skin jacket and

slumps on the floor. He turns to survey the interior, so I still can't see his face. For a moment, our firelight shadows play in synch on the wall and this disorients me; it's as if the shadows have a life of their own.

"Wait. I'll turn on the generator."

I step out and along to the end of the porch and stab the starter button with my thumb. It is probably foolish to leave this character alone in my house, even if only for a few seconds. Up by the henhouse, the generator winds up and chugs, a sound made glutinous by the snowfall. The hens will be fluffing into the straw, waiting for the warmth from the tube heaters. The green light steadies and I release the button. The living room window blares out yellow light and fat snowflakes plunge through. I look through my own window, and he's there, in my house, facing me but shielding his eyes from the sudden brightness.

On the way back, the porch light shows me his gear: a hand-me-down canvas pack on an external frame, a bone-handled knife in a pouch between canvas and frame, and the rifle. The safety switch is not engaged.

I reach the doorway. He turns to me, light now full on both of us.

The blood drains out of his face and he stumbles back, swearing hard and sharp, panic and hatred in his expression. He looks away towards his rifle then gapes back at me.

I'm unnerved by his reaction. "What's the matter?"

Abruptly, he shakes his head, ridding himself of something. "Fucking uncanny. Mistook you for someone. You should get better lights in here."

He's young, perhaps early thirties, though it's hard to tell behind his thick sideburns and black beard. His hair is down to his shoulders. He's a modern day Che Guevara, a little taller than me, and much fuller in the body. There's an excellent physique under all that clothing, but he's pale and drawn, and hollow-cheeked. He is deeply exhausted. His eyes have the restlessness of one who is never home, only ever passing through. But he's in solitary confinement within his own body; staring out through the bars, ready for the hot embrace of anger, yet carrying reproach like the orbs of a dying deer. And like the deer, he never meets my eyes. Once, twice, his gaze comes close, but stops on my cheek, or forehead, or the bullet scar behind my ear.

I push on the door handle, but he starts forward and barks. "Leave it open!"

"It's cold. I need to shut the door."

"I told you no," he snarls, bunching his fists and moving closer.

"You're safe here. No one's going to harm you." I shut the door quietly but firmly.

He breathes hard and fast, gulping, confused by my response. I plan to be in the next life shortly anyway, so I can hardly be afraid now, and besides, it's difficult to harm someone who is not afraid. Now, I will see to the wound, then I will see this unpleasant individual off the property. I won't ask his name; the less familiarity, the better.

A sudden breeze blows across the top of the chimney like a fog horn. Flames can-can in the fire. A loose sash rattles in the pane by the door. The light pushing out through the window now falls on snow flustering sideways.

He's swaying slightly.

"Sit down before you fall down."

"I'll stand," he snaps. He looks pointedly down at his right leg. He has done his asking for help; there will be no more of it and to ask again would be like begging.

"Then take the skins down," I say. "Let's have a look."

A wince pierces his sullen resentment as he takes his trousers and over-trousers down to his knees. Black dried blood is caked through half his underwear and down the outside of his right thigh, which is trembling with fatigue. Fresh venous blood, midnight red, seeps through a dirty singlet improvised as a bandage, and trickles over the dried blood. When he moves, his hobnail boot makes a sucking sound.

"Take them right off. I'll get you a fresh pair of socks."

"The cut is up here, not down there."

This has progressed well beyond stupidity; obviously he wants to be gone faster than I want him to be gone. I boil water, he removes the bandage and I hand him medical kit swabs as he deals to the wound. Except for a few granite splinters the wound is clean and needs only a little help to close. He asks for needle and thread, seriously intending to sew it together himself. Instead, I hand him butterfly stitches. For a moment, he looks puzzled, but if he is relieved not to have to sew his own flesh without anaesthetic, he doesn't show it.

Responding only to direct questions, he reveals that he sliced his thigh in a fall on a loose scree slope.

He gazes around with sour disapproval, probably a reaction to the trappings of wealth, possibly a reaction to the cheerfulness of the décor—Siobhan insisted that regardless of what winter assailed the outside, the inside should feel like glorious summer.

"Hungry?"

"Nah."

"A hot drink, then."

"Nah."

He breaks into a coughing fit that he has difficulty controlling, so I hand him water and he takes it in small, practiced sips, with his head tipped back.

Suddenly my universe tilts. My breath hangs still. With no word to him, I re-open the door and step out to the porch. With the porch light off, I stare into the darkness he came from and listen. Look back at him. Back into the darkness. Nothing. Nor will there be anything.

Of course. Of course.

Clarity. So this is how it begins.

It's like waking from a complex dream, when the symbols declare their allegiances, and meaning comes running downstairs with a glad shout and open arms. I go back inside, close the door and lean on it, grinning.

"What's going on? What are you laughing at?"

"At me. I'm laughing at me, because I'm a foolish old man."

"You'd better not be laughing at me."

"I'm not and I won't. You are not a laughing matter."

"Are you taking the piss?"

"No. I'm not taking the piss." I laugh out loud now, and the young man's upper lip curls noticeably as he stares at this cackling Croesus of the mountains.

"What are you? A nutcase?"

It's completely dark outside. All we can see is the snow immediately beyond the window, wet flakes, engorged, plunging in straight lines, creating the illusion that we have stolen aboard an elevator cage rising into space. This will be the reluctant hitchhikers' ride to the universe.

FOUR

We drove away from the hospital in Siobhan's blue Mini. And as we left Christchurch, I imagined a rubber band between the car and the city, stretching out hair thin, then snapping and dissolving in the spring air. *Gone. Nothing behind me.*

The rushing breeze made the bullet scar ache, so I had to roll up the window. Then the swooping paddocks and fences and telephone lines made me giddy; so I put down the visor to limit the light and, when that didn't work, pulled a towel from under the tiny suitcase on the back seat and put it over my upper face.

When everything stopped spinning, I peeked at Siobhan from under the towel.

"Copping an eyeful, are you?"

"It's therapy. The nurses told me I had to take care of my eyes."

"Not much wrong with your tongue, I'm thinkin'." She drove on, looking pleased. Her eyes, I noticed then, were the green of the darkest greenstone jade. Then there was her voice. Ah yes, to listen to Siobhan's lilt was to know that music should be written and a dance invented to pay homage to the sound.

It was a given that we were going to be lovers. But had we been lovers already? A disturbing uncertainty. I didn't want to ask her. I hunted in my head for some splinter of a past embrace, but a headache rustled its warning far back in a cornfield. So instead I imagined her clothes flying out the window as she drove, piece by piece except for her gold locket.

I discarded the head-towel and began to enjoy the self-assured parade of spring: arrogant magpies prancing on the pasture; a speeding farm ute with dogs peering round the side of the cab, blinking in the breeze and barking their eagerness to be there already; and lambs spronking, all four feet bounding at once in outrageous affirmation of life, then rushing the mother, bunting her udder, frantic to feed again.

I napped, waking when Siobhan reached into the glove box for a packet of mints. There was a half-smoked joint next to it.

"Help yourself," she said, then frowned. "On second thoughts maybe it's a bit soon."

I picked it up and sniffed it. The aroma was familiar, unmistakeable. I tried to call in a pre-accident memory for questioning, but again a headache rustled a warning. I would have to make decisions about many such intrusions from the past. We cruised, unhurried, through Darfield, through Springfield, and on into the foothills of the Alps. Now there were no towns at all, and even farmhouses were rare.

"Where are we going?" I asked, because somehow we had never discussed it.

"To the other side of those," she grinned, nodding at the Southern Alps, the peaks rising higher in the windscreen with every turn. I studied the jagged silhouettes.

"That's where we met," I said.

She darted a surprised sideways glance. "Are you asking me or telling me?"

"Telling you."

"Liar," she said. "Anyway, you're right."

"How long did we know each other before… before?"

"To be exact, it was less than two hours, boyo. You don't give a girl much of a chance, you don't."

Two hours? "What was…? What were we…?"

"Here's you with all the questions now." Siobhan changed down for an upgrade, punishing the gears. "I was wonderin' when you were going to get to that."

"Well?"

"All right then, let's get this over with. Here's the facts of the matter. The facts of the matter is I'm not going to tell you. No, let me finish. I don't think it'll do you any good to know while you're recovering. It'll just upset you."

"Why would it? Just hearing about something doesn't mean I'll remember it. You know that."

"Don't get tricky with me. You can dig it up on your own time. I'm not taking the risk; I really don't want to stuff this up, do you hear me? If I tell you and then you remember and you throw another scene like that in hospital, I wouldn't know how to handle it."

"But I already know about the bullet and it doesn't mean anything to me. What else could...? Wait... I know... You were there when it happened, weren't you?"

"Look, I'm not going to-"

"Ahah! This is really because it might upset *you*, isn't it?"

"Stop it! That's enough now, Jack. I've made my decision. I'm not taking you down memory lane for the sake of two missing hours, I'm not. So that's that. Don't ask me and I won't tell you any lies!"

We both scowled down the throat of the road winding towards us. But after a few minutes, she reached out and patted my leg anxiously. My hand jerked out to accept the gesture, awkwardly knocking hers, which she then withdrew to change gear. We grimaced self-consciously and glanced sideways at each other and grinned, and then it was all right again.

Mid-afternoon, we re-fuelled the car at Arthurs Pass village, deep in the mountains, just before the main divide. We re-fuelled ourselves on slab fruit cake, pies warmed in perpetuity, and stewed lukewarm railway station tea in cups that, if dropped, would crush your toes. The sun used the tallest peaks to rehearse its evening exit and a chill set in.

We crested the pass and descended the dizzy road, past the waterfalls, past the rock-fall barriers, through Otira and into the

West Coast; and there was the sun again, reborn in the afternoon. It penetrated the bush canopy beside us in long, oblique shafts, the most persistent lighting up pools of mist left on the bush floor by a recent shower.

Suddenly Siobhan pulled over and stopped.

"Will you feast your eyes on that?" she breathed. "Have you ever seen a finer sight than that?"

Between canopy and bush floor, fantails were flying through the shafts of sunlight, which pinned them in flight like stop-frame photography.

We scrambled out to look.

The fantail, *piwakawaka,* is the world's finest acrobat, on an endless, tumbling, chirruping search for insects. Some of the northern Maori tribes say that if one tumbles into your home, it is a harbinger of death. But here they flipped benignly from one light beam to another, flares of fuss and bother. Each appearance left such an impression on my retina that the birds seemed not to travel between the light beams at all, rather to disappear from one and re-appear in the next. There and gone, there and gone. Siobhan jangled her keys, drawing some of the busy birds out of the trees until they flitted around us. When we failed to deliver they returned to the light beams and pungent bush... there and gone... there and gone... their existence created and discreated by their own efforts. When a light sun shower also fell through the beams, the effect was heightened.

This, I thought, is how the field sings in the shower. Half humorously, I sent the question. *Well, is it?* The response was immediate, a wordless moment of internal experience. Back then I could not have translated it into words, but now I can: that the universe is, despite all appearances, a gigantic feeling, a yearning to express itself. And scientists, hunting for the fundamental building block of the universe, would never find a material object to fit the part.

I had to find a way to tell Siobhan about the field.

The sun sank further, the beams tilted, shrank pencil-thin and vanished. One moment the fantails were supernovae, then silhouettes, then they were gone altogether. As the bush pulled up its blanket and turned over to sleep, Siobhan found a sandfly on her inner wrist. When you find a sandfly on your flesh, it's usually too late to avoid the torment that follows. She squashed it and defamed its character, in that order.

We resumed the journey.

I did find a way to tell her, or at least to start. I was clumsy, conveying only a fraction of what I felt. In frustration, I told her that the field had saved my life. At that her facial muscles twitched, so I thought she was either amused or puzzled. Strange that I can remember such a fleeting detail now, half a lifetime later.

Then I got to the point, telling her how the field was answering my questions.

"What questions?" she said.

"Life, the universe. Everything. What it's all about."

"And this... field thing... speaks to you?"

"No. Never a word. It just makes me understand. It's..." I put a fist just below my ribs, over the solar plexus. "It's hard to explain."

"Why do you have to ask those questions?" she asked, frowning.

"I'm entitled," I said defensively. I had expected a little more respect for such a noble endeavour; if not admiration, at least a little deference. "I don't like what happened to me and I've got a right to call in the universe for an explanation."

She conceded the point. As we drove on, she did not mock me or make disparaging comments, but I could tell she was worried. As for me, I shunted my own doubts into the corner, where they muttered alone.

***

We rented a cottage on the beach, on the southern tip of
Westport, a 1920's, soot-lined original, reeking of the joys and
sorrows of four generations of coal miners. Just as the nearby
hills were riddled with tunnels, the cottage was riddled with
borer but still standing, thanks to paint and wisteria vine. Much
of the interior was lined with the soft pine-fibre usually slapped
up in the holiday shacks further down the Coast. We offered a
pathetically low rental and the owner promptly accepted it. By
then, it was obvious that he had worked out who I was, so he
knew what I was supposed to have done before the accident.
His manner indicated approval, in the bluff, dry way of the
Coasters. When we thanked him, he humphed and said he
wouldn't get too many chances to rent his cottage to someone
who took a bullet in the head and lived to tell the tale. Actually
I couldn't tell the tale, because the scraps of information forced
on me so far by well intentioned people had no meaning; they
were chaff on some other wind.

He looked at the scar behind my ear.

"Still in there, isn't it?" he demanded, as if I had been hiding
the fact. When I nodded, he humphed again, as if it were the
most ridiculous thing he'd ever heard, and trod away to his
truck.

Siobhan found a half-day-a-week job in Westport's book
shop, which took care of the rent but little else.

The cottage came with nature's air-conditioning. The walls
were damp, the ceiling mildewed, the furniture stained and
moth-eaten, and we ate off an old crate, sitting on upturned tea
chests. At first, the bed was only a mattress on the floor, but
each morning we woke to the sound of surf and gulls; one hand
would quietly join another and in that moment we wanted for
nothing else.

We fished off the rocks: silver-grey *terakihi* and snapper and
blue cod, delicious when raced from surf to frypan in ten

minutes. We took trout from the streams, and we netted whitebait near the river mouths—back then it was possible to fill a kerosene can with the tiny transparent fish in one morning. A sheep farmer invited us to shoot rabbits overrunning his property. I would not carry a rifle—just picking one up made my ears ache—but Siobhan could and did. We kept hens, grew vegetables, and found fruit on abandoned sections in the old mining district. In the summer, glossy blackberries grew by the creek sides, so swollen that it was impossible to pluck them without sweet juice bursting out.

My dizzy spells and headaches stopped altogether, becoming another personal memory in my new life.

My stick-insect limbs grew back their muscles, firmed and toned. I worked them hard, with weights made of beach gravel in paint cans suspended on a hoe handle, and sometimes while I worked, Siobhan would cup two hands round her mouth to bark, "Lunch is ready. Would Mr Schwarzenegger please report to the restaurant."

Every morning I shaved meticulously with razor and brush, without a mirror. Don't mistake me, the bathroom mirror was no more than an irritant; but it was an irritant I didn't have to tolerate, so I covered up the half closest to the door. Siobhan used the other half.

I took back full control of my body. I took to walking, then hiking, then running along the beach, where the Tasman Sea reared and boomed, and dead pebbles stood up and danced in the backwash, roaring their response. Blue penguins waddled down from nesting sites, awkward, fussy little gentlemen until they toppled into the water, then each would reappear just once, transformed into ballet master, leaping high into the next impossible wave.

And the field, my personal cornucopia of wisdom, continued to pour forth, sometimes unasked, sometimes at my bidding. I had only to hint at my desire to understand some matter and the answer would pour into me, usually at a level deeper than the original question. Still no words, just cool, clear, understanding, like a stream so pure you cannot see the surface of the water, but the pebbles below are more vividly present. Sometimes my body felt the answers physically, as if some chemical were flooding my bloodstream.

At first, Siobhan was cautious. Sometimes what I translated into words—always inadequately—made her narrow her eyes, or set her jaw and argue. Sometimes she became upset and told me to stop messing with her head. But more often she would listen, look hard at me and nod slowly, reluctantly.

One day, as summer tapped spring on the shoulder, I informed Siobhan that I wanted to tell the world about the field. We were in bed at the time, after lovemaking, cosy, rain tattooing the window. A sandfly was out there, beating at the glass, trying to get in while successfully dodging a flight of raindrops, which must be like a human dodging a shower of pianos.

I told her it bothered me that people were walking around, unable to see or use the field. The accident had allowed me to see, so I owed it to the world to announce it, so people could stop believing that they were at the mercy of external events and start to control their lives directly.

At first, Siobhan did not seem to react. She just stared through the ceiling. Then she closed her eyes for so long I thought she was making a point. Finally she popped up on her elbow, seized one of my longer and blacker chest hairs between thumb and forefinger and plucked it out.

"Ow?" I said.

She inspected the hair thoughtfully, then found another one.

"Ow. Pain. This means war."

"Listen, my beautiful boyo, this is too intense. You can't go gabbing in public about the field."

"Why not?"

She looked me straight in the eye. "Well, I'm thinking it might not go down so well, comin' as it does from a guy who was lined up for serious jail time.

"But-"

"Then there's the little matter of your holey skull, with the lead luggage and the brain damage, not to mention-"

"But-"

"Not to mention the massive amnesia—which is the only reason you aren't doing porridge right now. Tell me if I'm wrong but some people might be tempted to think there's a wee credibility gap in there somewhere."

"Oh. That."

"Aye," she said softly. "That."

It occurred to me that she had skilfully side-stepped the word *naïve*. I rolled over, face down, pulled the quilt over my head, and muffled a loud four letter word. But shortly, she lifted the quilt at the side and inspected my now normal and fit young body.

"Did I mention that you have the arse of a god?"

"No," I said, my head still under the quilt. "You didn't mention that."

"And did I mention that I want to shag you within an inch of your life?"

My head emerged. "No, you didn't mention that either."

So she mentioned both of those things and we engaged in a another frolic, fully testing the structural integrity of the bed. The musical group *The Doors* joined us and they were nice enough to keep time. Jim Morrison sang, *Hello, I love you, won't you tell me your name?*

***

A month later, everything changed.

At first, we didn't speak about the change, because the

coincidences were so bizarre that mentioning it risked lending reality to what could not possibly be real. So in the midst of our happiness, an asp of tension was born, and it squirmed between us, fattening on our silence.

Until Siobhan could stand it no more.

She ran us a bath. It was an outside iron bath on claw feet, positioned for an excellent view of the sea. Usually we did this with a romantic evening in mind. We would light driftwood underneath, then prepare food and drink, placing it on a crate beside the bath. Clothes were ripped off inside and we would run shrieking across the yard. On an extravagant, who-cares-about-the-cost evening we poured in half a cup of emerald green bubble bath and stirred frantically with our bodies until foam poured over the edge. That was usually the time to sit back and admire the crisp stars overhead and the restless white line of surf stretching away into the night.

Siobhan wriggled around to face me and took a breath.

"We have to talk."

"I know." I fought an impulse to hang my head.

She stabbed a finger back towards the house. "All these things...!"

I nodded immediately. The new sandwich toaster, the modern electric jug, the down quilt, the power drill, and the 10-speed cycles in the hall. On Siobhan's pay, we couldn't afford any of it, but over the last month it had been turning up shortly after we thought we needed it or wished we had it, for little or no cost: a drop-dead bargain here, a raffle win there, a neighbour shedding unwanted goods. The electric jug had simply appeared on the doorstep, the same day its predecessor rusted through the side. Yes, we had told a couple of friends about the jug. Yes, there was a rational explanation. There was always a rational explanation, but there were too many of them. Anyone adding it up would call it a spooky run of luck and ask us to buy their next lottery ticket. It wasn't luck; I knew it,

Siobhan knew it, and luck wasn't the point.

"Vonnie, listen. I think it's something to do with the bullet... I mean, the thing that came with it... the field."

She stared at me. "You're scarin' me, Jack."

And I knew precisely why it was scaring her, because it was scaring me too. Again she took the lead.

"So how do you explain all the other stuff?"

Finally, out in the open, almost a relief. Siobhan was talking about the fence that blew over hours after I mentioned the possibility. She was talking about the fire that broke out in the kitchen after she warned me not to leave an element on under the pan; we were both adamant we had not turned the element on. And the tools that went missing, only hours after I thought that I must get a lock on the garage door. Then there was the shrinking money: we had both spent an evening fretting about our lack of solvency and then discovered that we had eighty dollars less than we thought. We back-tracked through every possible transaction and couldn't account for it.

All that and much more in less than a week, way too much to write off as the flipside of luck. Our wheel of fortune was speeding up in both directions. Something unstable and wildly unpredictable had taken hold of us, shunting us back and forth between a rabbit's foot and a black cat.

Naturally, I demanded an answer from the field. My 'please explain' was loaded with anxiety, and back then I didn't realise the significance of such a loading. *What's going on? Is all of this stuff coming from you? Why is it not just the good stuff?* To my astonishment the response was garbled—a confusing stew of impulses. I could feel them, but they left no clear impression. I had tried framing the questions in different ways, but still could not understand the responses.

"Well?" Siobhan demanded. "What's happening?"

"I don't know," I said.

"Jack, what the hell is going on with that hole in your head?"

"Don't say that," I snapped. "I hate it when you put it like that."

After a while, we pulled the bath plug. The water splashed away on the ground, leaving clumps of foam on the grass and on our bodies. We fled back to the cottage, naked and shivering.

***

Then the field abandoned me. Us. In spite of its promise back in the hospital, the field faded away. I felt betrayed. As my pleading for explanation grew increasingly anxious, so the affective responses weakened in intensity. The more I said despairingly to Siobhan, "I'm not getting the answers," the less I got. The day came when there was no response at all. Not even a tickle in the belly.

Talk to me. Tell me something, anything.

Nothing.

Electric panic brushed me where the ribs meet. Then, grief. Throughout my short post-accident life, the field had been my only parent, always wordless, but always there. In my desperation, I made it personal.

Are you angry with me? Have I offended you?

No answer.

What have I done to deserve this?

No answer.

I was losing control. The wheel was developing a bias, lurching more into pain than pleasure. Everything conspired to take our money. Field mice found the pantry cupboard. Something—a possum, a large rat or feral cat—died under the cottage and I couldn't get to it. I tried taking up floorboards, didn't find it, then lost the hammer. Our oven forgot how to turn out risen bread. The terakihi and cod abandoned the rocks out on the point, leaving nothing on our hooks but bone-ridden guppies. A lubricated farmhand threw a stone which smashed one of the front window panes, letting the rain in. Promised replacement glass never arrived; I had to nail up a scrap piece of three-ply, using a stone in lieu of the hammer. Another gale blew it off before nightfall and spray from the sea came in, over the table and down onto the threadbare carpet.

When that happened, Siobhan stared at the water dripping off the table. She went to the window and watched a seagull drop a *pipi* onto rocks to break the shell. Then she turned back to me, pleading.

"Jack, please. It's that thing that came with the bullet... You've got to make it stop."

I turned inward, to the field.

Why is this happening? What are you doing to us?

No response.

Fuck you, then. Get out of my life.

No response.

I plunged into depression. Since leaving the hospital, I had experienced little but love, well-being and optimism. But now, I stopped weight training and running along the beach, and took to bed more often, climbing into the merciful anaesthetic of sleep. Siobhan and I fell into grindingly vicious conversations that lasted hours and took even longer to heal. Our lovemaking stopped being about love and took on the quality of fear. She came home after a difficult day at work and snapped at me, "I'm carrying both of us, Jack, I am. You'll have to get off your arse and look for a job."

Her words had the opposite effect, pushing my remaining energy out through the cracks in the walls. I read books, then magazines, then just stared out at the sea or the trees swaying in the wind. My brain would not rest.

The next northerly toppled the fat Nikau palm which had guarded the cottage for decades. On the way down, it clipped the corner of the kitchen, buckling the wall, and dropping a ceiling tile onto the stove. The side-window glass cracked from top to bottom.

Siobhan rounded on me as I lay in bed.

"I can't take this," she shouted. "That thing in your head is evil, Jack. You've got to get rid of it!

I lay there afraid to get out of bed in case I made the field do something else to us. It had to be something I was doing. But I was now afraid of my own thoughts, afraid even to be awake. I shut my eyes.

"Let's get a boat," she begged. "Sail away from this. We can start again, we can."

I shook my head. I couldn't even contemplate getting out of bed. She burst into tears and came to put her arms around me. "Jack, look at me! Is it me? Am I stuffing this up? Am I not loving you enough?"

My stomach lurched with new fear because I saw this as weakness on her part and Siobhan had never, ever been weak. I wanted to shout at her to stop making it about her, but then I was afraid that her weakness would sap any last strength I had, so I lifted my hands and pushed her away. She rose slowly and looked at me as if she needed reading glasses, and went out into the dusk and didn't return for a long time. While she was away, an elderly man went fishing on our point, each lazy cast pulling in a terakihi that thrashed and flashed in the evening light.

When she returned, she didn't look at me. She just spoke in a flat voice. "Nothing bad happened to me while I was away from you."

When we next came together physically, we poured all our anger and despair into each other so that at the climax we both cried out in pain, and then we curled up, back to back, equally wretched. Siobhan was wracked with sobs, and for the first time she covered herself when she got out of bed, turning her breasts away from my sight. As she dressed, I wondered why she bothered to stay with me. Then, in terror, I clamped down on that thought, not knowing what it would provoke.

She went to see friends on the other side of Westport, staying with them the first night, and then the second, then the third. I was alone. I hated the field for abandoning me.

And while she was away, the beast came. Even now, though I defeated it long ago, my writing hand remembers and a discontinuity appears between the 'b' and the 'e'.

I first noticed the beast when I was at the border between waking and sleep. It was a long distance away, gliding slowly through the field. I opened my eyes sharply, heart thumping. But after an hour I could not stop them closing and there it was again, a shapeless hole in the universe, the colour of a coal pit on the darkest night. Its equally shapeless appendages reached out towards me. At first I felt burning resentment. But then, as I watched it pulsating closer, I realized that if it reached me and drew me into its Stygian blackness, it would devour me.

So, right there inside my head, I became a child and hid under a mind blanket. When I peeked, I saw that the thing had not moved, but was waiting for my attention, which it now had, and so it pulsed a little closer, stopped, pulsed closer, relentlessly flowing in. From inside it came a muffled cacophony of pain and suffering, and threading through it all the keening of a terrified child.

I heard a scream, then realized that it had come from me. I was panting, my hands clawed. I thought briefly of finding Siobhan for help, but decided that I didn't want her to see me like this.

A neighbour? No, no one should see this.

In the afternoon, when the beast was almost upon me, it suddenly, unaccountably, moved backwards. The shift was almost imperceptible, but I seized on the supreme question of why. Intuitively, I knew that the push had somehow come from me. Something I had just done in my head. While I was exploring, there came a moment when I seemed to be watching my fear from a distance, and in that very second, the beast moved backwards again.

And a third time.

Then I knew I was going to win and exulted as the beast began to retreat, swallowing the despairing sounds that seeped from within. Hour after hour, I refined the technique and the beast grew smaller, until it was no more than a speck in a distant cavern. I was exhausted, still without the field, but I had won.

To this day, I have told no one about the mind-beast—not even Siobhan.

Finally, I fell into a different kind of dream. I still cannot claim to understand each moment in it, I just know that what it did to me was as necessary to the rest of my life as oxygen is necessary to lungs.

I dreamed that I was on the bow of a ship heaving through great seas. Each time it plunged, I free-fell until I crashed on the deck. Each time it rose, I was crushed to the dimpled iron, choking on the smell of salt and rust and old cable oil. I saw a large hole in the deck, and from inside came the sound of a telephone, calling and calling. I crawled over and put my head in the hole.

"You're late," a voice said.

Now the dream took me to a country lane under a blazing sun. A horse lay on its side nearby, panting, exhausted, its flanks streaming with sweat, it's nostrils speckled with blood. The lane was scored by the keels of war canoes and the dust bore the prints of hundreds of stamping, bare feet.

In front of me was a gate so twisted by wind and sun that it took effort to drag it open and walk through.

"You're late," the voice repeated.

I came to a musterer's hut, made of ancient timbers and sitting on poles shaped with an adze. And there in the doorway was a very old woman with a *moko* tattooed on her chin. "No discipline," she grated. "You blame the *hooiho*, even though it is you jerking the reins like a useless *poorangi*."

In the dream I was ashamed.

There was a baby in the cottage, in a rocking cradle, listening avidly to every word.

"What is the first truth?" the old woman snapped at me, barely tolerating my inadequacy. My tongue moved of its own accord and I was surprised by what it said.

"What is the quickening?" she demanded… she could hardly be bothered with me. Again my tongue moved. The baby chuckled and pumped its arms exuberantly, setting the cradle to rocking.

The old woman went to the cradle, and bent over the baby. And I understood that if I did not answer the next question correctly, the baby would die. When the woman finally shot her glittering gaze at me, her mouth was set in a toothless grin, and her voice dropped close to a whisper.

"And where is the seat of the fire?"

At that, wind rushed through the hut, around the crone and the baby. Blood pounded in my ears. But somehow I knew the answer, so I moulded it into a word and pushed it into my throat, onto the root of my tongue, willing the tongue to engage once more.

Then my eyes snapped open.

I sat bolt upright in bed and shouted the word, though the only reply was the rushing of the wind outside, around the cottage eaves.

Now I knew what was coming in the years ahead.

In seconds, I was running light and barefoot down the road, dressed only in cut off, ragged jeans. I ran all the way through the main street of Westport, past the shops, ignoring greetings from those heading home for the evening, to the houses on the far side. There, I jumped a fence and pounded on a door, raw feet burning on the doormat. When the door opened, I shouted past the woman to Siobhan who was standing, startled, in the corridor.

"Come home," I urged her. And she heard what was in my voice, stared at me, then we ran hand-in-hand, all the way back to the cottage.

Within hours, I was regaining control of our lives. The bias of events reversed, and over the next few days, the pleasant began to outweigh the unpleasant. Physical objects, household objects, continued to appear, but now they were things we wanted, responding directly to my new found knowledge. When I woke on the fourth day, the etheric field was simply there again, throughout everything, powerful and silent. And I realized that it had never faded, it was my inner sight that had faded.

It took Siobhan three days to trust that the change was real, then she allowed herself to lie down and weep with relief. Over the next few weeks, she too learned how to take the same conscious control of events and objects, until we shared the delight. And then... the good times—the magical and exciting times that would last more than three decades—were underway.

We grew close again. Our lovemaking became, once more, about love. Salt returned to the sea and green to the grass; fragrance found its way back into the air between us and we could not fill our lungs with enough of it.

And we invited the field to take part even in that, our lovemaking. Our bed became a portal. We found that we were looking not at each other but in the same direction, travelling through a landscape sculpted by slow and soaring rhythms, in a place indifferent to gravity and where the journey was itself the destination. Once, we watched our own bodies dancing in a far off ballroom, twirling more and more slowly until, on the peak, movement ceased altogether, and two distant voices remarkably like ours sobbed out in wonder, *It's lovely it's so lovely yes yes lovely* and we were not sure who was *you* who was *I* and where one stopped and the other began. And then there was nothing else and nowhere else.

And the revelations began.

FIVE

He hoists his blood-soaked trousers, refusing a shower and fresh clothes. With a brusque nod, he turns to the door. That's his thanks and goodbye. He fully intends to go back out there.

"You're not going anywhere tonight," I say.

"The hell I'm not."

"You've lost blood. And it's flat black out there. Even if you do find the track, there'll be slips and you'll ride a snowball to the bottom of the gorge. You need daylight."

He hesitates. "I'm not sleeping here."

"Then sleep in the barn, or with the hens."

"I've got a tent."

"The snow will wrap it around your head by morning. What about the hay shed, right out there away from everything?"

That he accepts with a grunt. Minimal shelter, away from the house, and less like hospitality on my part, for which he might be expected to simulate gratitude.

So I don coat and chullo—a rainbow-striped, alpaca-wool hat with ear flaps—and lead him through the fall, with a kerosene storm lantern that hasn't opened its eye in years. The hissing filament is yellow-tinged but somehow it lends a blue cast to the snow. To look upwards in the dark is to see the impossible beauty of snow—flakes rushing into existence out of black oblivion, something out of nothing. Each flake is a crystal of perfect symmetry and great beauty, full grown in its brief journey from the sky, and yet if you were to pass a million such flakes through a microscope, you would not find any two the same.

Sheba lies in the hay shed in the clear space beyond the

bales, She raises a head at the intrusion, blinks with bovine languor, and turns her head away from the lantern's glare. In winter, this is her home, and when snow covers the grass, she's either here or in the milking stall beside the barn.

The young man eyes her and hesitates. She would be warm to sleep near.

"She snores, belches and farts," I tell him. But Sheba settles it by heaving to her feet, walking out into the snow and standing irritably, side-on to us, waiting for the fuss to be over.

I pop the twine on a bale to provide a mattress and he re-arranges a few bales for side-shelter. He hauls a sleeping bag out of its stuff-tube, so sweat-stained it looks like a map. It's an established brand, rated for extreme conditions, and it's dry, so he will at least be warm tonight. The rifle lies on a bale of lucerne: a Sako Vixen 222, bolt action, Pegar scope, very old-fashioned but of such high quality that it still has a following amongst modern hunters.

I point out that the safety switch is off.

He shrugs, hauls out a cigarette packet, and opens it.

"No smoking near the hay; go over where Sheba was. Same with the lantern. You've got a gas cooker with you? Same with that."

He swears, the word hard and flat—he came to get his wound dressed, not his nappy changed—but the packet disappears back into his pocket. Then he stops still, surprised by a sedate stepping sound coming through the corrugated iron back wall. Several animals are moving at once, coming closer. A rattling of hooves, a muffled thump. Something brushes the corrugated iron. Then there's a cough and a bleat.

"Alpacas?!' The word bursts out of him.

"A few."

"Here? In New Zealand?"

I'm amused. I'm hardly the first to bring alpacas into the country, but he takes the lantern from me and walks around the

end of the shed to check for himself. The animals take fright
and scramble away into the dark, reassembling to watch from a
distance, so that all he sees is the lantern reflected back from
their eyes as an arc of sparks. He returns, impassive again,
regretting his outburst. Then he stands looking out into the
night, ignoring me, waiting for me to go away; there'll be
nothing as personal as cooking in front of me, or getting into
his sleeping bag. Man alone. Give nothing, ask nothing, expect
nothing.

"I'll see you in the morning," I say.

"No. I'm going to push on." He turns away and throws his
pack down where his head will lie. Mountain man's pillow.

"No problem," I say. Then, for just one moment, the
snowflakes suspend their drift to earth and fix themselves in the
air to listen to my next words. "If you change your mind, come
up to the house for breakfast and we'll talk about who you
really are."

"What?"

I put the lantern down and turn away, hearing him move
towards the rifle.

"What are you talking about?" he shouts after me. "What did
you say that for?"

I trudge on into the snow. The back of my neck prickles. I
listen for a sliding bolt, a round entering the chamber, but hear
only a muttered insulting phrase. I force myself to keep
walking without turning around. The house windows are a
sallow smudge in the darkness.

I wonder if I should listen to the next radio news bulletin.

On the porch, I'm shedding coat, hat and boots, when I see
that Siobhan is waiting inside. She's standing in front of the
fire looking up at the clipper ship painting, cheeks aglow with
the ruddy, reflected light as if she had the flesh to enjoy it. I
have asked her about that: yes, she says, she does feel the heat
of flames, she does see in electric light, though I do not

understand how.

"Hey, Vonnie."

"Ho, Jack."

We adopt our no-touch greeting, palm close to palm, forehead close to forehead, closed eyes. Then we draw back and regard each other. As always, I experience a melting sensation, a letting go, a knowing that all is well. I'm sure children must have similar feelings. I imagine it might happen when they snuggle into the pillow of a pre-warmed bed to feel the kiss of a loving mother and hear a loving father read the next chapter of a favourite story. That's what I imagine.

Siobhan's presence sometimes makes me dizzy; few young women, however perfectly sculpted, can compete with the depth of beauty possible in the old.

She is wearing *Je Reviens*, as much for her sense of humour as for me. But perhaps she too can appreciate the fragrance. And she has come to me with silver-grey hair set to mid length and carefully informal, as if some divine wind along the way had blown it into that shape. She always had the talent of dressing simply to dramatic effect—this time black jeans, and a jade green polo neck alpaca wool skivvy to light up her eyes. And the gold locket. If I asked her, she would open it and then it would show the black-and-white photo of her great-grandmother born more than a century ago, in Limerick, Ireland. The locket was passed down, eldest daughter to eldest daughter, through more generations than anyone in Siobhan's family could remember. It was always presented on the new moon after the first menstruation, always far from the presence of men, and always with this instruction: 'As long as you wear this around your neck, the little people will come visit your hearth while you are asleep, and they will cast spells to bring you happiness and fertility and men from the sea to give you beautiful daughters.' Daughters? Not fine strapping sons? Daughters, she replied firmly. At the time, I thought that a disquieting piece of information.

"Are you sure, now?" she asks. She's sultry and teasing, and I want to strip away the years and walk along the Westport beach with her and listen to the breeze waltzing with her voice.

"Am I sure about what?"

She glances towards the window. "About him."

"Yes. I'm sure. He has the intensity."

"Obviously. But are you sure you can you handle him?"

I dodge the question with a laugh. "Maybe in a past life I trod on a scorpion and the account is due."

"Well," she offers helpfully, "Maybe he'll turn out to be a figment of your geriatric imagination."

"Impertinent wench. Maybe I'll turn out to be a figment of yours. No, I have it—you'll turn out to be a witch, in league with Satan. Confess now, woman, and save your soul from eternal damnation."

When she laughs, her eyes light up and wrinkles deepen in the corners.

***

When her final prognosis came, we were well prepared. In fact we had already drawn up a one page bucket list, which Siobhan dubbed *the contract*. She stuck it to the outside of a kitchen cupboard.

The contract had two halves. The right hand side was what I agreed to do after she was gone, for example: build a wood shed, expand the herd, build a rotating shearing table, and—deemed by Siobhan to be the most important—talk to the infant swan plants growing in the glasshouse. The swan plants are for the sole purpose of attracting orange and black monarch butterflies into the valley. The monarch lays its larvae only in the swan plant. Each larva, knowing its complete self, becomes a gold, black and white caterpillar, and grows fat on the leaves of the swan. Each caterpillar, knowing its complete self, hangs upside down and dances, shimmying around itself a cocoon for the private magic of metamorphosis. Out climbs a fully formed butterfly which spreads its wings to the sun, and, knowing its complete self, lays its larvae only in a swan plant. The experts advised Siobhan that swan plants would not grow in this climate, but she did not pass that advice on to the seedlings; instead she chatted to them about their part in the completeness of the Earth. They believed her and began to grow in earnest.

"It will be a slaughter," I told her. "Those monarchs are eating machines.

"Completeness," she said, as if that were an answer. "When I'm gone, you must plant them every spring, and talk to them every day until the monarchs come." *When I'm gone.* So calm, so content. I have done my duty every spring since, but so far no one has informed the monarchs of the West Coast that completeness awaits them in my valley.

"When I'm gone," Siobhan also said, "I need you to say yes to every invitation that comes your way." To that I raised my eyebrows in lecherous inquiry, to which she replied, "Without exception." That item also went onto the right side of the contract.

The left half was everything Siobhan would do while she was still able, such as: build an eight turret sand castle with bucket and spade, meet a silverback gorilla face to face in the Virunga Mountains, make a kite with three tails and leave it in a children's playground, visit the Boboli Gardens in Florence, and—typical of her humour—float in the Dead Sea, which she did for nearly an hour, grinning at the white oven-hot sky.

It took six months to reach the last item on the left side.

We argued, we debated, we fought over the fine points through many an evening, until we made a pact, sealed with red candles and rhyming couplets. Then we installed state-of-the-art systems on our 60 foot cutter-rigged ketch *Dawn Treader*, systems that would allow me to sail her alone.

Siobhan was too weak to step on board; it took four men, a winch and a bosun's chair to ease her safely over the rail. Much of the population of Hokitika was there to wave her goodbye; women brought flowers to the rail and schoolgirls hung their feet over the edge of the wharf. Men were there too, in from farms and forest and coal mines. We had never told anyone of the pact, but they all knew they wouldn't see Siobhan again. She bid them goodbye with a voice that could barely be heard, but with a sparkle that could be seen halfway down the wharf. Many found tears on their cheeks, even some of the hard men of the coast, who quickly brushed the evidence away.

As we carried her to her bunk in the saloon, she sighed with pleasure. As I cast off, she waved through the porthole and beamed at the ceiling. As we ran through Cook Strait and reached north into the Pacific, she seemed like a small, happy girl, on her way home after a long absence.

It took fifteen days to find what we sought.

For most of that time, the contrary ocean defied us, delivering idyllic cruising conditions that we would normally celebrate. Day after day, the air drifted lazily over beam and stern; and the Pacific went to sleep, dreaming long, slow dreams of earth and sky. We entered the trance-like state known to long-distance sailors, in which some senses are muted and others acutely enhanced. Siobhan always knew where I was on the vessel, and I could always hear her stir on her bunk. I could hear her calling for me, wanting water, or help to relieve herself, though she did not speak a word.

Between Niue and the Cook Islands, we listened to whales, humpbacks, migrating east across our path, singing to us through the steel hull.

Once, she asked me to bring her the sextant. She held it to her chest and shoulder like a harpsichord, touching the brass, rotating the filters, running her finger along the arc. To

Siobhan, the sextant was the greatest of all inventions, a marriage of science and poetry, its use a discipline and an art. But now she knew she was no longer capable of using it.

"Take a last fix for me," she begged.

So, when the night began to empty of darkness, I pulled down the moon to kiss the knife blade horizon, then, four hours later, did the same to the blazing sun. Calculations done, I took the chart to Siobhan and showed her the result. That section of the chart was almost empty, with little to interrupt the blue, and the satellite GPS on the navigation desk confirmed, to an absurd level of accuracy, that we were in a particularly obscure place on the planet. Even so, Siobhan wanted to hear the numbers, so I intoned the rhythms of latitude and longitude, then she sighed happily, closed her eyes and dozed.

Later, she woke briefly, murmuring, "It will come today."

It came in mid-afternoon, in the shape of cyclone Charlotte. First, smooth but steepening swells on the starboard quarter, then rising wind, not gusty, but relentless, a warning of the force to come. I raised the side of Siobhan's bunk, jamming pillows and cushions around her. I tidied every potential missile into its locker, bolting the oven on its gimbals. Then I turned downwind, dropped main and stays'l, and rolled up the jib until it was no bigger than a mean tablecloth, just enough to steady us.

The fury mounted.

When breaking seas roared on swells higher than the spreaders, *Treader* began to race down the seething slopes. We could not risk broaching or pitchpoling, so I dropped the sea anchor off the stern to reduce speed.

After dark, the moment came.

I took off the last of the sail, retrieved the sea anchor and spun *Treader* in a trough, until the massive seas bore down on the bow. I put on just enough power to give bite to the rudder, set the autopilot, switched on the spreader lights. Then I went below, which, in a hurricane, is like entering a bass drum being used by giants as a football.

In full storm gear, I held onto the side of Siobhan's bunk. In spite of the cushions, the violent movements were tossing her from one side of her bunk to the other, but she was awake, and when my hand found hers she squeezed it. When I looked at her with the question, she nodded immediately and her eyes were shining.

In spite of our pact, in spite of all our preparation, in spite of the goodbyes already said in hundred ways, a spear plunged through me.

Her lips moved, "Be seeing you, Jack. Be seeing you soon."

Partially blinded by tears, I pulled her out and over my shoulder and lurched up through the companionway, hitting the sides, but she made no sound. On deck, even though she was in her nightgown, she didn't shiver, I remember that. There was no delay. I put her hands on the starboard jackstay and in the quarter mile gaps between raging peaks, filled with strength, she pulled herself along the deck to the bow.

There she stood up straight and spread her arms just in time to greet the next avalanche, which boomed down on deck and buried *Treader*. For half a minute, only the wheelhouse and the mast were above the water.

When the bow rose again, she was no longer there.

I kept my part of the pact. I didn't throw the danbuoy, or trail a sheet, or fling the vessel into a rescue turn. I didn't even look sideways, port or starboard; I dared *not* look sideways in the first few seconds. *Let me not see her,* I prayed, but my mind played tricks in the corners of my vision and I saw her shape many times in the seething water, long after it was possible. I knew her body was drifting slowly down into the void, to join those of her sea-going ancestors.

When the hurricane eased, waves still lumping like biceps, I came off the wind, resumed the original course, and sailed on across the remains of Charlotte's playground. I switched off the autopilot and stayed at the wheel for two days and nights, so numbed that I became the autopilot.

On the third night, Siobhan kept her part of the pact.

It was after midnight, with the half-moon climbing out of the sea; Boa was comfortably curled up in the wheelhouse cot, wedged between bulkhead and pillow. I was staring ahead, hypnotized by Orion's dance about the stays, when I felt Siobhan beside and behind me. My entire body tingled with electricity.

"Hey, Jack," said her voice softly.

Now I could pretend that I had never doubted, that the brimming certainty of our pact was with me at all times; but it would not be true. In the impossibly long and lonely nights, there had been moments when I caught myself despairing; so I would fiercely flick the doubt away, but could never flick away the memory that it had been there. So when she spoke, behind me, I lost my self-control. I could not look around. Instead my head bent forward over the wheel as I gasped and trembled and my hands shook on the spokes. Out of the corner of my eye I could see that Boa had woken and was looking at where Siobhan must be standing.

"And here's you thinkin' it's all in your head," Siobhan's voice chided.

So I turned and looked and there she was, no longer in her nightgown, but dressed for the occasion in her seagoing clobber, baggy pullover and frayed jeans and deck shoes. And grinning her widest leprechaun's grin. This was Siobhan before she fell ill, the light in her eye restored to the full wicked glint.

"Seein' is believing," she added, nodding. "That's what they say."

I couldn't speak past the clamp around my throat, so I reached out to her arm with my fingertips. They didn't connect, because she shook her head and spoke with a sad smile.

"But believing is not touching, Jack."

"Why not?" I whispered.

"Here now," she scolded, as hot tears coursed down my cheeks. "Is there not enough of the salty stuff outside already?"

Boa went back to sleep.

That night set a pattern for the rest of the voyage. She would never appear during the busy distractions of the day, but at night when all about me fell into predictable rhythms. Sometimes there would be no conversation at all. Most likely that was when the moon was up, illuminating deck and mast and the spray flaring out from the plunging bow, the wind a gentle friend on the starboard quarter, and *Dawn Treader* a lazy cradle set in motion. At such times the stars and waves, wind and vessel would conspire to reach up through the wheel to spin themselves and us into one vast being. Seconds or hours later, when I reasserted my individual, separate self, Siobhan would no longer be on board.

Sometimes, especially in the vast reaches of the Pacific, she could be two nights away, yet return to find me still on the same tack, the same tilt, the same attitude to the trade wind swells.

Boa took Siobhan's new presence for granted. Unlike most adult cats Boa had adapted immediately to the sea. Based in the aft cabin, or under the solar panel, she made the entire vessel hers. Any rodent that came sniffing down the port mooring lines could expect a one-way trip. Offshore, any tired migrating bird resting on the decktread was unlikely to see land again. Flying fish landing on deck had seconds to live, and once I saw Boa's lightning claws pluck a silver flying fish out of the air that would otherwise have clattered safely over her head. Once, she climbed the foremast steps to twice my height, before considering her position. No port authority would allow her to disembark, so she was on board continuously for nearly two years. When she finally came ashore, back in New Zealand, in the Bay of Islands, her hind legs staggered drunkenly for an hour.

***

Now, standing by the fire, Siobhan returns my thoughts to the young man with the rifle, who may or may not be settling down to sleep in the hayshed. I feel a brief impulse to lock the door, but immediately dismiss it. I will not begin that way.

"Tell me, Jack", she says. "I'm wonderin', when you look at him, what do you see?"

I rub my hands together, play-acting. "I see a boxing ring. An interesting contest. No, a duel in the dawn: loaded minds at two paces."

"Answer me."

"All right. What I see is an intelligent, disturbed young man. He's running from something, from someone, maybe from the law. I see a great deal of pain somewhere in his background, definitely an advantage; with his-"

"How do you feel about that pain?"

"I don't understand. What are you asking me?"

"I'm asking how you feel about him."

"What kind of question is that? What I feel about him is irrelevant. What he feels about me is irrelevant. I have the desire to pass on the knowledge; he has the passion and the intensity to focus it. That's a match. What else matters?"

"There is the little matter of persuading *him* that it matters."

"There is that," I concede.

"And," she points out, "you're assuming that he's going to show up in the morning."

There's no answer to that and she doesn't expect one. In the ensuing silence, we raise our hands again to the no-touch position, palm close to palm.

After a while my lips move. "Be seeing you, Vonny. Be

seeing you soon."

Her smile softens, deepening her laughter lines. It's her smile, more than anything else, that convinces me in my darker moments that she really is Siobhan.

***

I'm milking Sheba before breakfast. I was a few minutes late, so I found her in her stall already, and grumpy. She didn't settle until I played her classical music from the barn radio; I also had to pummel her flank and murmur—sooooo, Sheba…. Sooooo, there girl—and assure her that her beauty so surpasses that of the original queen of Sheba, she is an danger of arousing the jealousy of the gods. It's the sincere tone that stops her using a hoof to remove me and the stool. It also relaxes her and smoothes the flow, so the milk zips rhythmically into the pail.

My ears are full of music and pail noises, so I'm not aware of him until his shadow falls beside me.

"What did you say that for?" he demands.

I turn my head without disturbing the rhythm. He's leaning against the corner of the barn, arms folded. His hood is up again, against the wind curling across the snow. But he's in hiking shorts, a young mountain man's declaration of toughness. His pack is on his back, rifle strapped across the top. Every now and then his gaze flicks to the open pasture behind him, and to the bush behind that, as if he expects company. He's poised for fight or flight. If he chooses to fight me, then he has already started with the smell of his unwashed body.

"You mean about who you really are?"

"Yes, that."

"Because that's what you want to know."

Two hens have latched on to him already. There's bare ground in the shelter of the barn wall and they're waiting, heads cocked, for his boots to force worms out of the sodden ground. A reasonable bet, but if it doesn't happen, they'll tackle his boot laces as a substitute. I turn back to Sheba, whose flank radiates warmth. Cold suspicion radiates from behind me.

"What are you? A shrink?"

"If you're going to insult me, I won't give you breakfast."

"Don't bother."

I slip petroleum jelly onto Sheba's teats, slap her flank and she lumbers away through the mud puddles and snow towards a strip of exposed pasture under the trees.

"Well I want some; so you'll need to come inside."

I head for the house and he hesitates pointedly before limping along behind. On the porch, he lowers his pack, once again placing it carefully parallel to the wall. Inside, I ask to see the wound and he declines with a dismissive shrug. "She'll be right."

He watches by the door as I pour two plates of steaming oatmeal porridge.

"Told you, don't bother."

"I made it already. If you want it, it's yours."

I top both with brown sugar and clotted cream of Sheba, then put mine at my place at the table, his on the opposite side. He stares at it, shrugs, picks it up and returns to the door frame. There he wolfs every scrap in silence without looking at me or uttering a single word and I wonder how long it is since he ate. His odour occupies the room.

I pour large mugs of hot sweet tea, but he ignores his.

"Fancy yourself as some kind of mind reader, do you?" he sneers.

"Nothing so exotic."

"Okay, so who am I? Go on, enlighten me." This seems so unlikely, he sniggers. I'm on trial and the verdict could be delivered in a microsecond. One wrong word on my part and he'll be gone faster than the clap of a hand, and yet I can't see how to slide around the point.

"Let's get the question right first. For you it's a big one. You want to know how to take control of your life."

His eyes narrow. "You know stuff-all about me."

"I know that your life has hurt you badly. You're wounded and angry. You want answers and you haven't been getting them. You also feel helpless and alone and you wonder if being alive is worth the effort."

He stands abruptly away from the door frame, eyes blazing as if I had slapped him in the face. He looks at the door handle, then back at me, staring.

"I don't need to be a mind reader. It's written all over you."

"Who fucking asked you for your opinion?"

"You did."

"And I suppose you think you've got all those answers."

"I do."

"Who the hell are you to know stuff like that?" The anguish in the pit of his stomach stabs so strongly, I can feel its echo in me. He suppresses it ruthlessly and rocks with indecision. Go or stay. Go or stay. Sunlight floods in the window, made brilliant by the surrounding snow. It illuminates every perfect detail of him: the blood-stained boot, a ripped pocket seam, a tear in the leather belt, the bob of his Adam's apple, the pallor of his sunken cheeks, and his hair, so thick with grime it has straightened most of his curls. He radiates uncompromising, fierce intensity. He's a work of art that attracts and repels simultaneously.

A hundred paces away most of the alpacas press up against the fence of the enclosure, unable to graze. They're looking towards us, as if they can hear our conversation. In the male enclosure, Socrates' head stands out, higher than the others, coolly appraising all before him. Another male comes too close and Socrates sees him off with a spit audible from the house.

My visitor turns, suspiciously. "So what's in it for you?"

"Nothing."

"Crap. Nobody does anything for nothing."

"You're right. I'm doing this for me. I want to tell you how life works, how it affects you, and how you can take control of it. I want to do it because it'll make me feel good."

"Mr Doogooding Fixit, are you? You're wasting your time."

"That will be up to you."

Then he shrugs again and pulls a chair out from the table, well out, to reaffirm his declaration of independence. He can also keep an eye on the outside world through the window.

"The locals call me Jack," I tell him.

They have called me Jammy Jack ever since Siobhan and I started using the quickening to indulge our fantasies. Whatever unlikely venture we launched, our toast always landed jammy side up. In the late nineties, we even built a restaurant in the bush canopy at the bottom of the farm, thirty feet up on the stumps of four ancient kauri overlooking the sea. No advertising, no signs, hard to find—and outrageously successful. Everyone ate on benches at long tables and everyone got the same meal. The tiny stage was stocked with every possible instrument, including a length of drainpipe for kids to bang on. Talent was not required. If you felt like performing, you were guaranteed noisy and enthusiastic appreciation. Diners in period dress came all the way up from Milford Sound to experience bad music, pile-driver seating and superb food. Children would clamour to write out the simple menu using goose feather quills and ink bottles. One line always said *Mystery Dish*. It was a tradition, for those with the courage, to taste the dish, praise it, worry about it, then wait for the drum-roll and the announcement. It was always a cunningly disguised wild delicacy, such as huhu grub gratin, possum pâté, weta and cricket curry, or mountain oyster macaroni. Amidst the howls of dismay, children would rush to the window to pretend to throw up. One diner brought his own recording of the funeral march. We were notorious.

Even the media referred to me as Jammy Jack, but always added the other name, Conrad Fleming, relentlessly tugging at the past like a fishing line snagged in murky water. Reporters came to the restaurant, we couldn't stop that, but we never gave interviews, not then, not three decades later, when we were still getting a dozen calls a year, most from overseas.

"Locals?" the young man questions. "Up here?"

"Anyone within twenty miles."

He nods warily and we have marginal détente. "Well don't expect me to tell you *my* name."

"I don't need your name to tell you who you are."

"It's Smith," he says. "Matt Smith."

He's lying, and he doesn't care that it's obvious.

PART TWO

ONE

"Go on then, spit it out." He's leaning against the wall by the door frame, setting himself at an angle, one shoulder to me. He knocks his boot against the wall skirting, tap tap, tap tap, just loud enough to irritate. But as soon as I speak, he attends to my words the way Boa attends to a rustle in the undergrowth.

"What I'm going to tell you is not factual knowledge. It's about a passion that far exceeds anything you have experienced in this lifetime."

"What do you know about what I've experienced?" He stops the foot tapping, and shifts weight. "Take yourself pretty damn seriously, don't you?"

"Perhaps."

He gives me a knowing look. "Don't tell me, let me guess: you're the only one who knows this stuff."

"I'm the only one in front of you right now. But there's no hurry; if you don't talk to someone like me, then through many lifetimes you'll create the conditions that teach you anyway. You can't help it; it's built into the system. In the long term, it's impossible for you to choose a wrong path."

He blows air through his nose. "As if I had a choice."

"You did. You do, in every second. For example, you chose to believe that you're a victim and selected your path accordingly."

"*Believe? Believe* I'm a victim?"

"The paradigm of perpetrators and victims is a potent belief system that plays out around you. You can take it as real, or as a play with a blind director. You."

"This is crap!" His contempt is palpable.

"It's fertiliser."

"It's weasel shit."

"You're still here."

"I can fix that right now."

"I know."

His brow bunches into tight vertical lines, then he stabs the table with a finger. "So it's all my fault then. Let's play blame-the-victim, right? Tell that to someone who's been abused, or mugged, or raped. No wonder you live up here on your own, old man—they probably ran you out of town. I mean, get a life, for God's sake!"

"Exactly the point. How to get a life."

He blows air between his teeth, baffled that I am not angry.

In fact, he has succeeded in annoying me. If I relax my discipline, I could allow myself to dislike the boy. Which is what he wants, of course; it's his ticket to leave.

"What you're going to hear," I say evenly, "will turn common sense upside down."

He's so stressed by his competing needs to leave and to stay that he glares everywhere, works his lips around his teeth, and shifts weight constantly. It's as if he's standing on a hot plate.

"Matthew, you have *already* been directing your own life, without knowing it. You have been waving a powerful wand while wearing a blindfold, creating situations that damage you. But when you take off the blindfold and realize what you can do consciously with the wand, life becomes electrifying."

"Wand," he scorns. "Bedtime stories."

"Then don't call it a wand. Call it the *quickening*."

"Quickening," he repeats.

"Your potential is immense, far beyond what you have imagined. It's time for you to wake what has hibernated inside you for many lifetimes."

At that, he draws back in a slow cringe of discomfort. He shakes his head, swears softly, and mutters, "The way you talk…" But he hardens his tone. "So, let's have it. The quickening."

"You want to cut to the chase, directly to the power."

"I just want you to get to the point so I can get out of here."

"No, you don't get the quickening yet."

"Are you stuffing me around? I thought you were falling all over yourself to dump your shit on me."

"Suppose the answers come in a package with a label that says, *Warning! This device can be lethal if operated carelessly.*"

"Lethal?" he says, "You're pulling my chain."

"If it could be lethal, would you want the bullet point summary or would you read the instruction manual?"

Perversely, his interest is climbing.

"The manual," he shrugs. "How long is it?"

"It's exactly the right length. You don't even get to open it until you're ready, and you're not ready."

"So it's the whole sales pitch or nothing."

"Your choice… and it's your choice whether or not to be gracious about it." *Damn. A mistake.*

His mouth forms an 'o', his eyes narrow and speculate. Then, for the first time, I detect a glint of satisfaction. He has measured the enemy and already found a weakness. I am furious at my lapse, but he must not know it.

"You were going to tell me who I am," he says. "Go on, impress and astound me."

"You mean sum it up quickly? Cut and dried?"

"Yes, for God's sake!"

"Certainly. You are both the Creator and the Created. *Aham Brahmasmi.* The Hindu masters have known this for thousands of years. You are powerful beyond measure and you have only to remember the fact."

His face is blank. "That's it?"

"That's it."

"That's who I am?"

"In a nutshell."

He struggles for a response.

"What?" I say. "You're not astounded yet? You're not struck dumb with wonder? Of course not! Listen. The universe runs on feelings, not bullet points; the universe *is* a giant feeling expressing itself and you're part of it. If you want full mastery, you're going to need more than one-liners."

"Assuming I plan to stick around, which I don't."

"But you are still here. That's because you're starting to get a feeling, deep down, that you somehow recognise this."

He's startled and says, "Shit."

"It's as if something powerful that has been hibernating in you is beginning to open an eye."

"Don't! Don't say things like that!"

"Why not?"

"It's creepy... It's... getting in deeper than I thought."

"You were in over your head before you arrived; the word drowning comes to mind."

"You're pushing it, Grandad!' He rises abruptly, walks in a circle, eyes darting here and there. He takes a deep breath, letting it out slowly. His gaze swivels pointedly towards the rifle at the door and then back to me. He snarls, "If you're so smart, you know I've got nothing to lose."

"I believe you."

He's shaking his head as if I'm a blowfly that will not be swatted away. "You've got a lot of fucking nerve. I mean, look at you... a scrawny old buzzard with no feathers left and a beak that won't stop gabbing."

More irritation pings in my stomach, but this time it is easily controlled. Allow the feeling, observe it from a distance, release it to dissipate of its own accord. Soon, this ancient discipline of the masters will be his.

He shrugs, sits slowly and peers at me as if I will, any

moment, reveal myself as fraudster or fool. He sneers, "This talk of wands—sounds like black magic."

"It is."

"What?!" His head jerks up.

"And white magic, and prayer and visualization and affirmations and many other devices used by those who seek to master life. But I am talking about their essence, not their form. The quickening can include props and ritual, but no master of life is bound by it. Real power comes from within."

"It's some kind of religion, then."

"Definitely not. Religions are a scourge. The worst treat you like a sheep and shepherd you away from your power, not towards it. They would have you believe that you are inherently weak, unworthy and offensive to a greater being, that humanity is dysfunctional and the sum of its misdeeds. It is not. Humanity doesn't need fixing. It's perfect and it always was."

"Are you soft in the head? You never read the papers? What about child abuse and child slavery and terrorism? What about the children who die because drug companies want bigger profits? What about those beheadings and stonings and the corruption and all those lying politicians? That sound like perfection to you? And you call me blind. Hah! You need to get out more, old man, find yourself a better guide dog."

I smile. "Those events are like pieces of a jigsaw. In isolation they look ugly, but when you combine them, you get a picture of great beauty and depth."

He leans forward as if he must be hearing me wrongly. "You know this is hard to take from someone who's loaded. You sit up here with all this imported luxury stuff. You probably own the whole valley. That alpaca herd is too small to be commercial. It's a hobby, isn't it? You're rich. You don't know what it's like to have to work for food."

"You mean my words sound like callous indifference or naïve ignorance."

"Now you're talking," he says. "On the button."

"You've heard the phrase, It's all an illusion? It's not true. Your pain is real, your pleasure is real. The illusion is to think that the reality you experience is *all* there is. In the reality behind reality, a much more powerful version of you exists, an expanded self, of which your mind-"

"Oh, and my expanded self lines me up for this life? For this bowl of bat vomit? Some kind of spiritual sadism, right?"

"No. Your mind and your expanded self are not separate. Your mind is part of your expanded self, just as the crescent moon is part of the whole. If you experience pleasure or pain, then your expanded self experiences the same."

"Okay, then it's masochism."

"Ask an Olympic runner if the pain was worth it. Ask a mountain climber if the fatigue was worth it. Try suggesting to the audience of *Romeo and Juliet* that the play might be more moving with less agony. Pleasure can only grow out of pain. If you see a pohutukawa emerging from the dirt, do you cut away its roots to prevent it contaminating the future flower?"

His mouth opens, closes, opens again. "You're the one with the illusions."

"What do you mean?"

"There's nothing there! There's no grand design… it's just mindless, random cruelty. That soul stuff is for people shit scared of the light going out. Expanded self… hah! All I am is what you're looking at right now. Nothing more."

"And what am I looking at?"

"Atoms." His eyes flicker. Aluminium, arsenic, bromine, calcium, carbon, chlorine, chromium, cobalt-"

"Yes, I get the picture. So you can probably tell me what holds that assembly of atoms together."

"Damn right. Inter-atomic and inter-molecular bonds."

"And what holds it all in the human shape…? What heals you when you're injured or sick…? What causes your thoughts and feelings?"

"DNA." He's getting angrier by the moment. "Evolution. Complex specialisation. Survival of the fittest."

"And what causes the feeling you have right now—even as you argue with me—that there is more to your life than the cold complexity of atoms?"

He comes off the wall, eyes smoking, gaze darting about my face, trying without success to look directly into my eyes.

"Matthew, through many lifetimes your mind has nurtured a desire to re-connect with your expanded self, like a carefully tended ember in the deepest recess of the cave. Now it's time to bring the ember forward and blow on it. I will help you do that."

"Oh you will, will you? And what's the catch?"

"No catch, no conditions. You have nothing to lose but your suffering."

"There's always a catch. You want money?"

I smile faintly. He knows I don't need it.

He takes on a shrewd look. "You want to be a guru, then, right? You want me to be a humble student at the feet of the great master? Right? Fat chance." He shakes his head, furious that he delayed this moment so long. "I've got your number, Zimmerman; you were desperate for someone to turn up, weren't you? And I'm the sucker got handed the short straw. Nah! This is too weird for me, you're away with the fairies. I'm outa here."

With not even a glance of farewell, he hoists pack and rifle off the porch and takes off across the snow towards the track. The sun has repainted the sky the blue of a thrush egg, the melt is under way, but snow will still be set in deep, unstable drifts where the track hugs the upper gorge. There's no exit that way.

While he's gone, I discover that the power has been restored, but the phone is still dead.

***

He's back in less than an hour.

"I'm stuck for another night," he barks from out on the snow. "I'll stay in the hayshed again."

He takes over the hayshed, ejecting Sheba. In the early evening he hunches over a white spirits cooker. He fills the billy with snow and it's more than an hour before I see him holding a mug, hands inside sleeves, huddled, collar up against the cold. Then, no more cooking. I suspect he has no food with him.

Before nightfall, he leaves the hayshed and strides across the middle paddock to the reservoir. At the outlet stream, he leans the rifle amongst dripping icicles and throws off all his clothes. He washes himself in the snow-fed water, fighting cold with frenetic energy while the two keas, Rangi and Papa, swagger and preen nearby, scratching behind their heads and commenting on his performance. He puts on only his outer layer of clothes, then washes the remaining garments so vigorously it looks like an act of violence, beating them on a rock he has kicked free of snow, wringing them out with hands that must have lost all feeling in the first minute. Then he snatches up clothes and rifle, runs back to the hayshed and lays the wet clothes out on the bales. There is not the slightest chance that they will dry overnight.

And now he will be deeply cold, down to the bone. Perhaps he thinks this machismo will make an impression on me.

I turn the duct heating onto full, then fan the embers in the fire, feeding them with twigs from the bin. When they blossom, I feed them thicker branches, then stack logs around them in a U shape and soon they shimmer in rescue orange and radiate heat into the room.

He walks in without knocking, wild-eyed, leaving me to close the door.

"I have to get warm," he says.

He crouches in front of the fire, torso and limbs shaking. He has to be urged to take off his boots and with his nerveless fingers, it takes minutes to reveal feet the colour of candle wax.

"You want a shower?"

"No. But if I've got to be stuck here, you might as well tell me your stuff. It's entertaining, I'll give you that."

"You can have dry clothes if you want. Socks? Pullover?"

"Nah."

"All right, you've made your point," I say. "But, remember I'm doing this for me. You don't owe me a thing."

He looks up swiftly. "You're doing it for you, all right. You've got something to prove to yourself, haven't you... some kind of inadequacy thing." He sniggers. "Or maybe you have delusions of adequacy."

A sour stab in my stomach silences me—and puzzles me; how can an individual I've known less than a day rouse such a reaction in me? Why am I not just amused?

Matthew nods with satisfaction. "You hate me, don't you?" he says. Then he shrugs, intending to convey indifference. What the shrug actually conveys is a declaration of need so loud it rescues me from another wrong move.

"Not even close. It's you who hates you; you're at war with yourself."

"You being the peacemaker, I suppose."

"Possibly." I glance towards the hayshed. "But first things first; if you don't accept a little practical help, you'll get hypothermia and be stuck with me longer than you want. We need to get your clothes over here and drying. I'll get them now and I won't touch anything but the wet clothes. Stay here and get your body temperature back to normal."

I'm through the door before he can argue.

When I return, he intercepts me on the porch. His clothes will not be going into my dryer. Instead, he hangs them on the porch line where they will be starched by tonight's frost and steamed in tomorrow's sun.

He returns to the fire. It's half an hour before he stops shaking, even more before colour returns to his skin. He accepts a mug of hot, sweet tea without comment, sits up on the couch and eventually allows himself to lean against the backrest. His hand is so awkward handling the mug that it draws my eyes. There's a recent scar on his thumb and another on his forefinger. They look like burns.

I pull an armchair around to sit adjacent to him, lean forward and speak softly.

"Matthew, listen to me. I need you to place your anger to one side for a while. Stop shooting from the ramparts, lower the drawbridge, and come on out where you can truly hear what I'm offering you."

His defences are not ready for this approach. He puts his tea mug down on the armrest, crosses arms over his torso, and his body rocks almost imperceptibly. He catches himself in the act and kills the movement. He looks desperately tired now.

"Then," I continue, "as you listen to my words, I need you to watch carefully for more of that deep down feeling of recognition. Accept only the words that generate that feeling, reject anything else."

"I don't… I'm not… I mean how will I know?"

"You already know. You already sense something happening, as if an invisible train is passing through, waiting for you to catch sight of it and swing up on board."

His mouth hangs open. I can almost feel the prickling around his cheeks and temples. He looks down at his hands and back at me, accusing.

"You're making me feel weird. What are you doing?"

"Good weird or bad weird?"

He darts glances all around my head as if he is working out how to place me for a photograph. "It's the way you're speaking. You're using psychology on me."

"No psychology, just truth from the highest shelf I can reach."

"Some kind of hypnotic suggestion, then?"

"No, you'll make your own decisions. Underneath, you know where this is going, but you're afraid that life will let you down. Again."

Matthew's eyes close, but instantly open again, a lapse he covers with energetic blinking. He moves his tea mug so the edge of the handle is precisely above the edge of the armrest; to achieve this, he leans so that his eye is directly above the handle.

"So tell me. Get on with it," he says. "Tell me something to stop all the... all the... thoughts running around...yakking..." He runs out of words and raises two hands and makes them into jaws that attack each other.

"I can describe the state of mind you can expect when you master your life, but you'll have to be willing to allow the images to enter your mind."

He nods brusquely, leans back, stretches out his feet to the flames and doesn't move them even when a spark hits his toe. I speak slowly, with long pauses in which the only sound is embers re-positioning in the hearth.

"Imagine..." I say. "Imagine... that you're walking on a path through the forest, in a future very close to now. Imagine, as you walk, the calming ebb and flow of your breath, the relaxed rhythm of your body, and the soothing swing and tap of the walking staff in your right hand. As you walk, your thoughts come to rest and gradually your mind clears until it's like the surface of a tarn when the wind dies in the dawn. You become what is around you: the shale crunching at your feet, the *totara* guarding the path and, in its uppermost branch, the bellbird singing summer to the sky. All things, seen and unseen, come to fill your being and tell you that heaven was always here, where you are, on this very bend in the path. You are where you want to be and you want to be where you are."

Matthew's eyes close.

"When thoughts finally return to your mind, you are their master, and it is you who chooses to accept or reject the thoughts. You accept only those thoughts which connect with the great field, the source of all life, so that you can have, do, or be, whatever you desire, and so that your path lays itself through the forest according to your will. You are excited to be alive, filled with purpose; and others who cross your path are drawn to you, though they do not know why.

"Others may seek your approval, but you do not seek theirs, and you cannot be flattered or wounded by their words. Others may seek to condemn you, but though you may feel regret, you have no use for guilt or shame. Others may hold a compass before you, but your only guide is the great field within, which knows nothing of sin, and cannot be offended.

"Yet you do not feel superior or inferior to any living thing, because you and they are different faces of one Being, which knows itself through all adventures and all paths through the forest. And..." I whisper the last words, "...you are no longer afraid."

Matthew doesn't move. Boa watches me steadily from the top of a pile of books near the grandfather clock. Getting up or down, she never topples the pile. Since Matthew arrived, she has not been back to her basket by the fridge. I have noticed also that she never looks at him directly.

He turns to me, startled. "What did you stop for?"

"How do you feel?"

"Like you were swinging a fob watch in front of my eyes."

"Call it meditation."

"You said there was no sin. You're saying this field thing is godless?"

"I am—if you're talking of a separate god, out there

somewhere. The idea was useful for its time, but that time is passing."

"You're rubbishing the Bible."

"Definitely not. Read the Bible, the Koran, the Torah and the Bhagavad Gita and look for the wisdom buried in them. But read them as if *you* were a great and wise being. Do the words agree with this wise being in you? If so, accept them. If not, let them pass by."

"That's arrogant," he objects. "That's conceited. To set myself up as-"

"Matthew, your fullest, most expanded self *is* God. Your separation is an illusion maintained by your thoughts."

"Haw! My ego will throw a party."

"No, it will throw a wake, because it cannot tolerate the idea that you are re-connecting with your expanded self. Your ego's job is to keep you believing exclusively in your Earth drama. To do that, it must keep you separate and capable of being hurt by what seems to be other than you."

Several different expressions cross Matthew's face in quick succession. There's a moment of unguarded interest.

"Try this," I continue. "Imagine that at your core you are deeply happy. What would you be doing if you were deeply happy?"

"Deeply happy? All the time? I'd be getting compulsory medication."

I chuckle. "You're dodging. But don't mistake me; when you have mastered your life you will still experience pain, but you'll experience it without suffering."

"Pain without suffering? Come on!"

"They are not the same. Pain is the direct outcome of an event, but suffering comes from the attitude you adopt to the event and to the pain. And you will learn how to release even the pain, allowing it to pass by without detaining it, the way a willow branch sways with the wind and then straightens. The

willow does not perceive a boundary between itself and 'other';
it knows itself not only as leaves, branches and roots, but also
as the earth and the stream which caresses the roots of all living
things."

"Stop."

"What is it?"

"You're making me... it's... like that invisible train. Passing
through."

"Good. And when you have sighted it and swung up on
board, you will walk towards the engine as an apprentice
master of life. To do that, you will learn to master your own
thoughts. You will become extremely disciplined."

"Too late," he smirks. "I've already been extremely
disciplined. I wasn't raised, I was broken in." He waits for my
inquiring glance, his grin cornered like a hospital sheet, his
tone altered. "'What will it be today, Whippy Willow or Cutty
Cane?' 'Oh, I'll have Whippy Willow, thank you Mother.'"

"Ah. I see. That was agreeable of you."

"Of course," he says mockingly. "We were a model family,
weren't we? So unhappiness was a punishable offence. I had to
use a happy, kind voice all the time. Like Father's, so kind, so
gentle and compassionate..." He's in another state now, not
looking at me. His anger takes another form, his voice light
with affected carelessness. "Father would put his forehead
down on my shoulder so our heads would touch and he would
say, 'You know your mother and I have to teach you how to be
a good boy and love God and us, don't you?'

He adopts a humble small boy posture. "'Yes Father.'

"Then Mother would pick up Mr Whippy and say, 'The
golden rule is....?'

"'A helping of hurt now brings a heaping of happiness later.'

"'Correct. And this act of love is necessary because...?'

"'For perfect love I must perfect be.'

"'Correct. Now touch your toes. Right down.'"

His hostility to me has been suspended for now. I ask, "Your mother did it?"

"Yep. Forehands and backhands; she used to be a tennis champion. Father would inspect to see if I had put a tea towel in my pants, then he would sit and watch while he ate salted peanuts out of a jar. He didn't like the peanut skins, so he would pull them off before he popped the nut in his mouth. After the whipping he would get down on his knees and hug me and put his head on my shoulder and tell me how my pain was hurting him and Mother deeply. He always said that. Instead of crying, I had to thank Mother for her act of love."

An insect scuttles somewhere in a corner and Boa's head lifts. Matthew studies the back of his hand, which is trembling, and then the other, which joins in.

"He left the priesthood in Australia and came here and took up counselling at a health camp for delinquent boys. Then he met Mother, clever, clever Mother; she was a psychologist and a time-and-motion efficiency expert. When I was ten she wrote a book called *The Creation of Genius: how to turn your child into a prodigy*. They took me round the country giving public lectures."

"With you as the star."

"Yep. I was top billing at the freak show. I wore a little suit and a black bow tie and gave pre-pubescent accomplishment speeches in church halls. Played Mozart, parroted dates, did sums in my head, explained the connection between energy and matter. Audiences loved it, didn't they? Especially when clever Mother told them that prodigies are not born, but made by their parents. Every time she paused, they gave her a standing ovation."

"So her method worked."

"Worked!" he scoffs. "That's one way to put it." He sits on his quisling hands, but now he can't stop his mouth. "Filled me full of fish oil and blueberries and ginseng and a yellow powder from Sumatra that made my tongue furry. They flashed pictures in my eyes, and played sleep-learn records at night. No children's stories allowed, no negative emotions, no raised voices, only dignified discourse on philosophers and thinkers. On the book tours, Mother flashed up intelligence-time graphs and—surprise, surprise—they always rose from left to right and made audiences gasp. And Father would stand there admiring her with one hand on my shoulder and the other holding a Bible. He told them God had been waiting for sinful mankind to find its way home through the disciplined intelligence of its children. He told them small boys were like canoes which should be paddled from the rear, and I was expected to smile. The audiences loved it, and so did the media; one paper said my parents were the cure for the liberal ideas sucking moral fibre out of the new generation."

"Did your mother do all the beatings?"

"Hah! Wash your mouth out, it was called *behaviour motivication*. Behaviour motivication at 7.15pm, Proverbs 7.30, piano practice 7.45 sharp, no shifting about on the seat. At 8.15, Mother practised the piano and at 8.45 Father would get on the trumpet and play *Greensleeves*. Always *Greensleeves*."

I realize that I am also sitting on my hands and bring them out.

"All very precise," I observe.

"Everything by the number. For behaviour motivication they set the piano metronome to slow, down to one second. I got it every fourth second." He waves his hand back and forth. "Whack, tock, tick, tock. Whack, tock..." He shrugs. "But I had an escape. I would make a film in my head. We would be on safari in India and a tiger would attack from a high tree, ripping off Father's arm so that blood spurted all over the porters and elephants. I would fight the tiger and drive it back into the jungle. Then Father would cry and whisper that I was a grown-up hero and from now on I wouldn't make him play the game any more."

"The game?"

He pulls his hands out and studies them again. He pushes the middle three fingernails of his right hand hard into the palm of his left, then inspects the resulting marks. They look like stab wounds that have healed over. When he looks up, suspicion and hostility return.

"How did we get into all that?" he accuses.

"We were talking about how disciplined you were."

"You're supposed to be talking about your stuff." His voice rises. "Don't be so bloody nosey. I don't want to talk about me any more, okay? You got that?"

***

In the country of sleep my dreams are a two-storey house. I dream on one floor, watching from the other.

I am looking for something, urgently. It's terrifying that I might not find it—doubly terrifying that I don't know what it is I must find. Perhaps it's a toy that I left outside. I can't think what it's called, or even picture what it looks like.

While looking, I am distracted by Boa who has caught a jet-black piwakawaka and brought it inside. If it escapes and flies around, I will die. I try to make her release the bird, though I'm afraid that it will then spread its wings. She refuses; I try to pry her jaws apart, but she rumbles in her throat and her jaws tighten. I'm furious with her and throw her in the air, close to the ceiling, hoping to make her release her prey. It doesn't work. She lands on her feet, fantail still clamped, her growl roller-coastering up and down, warning me of dire consequences.

A python slides out of a hole in my head, just behind my ear, twin tongues tasting the air independently. The tongues become my hands which clear snow away from ice which covers the surface of the reservoir. As I look down through the ice, a Neanderthal woman floats by beneath. She has shaggy hair and receding forehead, and ridiculously long breasts which float out from her chest. She peers up at me with shock and amazement and shouts a question, but I can't hear the words.

TWO

I trudge across the snow to feed the alpacas by hand. It's a pleasure I would keep to myself, but since Matthew is still in the hayshed, I can hardly avoid him. He's sitting on a bale of lucerne, looking through the telescopic sights of the Sako at various objects around where the track comes out of the trees. The weapon makes my teeth ache. The red dot behind the safety slide is all too obvious.

"Sleep all right?" I ask.

"Not bad," he grunts. It would be the same answer if he had lost a limb to gangrene.

I hoist the first bale. He starts to follow me, but I look at the rifle pointedly and shake my head. He glances back to the track, shrugs, and puts the weapon down behind his pack. Then he picks up a bale and walks with me across the snow, beside me to avoid the indignity of following, but well separated to avoid any hint of companionship.

The entire herd steps hesitantly towards the fences in both enclosures. The highest in the pecking order take the front positions, heads aloof, a fringe of wool over knowing, luminous black eyes. These are *suri*, the nobility of the alpaca world. The Incas and the invading Spanish prized the wool because the silky fibre has high tensile strength, and is hollow, giving it extraordinary warmth for its weight. The Incas bred alpacas from llamas and wild vicuña. Mine have waited through this snow with patience bred in the blizzards of the Andes.

One approaches now, with inch-by-inch caution, peering past me at Matthew. She nuzzles my arms and neck spasmodically, unable to keep her eyes off him.

"Morning, Popper." I nuzzle her back. She demands affection on every visit—unless she's pregnant, in which case she treats me like a bad smell.

"You know them all by name?" Matthew asks.

At the sound of his voice, Popper scrambles away to the safety of the herd. A message is passed; the herd retreats half a dozen steps, but turns again in unison, choreographed, heads perfectly still, keeping Matthew in sight.

"These are not sheep," I reply.

He nods. "Meat or wool?"

"Here's a clue: they die of old age."

In fact, there was one exception. Two years ago, Siobhan and I were up at the henhouse when we heard a fuss from the compound. When we got there Rousseau was missing, there was blood on the grass, the rest of the herd milling and terrified. It had to be hunters, down out of the tops empty-handed. I didn't bother with the track, I cut straight down the gorge, boulder bashing, and waited for them by their ute on the main road. Two men appeared, heavily tattooed, one with the tears of the prisoner below his right eye. Rousseau was over one set of shoulders, throat slit and his head banging against the pack. I pointed out that they could shoot me, they could drive away and have the cops waiting, or they could take Rousseau back to the farm and give her a decent burial. They chose the burial, dug the grave and stood by in extreme discomfort as Siobhan gave Rousseau part of the Irish blessing: *May the sun shine warm upon your face, and the rains fall soft upon your fields.*

Then we fed them. As they set off down the path afterwards, the one with the tattoo tears muttered, "Fuckin' freaky." The other mumbled to me, "Sorry, mate."

Matthew and I throw three bales over for the females and drop barley nuts into the trough. That produces a sedate pushing match, ordered by strict hierarchy, almost dignified, except that the occasional dispute is settled by spitting. When an alpaca spits, it's straight into the face and includes a spray of saliva and sometimes a peppering of barley nuts. The young ones are independent of status and always allowed through to the feed.

After the semi-controlled frenzy, Popper returns, keeping her distance from Matthew. I scratch my fingernails under her jaw and down the front of her throat, a sensual delight which nearly drops her to her knees. Matthew's tension eases. Other alpacas come closer—Leibniz, Mahasaya, Berkley. Disreputable Berkley, lowest ranked amongst the alpacas, on the outer, always in a dream world as if nothing around him is real and he has to be reminded to eat and breathe.

The males get a single bale through the fence at the other end of the trough. Socrates, as always, comes first. Every now and then, to underline his authority, he stands tall, broad-shouldered, shaggy-browed, questioning all and finding all wanting. Then a graceful dip of the head, a grasp and pull, a thoughtful chewing and contemplation. Macchiavelli, second male, positions himself in Socrates' peripheral vision. He makes a sudden movement, looking downhill as if to an object of considerable interest. As Socrates' head rises in response, Macchiavelli's teeth extract a sizeable chunk of hay from the bale. The deception succeeds and a lunge and spit from Socrates is too late to stop him.

The air slips on crystalline snow and rasps on our exposed flesh.

In the back of the herd, Simone is the only one holding back. She's humming, when the others are silent. Her teats are swollen. Lately she has been eating less and adding to the dung pile more often. She'll be in labour soon.

Matthew seems obsessed by the animals, almost proprietorial. He tells me a lot about alpacas, wanting me to know how much he knows. He first met them in the Andes, when he was walking across the *altiplano*, a high altitude, frozen plateau. It was the middle of the night and he stopped to relieve himself. To do so, he threw his snow sodden poncho over one shoulder, spooking a large herd, unleashing a mini-storm of cloven hooves and a thundering in his chest.

"Almost forgot to piss," he says.

I glance at him sharply to see if this is humour, but it isn't.

His mood changes suddenly. He says, "There's something weird about you."

"Undoubtedly." I growl. "What in particular?"

"It's like you were hanging about waiting for me to arrive. I still don't get who the hell you are."

"You don't have to."

"You're unloading your stuff on me. I need to know something about you."

I sigh. "All right. Here it is in brief. In my early years, around your age, I had an accident that nearly killed me. I was in a coma for months. When I woke, I couldn't remember the accident and I couldn't remember anything of my earlier life. But I also woke up directly aware of the infinite field of consciousness and discovered that the true cause of my suffering was me. That's it."

He grumbles, "I still don't know who you are. What was the accident? Something to do with that scar behind your ear?"

"Yes. Well, I don't recall anything up to that point. I've been told a few things, but they mean nothing to me, so I'm not going to give you a second-hand story."

"Up to that point?"

"I have no memory of the accident or my life before it."

"What?" He grapples with the implications and becomes angry. "So here you are promising me the wisdom of the ages and all the power in the world and the first half of your life has gone AWOL? Permanently?"

"That's right."

"That's… That's…'

"Ludicrous?"

"My God, all this time I've been listening to a head case! Why should I take notice of anything you say?"

"Good question. And the answer should sound familiar. It's not about who or what I am. The only thing that counts is what stirs in you like an echo. Stay only for that. When you no longer feel it, go."

"Damn right."

"You're still here."

"You still piss me off."

"Sometimes the feeling is mutual."

"You want me to go now? Is that it?"

I grin. "Of course not. Now, here are the ground rules. I'm not going to answer any more questions about me, unless they're to do with the farm."

"Oh. Rules now? You hand out detentions, maybe? Shall I write out fifty times, *I must not piss off the teacher?*" He's pleased with himself for that thrust.

"No. But here's the next rule: it's time you told me what's wrong with *your* head."

His grin collapses and his eyes swivel away. Suddenly his breath is unpredictable and shallow, tripping over itself. I can almost hear his heart banging in his throat.

"Yeah, well, you don't know how *much* of a head case I am," he says darkly. "You won't wait for the snow to thaw, you'll kick me out." Amongst the alpacas, Berkeley dips and raises his head in agreement.

I wait.

"All right," he says, "I have visions." His laugh is as brittle as the icicles hanging along the edge of the hayshed roof. He's tense, strung to high pitch, anticipating my reaction. "Well?" he demands.

"Just tell me."

"I got myself locked up because of these fucking visions, all right?" It's still a warning.

"Were you insane?"

"I had so many screws falling out you could store them for winter."

"Are you insane now?"

He scratches at his beard, studying my face. He says, "You can work that out for yourself."

"It's cold. I'll work it out inside. Come in."

***

He checks his clothes on the porch. They're not much drier than when he put them there, but I don't offer the dryer again; once is definitely enough. Inside, he appoints himself keeper of the fire, bringing in an armful of wood, fussing with the arrangement of the burning logs. All the while, his face is pale and when I look expectant, he mutters to the fire, "Never told anyone." Then he takes a deep breath, letting it out with a shudder.

"It started when I was ten," he says. "In the middle of Father and Mother exhibiting me round the country. I started having crazy dreams every night. I mean *really* crazy—don't say I didn't warn you." He swallows, breathes in and out. "I wore a robe. I produced fish and bread cakes for hungry folks without spending time in the kitchen. Getting the idea?" He grins fiercely.

I nod.

And he frowns, not quite believing that I could take it so calmly. Then he is suddenly bold; as if it was all a cosmic comedy in which he landed the part of fall guy. "How about this? In my dreams I walked on water. Do you like it? Hell, in the daytime I couldn't even stand on a *frozen* puddle. Sick people were brought to me on stretchers. I even did the cross thing with the thorns and nails and blood running down my face. Woke up with my hands trying to tear the sheets. Sometimes I splashed water on the pillow so Father wouldn't notice the sweat when he did the washing."

I can feel the fluttering in the middle of his rib cage, like echoes in a chasm.

"I knew if I told anyone, the worst kind of shit was going to hit the fan. Even if I didn't, I thought forked lightning would come out of the clouds any time." He shoots a glance at me. "You can't tell anyone this, I've got enough shit happening already. If you tell anyone I'll fucking kill you!"

"I hear you."

"By the time I was fourteen, they weren't dreams any more, I got them during the day. I hid in the school toilets, or if I was at home, under the bed. That image of being JC was my *bad thought* like a Tyrannosaurus Rex stomping about, looking for a boy snack. I had to jink and swerve around it with jaws clashing behind me. I actually would do that, I mean physically, dodging about, escaping my bad thought. I couldn't tell my parents, obviously. I couldn't even begin to tell God."

"Why not?"

"Because He had anger management problems, that's why not."

"Ah. Old Testament. *Their children shall be dashed to pieces before their eyes. Take disobedient children to the gates of the city and stone them to death.*"

"You got it. Only Hitler and Genghis Khan were that vicious."

"So, no answers for you in church."

"None. So instead I sold my soul to science, to physics, which was supposed to reveal the mysteries of the universe. But all that happened was I got to know more and more about less and less."

"Go on."

"When I got to 16, the T Rex started closing in. I used to calculate, you know, if a T Rex got a cone-shaped tooth into me right through from chest to back and the cone had an angle of 10 degrees from the central axis, how wide the hole would be in the chest. I measured the-"

"Yes. I've got it. Why didn't you get some help?"

"And get thrown into a padded babble bin? Which is kind of funny because it happened anyway..." He breaks off, newly horrified by the words emerging from his mouth.

I prompt him to continue.

"It was my last day under my parents' roof. A bumblebee was caught inside, throwing itself at the window, and the sound made a snake in my stomach that was eating me, you know? There was a horror TV show on. A little kid had been buried alive. I can't stand that kind of thing, happening to kids. Then it was like a hundred snakes, all eating me from the inside. I went to bed to close my eyes, but it lasted only a few seconds and I... It was like a black tunnel pouring over me faster and faster. There was a light in the distance, but that T Rex kept getting in the way, blocking it out, hunting me down faster and faster. You know what's really weird about this?"

"No."

"That stuff you've been saying about choosing... I felt like I was choosing to do everything, but I didn't have any choice either... uh... shit, I'm not making sense."

"You're making perfect sense. Go on."

"Next thing I'm in the car, burning rubber across the city, out into the plains and on the way to the mountains, convinced that I had to climb Mount Rolleston. This choosing thing... I was kind of following developments. I mean I knew I was certifiable at the time and I wondered how I could be so clear about that. It was kind of funny, but there was no one to tell. I fuelled up the car, watching petrol go into the tank like a purple snake down a gullet, then I played chicken with an oncoming car. After that I ran every car off the road."

Now Matthew is certain that I will know he's a lost cause. He takes on an air of carelessness, his voice lifting and his hands moving with the story.

"A cop car came towards me and I ran him off the road too. He did a U-turn and came after me with everything lit up and the orchestra playing. He got up there beside me, red-faced and signalling me to pull over. You know, I whispered the words *fuck off* because I had never used them before, then I screamed them at him. And I gave him the finger—I had to practice that as well—can you believe that? While he pulled back and talked into his mike, I ran a motorbike off the road. Then he got really serious and came back and rammed me from the side. So I rammed him back and his car turned into origami. I thought: Stupid bugger; I had a Peugeot and he had a tinfoil Ford.

"They got me on a one-way bridge well into the mountains. Half a mile before that two guys shot to their feet out of the tussock and waved... friendly yeah? So I waved back. But when I rolled onto one end of the bridge, a Land Rover rolled onto the other end and the driver leapt out and sprinted away, leaving the door open. That hurt, because I didn't want to kill anyone, not then. I skidded to a halt and jumped into the Land Rover. The key was in the ignition, but I couldn't find reverse, and then there were park ranger uniforms everywhere and hands coming through the window—hah... like the attack of the triffids.

"I threw myself into the back and picked up the RT mike. I called up control tower for permission to take off. And you know, I was faking. Crazy, faking crazy. It's hard to explain.

"No, it's making sense. Your thoughts were in two arenas at once, we'll talk about that when we get to the disciplines of mastery."

Matthew gapes at me. "You still want to do that?"

"Of course. Keep going."

He absorbs that, then continues. "All these faces were gawping at me. One of the park rangers said I must be from the air force. And another circled a finger round his ear and said, 'Loop-the-loop.' I didn't think it was funny, but his mates did. Anyway they tied me up, wrists and elbows, ankles and knees—they used my belt for the knees. They even attached me to the tow bar because they had no idea what a full-on nutbar might do next, then they waited for uniforms to come from the city. Children came and stood on a mound of shingle and gaped at me. One of them fell down when the edge collapsed and scrambled back as if I was about to leap over and eat him.

"I told the rangers I had to get to Mount Rolleston. One of them shook his head and said, 'Jesus', which really *was* funny wasn't it? I timed how long it took for spittle to fall from my mouth to the road surface. Three seconds. Which was pathetic, because a free-falling stone would do 45 metres in the same time. My body was too big. Hah. I read somewhere that a T-Rex is so big you could hit its tail with a hammer and run behind a tree before the pain message got to the brain. Which is bullshit because nerve impulses have been measured-"

I interrupted him. "You were still aware of yourself acting crazy?"

"Yep. I watched it all from a distance and knew it for what it was. How about that?"

"Yes. That's important. Go on."

"The ride back to the city was a kind of blur. I asked the cop beside me if I had hurt anyone, and he looked at me like I was Typhoid Mary, but he shook his head. We stopped in Darfield. They took me into a private house, into a dining room where a woman gave everyone a cup of tea. She looked at me like she wanted to ask me a question, but instead, she offered me a cup of tea and some cake. The red-faced traffic cop came in, the one I rammed, and everyone shut up. He tossed his cap onto a bench, without taking his eyes off me and sat on a chair opposite. The woman gave him his own tea, dropping in two lumps of sugar without asking how many he took.

"He stirred it and took a sip, looking at me all the time. Then he said in a real quiet voice, 'You could have killed me. You know that, don't you?' Everyone was watching me, or watching him watching me. Except the woman. She was gazing out the window with the tip of one finger of her left hand touching the little finger of his right hand. I looked down at my fruitcake. My cup was sitting a bit off-centre in the saucer. I wanted to straighten it, but I didn't because my mind was trying to lie down on the floor."

He is silent for so long, I think he has forgotten me. But he suddenly resumes.

"When we got to Sunnyside Hospital, I went into orbit again. Six guys in short white coats closed in with blankets and I could tell they'd done this before. I said so, and they agreed. They held me face down, starkers, on the floor of an observation cell, trying to inject me with a blunt needle... and moaning that I had the hide of a rhinoceros. They sank it in on the third stab, then they shot through the door and bolted it.

"But I wasn't alone. There were heads jostling in an observation window—tall window—three heads one above the other—nurses, watching me standing there butt naked. I ignored them at first, because I didn't think they could be real. I needed to know what was real. I touched the walls, thinking that I could get some... some... *real* back. I blinked at the stacked heads but they didn't blink back. I stepped towards them suddenly, spreading my hands to tell them to go fuck off and they all jumped. I couldn't think of any place lower than that. Can you?"

I shake my head. I can feel something of the surging blood in Matthew's temples.

"Well, there was. Clever Mother came into my cell the next

morning, Father behind her. They asked two guys in white coats for chairs, then sat back by the door. As far away from me as they could get and still be in the same room. Father was holding his Bible in both hands, kind of scraping the leather all the time with a fingernail. He said he knew I must be suffering, but my sin had caused them a great deal of distress… oh yes… He said I had to get down on my knees and ask the Lord in his infinite mercy to forgive me. While he said that, Mother looked out the window with contempt—for him. It was for him, I never noticed that before. She told him to shut up. Then she asked me, Did I have *any* idea what this spiteful little charade of mine would do to their reputation if it got out? They would become a laughing stock. I could ruin them. If I had the slightest gratitude for the intelligence they had given me at great sacrifice to themselves, I would get myself together, starting right now. So…"

This time he's silent for so long that I prompt him. "So…?"

"So there was a lower place, after all, wasn't there? I picked up a chair and smashed it against the window, really hard, but nothing broke… I think they made the cell for people like me. So then I threw it at my parents instead, and they screamed, and the men with the white coats rushed in with the blankets and stuck needles in me again.

"My parents didn't come back. I just got a note telling me that I had got what I wanted. I had ruined them. They hoped I was happy now."

He fills the silence with tapping, forefinger on wood, body twisted in the chair.

"So I dug myself the deepest pit in the mine, didn't I? I took my clothes off and lay in the corner like one of those hairless rats they breed in laboratories. I estimated how many hairs a normal rat might have on its body, assuming 150 square centimetres of skin with three hairs per square millimetre. Forty-five thousand. That's a lot of hairs. I was surprised. So was the psychiatrist."

"That's quite a load you're carrying," I say.

Matthew stares at me. "You don't have any idea what I'm carrying." There's a threat woven through the words, a fine steel thread, and he wants me to hear it.

"They gave you medication?"

"Chlorpromazine," he replies, switching to the far-away gaze that penetrates walls and mountains. "After I threw that chair, they doubled it to the full drooling dosage. Didn't have any thoughts left, just pictures like dots you can't join up. Wanted to scream all the time without knowing why, except for the itch—like a thousand monkeys with a million fleas. I had to take the pill in front of them, and they'd watch my mouth and throat while I swallowed. If I refused, I got shown that some places in hell are more shocking than others. I only refused once."

I study him for a moment. "You never told the psychiatrists about the visions?"

He pulls his gaze back towards me and sneers. "I would have to be out of my mind to do that, wouldn't I?"

"When you were released, did you return to your parents?"

"Never. Never saw them again, because they sent all my things to the hospital in a box. The minute I got out, I set fire to my books and took up work with the national parks: track cutting and hut maintenance in the mountains. When I wasn't doing that, I was hunting deer and tahr, and possum for the fur. And I travelled in South America."

"Still with the visions?"

"Yep."

"Which you still have."

"Yep." He rubs the back of his neck furiously as if it's giving him pain. "So, now you *know* you've got a top-shelf nutter on your hands. You want me to bugger off back to Lobotomy Bay, right?"

"Not right."

"Look, I know damn well I'm not JC. So what are those visions for?" His eyes blaze. He storms to his feet and rams a fist into the wall, somehow by-passing the stud but leaving a neat, fist-sized hole in the plaster. The missing piece has dropped away inside. Then he rounds on me. "What the fuck are these visions for? Why would a ten-year-old kid get them? Ten! I didn't ask for them. I didn't want them and I still don't want them. Why won't they leave me alone?"

And, suddenly, I know why. I tell him, "Before you leave here, you'll have the answer and the visions will stop."

"How? Don't fucking play with me. If you know the answer, tell me now!"

"That's impossible. You'll work out the answer yourself, by listening to what I would tell anyone who thinks the universe has delivered them a losing hand."

"Thinks? What the hell does that mean? Stuff you." But the tension is draining out of him. He seems exhausted, as if he would lie down on the couch and sleep, but he won't allow himself to do that in front of me. He remembers the plaster and looks at it, rubbing his knuckles. "I put a hole in your wall."

"I noticed that."

He turns his head back abruptly, narrowing his eyes. "All your fancy words… but you don't actually give a shit about me, do you? You could have gotten your hooks into anyone passing by, just happened to be me. Only I'm not what you expected, am I?"

"No. You are definitely not what I expected."

"You're really something, you know that?"

It's not a compliment.

THREE

"Look around you," I demand, sweeping my arm in front of me. The sound resonates, the first echo returning before the word has completely left my mouth. "What does this place remind you of?"

We're on the blarney rock, the monolith that juts into the farm reservoir as a natural peninsula. If you were to join up a dozen Stonehenge slabs and topple the result to lie half in and half out of the water, you would have the blarney rock. Siobhan and I have picnicked here, painted watercolours, solved the world's problems, and made unrestrained love here, much to the astonishment of the alpacas. One time, at the critical moment, an avalanche started over on Ringa Mountain and we laughed so hard we nearly fell into the reservoir.

When I leave my body here on the rock, it will merge with the elements and eventually disappear, leaving just the bullet. I like that.

The reservoir is a very deep, natural tarn, formed by a geological fault running across the middle of the valley. Siobhan and I once dropped a rock off the blarney stone and watched it shimmy away into the depths, growing smaller until it vanished. So we tied another rock to the end of a full reel of builder's twine, and dropped that too. It didn't touch bottom, so all we discovered is that the farm would never be short of water.

Matthew inspects the way the valley has formed around rock and reservoir, a sweeping, rising curve.

"It's a natural amphitheatre," he muses. "We're on stage. We should turn on a Greek tragedy." For now, he has suspended hostilities, his tone almost friendly, as if he has allowed the sun's warmth to reach inside him.

Where an audience might sit, alpacas are either studying us, or grazing, and more are arriving, drawn by the human activity. They spend most of their time grazing the grass, supplementing with alpine daisies and buttercups that emboss the pasture with white and gold. When summer settles in, the display will be even more extravagant, because Siobhan spent a small fortune improving on nature.

Following my lead, Matthew strips off his shirt and lies back on the warm rock, using the shirt as a pillow. In times past, a hiker has scratched *Kilroy was here* into the surface near his head. There's an upward tilt at that end of the slab, inviting humans to lie back and contemplate the abandon of the Southern Alps. In recent geological history, some exuberant giant flung peaks, bush and lakes into the air to fall where they would. In Maori legend, the Earth mother is reaching up, yearning for her lover, the Sky Father.

In the distance, the sun shines down on Ringa Mountain. *Ringa* means arm. With three gullies reaching for the peak, it takes little imagination to see fingers pointing high. This side of the hand is in shadow, but the gullies are snow-filled, sharply defining the gaps between the fingers. The thumb is a stumpy misshapen outcrop; the palm a rain-hollowed slope. The arm is greywacke scree running down to the beige and green garments of tussock and beech. Arm, hand and fingers beseech the sky, asking why.

When he first clambered up, Matthew stayed crouched until he found a safe spot away from the water. He explained that if he looks down into the deep water, he'll turn dizzy and breathless and his hands will shake. At five years old, he was playing on the beach by an ill-tempered Tasman Sea when a freak wave reared up, fell on him, and pulled him back in the undertow.

"You got yourself out, or were you rescued?"

"Rescued. Howled my head off. I never could go near deep water after that."

We bask in the warmth, but after a while a thought occurs to me and I speak lazily to the sky. "So you'll know how to *really* appreciate a lungful of air."

Just as lazily, he rolls over and looks at me. "If you mean do without it for a while, then yes. Is there a point?"

"There is. Want the best experience of eating and drinking? Do without for a day or two. Want the best shower you've ever had? Do without. Likewise, the full experience of hot must include cold. Up has no meaning without down. You appreciate light when it has been dark, and starlight as the mist melts away, and happiness when sadness has carved a cavern within you. On this earthly plane, nothing can be fully experienced, appreciated or understood or have any meaning without its opposite or lack. Your mind performs on a stage built of opposites and contrast. Listen..."

In the beginning, there were no stars or planets, there was no space and no time, no opposites, nor any contrast. There was only the stillness of a deep longing, and the deep longing was the Great Spirit.

The Great Spirit longed to know itself, because there was nothing else to know. So it asked the question, What Am I? It wanted to experience the answer in many ways, so within its stillness, it created many smaller spirits called souls, each asking the question, What Am I? So the one became the many and yet they were still one.

And each soul created within its own stillness a separate region called mind, and each mind asked the question, What Am I?

And each mind was given the gift of space and time

and contrast. Each was given light and dark, here and there, past and future, big and small, up and down, hot and cold, right and wrong, male and female. And each contrast brought desire, and each desire was the asking and the answering of the eternal question, What Am I?

And each mind was given the gift of forgetting. So that its experience could be real, each would forget that it is a creator surrounded by its creations. Each would experience itself as separate, and restricted to a vibration called physical, and each would believe itself contained by a shape with head, arms and legs.

A bush robin, *tououwai*, flits past, so low over the outlet stream that the pale underbelly is barely visible. It lands on the stream bank, an ebony pebble against grey stones.

"Forgetting," Matthew says. "Why does that make it real?"

"Imagine that you're playing chess with yourself. You make a move on one side of the board, then go around to the other side. What has to happen before you can truly-"

He interrupts. "Okay. I have to forget the other guy is me."

The robin's mate arrives, and the pair pursue insects under twigs and small stones, the female so enthusiastic that her discards bounce off nearby rocks.

Matthew says, "I feel about as important as a sparrow."

"You're about as important as a being which casts itself out as a sparrow and returns as a bird of paradise. You have only to remember what you forgot."

"Hah! This from someone missing the first half of his life."

"That from someone missing the second half."

"I could go crazy listening to you."

"Crazier than your visions made you, or not that crazy?"

He glares, but says nothing.

"How long before they let you out of the psychiatric hospital?"

"The bin? A month."

"A month? *One* month?" My disbelief must be written all over my face. "After you wrecked a police car and ran other-"

"Well, after three days, I stopped fighting them. Instead, I became a model patient and got to know what the shrinks wanted. You know, talking openly and calmly about my own feelings, a little regret for how I had scared people, a bit of humility, a touch of wry humour about my situation, eagerness to make a new start. Not difficult."

"But how could you think so clearly? Didn't you say you were on the maximum-"

"I reduced my dose."

"*You* reduced it?"

"Broke the pill in two on the way to my mouth—between the thumbnail and forefinger—chewed and swallowed one bit in front of them, with the other bit tucked in the side at the back of my tongue. Bitter as the devil, but worth it."

"And you got away with it?"

"I was so well behaved, they stopped watching me so carefully at drug call. Then I had to get a balance between acting zombied and looking like I was improving. They bought it. After a while, they reduced the dose themselves. Then I reduced that. Which freed me up to work my way out."

"Even so, they can't have released you in a month. You escaped?"

"No. They showed me the door. Actually my psychiatrist came to the door with me and opened it. I think he wanted to make sure I went through it. He looked a bit disturbed." There's a hint of a smile at the corner of his mouth.

"Wait a minute. It doesn't add up. There's something you're not telling me."

"Nothing important." He shrugs dismissively.

So I let it go and change direction.

"Brain chemistry is an effect, not a cause. The root cause of insanity is the belief that you are alone. But when you understand my kind of craziness, you'll know you're far from alone."

He's amused. "It's all psychology, isn't it? No hard facts. You can't substantiate a single thing you're saying."

"Of course not, and be glad of it. Empirical evidence, logic, and deductive reasoning don't even begin to help you remember the being waiting inside you. The human mind does not become wise through reason. History is littered with those who used reason to corner the Truth, but who would come to blows if they met."

"And you," he says, "have transcended such limitations."

"Yes. I have."

He rolls on his side to look at me. "Do you know how arrogant you are?"

"It's the opposite of arrogance. Once you master your life, you won't see your self as superior or inferior to anyone or anything."

"So you would not be superior to a dung beetle."

"Superior at hammering nails, inferior at rolling dung balls to impress my mate, but inherently superior? No."

He presses the point. "And you wouldn't see yourself as inferior to, say, the Buddha."

"Inherently? No. Of all people, the Buddha would say that if I think I am inferior, I will become so and then mistake it for reality. No. There is no higher or lower."

He sighs, closing his eyes against the sun, which must turn his blue sky to salmon pink. "Can your expanded self talk to you directly? Like with a voice?"

"Yes, it can. But... " My tone is rueful. "... it's *very* choosy about when."

"Then what about people who hear voices telling them to do really crazy shit. You know, kill someone."

"You associate the expanded self with only pleasant, nonpainful things?"

"Of course."

"No. Your expanded self—your soul if you like—often brings you painful events deliberately, most of them at your direction. As you'll see."

He mutters. "Who the hell's the crazy one here?"

"Obviously you. You're the one mumbling to yourself."

Abruptly, for the first time, he laughs out loud. That makes him cough, so he clambers down the land end the rock, well away from deep water, and goes to the outlet stream. Still coughing, he kneels in the stones and scoops cold, crystal water into his mouth, cooling his throat. Both tououwai flit to the top of the opposite stream bank, then loop away into the bush in different directions. Their wings make no sound at all because melt water is on the move everywhere, bustling down the stream, bubbling through and under the soggy pasture.

***

In the last hour of light, Matthew moves out of the hay shed.

He sets his tent up in an alcove of trees on the other side of the barn, nicely concealed from anyone who might approach from the track. He places it on a patch of one-mile moss—exhausted hikers will always go the extra mile to find it—soft as a mattress, with an upper surface that stays dry in light rain. He also has the hiker's luxury of a fallen log for sitting on and sheltering a camp fire. There's a flat, black mound of ash already there, left by someone who passed this way long before and stayed for many days; also an ancient camping billy behind the log, crumpled and half-buried, with two bullet holes in it, one bullet, in and out the other side. Someone's target practice.

Matthew orients the tent, with its external stays, so that when he wakes he will look directly across the meadow above the reservoir. If he stays, he will see hyacinths spread among the alpine daises, then bluebells, bringing edge and depth to the tapestry. Then, if he is still here when summer settles on the valley, he will see the full extent of Siobhan's follies; not just flowers, but vivid flowering bushes lining the fences, and aromatic herbs, which she cast so far into the bush that I have found deer lunching on sage a kilometre from the house.

He prepares the campsite meticulously, watched by Rangi and Papa. He gathers twigs and branches for a fire, and builds a fire rack—a simple device to control cooking heat: two upright dead branches, each with several deep notches, then a straight stick to sit in the notches at the level of his choosing. When billy and cooking pan appear, the two kea skip closer, waiting for an opportunity to raid.

About then, I notice new behaviour in one of the alpacas. Simone is restless, constantly sitting up, lying down and rolling. Then she stands, the contractions begin and her vulva bubble grows. She is calm; I am the one with the urgency of an expectant parent. I walk at full speed to the barn for the birthing kit: towel, gloves, iodine and a cold weather coat for the *cria*, the baby. By the time I reach the enclosure, Matthew is close behind, and Simone is standing, ready for the delivery.

After ensuring that Matthew is at a safe distance, she begins contractions. She looks ahead, seemingly uninterested in what is happening at her rear end. First the cria's nose emerges, then the forelegs, then the skinny red-brown body touches the grass before the rear legs rush out and slump to the ground.

"Well done Simone. Hello, Mikey, welcome to Earth. Passport please."

Simone turns and sniffs carefully, and other dams approach and do the same. Mikey squirms and rolls in the grass to clean off the membrane, then stands shakily for his first suck. A completely normal birth, without fuss. I would prefer to leave it to them, but with another cold night looming, I'm not going to take the risk. I towel Mikey dry and tie on the coat, with a perfunctory bleat of protest from Simone.

Matthew is fascinated by the cria. He stays while I return the kit to the barn and go about other farm chores, and he's still there when I return to check, an hour later.

But then, a surprise. Just before nightfall, I find him sitting on the porch steps. I tell him I'm doing a final check on the new arrival and he opts to stay where he is. I head off, but when I glance back to the house from the enclosure, he's not in sight. When I return twenty minutes later he's back in the same spot. Then, when I enter, he follows me.

It might be innocent, but it doesn't feel right. I look around the living room, but see nothing out of place. He sets himself to fussing with the fire, but remains intensely aware of me.

Something significant just happened and I missed it.

So I use a mind trick once known to the aboriginal trackers in Australia: it's a form of remote viewing, spanning time, looking into the relative universe from the absolute. I walk out to the porch, to where he sat, just a few minutes ago. I imagine him as he was then—watching me tread across the snow—then, in my mind, walk 'with him' as he jumps up and strides off to the barn tool bench and grabs pliers and insulation tape, 'with him' as he takes them around to the back of the house and climbs the elm tree towards a wire tied to a branch. The wire loops out of the tree and up to a telephone pole. Ahah!

No need for more remote viewing.

I go to the phone, feeling his eyes on me all the way. When I lift the receiver, the dial tone hums in my ear with the usual crackles of distance. We are re-connected. Perhaps I will not, after all, blame the phone company. Still holding the receiver, I turn to look at Matthew. Our gazes lock. He tries to maintain an expression of casual interest, he is telling himself that it was a fluke of timing that I chose to check on the phone right then.

Do I make it obvious that I know? Yes, I do. All it takes is the lightest touch of wry amusement while holding his eyes.

For a moment he masks surprise. Then he adopts his own air of amusement, with a nuance that says, Okay, so you've worked it out. What are you going to do now? We understand each other perfectly; I smile, put the receiver in the cradle and return to the kitchen.

"Eat with me," I say. "Nothing fancy."

He accepts the invitation. While I concentrate on the cooking, he tours the living room. He inspects the bookshelves. He spins the earth globe. He stands immobile before the grandfather clock, eyes tracking the pendulum. He then tries approaching Boa, on her pile of books, but she arches her back and topples the pile on her way out the door. He gives her the middle finger, and returns to fiddling with the fire, using the poker to manoeuvre the burning wood into the shape of a perfect triangle.

The phone rings four times in the next twenty minutes. The first time, Matthew stares at it wildly; the next, he controls his reaction, but can't hide a momentary freeze. Friends are checking that I have survived the storm; they don't mention my age, but they are somehow relieved to hear my voice.

The last caller demands—please answer either yes or no, Mr Fleming—do I want to be rid of my colossal burden of sin? I don't, I tell him, because I'm an agent of Satan, though it is mostly a ceremonial role. I put the phone down, then take it off the hook. I'll have to change my unlisted number. Again.

Matthew and I cross glances and I don't have to be a mind reader to see that he's thinking it might be helpful to go back out and re-disconnect the line.

His mood at the table is subdued. He responds to the small talk, but only because silence is intolerable. He breaks one silence by telling me how much he hated his teachers at school. The more teachers praised his prodigious brain, the more he hated them.

He reserves greatest contempt for a fourth form French

teacher with the first name of Louis. Louis saw his pupils as untidy mounds of excrement. But he treated Matthew as an exception, the golden boy, and toadied to him in front of the class. One day, Matthew stole bottles from the chemistry lab, mixed ammonium tri-iodide and dried it out on blotting paper. Just before the arrival of Louis, Matthew persuaded his classmates to take their places, then sprinkled the chemical around the teacher's pacing range. It was invisible against the linoleum, but had the explosive power of a fire cracker when trodden on. In the ensuing chaos, the French teacher noticed two large signs chalked on the blackboard: *Vive la révolution* and *Rapportez la guillotine pour Roi Louis.*

The hue and cry that followed included interrogations of chemistry lab monitors and every member of Matthew's class. When not one broke, the deputy principal caned the entire class in the gymnasium, including the now very popular golden boy. The local newspaper carried a report two days later, using words like deplorable and regrettable to discuss the declining standards of behaviour and the teacher's resignation. Matthew has embellished the tale, no doubt—mass canings were more a feature of my era than his—but I'm not going to spoil a good story by questioning the detail.

Matthew leaves less than a minute after finishing his dinner, refusing a hot drink. In five minutes I can see a blue glow beside his tent. He's brewing his own.

***

"Progress," Siobhan's voice says behind me. I can tell from the direction of the voice that she's sitting at the spinning wheel. Sure enough, she has both feet on the treadles, upper back straight, hands poised. She's grinning, anticipating my command.

"Do it," I breathe.

She laughs, flicks her fingers at the spokes, appears to press with her right foot and in an instant wool appears in the bobbin and in her right hand. The wheel whirrs, the bobbin clacks. The wool passes out of her practised right hand, through the thumb and fingers of the left, then winds into the machine—a sublime invention plucked from the etheric field more than a thousand years ago. When she was here in body, when our lives emptied of extravagance and filled with simpler pleasures, Siobhan became expert in spinning alpaca thread, which she sold to buyers in the Hokitika market. From the start, I loved the sight and sound of her spinning; I found it erotic—so much so that many a ball went to market with an uneven lump that came from stopping the wheel and starting again later. She would tease me that I only loved her for her bobbin.

"Will you marry me?" I ask.

"You'll have to ask Pa," she says, as the wheel whirrs.

"I did. He says I should make an honest woman of you."

"Ho," she scoffs. The urge to touch her rises, peaks, then fades. If I were to try such a thing, she would vanish as surely as if I switched off a movie projector. She spins on. The lorag, the cylinder of wool in her right hand, keeps giving of itself without getting smaller. Something out of nothing.

Now she gets to the point. "You're about to start him."

"I am."

"You're sure he's ready now?"

"Yes and no."

"Tch tch, and you not in politics. What a waste."

"Impertinent hussy. It's a risk because I don't know what it will prompt. He's sitting on something crucially important, I'm sure of it. I think there's a crisis ahead."

"So why take the risk?" The bobbin is full, but keeps accepting more wool without overfilling.

"Because we can't progress until he faces it. It would be worse to do nothing. In any case, we're past the point of no return. Ready or not, he begins tomorrow."

"And what about you, Jack?'

"Me?"

"Are *you* ready?"

Me again. And the look in her eye makes me pause. I have noticed recently that Siobhan's manner has nuances that don't match my memories of her. There are moments when it's like talking to someone else. But then I reassure myself; considering where she dwells, she cannot help but have qualities and perspectives I never saw in the flesh. Now she seems convinced that my mental state is worth discussing. It's not as if she even needs an answer—she knows it already. Perhaps she thinks there is value in my saying such things out loud. Well, why not?

"I am a little concerned," I concede.

"Talk to me."

"I feel as if I have walked into an unpredictable river. Whenever I try to face into the current, it changes direction. I may not be entirely in control of what's happening. I'm about to tell him how to master his life and I'm not sure I'm in full charge of my own."

"So you feel like a hypocrite?"

"Never mind that. Why am I experiencing this? What's going on?"

She shakes her head, clucks her tongue. "The rules, Jack, the rules. I ask the questions, you give the answers."

There. That's another difference. She didn't have this perverse trait when she was with me in the flesh.

"You're a cruel woman."

"I know," she beams. "I have other qualities as well."

She spins on, silken wool ghosting out of a cloud of nothing, gliding through her fingers to become something. When she goes, the loom will fall silent, the bobbin will be empty, and there will be not a scrap of alpaca wool anywhere in the room.

***

I dream that I am wading in tropical swamp, wearing only a tattered leather coat that hangs down into the water.

A female spider is crawling just under the transparent skin of my hand, eating subcutaneous flesh, regurgitating it for baby spiders racing along raw nerves. My skin is starting to come away in strips. I stop to urinate and a tiny fish leaps, flickering silver, up the stream of urine and into my penis. It sinks hooks into the inner flesh and starts working its way in and no matter how hard I urinate, I can't dislodge it. I grip my penis to stop the intruder penetrating further, but when I look down, I am holding someone else's penis, which is bloated and angry, and I can't find my own.

Far off, on a floating island, peacocks roam in the reeds. Simone is there, waiting to give suck, but her cria is crying over on the river bank, calling frantically, dashing between trees to keep her in sight. The island drifts downstream, reaches the ocean and begins to rise and fall in the swell. It's edge is lined with a brightly coloured floral dress. What I'm searching for is under the island, hidden by the dress. Piranha find what is underneath and attack in their hundreds until the water boils with their feeding frenzy.

The wind is rising.

FOUR

At four-thirty in the morning I'm on the way to his tent, huffing steam which slides around behind my head, hangs a wraith in the air and vanishes. A silver and gold hunter's moon dives into the western sea, hiding from dawn. Matthew's tent is sagging in the frost. I pluck on a corner guy string and tiny particles of ice spray to both sides, some pattering on the tent fabric.

"Matthew."

There's a swift rustle and an unmistakeable click.

"It's Jack. Get up."

"What? Whaddaya want?"

"Put that thing down and get your gear on. We're going for a walk."

In five minutes he's following me through the trees up towards the valley saddle, stamping to get his blood moving. He insists on bringing the rifle, strapped across his body. Soon, he offers to carry my pack as well, but instead of gracefully handing it over, I pretend I haven't heard him and push myself hard, working knots out of muscles and sandpaper out of joints. Graceful aging is for those with nothing left to achieve but graceful aging. I can see the look on Siobhan's face already: may the best testosterone win.

The dawn chorus begins with a single call, then a dozen; then hundreds of calls seek places in the air, some as startlingly close as the next tree, some penetrating dense thickets of leaf and wood, some reaching from far up the valley and barely on the threshold of hearing. By the time some songs reach us, the songsters have composed new phrases and broadcast them to follow the first.

I look back at him only when we're above the tree line, trudging through a snow drift near the saddle above the farm.

"You're fitter than you look," he grumbles.

The first spear of the sun strikes us full in the face as we crest the saddle and turn south east. That gives us ten minutes to luxuriate in its warmth, preferring to stumble, half-blind, rather than shade our eyes. Then we lose it again as the track takes us swiftly down the other side, criss-crossing a noisy cataract. Southern Alps water is the purest in the world, hasty now, dashing downhill before the cold tricks it into becoming its own prison. The track is more a series of knee-pounding jumps than a path, dropping so swiftly that when we reach the flats, our lungs feel the difference.

This ancient forest is disconnected from civilization. Around us, the buttresses—deformed by bunions and draped by moss— are taller than the two humans walking amongst them. There are green giants here that yawned above the canopy before the first Maori navigators pushed their canoes onto the shore: *kahikatea*, totara, *matai*, rimu, and even a lone massive kauri whose seed must have been dropped by a south-bound bird. If, by chance, the bird stayed and died here on the forest floor, then its atoms will be distributed throughout this tree and others. The forest is one being, made of many. New bright green saplings rise from between its toes, straining for the light far above. And here, the dawn chorus knows no restraint: all songsters celebrate winter's end with squeaking, tapping, piping, and chirruping, revelling in the audacity of their existence. The yellowhead plucks its balalaika, the bellbird swallows its echo, the saddleback ponders its own reflective melody. A solitary owl calls the night hunter's farewell in double-descending tones, *I... am. I... am.* And then a rare sound; I hold my hand up to stop Matthew in his tracks. It's that operatic diva the *kokako*, which surpasses even the bellbird in its versatility and purity. Matthew's lips round in a soft whistle of admiration and I bow, as if I had personally wielded the conductor's baton.

At a cairn—a stack of shale Siobhan and I placed years ago—we cut to the right, off the established track. After another kilometre, I slow and change my walk to a soft rolling of heel and toe, placing feet carefully, avoiding fallen twigs, gently pushing branches aside and just as gently releasing them behind.

Matthew catches on. The full dawn chorus is over, but calls continue in the canopy, covering our approach.

Then we're up against a rock outcrop, climbing, crawling forward on hands and knees until we can peer between rocks, over the edge.

We're looking down through tall beech into a clearing, a wide, grassy flat by a stream. The sun is still so low that only a fraction of the clearing shows its full palette of colours. That portion dazzles our eyes and by contrast the rest is murky, still favouring the night. So it takes Matthew a few seconds to register what he's seeing. Then he draws his breath in sharply.

The herd of wild horses grazes quietly, long practiced in silence. At this distance we can only just hear the rip of grass from turf, thud of hoof and nicker of contentment. Heads are down, except for the sentinels. Without visible signal between them, when one head drops, another rises. Some in the herd are black, some are white, most are roan or dappled. Only a few are in full sunlight, but as our eyes adjust we see the rest of the extensive herd away in the shade. There are scores of them.

Matthew is open-mouthed.

Under the trees, in the shadows but close to the sunlit grass, is the largest horse in the herd. He spends more time as sentinel than any other in the herd. His head is raised now, ears straining, suspicious. He senses us.

I touch Matthew's arm and signal. We slither back, out of sight and then tread carefully back down into the bush.

We find a patch of sunlight and dry ground. Matthew leans his rifle against a fallen tree, safety slide on, red dot obscured. I light the cooker, he fetches stream water, slow about it, almost detached. We sit and listen to the birds lay sound patterns on the hiss and crackle of the cooker, like flute music on an old long playing record.

We cook oats porridge hot enough to strip flesh, but cooled with powdered milk and sweetened with raw sugar. He knows I am waiting for the right time and does not push me. He taps the bowl with his spoon and observes that his Scottish grandmother wouldn't let him have sugar on porridge, only salt—a detail of Scots austerity that had escaped me until now. I picture sepia photographs of matriarchs with grim, disappointed mouths.

When the coffee is poured, he stirs in milk powder and sugar with a twig, clockwise, until the liquid starts to wheel. A mosquito drops into it and dies, an orbiting black speck. He watches it until he realizes that something between us has shifted. He drops the twig and grips the mug in both hands, ignoring the heat on his palms and looks up at me expectantly.

It's time.

"Matthew, the first truth is the big one, because you will not begin mastery without it."

He nods.

"You are entirely the creator of your reality. All of it. At some level, mostly subconscious, you create every event, detail and nuance of your life. The day you live this truth and take conscious control is the day you declare your freedom and power. It's also the day you cease to be a victim."

Matthew absorbs this with an expression straight as slate, as if nothing of consequence has been said. But he's listening, very carefully.

"You don't yet know the power of your conscious thoughts. But Hindu teachers have known for 3,000 years. It's the law of attraction: What you think, you become; what you feel will follow; what you believe will be manifest around you."

Matthew glances significantly, inquiringly, back in the direction of the horses.

"Yes," I agree. "They represent your accumulated thoughts, feelings and, above all, your beliefs. Your beliefs have more power over your life than a hurricane."

He sees the dead mosquito through a slow circuit of his mug, then objects, "What about free will? I'm free to have any thought I want."

"Your thoughts are only free when you master the beliefs that dictate them. Did you see that some horses were in the sun and most in the shade? And yet you raised all of them. You fed them thoughts in the stable of your mind, never knowing what powerful creatures they would become. And the most powerful of all are in the dark—your invisible beliefs."

"How can a belief be invisible? If I have a belief I must be aware that I believe it."

"That's only true of your weakest beliefs. If you precede an opinion with *I think that...* then, yes, you're aware of a low-power belief. If it's *I believe that...* then you're aware of a belief with more power to direct your choices. However, if it's *I know that...* you see it as the truth and fail to recognize a potent certainty-belief. If you *know* that eating animals incurs karmic debt, you cannot visit the butcher's shop. If you *know* that teenagers are trouble, you create parenting problems. If you *know* you will lose your faculties as you age, it is the knowing, not the age, that damages you. And the most powerful of all beliefs is the simplest: the assumption-belief. That's a certainty so deep it is laughable to question it. Countless millions are steeped in assumption-beliefs that make their lives a misery. You noticed the alpha male? The lead stallion?"

"I wouldn't want to be caught in a corner by him."

"You are always caught in a corner by him, because he is

your ego. He's that biggest and most cunningly disguised belief of all, that you are an individual, separate, isolated and alone. He must exist for you to be human; but he must be exposed for you to master your humanity."

Matthew swallows coffee carefully, then retrieves the twig and uses it to restore the insect's tour of the mug. "So what do I do to take conscious control?"

"You could start by listening to this, from the Sioux Indian campfires."

A story. His eyelids drop immediately, a wistful, almost mournful, reflex.

An old man and his grandson are sitting by the fire outside the tepee, wrapped in furs and gazing into the leaping flames. High on a snowy ridge, a wolf howls at the moon and another answers from far away. Soon after, the old man removes the pipe from his mouth.

'Grandson,' he says. 'There are two wolves inside you. One is white and the other is black.'

'What are they doing there, Grandfather?' asks the wide-eyed boy.

'They are fighting each other,' says the old man.

The boy considers this, then asks, 'Why are they white and black?'

'The white one is your love, your peace and your truth. The black one is your fear, your anger and your lies.'

The fire crackles and sparks flare in the night. The wolf on the ridge howls again and the old man puffs contentedly on his pipe.

Finally, the boy says, 'Which one will win, Grandfather?'

'Ah,' says the old man, removing the pipe once more. 'The one that wins is the one that you feed.'

"Neat," Matthew says, a reluctant smile pulling his cheeks.

"It is. And when you understand it fully, you will stop blaming your upbringing, the government, the boss, or God or the devil. Externalizing cause is a habit masters of life abandon as self-defeating and, literally, sickening."

Matthew's smile fades. "My beliefs affect my physical health?"

"Yes. Including injuries."

"So if I get cancer, you're going to tell me I caused it."

"Yes."

"This again! Just when you were making sense. Look, in Karamea there's a mother with four little kids and she's dying of leukaemia. You're saying it's her fault?"

"Of course not. The word is not fault, but cause. First cause is your pre-set life template, second cause is your beliefs. No blame or judgement is appropriate because most beliefs grow in the shadows and your mind usually has no idea of its own creative powers."

"But what belief could possibly cause leukaemia?" Matthew homes in.

"You want a river with many tributaries to come from one spring? It's only safe to assume that persistent thoughts like *I am powerless* and *I am a victim*—compounded by suppressed emotions like anger, hatred, and fear—will express themselves dramatically in your body."

"If I get what I focus on, why am I stuck with so much I don't want?"

"Because you are focusing on what you *don't* want. But what if you were to reverse that? What if, for example, you were to focus on trusting others? Then you create a trusting universe, in which you are also trusted."

"Pah!" His temper is ratcheting up. "I've tried trusting people and I've had my fingers burned. You've got to be pretty damn stupid to keep coming back like some besotted puppy that's been kicked against the wall and can't take the hint."

I keep going. "What if you were to focus on forgiving others? Then you create a forgiving universe, in which you too are forgiven. As you do unto others, so do you create for yourself."

Matthew's head jerks up. He hisses. "I don't do forgiveness. Some things can't be forgiven."

"You want to explain?"

He uses the twig to eject the insect, then gulps coffee. "Nope."

"Matthew, how long will you go on tolerating thoughts that damage you? How long before you shrug off the victim's sack cloth and begin a lifetime directed by you?"

"That's enough now. Get out of my head. I don't-"

Somewhere downhill, there's a brief tripping of hooves, bush punctuation, light and precise. A single deer: a big hind or possibly a small stag. It moves again; an unhurried canter which slows and stops.

Matthew reaches for his rifle.

"Not the right time," I say.

He stands over me, working a round into the chamber. I can see the red dot, safety off. He shouts, "You don't tell me when I can and can't shoot in these mountains. Got that? I make my own decisions." The hands holding the rifle are trembling, the tremors travelling up into his shoulders.

"You do," I agree. "So do I."

"Self-created man, are you?" he sneers. "Worship your creator, do you?"

I say nothing.

"Shit," he says, breathing hard. He hesitates, his free fist clenches, his eyes close and open slowly. Then he returns the rifle to the tree, the red dot still exposed. His shoulders twitch as if struck by an invisible hand, and he throws his drink out across the bush floor. Within hours the teeming life in that carpet will have absorbed every molecule of nutrient.

He sits, a slumping motion.

Two yellowheads burst out of the nearest foliage, flapping and scrapping with the sound of furious balalaikas, then disappearing again. For all the notice they took of us, we might as well be ghosts.

"You're turning everything back to front," he complains. "It defies common sense."

"It also defies classical science, the 300 year story of existence, which says we are the sum of our tiniest parts— machines driven by trillions of microscopic interactions. But it is not your atoms that decide whether to pick up that rifle or put it down. We are points of consciousness, suspended in space, creating around us what we call physical reality. Your level of mastery depends on how consciously and deliberately you create. You can even pick which level you are at now. Shall I explain?"

He assents cautiously.

"Here's the lowest, most helpless level of creation-belief. That you're *not* the creator of your life, but a victim of circumstance. You blame your condition on something other than yourself: God, the stars, fate, birth, parents, lovers, the government, accidents, sickness, the police. You never stood a chance. You are inherently worthless. Life is a torment. Is that you?"

"No," he grates, in order to resist me.

"Then try the next level, more evolved: you are *sometimes* the creator of your life. You can influence some events, but mostly, external forces are too strong to fight. You blame most of your condition on something other than yourself. You take some responsibility for what happens to you. You have some worth, some potential. Life is a painful struggle with a few highlights. Is that you?"

"Maybe, but I don't go for calling it a belief."

"Here's the next level: you are *mostly* the creator of your life. You can influence most events, though sometimes external forces are too great. You take responsibility for most of your actions. You spend little time blaming others for painful events. You are a worthwhile person with faults. You have a lot of potential. Life is an interesting and often enjoyable challenge. Is that you?"

He shrugs.

"Or is it this? The master level of creation-belief is that you are *entirely* the creator of your life. You are both your mind and the field. You do not see your Earth character as you, but as your work of art. Your every thought and action is your choice. You are fully responsible, not only for your creations but for your response to your creations. You never blame or judge others for your experiences. Your inherent worth and potential are vast. Life is an exciting, sometimes surprising, sometimes painful, yet joyous adventure. Is that you?"

"No it isn't..." He frowns. "Wait. What you're saying is that whichever of those four I believe, that's what I'm going to get."

"Exactly! And how ironic. You will create the conditions that appear to prove you right. Now do you see the potency of the first truth?"

"It's got... interesting muscles," he concedes.

"Every direction you head in—spiritually, psychologically, physically, every event and detail—is your creation."

"Every detail? You can't mean it literally."

"I do."

"Now you're going too far."

"All that surrounds you is your own finely spun thought."

"You know, this is the ultimate in self-centred. I used to get told not to act as if the whole universe revolves around me. You're saying it really does, and that I'm the one that makes it spin."

"Exactly, The only issue is whether or not you take conscious control of the spin."

He sighs. "Are you *sure* you're not running the funny farm?"

***

We scrape the bowls and refill the pack. Without asking, he straps his rifle to my pack and hoists it, then we set out back towards the stream and the track uphill. No longer content with following me, he sets a fast pace ahead. He doesn't speak, but I can see his brows furrowed, his gaze directed at the ground in front of his boots.

On top of the pass, we stop to rest, on boulders the size of small cars. Cloud steals the sun, and a breeze slides up from behind us, bringing its memory of thawing peaks and waking valleys. In the distance, Ringa Mountain asks the sky the question it has been asking since the backbone of the South Island bristled up from the sea floor.

Matthew spots something on the ground, picks it up, then turns to me. He's holding a leaf, copper red, with black veins shaped like the branches of the mountain beech that bore it. He stabs at it with a free finger.

"Look at that. A scrap of nothing. You're seriously telling me I created that?"

"Yes. When you look at it, you are looking at piece of you."

"But what's the point? Why would I bother? It's not the Magna bloody Carta, it's just a dead leaf."

"You created it out of your intent, which is to make a point to me."

"That's just brainless. What about every tiny detail when I'm not making a point? A stone. A feather. A dust particle. Anything."

"They are *literally* not there until you notice them. You create every detail you notice in the instant you notice it, and your mind assumes it was there all along." I take the leaf from him and place it between us, where it rocks and shifts. At any moment the rising breeze will whisk it away. "In this moment, which of your senses knows the leaf is here?"

"Sight," he growls.

"Yes. Sight only. Right now, this leaf does not possess any physical properties other than visual. It has no texture until you touch it, no taste until you put it in your mouth."

"No, no, no!" He snatches up the leaf, astounded that I cannot hear the stupidity of the words emerging from my mouth. He puts it out of sight behind him. "There. It's gone. Our senses can't detect it. What you're saying is that it doesn't exist any more."

"Physically, no."

"Hah! So if I look around...'

"You will see it, of course. Matter and energy are instantly interchangeable. You gave it energy which still exists in the great field of consciousness, and it returns to physical form when you give it your attention. It's like the common household spider, freezing when you look at it, scuttling on when you don't. The perceived cannot exist without the perceiver. Just by looking, you prompt your field to collapse potential existence into physical, re-manifesting the leaf; then your mind reacts as if it had been there all the time. You are like a butterfly inside a bubble of your own making."

"Oh, now the funny farm breeds butterflies."

"Now there's a thought," I say, thinking of Siobhan's swan plants, and the pep talk I gave them yesterday.

Matthew glares at the leaf. "But we can both see this leaf at the same time. You're saying-"

"Yes. Our bubbles overlap. We co-operate."

"Any connection between your bubble and mine is an unfortunate accident," he growls. "What about the wind? The wind didn't drop this leaf here?"

"The wind is a back-story we tell ourselves, like millions we use to perpetuate the illusion that we occupy one planet filled with objects that respond only to other objects."

"So nothing has any meaning."

"Nothing has absolute meaning, there is only perceived meaning. There is no objective truth, only subjective experience. You don't see things as they are, you see things as *you* are."

Matthew lets the breeze take the leaf, turning it over and over until it drops between two rocks.

"Try this," I suggest. "Think of any new object, something that doesn't exist yet."

He waggles his head, then shrugs. "Okay, a mug of hot mulled wine."

"Why not? All right, pretend that you're holding it in your hands now. Give it a shape and weight and colour, feel the warmth, smell the spices. Go on, take a moment or two. Now, you can't hold it in your hand yet, but it has just begun its claim on reality. Physical expression can follow."

"So, you're saying that it's possible to directly-"

"Yes I am. Now you're onto the full implications."

"The quickening."

"Yes. A fully evolved master sees through, lives in, and uses the illusion of physical existence to create whatever he or she wants."

"I don't believe it."

"The separation we feel from our greater being has flipped reality inside out. But let's keep this in perspective; throughout history, only the rarest few masters have been able to manifest directly. What I'm doing now is giving you an advance taste of indirect creation. Think of the mulled wine again. Make its shape and weight and colour *vivid* in your mind. Think how pleasant it will be in this cold weather. Feel the pleasure of the warmth on the palms of your hands, breathe deeply through your nose and experience the sharp aromas of cinnamon and cloves and taste them on your tongue. For a moment, lose yourself in the pleasure of mulled wine."

He does. Then, archly, "Surprise, surprise, nothing has appeared in my hands."

"Of course not. You're a beginner. Direct manifestation is ahead of you."

"What does all this say about other people?" he demands. "Here you are sitting in my bubble. I didn't hear you knock. Hah! Did I create you? Or did you create me?"

"Both. You attract into your bubble universe that fragment of my soul that most reflects your inner beliefs. And vice versa."

"So even if we hate each others guts, we're stuck with each other by our inner beliefs."

"True," I say, ignoring the bait.

"So far."

"So true."

"Look, if I meet the right woman one day, and live with her, will she really be there?"

"Yes, she *will* be there and so will you. Your problem is in the word *really*. Perceived reality is all there is—do you hear this? Your mind cannot perceive her complete soul, which dwells in the mansion of her own universe. Common sense and traditional science insist that all those bubbles must be one, but in the house of consciousness there are many mansions."

"So if a speaker talks to a thousand people... a thousand universes... that's one crowded theatre."

"It's 1001 theatres on the head of a pin, with no real estate boundary problems."

He stares away to the peaks and passes laid out to the north and east, lips moving with no sound. Then, out of nowhere he says mildly, "You think I'm an insufferable son-of-a-bitch, don't you?"

"Would that be more or less insufferable than someone who

says he's got all the answers?"

"Yeah. Well. There is that."

"Matthew, you have more thorns than a thistle."

"You could just tell me to shove off."

"You'll make your own decision on that. In the meantime, your questions test me; I don't need you to be polite."

"Didn't say I was going to be."

We rise for the downhill leg to the farm, about an hour away. I reach for the pack, but again he snatches it up, and no more words pass between us.

***

It's late afternoon before we emerge from the trees. The alpacas are wandering their way to the night enclosures, following their leaders, females from the bottom paddock, the males from the middle. Near us, the hens are patrolling for scraps and titbits, watched by Boa from the porch. They're never afraid of Boa. There's some kind of mutual understanding there: she doesn't take out their jugulars and they don't take out her eyes.

I notice the beginning of a scene I recognize, put up my hand to stop Matthew and point out a plump brown hen close to the house wall.

"Watch this."

The hen is scratching contentedly for grubs. The young red rooster, pretender to the chicken throne, advances on her with clear and present intent, prancing, chest out, feathers high. The hen, not in the mood, scolds loudly and sprints away, without noticing the reigning rooster, the mature black, high-stepping around the corner of the house, equally firm of purpose. The fast-moving hen gets the message when there are less then ten fowl paces between them. It squawks piercingly, reversing while still at full speed, frantically scrabbling for forward purchase.

A snort breaks out of Matthew like steam from a fractured pipe. He tries to smother it, but it bursts through again, and then he is reduced to helpless whoops of laughter. Between gasps, he says he thought it only happened in cartoons and asks where I am keeping Roadrunner. The evening migration of alpacas comes to a halt for the performance, heads tennis-necking to give one eye a view and then the other.

When Matthew can speak again he says, "I suppose you're going to tell me I created that as well."

"I am. You did."

"I'm willing to share the credit," he says, looking at the frustrated roosters.

***

In the house, his mood soars and I decide that predicting his disposition is an impossibility. He walks around inspecting things: the spinning wheel, the sextant, the chess set. And the ivory and brass hourglass I bought in a village market north of Mumbai. The brass ends are tarnished, but the ivory columns are still the same cream-white as the sand; and the sand lies in a perfect, undisturbed cone, a living thing in hibernation, dreaming of the return of Siobhan's hand to make it run free again. The brass is tarnished because I can't bring myself to disturb the sand.

Then Matthew has an idea. Without asking, he opens kitchen cupboards and looks on the shelves.

"You got any oranges? Or lemons?"

"No oranges, but there's lemon juice in the fridge door."

"I could make us that mulled wine."

"Of course. Go ahead."

"Then," he adds darkly, "you can claim that it was actually created by my thoughts about it earlier."

"I will," I agree.

"Or I could just refuse to make it."

"You could," I agree.

"Bollocks," he says, then goes to work, pulling the ingredients together with the subtlety of a schoolboy attempting his first meal, throwing everything into the same pot at once, including the cinnamon. But he knows his ingredients. He says he used to make mulled wine in the mountain huts for students on ski week. He volunteers cheerfully that women loved it, and it was always a bargaining chip for side-stepping hut duty.

I remember too late that he has only one source of red wine, and watch as one of my two remaining McWilliams Cabernet '65s—the finest cabernet ever landed on the planet—is wrenched out of decades of velvet slumber and violently chugged into the pot. I had been saving it for an occasion rather more special than the production of student-grade mulled wine.

"What?" he demands, aware of my intense gaze.

"Interesting technique."

"It gets better," he promises airily. He asks if I have any old electric jugs lying about—a good bet because the barn shelves are crammed with old appliance gear. He disappears and comes back five minutes later with a bare jug element attached to a stick. He plugs it in, waits for red heat, and plunges it into the pot. Most of the brandy vaporizes, producing an atmosphere that makes Boa's eyes pop open and roll independently. Perhaps it had that effect on the young women in the ski huts.

"Don't light a match," I suggest.

Matthew winces, then glances swiftly at me to see if I noticed. I decide that I didn't. He stirs quickly to dissolve any remaining sugar and the cinnamon, then he pours the concoction into two coffee mugs. He sips his carefully, then smacks his lips, surprised by its surpassing excellence. In his ski-hut days I imagine that the available wine would have served equally well as paint stripper.

"Maybe it was the quality of the wine," I suggest sourly.

"Maybe it was the quality of the chef," he corrects.

I don't argue, because I'm seeing a warmth in his eye I haven't seen before.

But then it's more than warmth. It's exuberance. He walks outside, holding his steaming mug in both hands, breathing in the vapours, gazing out to far places. He sings snatches of songs to himself, including *Honky Tonk Woman*, with the worst lyric line ever written: *"...she blew my nose then she blew my mind."*

While he's out there, the phone rings.

"Gidday Jack, it's Moose. How'r'ya doin'?"

Wiremu Moheke from Moheke Motors in Hokitika. Better known as Moosehead Moheke since he hoaxed wildlife experts that there were live moose living in the Fiordland bush. He brought back a hoof template and droppings from Canada, left strategic evidence on the bush floor, and played the experts a recording of a randy moose. There were headlines for days. Then a suspicious expert wondered why a man like Wiremu would take a tape recorder hunting, and oscilloscope analysis showed that the sound was identical to a recording in the Greymouth public library. Then there were more headlines and laughter from Karamea to the Haast. Now, wherever he goes into a local tavern, Moose doesn't have to pay for his drinks.

"Jack, good news old son. You won't believe this. Been all over the net for your drive shaft, and guess where I've found one? Right here in town! Perfectly good engine sitting in a wreck in a back yard."

"So close? That's great, Moose."

"Only thing is, I'm flat stick. Can't get onto it until the end of the month. You wanna courtesy car?"

"No. Don't bother. End of the month works for me."

"Eh? You're pullin' my tit." There's an awkward pause. "Your funeral, then. Okay, godda go, mate; the wife's bellyachin' for a feed. See ya." Click.

I have just boosted my reputation as an oddball, which, on the West Coast, is a badge of honour.

Inside half an hour, the phone shrills again.

"*Kia ora*, this is Detective Constable Janie Driscoll, Greymouth Police. Sorry to bother you. I'm calling all the back country farms in your district to ask you to look out for a young fella on the run. He has a psychiatric history, he's armed and highly dangerous, so don't approach him. We want to talk to him in connection with the death of a Hokitika man." All of it is rattled off at speed. She has rung many people and is fed up with the job.

"A death? Who?"

"Sorry, Sir, I'm not at liberty to tell you that."

"You mean murder?"

"I'm not at liberty to tell you that either. The coroner's still working on it."

"What's the name of the man you're looking for?"

"Been calling himself Matt Smith. Or Matthew Smith. He's off his nut and you're best to keep out of his way. Here's the physical." She describes Matthew accurately, except for the extent of his beard. "This is one weird fella. Could be a firebug too. You got a water supply to put out fires?"

"Yes, I have."

"Lock the doors at night, shut the windows, lock your outbuildings. You see him, you call us, we'll get there… thank you for your time." Click.

Matthew returns with the mug just as I put the phone down. He's in high good humour and says that if he's to believe my talk of butterflies and bubbles, my phone is connected with five billion universes. I resist the temptation to point out that when he arrived, he disconnected my phone from all those universes. Instead I correct his figure. It's six billion.

Five, he insists. Smart phone, he adds cheekily. He then wishes me goodnight, and departs to wish the same to the alpacas. I have not seen him like this. It's too much. It's disturbing. I can't put it down to the mulled wine because he was well on the way before he took the first drop.

The sun sets modestly behind a grey screen.

I decide to call Siobhan, not for any reason other than missing her company.

I place my untouched wine on the piano. I bring over a silver candelabra with two red candles, place it next to the vase, light the candles, and sit at the keyboard. For a few minutes, before playing, I imagine Siobhan sitting in the armchair at the end of the piano. I imagine, vividly, that she sits just so, chin in hand, listening intently, her presence allowing the room to breathe deeply and to sharpen its colours and textures. Now I dwell on my desire to be with her. I project that desire out to the armchair where she will sit, imagining that she feels my desire and is thrilled by it. I build and build that passionate imagining, until my whole body feels the intensity. And only then do I allow my hands to liberate her favourite piece, Camille Saint-Saens' *The Swan*. Outside, the air is already awaiting sunset, so I slow the glide of the swan and trickle the water so lazily down to the lake as to cast doubt on the law of gravity.

Then she is there, in the armchair, sitting just so, listening, radiating pleasure.

I keep on playing through the part where the busy stream joins the depths of the lake, and on to the end where water and swan come to elegant rest. Then I reach for my mulled wine, and raise the mug to her, pinky finger raised as if I hold the finest champagne at the perfect temperature. And how she smiles in return! Those eyes; how I long to travel through those greenstone jade windows to where she really is. They are *pounamu* eyes; the precious jade the Maori used for everything from symbols of love to weapons of war.

"Vonnie, my darling woman, say the word and I will transport you by magic carpet to the royal suite, where I will light you a hundred candles, and fill the air with jasmine, and read to you from *One Thousand and One Nights*. I will remove your clothes very slowly, and rub exotic oils into your alabaster skin, and cover you with rose petals, and kiss every millimetre of your-"

She laughs out loud and claps her appreciation. Then she says, "Chance would be a fine thing, Romeo, but Pa still has the shotgun."

I look about in terror. "In that case, you leave me with no option but to reject your shameless advances."

"Ah," she says, "What a thing it is to live in fear."

We hear a snatch of singing from outside. *Suzanne takes you down, to her place by the river...* His choice of song has jumped from ridiculous to sublime.

I look out through the window. Incredibly, Matthew is singing to the alpacas.

We move out onto the porch; rather, I go out and sit on the steps, and Siobhan appears there beside me, her skirt already tucked under. Matthew has a pleasant tenor voice, with true notes that carry well in the confines of the valley *...She lets the river answer, that you've always been her lover...* He doesn't see me, and now hams it up for the alpacas, one hand on his heart, the other open to the universe *...And you want to travel with her, and you want to travel blind...*

The alpacas gather in a wide arc separated from him by the distance where fascination and fear are equally balanced.

...There are children in the mirror, they are leaning out for love. They will lean that way forever, while Suzanne holds the mirror...

When he finishes, he sweeps an imaginary hat off his head, twirls it, and bows deeply to the alpacas. Then he blows them a kiss, and departs towards his camp, whistling. On the way, he notices me on the porch. His step falters momentarily, then he walks on, light of step and heart.

I look expectantly at Siobhan, inviting comment, but when she looks at me, she shakes her head slightly, then returns her gaze to the front. The message is clear: I have to think for myself.

It would be tempting to take Matthew's sudden high spirits at face value. Even more tempting to assume that the cause of his happiness is the first truth. But I don't believe it, because it's not happiness. Matthew is high on the wings of euphoria and I fear for his landing.

Siobhan and I watch the valley drift into dusk. Sheba grazes on clumps of long grass around the tree line. As she turns for a new clump, her hindquarters bump a low branch, and bush bees erupt from above to drive her away, forcing her into a brief, lumbering trot. Two harrier hawks, on a last sortie over the bottom paddock, quiver in flight and spiral down, a double helix. Something interesting has moved down there, perhaps as small as one limb of a field mouse. But the lowest hawk suddenly folds its wings and plummets, which means that something is about to commit to the food chain unless it finds shelter at great speed.

A pale, sickle moon winks at complicit Venus as they sink together into the sea. A blanket of stratus reaches out to extinguish the stars.

FIVE

Gloomily, he draws a finger across the immaculate surface of the piano, leaving marks in the polish. He brushes his fingertips lightly down the keyboard, frowning, as if it had made an inappropriate suggestion. He presses a few keys together, a three note chord, then plays random phrases, disconnected trills, little answers that never agree on the question.

"Play," I suggest. His hand stops immediately.

"Nah."

He notices that the red candles on top have been burning in his absence, then turns his attention to Siobhan's picture beside them. In it she's looking up from her spinning wheel, laughing at some joke that passed between us. He inspects the image carefully. He seems puzzled by it, as if there was something about her expression that he might understand if he could only tilt his head at the right angle. A fingernail burrows into his beard and scratches there. His beard grows shaggier by the day, framing his eyes, accentuating the hollowness of his cheeks. In another week, he'll look like a wild man of the mountain. I'm tempted to offer him the alpaca shears in the barn, but perhaps I will wait until the next mood-swing restores his sense of humour.

"We eat in ten minutes," I tell him, opening the oven to move a tray up one shelf. Then, casually, "Use the shower if you want. There's a spare towel in there."

"Nah."

No shower. I have seen Matthew use his camp cooker to warm water to give himself a body wash, rather than use my shower. But he does, for the first time, deign to use the toilet.

When he emerges, he asks what kind of bathroom has no mirror. When Siobhan went, there was no need of one, but I see no reason to explain that to him.

I lay the meal on the table: empañadas, hardy spring broccoli, and fillets of elephant fish trawled from the depths of the freezer.

He knows I will not begin while we eat, so he will have to endure small talk, perhaps even silence, which alarms him. He fills natural pauses with awkward comments about Boa and Sheba and the hens. Then he moves on to our hike into the valley of the horses, trying to provoke me into serious conversation. I will not be drawn, wanting nothing more than to savour the meal, which—and he will certainly not say so—I have cooked to perfection. The moment he finishes eating, he places knife and fork down parallel to each other, angled precisely to the centre of the plate, then looks at me expectantly. But I make him wait longer, running water for the dishes and handing him a tea towel, which he holds as if I handed him the controls of an unfamiliar machine.

When we finally settle in front of the fire, he jams himself into the corner of the couch as far from my armchair as he can get. Braces himself. Looks at me apprehensively. Waits for me to speak.

"Here's the second truth. Your life is your mirror."

His eyes flick back to the bathroom—an annoying distraction from a literal mind. To reclaim his attention, I repeat myself.

"Your life is your mirror. It shows you what you're creating and who you're choosing to be. Every object and event is a reflection of you. This is the secret language of things and events. The day you remember is the day you start to place what you want in your mirror."

"A custom-made universe," he says dryly.

"For each and every one of us. *Ko au te taiao, ko te taiao ko au:* I am the world, the world is me."

Matthew shakes his head and flaps a hand at the room. "Right now I'm looking at your house, but tomorrow I could be down on the flats driving a truck. Both scenes show me who I am? How could I change so much overnight?"

"You don't. Your physical surroundings are only the shallowest reflection of you. If you want a deeper reflection, look at your psychological surroundings. Look at your relationships, at the attitudes you take from one place to another. Look especially at the events you attract and you will see that you do, comprehensively, take your mirror with you wherever you go. Listen to this Sufi story…"

Another story. His eyelids drop instantly and I fancy I can hear a click as they close.

A stranger enters a village, and immediately looks for the Sufi master to ask advice. He says, 'I'm thinking of moving to live in this village. What can you tell me about the people who live here?'

And the Sufi master replies, 'What can you tell me about the people who live where you come from?'

'Ah,' says the visitor angrily. 'They are terrible people. They are robbers, cheats and liars. They stab each other in the back.'

'Well now,' says the Sufi master. 'Isn't that a coincidence? That's exactly what they're like here.'

So the man departs the village and is never seen there again.

Soon, another stranger enters the village, and he too seeks out the Sufi master for advice. He says, 'I'm thinking of moving to live in this village. What can you tell me about the people who live here?'

And the Sufi master replies, 'What can you tell me about the people who live where you come from?'

'Ah,' says the visitor in fond remembrance, 'They are wonderful people. They're kind, gentle and compassionate. They look after each other.'

'Well now,' says the Sufi master, 'Isn't that a coincidence? That's exactly what they're like here.'

"So much for skipping the country to start a new life," Matthew observes.

"Exactly. It's impossible without the corresponding inner change. You are the Great Spirit, individualized time and again, creating and experiencing, in the mirror of life, who you are. In the Bible, it is reduced to a short phrase. *And God said unto Moses, I AM THAT I AM:* It's a five word description of the mirror we call physical existence."

"You're saying everything around me is Me, capital m."

"I am. That I am."

"It seems like nonsense that what appears around me is showing me what I think."

"That's because you assume that thought has no substance. But thought is a thing, leaving a physical signature you don't normally recognize as your own. Thought, or more accurately, feeling, is the fundamental building block of the universe. Imagine that you throw a boomerang, but then forget that you threw it. When it comes back, at a different time and angle, you look around and wonder who threw it. So you keep throwing boomerangs, some returning to bring you pleasure, others to bring you pain."

"The law of attraction," he says.

"Exactly. Implemented by your accumulated thoughts, feelings and beliefs."

"Even if I buy that," he objects, "How does it help me to know it?"

"In any garden, if you water only the noxious weeds, what grows fastest?"

He pursues this. "You want me afraid of my own thoughts?"

"Definitely not. Fear is potently creative."

"You don't let up, do you? You turn everything back on me and you leave God out of the equation. Have you tried this stuff on Christians? I'll bet they back away from you and cross themselves."

"Some might, especially those who are blinded by their own forms and rituals. Heh! It's always been so. Listen. In 1553, a Spanish theologian called Michael Servitus was burned at the stake as a heretic. As he felt the first flames, he called out 'Jesus, thou son of the *eternal* God, have pity on me.' And a minister, watching the event, remarked sadly to another bystander, 'If he would only say eternal *son* of *God*, we could cut him free.'"

Matthew is incredulous. "That was a burning offence?"

"Not so strange if your religion—as defined by your forms and rituals—is the only one permitted by God. Then those with other forms and rituals must be His enemies. And yet all religions, are themselves part of a much greater Truth."

"Which is?"

"Which is closer to you than the breeze passing through your hair. Listen."

Three blind men find themselves in the presence of the Great Elephant. Each, trembling with fear and awe, stumble forward and reach out their hands to discover its nature for themselves. One takes hold of the tail, one a leg, one a tusk. And each is overcome with joy at having directly discovered the nature of the Great Elephant.

The blind man holding the tail announces, 'The Great Elephant is a broom that cleanses and sweeps all before it.'

The blind man holding the leg is surprised, and

protests, 'No, the Great Elephant is a magnificent pillar towering above us, guarding us and keeping us safe.'

The blind man holding the tusk is astonished and shouts, 'No, you're both wrong. The Great Elephant is a plough that furrows the earth that we may grow crops and have plenty.'

And they fell to fighting and there was no peace in the land.

"So," Matthew says, "All religions are equal."

"Yes. Part of the completeness of the field."

"So all paths are acceptable."

"Yes."

"So there's no right or wrong. No boundaries. Anything goes. I can do whatever I want."

"Yes. You are not and never will be judged by an external deity."

"In church, the minister was hot and strong about the beguiling tongue of Satan. What you just told me sounds like a sugar-coated definition of evil."

"The thought of no spiritual boundaries terrifies many, in the same way that it terrifies a kitten to be placed in an open field. But once the kitten is grown, the open field is its natural habitat."

"Then the masters of life are immoral," Matthew says.

"No, they are amoral. They see nothing in terms of right and wrong, good and bad. Who would you rather deal with: someone who reads a holy book that instructs him in right and wrong behaviour? Or someone who knows you as another face of the Great Spirit?"

"You know," Matthew says slowly. "you're smooth and you're dangerous. Society should lock you up and throw away the key."

***

Just after midnight, a crash and a rumbling sound jerks us both out of sleep and we stumble into the dark, hunting about with lanterns. We find nothing and go back to bed.

In the morning the cause is obvious: a boulder, as high as my waist, sitting in the frost-whitened pasture close to the reservoir. One face looks un-weathered, which suggests that the boulder must have split off from a mother rock, undisturbed for millennia up the northern side of the valley. Last evening's rainwater froze deep inside a crack, swelling as it turned to ice. The boulder broke off and plunged down the hillside, mowing a tunnel through the bush, passing through my wire fence as if it were nothing but strands of wool, gouging a track out into the farm pasture.

We can't move the boulder, even with the tractor. But the fence is an easy fix. All it will need is half a dozen light manuka staves, a roll of number 8 wire, and joiners and strainers. And a new sign to replace the one that was hanging on the fence near the gate and directly in the path of the boulder. *No reporters.* Some reporters never gave up on the chance to be the first to land an exclusive with the bullet that walks.

We start after breakfast.

But repairs slow right down when Matthew looks thoughtfully at the first new wire and plucks it. The result is a pleasing, pulsing musical note, the pulse thrumming back and forth between the strainer posts. He breaks into a grin. The sound is even better when he plucks it one pace out from a post, something like putting your head in a drum and singing a single note *wowowowow*... Then he discovers that he can alter the pitch of the note by controlling the strainers. Soon, he is absorbed in making a giant five-string harp out of the new fence. He's utterly present, other places and other times temporarily dissolved back into the field.

And suddenly he is taken over by more euphoria. He runs back and forth to the barn to find materials like string and sticks, then taps and ties and tinkers to get precisely the right pitch. Along the way, he tells me the principal frequencies of each wire, and throws in most of the harmonic frequencies as a bonus.

Then he bids me to take my seat in the dress circle. He mimes spitting on his hands, rolls and flexes his fingers like an artiste about to attack a keyboard, then plucks—top wire to bottom. D, E, C, low C, then G. The sound is well worth the wait, eerie but satisfying, rolling back on an echo from the other side of the valley.

The frightened alpacas wheel and rush to the furthest boundary fence, then gradually calm to mere astonishment. A few of the braver individuals come forward, a few steps at a time.

When Matthew tires of it, I try the massive instrument myself. There's a remarkable amount of pleasure in making such rich sounds come from one's own hands. Even wrapped in his euphoria, he notices my pleasure and his own increases as a result.

Then I leave him to staple the new battens and I head for the workshop.

I don't reach it. I'm halfway across the paddock when there's a commotion behind me—snarling, and a shout of surprise. I turn and see Matthew on his back, holding arms up to fend off a dog. It's a golden Labrador doing something I've never seen or contemplated in the world's most loved and loving dog. It's bent over him with lips drawn back and the slavering, deep throated snarl signals imminent attack.

But even as I begin to run towards them, the dog hesitates and draws back. It rasps out a last snarl, then effortlessly clears the fence and lopes away towards the track. Shocked, Matthew clambers to his feet and backs further from the fence, but the danger is over.

In a few seconds, I'm beside him, and we see the dog's owner: a middle aged woman with blue-rinse hair, a smart walking jacket and sensible walking shoes. She fondles the dog's neck with rough affection, seeming not to notice that the dog is trembling and looking back at Matthew.

"Hey!' Matthew shouts.

She stops, but only to take in the scenery.

"Hey! Your dog attacked me."

She doesn't hear or see him. She pulls out a cigarette packet and matchbox, and with methodical care puts a cigarette in her mouth and removes a match. She strikes it and lights up, dragging deeply while the match still burns. Then she flicks it away to one side without looking at where it lands. She clips the dog onto a leash, then continues down the track, jerking the lease to make the animal fall in behind. And it does so, ranging side to side with lolling tongue.

Matthew stares at the damp grass where she threw the match. A wisp of grey curls up in the air, smooth as wrought iron. When the match is completely spent and the smoke signal gone, his rigid muscles relax. Then his body slumps even though he is still on his feet.

***

The night sky clears, the cloud swept away by an invisible broom, the air standing still like an extension of the earth. When I think Matthew has turned in, I set a ladder against the barn and climb up to sit on the roof. But within seconds the ladder beats on the guttering, the corrugated iron creaks, and there he is.

He sits beside me, without asking. And he immediately accuses me. "You talk about the field, but you don't talk about love. You're cold. Your knowledge is cold."

I look at him. "You are wondering if the field... loves you."

"I... no... it's not..."

"Do you love your right hand?"

He looks at his right hand, starts to speak, but changes his mind and gazes at the star fields of the Milky Way blazing above—and below, because the surface of the reservoir is a mirror. Now and then a speck of life disturbs the surface, creating a supernova that quivers through entire galaxies. He informs me that there are so many stars in our galaxy alone that if a single one is like a grain of salt, then the entire galaxy would take enough salt to fill an Olympic swimming pool.

"Too much information," I grumble.

"Look who's talking," he replies easily.

Even the bush is hushed, in silence so profound that we seem to be falling through the night. A light with a tail swims across the sky, too slow for a meteorite, yet too fast for a satellite.

Matthew asks, "You still remember nothing from before your accident?"

"No. Well, nothing personal."

"Do you try to remember?"

"No." I tell him that I see my missing years the way I saw a painting in Malaga Cathedral in Spain. It hangs in an unlit alcove and the colours are shades of black on black on black. You can't see any detail, let alone the whole picture, but it creates a feeling of dread and you want to back away. That's what it's like. That's why I don't try to remember.

He considers that, hugging his knees, looking ahead. "But you're sane, aren't you?"

I look sideways at him, seeing that he needs me to be sane. "Yes, I am. I am completely sane."

"I'm not," he says. "Aren't you afraid to be sitting up here with a madman?"

"No. I'm not. Are you warning me?"

"You don't know... I did something..." He breaks off. Then, "Why do you persist with me?" And when I don't answer, his voice drops to a thin thread in the darkness. "What's happening?"

"What do you mean?" I ask.

"Will something make it right?"

In the darkness, one part of him can pretend that I will not hear his vulnerability, but another needs the answer. Will something make it right? Will something make it right? I want to put a hand on his shoulder, but I cannot because I remember that I dislike him. But as I think this, I imagine what Siobhan would say. *Don't think, Jack. Just understand.*

"Yes," I say. "Something will make it very right."

SIX

He washes his breakfast pan and billy in the stream, scraping them with wood whittled to the shape of a broad chisel. Then he clambers back up to his camp, and secures pan and billy and food supplies in the tent, out of reach of Rangi and Papa. He has accepted some of my supplies now, but only as a way to both stay and remain apart.

Some mornings, he wanders into the bush, rifle in hand, returning hours later. This time he turns towards the house, but hesitates, looking down at his rifle. What he decides now will determine the next lesson. If he brings the rifle, I will take one track. If he leaves it, I will take another.

He leaves it.

I go to my bedroom and look under the bed for two magazines. They're not immediately obvious and I have to move several objects around in the dust before I spot them. They're on top of a tiny, very old suitcase, which I pull out far enough to retrieve the magazines. The label says *Conrad Fleming*. After all this time, I had forgotten about it. But right now, I have a more immediate purpose, so I push it back under, keeping the magazines.

By the time Matthew reaches the porch, I'm lying back in one of the deck chairs. He sits, cheerfully returning my greeting. If he regrets last night's words on the roof of the barn, he's not showing it.

I point him to the magazines. One cover shows a picture of a pueblo Indian woman blissfully playing a *quena*, a bamboo flute. The quote attributed to her says, *We shall be one person*. The other volume is open at a picture of a New Guinean tribesman, with loincloth, feathers in his hair, and bones around his neck. His appearance rouses the instant stereotype response: savage, primitive. But he too is warm of eye and light of mood. The quote just below his photo says, *We are one person.*

Matthew throws down the magazines and sits back, his expression pre-set—as always—to impassive.

"The third truth," he guesses.

"The third. All things are connected. All things are different faces of one thing, which is Consciousness. The Field, the Great Spirit, the Source, the Tao, the One: these are all names for the same thing. The universe *is* Consciousness: an ocean in motion, a river of eddies, an infinite field of creative works in which the art is the artist and the artist is the art. Consciousness, longing to experience itself, imagines us into existence, individualized, so that we can interact as if we were separate. What we create in that experience is also consciousness, and whatever object you can name—a galaxy, a mountain, a mouse, a fish or a fowl, a blade of grass or a puff of air—all of it is consciousness waving to you in your mirror. Listen to this…"

Two monks argue over a flag waving in the wind. One says 'It's the flag that is moving.' And the other says, 'It's the wind that is moving.' So they put the problem to their teacher.

'You are both wrong,' the teacher says. 'It's only consciousness that is moving.'

Matthew's hands hang over the side of the wicker chair, close to the porch planks. He frowns, then taps a finger on the wood. Hard matter dismisses soft consciousness.

"Seems solid enough to me."

"It does. But hold your judgement. I want to show you something."

We remove all clothing and pegs from the clothes line, a

heavy braided nylon rope running the full length of the front porch. I slip a stick into the loop at one end of the line and twist it, until it's so taut it barely dips in the middle. I pluck the line and it thrums.

"Another giant harp?" Matthew asks.

"No. Now watch this."

I position Matthew in the middle of the rope, then go to the end and pluck it sideways like a guitar string. A pulse flashes down the line, bounces off the far end and dies on the way back. I turn to Matthew.

"Tell me what that was that went down the line."

He shrugs at the elementary question. "A pulse. A wave."

Now I take a single peg and re-attach it to the line in front of him. "The peg is just to help you keep your attention on one point of the rope. Watch to see how it moves." I pluck the rope again. Another wave pulse flashes down it and the peg twitches sideways.

"Okay," he says, "It kicks sideways as the wave goes through, then it does nothing again. So what?"

"Sideways. Did the peg move in the same direction as the wave? Does *any* part of the rope move in the same direction as the wave?"

"No."

"Is the wave the same thing as the piece of rope?"

"No, obviously not."

"So what is this wave, if it's not the rope?"

"Energy. Travelling along the rope, kicking it sideways."

"And where did the energy come from?

"From you. From your hand."

"Exactly. So, here's what we've got. Energy arrives from somewhere else, picks up the rope and makes a wave shape. As the wave travels, it takes up bits of rope at the front end, replacing those dropping out the back. So far, nothing we've said would offend a scientist. Agreed?"

"Yes." He's impatient for the point, looking for the catch.

"Hold that thought. Now, the rest is in your head. Instead of a peg on a rope, change to a dinghy in open water. For long, slow waves in deep water it's the same situation. The dinghy bobs almost straight up and down as the wave goes through. The wind over the horizon puts energy into the water. The energy picks up the water and makes a wave shape. As the wave travels, it takes up bits of water at the front end, replacing those dropping out the back. Again, nothing to bother a scientist. Agreed?"

"Yes." He's puzzled.

"Now we come to the human body. Here are facts, accepted by traditional science. Your stomach lining is replaced every four days. Your skin is replaced every month. Your skeleton is completely new every three months. At least ninety-eight per cent of the atoms of your body are replaced every twelve months. All in all, you have a completely new physical body at least once every two years—including your brain cells. And once more, taken in isolation, that's nothing to bother a scientist."

"Ah." Comprehension dawns on his face.

"Now," I urge him. "Put it together."

He chooses his words thoughtfully. "What drives our bodies is an energy form which does not arise from the body itself. The energy picks up the earth—food and water—and forms a human shape. As it travels, it maintains that shape, taking in bits of earth to replace cells that die and return to the earth."

"Exactly. We are not our bodies. We are the energy of consciousness, wearing our bodies like glove puppets, continuously discarding old parts of the puppet and replacing them with new until we withdraw the hands."

"That's a mighty big jump," he objects. "If we turn over every body cell every two years, how do you explain someone who has a cancer tumour in their body for five years?"

"The consciousness that formed the tumour also keeps replacing those cells."

He broods, then lets it go with a shrug. Get on with it, his shoulders say. So I continue.

"Traditional science—let's call it the old science—says the universe is made of isolated dead things called particles, atoms and molecules and, therefore, so are we. It says the universe is a complex mechanical toy that has been winding down ever since the big bang. It also says there is no ghost in the machine.

"Which means no free will." Matthew says.

"None. Old science says we are the sum of our parts, our paths utterly dictated by the tiny atomic interactions that make up our bodies and environment. It says the future is fixed by the past. Michelangelo's *David*, Beethoven's *Fifth*, Shakespeare's *Romeo and Juliet,* all created by the mechanical processes of physics and chemistry. And so is our appreciation—except perhaps for Charles Darwin, who thought Shakespeare dull to the point of nausea."

"That would make us all robots," Matthew says.

"It would. Old science sees DNA as original cause in the human body, but DNA is the instruction code, not the instructor. The instructor is consciousness. Which comes first, the happiness or the smile? The sadness or the tears?"

Matthew nods warily.

"Now, if you're going to grasp what comes next, you'll have to grapple with modern science discoveries that seem like theatre of the absurd. Science is poised to reverse its most fundamental assumptions. Physicists have been using their atom smashers to hunt for the smallest particle of all, the fundamental building block of the universe. But the results are so disturbing that the West has closed its collective eyes and ears to the implications."

He's scornful. "You're exaggerating."

"I'm understating it. The discoveries will transform the story humanity tells about itself. Science and spiritual knowledge are now racing towards each other and the meeting will cause worldwide joy and relief when the implications sink in. I'll compress a century of scalp-tingling conversations into one chat in a science lab. Imagine a worried physicist, bursting into the office of his Head of Research, waving a fat sheaf of experimental results.

'Boss, I've got bad news. About that smallest particle, the fundamental building block of the universe I was supposed to find...'

'Yes, what?'

'There isn't one. There's nothing there.'

'What? Of course there's something there.'

'Well, it exists when we're actually observing it, but before and after that it just isn't there. It has no physical existence without us.'

'Oh. I get it. This is a joke.'

'No joke. It does still exist, but only as part of an energy field that waits for us to start looking before it obliges us with a physical object.'

'Some under-washed undergraduate put you up to this, right? Very droll. Now go away and-'

'Wait. There's more. When two particles have interacted, they stay in touch. No matter how far apart they are, each responds instantly to whatever happens to the other. And I do mean instantly—it makes the speed of light look like a sick snail.'

'No!'

'Yes. We've even got objects appearing in different places simultaneously.'

'Stop!' The Head of Research stands abruptly, a nervous smile twitching at the corners of his mouth. 'For a moment there I thought you said that one object

can appear in two places at the same time.'

'Actually any number of places at the same time.' (Stabs finger at sheaf of results.) 'It looks as if there are many universes. Many dimensions in parallel. There may be millions.'

'No!'

'Oh, and these particles have no respect for our time equations. Time is showing up like a human invention. We can even change the history of an experiment. History is changeable.'

The HOR's voice turns husky. 'We'll be a laughing stock. There's got to be a flaw in your methodology, you'll have to re-calibrate the atom-smashers. These results... These results-'

'These results have been replicated again and again around the world. And there's something else... Uh... Boss—you're really going to hate this—it's not just an object's existence that depends on the observer; its behaviour depends on the intent of who's looking!'

'Now stop right there! This is all sub-atomic, so what's it got to do with real life?'

'Boss, I can't believe you said that. If you feel the ground shaking, hear loud trumpeting and see a large animal with tusks bearing down on you, wouldn't you be tempted to think about elephants?'

'What I'm thinking about is having a migraine. Do you have any idea what this will do to science?'

'I think so. We dug into the atom and found a mirror. We've found our own minds in there, causing things to appear and move about and vanish.'

'But we can't just go public and tell... and tell the world that... that...'

'That we humans are, somehow, directly creating the physical universe?'

The Head of Research is stunned. His jaw sags. He sits abruptly and murmurs, 'My God!'

'I think you've hit it on the head, Boss. That may turn out to be the point.'

"Whoa." Matthew's jaw has done its own sagging. "Is this for real?"

"The science, yes. Einstein saw it coming back as the fifties. He did the science equivalent of crossing himself and said, 'I like to think the moon is there even if I am not looking at it.' He also described everyday reality as a persistent illusion."

"The leaf! It's what you were saying about the leaf!"

"Yes."

Matthew is incredulous. "This changes everything. Why isn't this known around the world?

"Because rapid change has already thrust humans into future shock, and these discoveries will lead to the biggest and fastest human transformation in history. No scientist can utter the implications and still sound like a scientist; but some are starting to break ranks and say that this is the first sighting of the universal field of consciousness that pervades all things and is all things."

"So the joke about finding the God particle inside the atom is no joke."

"You have it. The fundamental building block of the universe has been found. It's not quarks or leptons or bosons or charm particles. It's-"

"Thought."

"It is. Thought—especially passionate thought—is the cutting tool of Consciousness. It acts on the great field like a sculptor's chisel on a rock which contains all possible shapes. The sculptures move around, and shift in and out of existence according to the rhythms of thought. Scientists say energy can be neither created nor destroyed, it can only change its form.

But when they recognize the field, they will rewrite that law: consciousness can be neither created nor destroyed, it can only change the form of its expression."

Matthew shoots me an accusing glance. "You're making me feel weird again."

"Weird good, or weird bad?"

He doesn't answer. Then, "So, if we know how it works, we can use our thoughts to directly control what appears and disappears around us."

"Yes. With discipline and focus, it's all waiting for you."

"The quickening."

"Yes."

"Which you are still withholding from me."

"So you keep reminding me. But you're not ready yet."

"So you keep reminding me," he retorts. He turns away, brows lowered. He pulls a multi-purpose tool from a pocket, turns it over and over, pulls out the knife blade and uses it to explore a deep crack in a porch board.

"What is the meaning of the word knife?" I ask.

He wrinkles his nose. "Something you hold in your hand that cuts objects."

"And the meaning of cut?"

"Slice into bits."

"And the meaning of bit?"

"Portion, fragment... okay, okay, get to the point."

"Each word is defined by all words. Each thought by all thoughts and each thing by all things. Nothing has meaning without the existence of all else. What is everywhere else has a presence here, and if it is not here, it is nowhere. All things are so utterly connected that they are *of* each other. Even if you were to travel in a spaceship further than the most distant galaxies, you cannot be disconnected. Even if you were to inflict deeds too terrible for the imagination on others, you cannot be disconnected. What you do unto others *is* what is done unto you."

"Don't say that. *Don't talk like that!*" His mood is, once again, in free fall. I can hear the movement of his breath, a clicking sound in his throat. "...acting like God Almighty."

He rocks the knife aggressively into the crack, finding a splinter and making it longer. Then he levers it aside so he can see what he has disturbed. "I bet there's insects in here," he says. Then he presses hard on the handle so that the blade anchors itself in the crack; and with eyes hooded, he accuses the blade.

"Why did you have to look like Father?" Then he looks up at me and snarls. "Why did you have to go and *do* that?"

***

Just before dawn, pandemonium breaks out in the henhouse. Matthew and I get there at the same time and dash in to find the air filled with feathers and fear-crazed chickens half-hopping, half-flying. They burst out past us, emptying the space in short seconds. Our torches slash and stab the air, looking for the cause, and we find it in the middle of the floor.

The stoat rises on its hind legs facing us, and spreads its forelegs. Come and get me.

For its body size, little more than the length of a boot, the stoat is the most ferocious mammal on the planet. If cornered it will attack anything and when it kills, it torments its victims. It can dispose of a rooster ten times its size, and when it gets into the henhouse, you expect dead bodies and quickly. We can't be sure of the toll yet, because neither of us is willing to take our torch beams off the stoat. We back into the corner to give it maximum room to pass without sinking teeth into our legs.

The stoat is in no hurry. It snarls at Matthew and waits for a response. Getting none, it turns its head, hops a pace towards me, and snarls again, this time drawn-out and throbbing. Then it drops to all fours and vibrates out the door and into the night.

I flick the torch around. Remarkably, there's not a single dead hen, not so much as a cracked egg, even though the stoat surely had time to create havoc. I search with the torch and find the entry point; an old weatherboard, warped away from the frame in the corner. When I reverse the torch, Matthew hasn't moved. He's staring at the floor where the stoat was. I touch him on the upper arm.

He jumps, and rounds on me, "Keep your hands to yourself."

We nail the warped board to hold until morning.

After breakfast, his roller coaster emotions soar again, this time on another set of wings.

He replaces the warped board himself, whistling as he fills the nail holes and primes the result. To tempt the hens to return, he lays kitchen scraps inside, and a pellet trail back through the hatch, down the plank and out into the yard. Then we sit on the woodpile to watch.

At first, the hens peer suspiciously round the corner of the house, roosters pacing in the rear. Eventually, they approach and step onto the plank rising to the hatch. Hilda is first to the top. She peers through the opening and encounters two things: kitchen scraps and lingering essence-of-stoat. Her head inclines forward, but her feet refuse to budge. So she pulls her head back out. The others pile up behind, until the entire brood is crowded on the plank going nowhere, eyes blinking, heads and necks twitching nervously in every direction.

Matthew and I look at each other, then back at the brood.

"I want to make a sound like a stoat right now," he murmurs, and is pleased when I laugh.

He walks over, grabs Hilda in one swift action, and pushes her through the hatch. She gets out a cry of protest, but the feather jam is broken; the others pour through the hatch after her and throw themselves on the scraps in an orgy punctuated by the rattle of beaks on the henhouse floor.

***

In the last light of day, he spots a thick, dead branch near his tent and props it against the nearest tree. It stands there on two limbs and has two more higher up, so it simulates a thin human body. Then he takes his hunting knife from the pack. The first throw fails, the knife bouncing off the branch and falling to the moss below. But then he finds the range and the blade sticks. He strides forward, works it free, strides back seven paces, turns, throws again. And again. And again. Each throw is launched with more energy than the last. Rangi and Papa arrive, hopping sideways, skipping closer. Then Matthew is shouting, each shout a crescendo of rage, the blade leaving his hand at the climax and flashing through the air to sink deep into the rotting wood.

A shiver hunts for tributaries in my spine and I turn away from the window. I take a plate from the table to the kitchen, pick up a cloth to wipe the bench, put it down, run water for too few dishes and leave it unused, and straighten the chairs around the table. None of which eases the twisting in my gut.

When I return to the window, he's still there.

Then, even though I did not call her, Siobhan is beside me.

We stand side-by-side, shoulders close. Even now, with Matthew drawing our gaze, I'm intensely aware of her. I feel drawn to the edge of the abyss between where I am and where she is. If I could, I would draw her this way across the gap, to where she could once again wear real flesh to touch, lips to brush with mine, hair to run silk through my fingers, and a heart to hear when I press my ear against her breast.

Matthew is now just a black shadow against the trees, the blade a flash from the shadows, the shout guttural and primitive.

"You're still pushing ahead," she says, her tone neutral.

"I am."

"You've obviously decided that the Truth is not just for the benefit of the sane."

My reply is petulant, even sarcastic. "In the absence of clear advice otherwise, yes."

"But you're worried."

"Yes. I think we need a crisis to clear the air. But I don't want it to get out of control."

"And?"

"And I could fail."

"Ah," she says. "Failure. I'm thinking you wouldn't be taking too kindly to that." She doesn't elaborate. There is so much she does not tell me.

The shouting ceases, the blade stops flickering and Matthew squats by the remains of his camp fire, warming his hands, slapping sandflies off his wrists. His jacket hood is up and the flames make his hands and face glow red against the black bush.

"Jack. If you were to fail, what then? What would that mean for you I'm wonderin'?" She's an expert at this—either straight questions, or statements that are actually questions in disguise. But never an answer. She is so accomplished at the Socrates technique, drawing me out, that I can easily find my tongue blurting what should first be carefully considered.

"I won't give that thought any more attention," I say.

But she is merciless. "Talk to me, Jack, or must I fetch a mirror?"

"You and Socrates have a lot in common," I grumble. "He was a pest."

"So are you planning to offer me hemlock? I hope not... it's hell on the digestion."

"Hah." I turn away from her and stare gloomily at where Matthew is now almost completely absorbed into the darkness.

I don't want to tell her the truth, because the truth is... that I have become afraid. There. Just admitting it to myself is enough to send insects scuttling through my bloodstream, partly because it's been a long time since I was afraid of anything. But also because I cannot explain what causes it. Siobhan is on the wrong track; of course I want to succeed with Matthew, but fear of failure does not explain the knot in my stomach.

"And if you succeed," she asks. "What will that mean for you?"

"What kind of question is that?"

"Answer me."

"Well then, Vonnie, I'll depart this life, bring champagne to your door and say 'mission accomplished' and ask you to let me in for an eternity or two. Of course your pa will have to put away the shotgun."

She will not be distracted. "No, Jack. It's not the point."

"What? What's the point?"

"You're missing something."

"Missing? What are you talking about? What am I missing?"

"Something that's prancing right there in front of you tweaking your nose and you're not seein' it, Jack. That's what you're missing."

I sigh heavily. After learning how to master my life on this planet, must I now be made to feel like an ignorant schoolboy? "Let me guess. You're not going to tell me, are you... what this thing is that I'm missing."

"Not even a clue."

"You have no heart."

"Well, that's true enough."

"I want a divorce."

"I'll be sure to look into it," she says.

***

I dream that Matthew and Siobhan are having sex in a marble bath. It's awkward and painful for them, because the bath is broken in the middle and the water has drained away. They pause in their exertions and look at me expectantly.

I ask them, "If my heart beats fifty-seven times in a minute, how many times does it beat in seventy years?"

"Two billion, ninety-eight million, five hundred and eighty thousand, four hundred," Matthew replies.

There's something important I am supposed to give them. I search my clothes, but find nothing except a movie ticket.

Now I'm running down the street with Archimedes, who is naked, except for a clerical collar. I am trying to explain that his concept of upthrust and displacement simply does not hold water, but my tongue is thick and slow to move. A King Charles spaniel puppy with a stick in its mouth runs in front of us, eager to play. Archimedes crushes it with one foot, flattening its head. I attack him, flailing at him until he falls to the ground. But my anger is not satisfied. It vaults on itself, until I am screaming with rage and hatred. I lift a rock high and bring it down on his head. Again and again and again. His blood splatters over the spaniel's teeth and vacant eyes.

And I wake, heart lurching, sweating and panting. *Just a dream, just a dream.* But the loss of control is terrifying. I can still hear my screaming like an echo. *Too hot.* I throw the quilt off.

But the screaming continues somewhere.

Vertigo swirls into nausea. I think I must still be in the grip of the nightmare, then I realize that someone really is screaming in the distance. I leave the bed and run out the front doorway onto the pasture. The screaming is coming from Matthew's tent, slashing across the darkness.

As I near the tent, the sound cuts off abruptly.

I stop. The tent is mute now, a grey patch against black bush. I wait, gooseflesh rising against the chill, until the bush forgets and breathes again. A possum grunts. A kiwi calls, so close I can also hear the rustle as it forages in old leaves. I turn around and go back to bed, to lie awake until the roosters catch dawn in the act of sneaking in the window.

SEVEN

Every afternoon now, there are two of us at the alpaca enclosure.

Popper is first up for affection, nuzzling my chest and neck, pushing her nose into my armpit. When Matthew comes closer, hoping for contact, she backs off, leaving him to pretend indifference. Plato discovers his shadow on the side wall of the hay shed and studies it, moving his head about to watch it lollop across the corrugations.

We bring a bale of lucerne out of the shed.

It's not because they need it. To an alpaca, a lucerne feed is a lolly scramble, so when we break the bale and dump it over the fence, there's an unseemly rush. A mini chorus of spitting breaks out as a dozen jostle for position. Kant stretches his neck forward with mouth open, waiting for lucerne to somehow materialize in his jaws. Pangloss loses his position but his inane grin never falters. I dreamed once that I had his smile surgically removed, for which he thanked me in the cultured tones of an Oxford-educated, Italian gentleman. Even further back, Descartes stands at the junction of two fences looking bewildered, as if he can't think his way out of the corner.

Socrates uses his teeth to mete out punishment to other males whose judgement is so lucerne-disabled that they enter his circle of authority. Alpacas may be cuddly and curious, but they can also be ruthless. When they perceive a manageable threat, they can attack as one, rising on their hind legs like deer, stabbing with twin-toed hooves, then bringing their heads down hard with teeth agape. The hierarchical males will take out each other's hamstrings and testicles just to maintain status and access to the females. Combined, these apparently harmless creatures can easily dispose of an intruding cat or dog, and in Peru they've been known to turn pumas into rugs.

The sky is overcast, the air pressing on the grass. The usually surprised brows of the alpacas seem low, and sleepy. The hens forage with almost no sound, close to the protection of house and barn. A native wood pigeon, *kereru*, thuds past overhead, feathers whistling, wings working hard to stay aloft. When it reaches the elm behind the house, it does not rise to drop into the foliage, but blunders into it horizontally, as if desperate for a way to stop. In the season, the kereru gorges itself on ripe *karaka* berries and staggers, drunk, from branch to branch. Some kereru fall out of the tree. I have found them on the ground in a stupor—living marinated pigeon.

"How did you sleep?" I ask Matthew.

"Good," he says, surprised by the question.

"You don't remember?"

"Remember what?"

"You were shouting."

"In my sleep?" He feigns lecherous interest. "Did it sound like I had company?"

"No."

"I might as well be a monk," he complains. "Even Sheba is starting to look attractive."

But I'm distracted by the sight of the newest cria. Mikey is dishevelled and thin and has not followed Simone into the feeding frenzy. She turns and bleats to him, but though he makes a shaky effort, he can't move. She returns, he tries to suckle, but gives up in seconds. She nuzzles him, attempts to push him, but then stands around uncertainly.

"Damn," I mutter. I enter the enclosure, walking around the busy herd towards Mikey and Simone. Abruptly, Matthew heads in after me and the alpacas nearest him startle. The whole herd scatters, abandoning the lucerne to watch him warily from the far corners. He grimaces, but continues to follow me, coughing on the way.

Simone and Mikey are the only animals who haven't bolted. Both peer this way and that, but stay still.

"What's the matter?" Matthew asks.

"Mama's milk bar is dry. It's hand rearing time." I stroke Simone for a while, explain the situation to her, then lift Mikey, inviting her to follow. She does so, all the way out of the enclosure and up to the house steps. There she watches her baby taken inside, bleats once, then drops her head to graze. Back at the enclosure, the other adults return to the last scraps of lucerne.

Inside, Mikey gets centre-spot on the couch in front of the fire. Matthew is impressed, but Boa emits an indignant blast of air from her nostrils. The tiny alpaca shows no distress at all, even though this must be the alpaca equivalent of finding yourself on an alien planet. He lies on his side, head up, interested. He sniffs the blanket under him, then the leather behind him. Matthew lights the fire and Mikey watches it grow as if it were an astonishing revelation. Seated in the centre of each black orb is a tiny but glittering reflection of the flames. *El fuego.*

I mix lambs' milk formula in a bottle.

Matthew loses every scrap of his reserve; he asks to do the feeding and I show him the technique—right hand behind the head and supporting the back of the jaw, left hand holding bottle and front of jaw. Mikey hesitates, fumbles the teat, then sucks greedily and finally falls asleep with his head on Matthew's thigh, Matthew strokes the silky fur and blinks and swallows. His eyes moisten, so he angles his head away from me.

His index finger taps repeatedly on his kneecap: three fast, three slow, three fast, three slow. He doesn't know he's doing it.

I can't delay any longer.

I consider stacking the odds by selecting the right music, but decide against it. Instead, I pour two glasses of a good pinot noir and pull a comfortable chair up close to the couch. Matthew blinks furiously to rid his eyes of Judas moisture. His index finger is still tapping.

He's not looking at me, but I start anyway.

"When we are born, very little of our expanded being can be seen by other humans. A mother can sense it; sometimes, she can even sense the broad intent behind the incarnation. But within the boundaries of that intent, the new Earth personality is a blank slate. Life events start immediately—the feel of air on the face, the scrape of clothing, the suckle at the breast, the touch and smell of the mother's skin, the sound of her voice, the love in her eye. The new mind begins to write on the slate, building attitudes and beliefs, which then generate their own events. What the mind writes on the slate is increasingly influenced by what it has already written there. So most move in lockstep to a world-view they unknowingly wrote themselves. They are prisoners in cells they built."

Matthew shivers. "I wish I could zap my brain, wipe out the past and start again. I tried to do it once, with acid, but I just had a bad trip."

"You can't cancel a painful past. If you try to destroy the prison cell, the bars get stronger. Instead, there's a way to unlock the door and step out. To find out how to do it, we're going to go back and look at the intent your expanded self might have for you in this lifetime."

He gives silent assent.

"Imagine that you're considering your next incarnation—the where, when and how circumstances of your birth—in other words, your life-template. Let's suppose you want to experience, say, courage. How would you go about that?"

"I don't understand the question."

"If you were your soul, what might you arrange for your Earth personality so that you could experience the quality of courage?"

"Feel fear and overcome it."

"Right. Give me an example."

His mood pendulum swings instantly. "I arrange to be born in a time and place so I can be around when a bus-load of gorgeous women crashes off a bridge into the river. Spurning all thought for my own safety, I dive 200 feet into the water, swim like a dolphin, bringing them out to-"

"Fine," I mutter.

"-bring them out to safety, one-by-one. They're clinging to me, weeping with gratitude, clothes in disarray, some of them barely decent... yeah... Oh yes, and I'll arrange to have cameras around so I can say that I'm no hero, I only did what anyone else would have done. Courage, yeah. Hey, I should be a movie director."

"All right, Mr Spielberg, how would you set up a life-template to experience, say, gratitude? Show me the rushes."

"Okay." He frames his hands into the shape of a viewfinder. "I set up to be born as a child in a remote village in the Congo. No phones, no electricity, no roads, just a foot track through the jungle. I'm restless, I know I have a brain, and I want to use it. The village council knows this also, but doesn't know what to do about it because the only school is taught by a teacher who is barely literate himself. But one day, let's say... a surveyor passes through. The village council pushes me in front of him and asks advice. He asks the council if he can take me away to be schooled. The council agrees and every village family brings gifts to help me on my way. Fifteen years later, I return as a doctor, and serve villages up to three day's walk in every direction. I think that would be gratitude."

"Couldn't agree more. But you would need some cooperation."

"I guess. From the village, the council... the surveyor."

"Tell me more about the cooperation of the surveyor. Was it coincidence that he just turned up?"

"Ah." He sees where I'm going. "It has to be arranged in advance with the soul of that surveyor."

"Exactly. That soul lets a specific fragment of itself enter your universe, a gift to you. How you handle the gift will be your creation and your adventure. Let's do another one. How would you set up an incarnation in order to experience compassion?"

"Compassion." He's instantly uneasy. "Maybe I don't do compassion."

"Why is that?"

"It's... it's like setting up a picnic on an anthill."

"Then it's not real compassion. Paint me the real thing."

He looks at me speculatively, tongue pressing the inside of his cheek. He senses—correctly—that I'm setting him up, but can't predict how or why.

Mikey, between us, breathes almost silently in his sleep, with a sigh now and then.

"All right then, compassion," Matthew says slowly. His imagination fires again. "I would arrange that when I'm ten years old, some drunken dickhead kicks me in the spine with steel-capped boots. That puts me in a wheelchair as a quadriplegic. My voice box is affected and I can only just get words out. Some people can't face me at all, some are revolted, some shout as if I'm deaf, some of them ask my foster mother—in front of me—if I want a biscuit. I get years of this until my eighteenth birthday when I get a new daily help. Myra. Myra's different. She talks to me without shouting and she assumes I've got a brain. She doesn't change her decisions if I throw tantrums. She doesn't stand any nonsense from me. I can't manipulate her. She's not po-faced around me. She's happy. She whistles and sings when she does things around the house. She even tells me dirty jokes when no one else will. When Myra looks at me, she's got respect. She asks my opinion on things. She expects me to come up with interesting conversation. She doesn't pity me, she's not sorry for me. She seems to know what I'm going through, but it doesn't stop her feeling happy or being happy. It's like she can see a bigger picture. This is a shock to me and it puzzles me. I talk with her about it. Then, one day, she doesn't come alone. She brings a little girl who had her leg amputated and is still recovering. The little girl is pale and quiet. Withdrawn. I start treating her the way Myra treats me, and after a few days I realize that I feel better than I have felt for a long time. Almost happy. I think that's how I could experience compassion."

"I agree," I say, encouraged. I take my chin off my hand. "And which of those characters would your soul need to set up the key events at field level?"

"Myra. And the little girl."

"Who else?"

"My foster mother."

"Who else?"

And then he knows. He knows what I'm up to. He pales visibly and a muscle twitches in his cheek. He has his glass up in front of him and he's been looking at the fire through the red liquid. But the hand holding the glass is trembling. Mikey wakes, lifts his head. The diminutive alpaca tries to get up, but still doesn't have the strength.

I can feel Siobhan's presence and glance around. She's sitting in half-lotus position beside the grandfather clock. Her Mona Lisa smile confirms that she will not be telling me what to say or do. Of course. My decisions. I feel like telling Matthew that I'm trying to help him, not hurt him, but instead, I take advantage of the silence.

"Matthew, what events might *your* soul set up in cooperation with another soul so that you might experience forgiveness?"

He closes his eyes emphatically, screwing them down hard. The glass stays poised in front of him. Some mothers tell their children, Don't screw up your eyes so tight or the shampoo will get in through the cracks and sting you.

He says, "Not everything can be forgiven."

"Not only can be, but will be."

"Turn the other cheek, eh?" His eyes stay closed. A vein throbs on his temple.

"Forgiveness does not mean turning the other cheek. It means knowing that there is nothing to forgive—that whoever brings you sorrow brings you the gift of rich, limitless possibilities."

"Gift," he murmurs.

"Matthew, when you can't forgive, you're the prisoner. When you can, the chains fall off you and you step out of the cell."

"Gift. Gift. Gift." He works his tongue around the word, as if it were a strangely shaped pebble. Slowly, deliberately, he lets his hand fall forward and his glass smashes in the hearth, the wine splashing out onto the carpet.

Here it is, then. No turning back.

Boa slinks under the table, fur a ruff on her neck. The light is falling already and the spilt wine glistens like black blood. When Matthew finally looks up, something turns over inside me. The lines on his brow are like wheat stalks in a fist. His pupils are hard points of firelight, red on black, and his voice is eerily soft and flat.

"A gift, eh? Well, old man, if you met someone as compassionate and caring as my father, you might think that was a gift. You know what he did whenever clever Mother went away? Father gave me the gift of full-on, quality time, that's what he did. He would turn up the heater in his study and make it warm and cosy and sit me down on the sheepskin rug and put his arm around me, and tell me that I've been a wicked boy again, making him have to play the frog game. And I would say, But I don't want to play the frog game. But he would look at me with so much understanding and compassion, and say it was too late now but if I prayed, the Lord in his infinite mercy would forgive me for making him do it, so I... so he was-"

I try to calm him. "Matthew-"

"Shut up!" he screams. "Shut your fucking drivel!"

Mikey gives a high-pitched bleat.

Matthew groans, and sinks forward with hands around his head. He stares down at his own elbows and legs which have begun to shake violently of their own accord. Then he surges to his feet and rounds on me in outraged wonder, as if he has just recognized something both extra-ordinary and horrifying. His face seems to have changed shape.

"Matthew, I'm not your-"

But he roars with pain and rage, clutches his stomach, backs towards the door, whirls, and is gone.

My heart booms and surges in my ears, so I can't hear myself think. Mikey bleats again, making a momentary effort to rise. *Vonnie, Vonnie,* I breathe. I can't see her by the grandfather clock any more, but she must be here somewhere, breathing along with me.

I hear running feet, panting, a click, then double-click of a round being loaded into a chamber, then Matthew is back in the doorway with his rifle. He swings it up to his shoulder and aims at my head, his body quaking as if in high fever, breath ragging in and out of his lungs. His gaze goes through me, focusing somewhere behind. For no apparent reason, a detail about the rifle occurs to me: Sako Vixen 222, standard round muzzle velocity up to two thousand eight hundred feet per second.

"You're *dead*," Matthew shouts. "You're supposed to be *dead*." The sight steadies and the blackness in the end of the barrel grows towards me like an opening vortex.

"Matthew, I'm Jack. I'm not your father and you're not going to become your-"

"Liar!" he roars and Mikey bleats again.

Now I'm afraid; which is curious because I really didn't think fear for my physical body was possible any more. But the fear seems only to belong to a small part of me and rest of me is observing it. I turn my head away from him towards the fire to ponder this discovery. It's almost as if I am a hallucination of my self, wondering why this disturbed young man would be pointing his rifle at something so insubstantial as me.

With that thought, I find myself behind Matthew, looking past him, past the rifle, at my physical form on the couch. I can see his finger tightening on the trigger, knuckle whitening, approaching that cusp of pressure that is the point of no return. I see with his eyes now, down the barrel, through the telescopic sight, to a fuzzy view of my old scar, the bullet-hole crater behind the right ear. The barrel wavers, steadies. Matthew refocuses. The scar is still there.

He shakes his head abruptly, as if the scar should vanish with the movement. He whimpers, a mixture of puzzlement and pain, then jerks his head up and looks at my scar without the scope. The barrel wavers again. Then it's over. The rifle crashes to the floor, He howls out in torment, stumbles through the door and vanishes.

This time he doesn't return.

Now I'm back in my own body, watching my hand stroke Mikey under the throat, calming him. His eyes are so black and lustrous that the fire plays perfectly in them, flames tiny but distinct, the embers in tight clusters. Then his eyelids come down and his head sinks to the couch, returning him to sleep. Boa is standing under the table. I approach her, but she slashes at my ankle and blood trickles under my sock. I don't look down, instead I listen to the swarm of tiny sounds as the house settles into the evening.

From outside, I hear nothing.

There's a muffled thump on the glass of the tiny back window. Boa and I cross paths, the cat sprinting for the door, and me walking slowly to the window. There's a stunned bird lying on the outside sill. It's not the first time this has happened. Sometimes, in the evening light and with the front door open, birds think there's a hole right through the house. This time, it's a young black piwakawaka, a scrap of disorganized wing and feather, surely too tiny to sustain a beating heart let alone wings. Boa is already out there, leaping against the wall, attempting to get a claw up to the window ledge. But the fantail recovers, arranges its wings, blinks twice, and then loops drunkenly up into the elm.

I go to the door. No sign of Matthew. I go down to his tent and pull the flap aside. His pack is still here.

I get busy then and don't stop. I switch on every light, even those in the back bedrooms. The house must be a beacon. I pick up the rifle, remove the round, return it to the internal magazine, and push the safety slide on—surprised by how smoothly my hands manage the process. I feed Mikey and carry him out to a stall in the barn, strap on a back blanket, then bring Simone in to keep him company for the night. I leave food scraps for the hens, then force my way through the rest of the evening chores. Even when they're done, I can't stop moving. I find myself in the barn workshop touching the tools; there's something reassuring about the unforgiving hard surfaces: the lathe, the drop-saw, the drill press, the router and the nail gun. I pick up the router and look at it and put it down again. I switch on every light in the barn and leave them on.

I haven't eaten for many hours, and I don't want to.

I sit out on the porch steps. From a standing start in the south east, a warm wind springs up, making the nearby tree tops sway and call out. Night clouds sweep over the nearest peak, making it topple towards me without ever arriving. The Milky Way, satin river of souls, slides across the blackness behind the clouds. Astronomers say that we are intruders from the Sagittarius Dwarf galaxy, which made the fatal mistake of tangling with the Milky Way and is in the last stages of being consumed.

PART THREE

ONE

The car is far away, but the sound is crisp and crystalline like the morning frost. It's a peculiarity of this hanging valley that when a vehicle turns off the road in the upper foothills, the sound bounces up through the gorge walls and emerges clearly at the farm, more than a kilometre higher in altitude.

It lasts only a few seconds, then it's gone. The car is working its way north east of the gorge, soon to begin the real climb: the tortuous, low-gear crawl up the gullies, round the bluffs, through the bush, hidden by the canopy. To call it a road is to flatter it; it's really a wide track, riddled with roots, potholes, slumps and fallen rocks. Higher up, some parts have bowed to the equinox rains and plummeted into the gorge for a more direct journey to the sea, leaving a track barely wide enough for a vehicle.

The flawless, egg-shell sky is everywhere, calling down to a landscape laid out in supplication. The sun reaches down first to the fang-like peaks, then along gunmetal ridges with scimitar crescents of remaining snow, across amber slopes of tussock, through rumpled bush blankets of olive and hunting green, across the patchwork plains, across the beaches cast like a necklace of bones linked end-to-end. Then out across the polished sea. A rust-red container ship is a careless scratch in the polish, tracking south on the great circle route to Cape Horn. Far away in the west, a lone tongue of cloud sticks to the wall and hangs, ready to fall.

Before time began, Ranginui, the Sky Father, and Papatuanuku, the Earth Mother, lay in close embrace.

So tightly were they entwined, there was no space between them; their god children were trapped in darkness and the world could not be created. Tu, the god of war and father of mankind, argued that they should kill their parents. But, Tane, god of the forest, refused and said that in order to create the world, their parents must be separated. He put his head against his father and his feet against his mother and strove mightily, tearing them apart so that the children could move and breathe and experience the nature of light.

But one of the children, Tawhiri, the storm god, could not bear his parents' cries of grief and agony. He became angry and poured out his wrath with mighty whirlwinds and hurricanes so that Ikatere, the father of fish, fled to the sea and Tutewanawana, the father of reptiles, fled to the forests.

Yet Rangi and Papa stayed separated, each reaching out to the other.

Tane made stars in the heavens and the sun and the moon, so that his father could be appropriately dressed. And he supplied the descendents of Tu with canoes and fishhooks to catch the descendents of Ikatere, and with snares and spears to catch the descendents of Tutewanawana.

And so the Sky Father and the Earth Mother continue to grieve, longing to return to their embrace as it was before time began. Sometimes his tears fall upon her as rain. Sometimes she heaves and strains to reach her beloved, but it is to no avail. And when mist rises from the forests, these are sighs as her warm body longs for reunion, and by that longing she nurtures all mankind.

The day ripens. Scents waft by on the merest excuse of a

breeze: vegetation aromas from the bush, earth and animal smells, mint and sage and rosemary from the garden. But no scent overwhelms or is overwhelmed, and I can detect the tang of water from the stream more than a hundred paces away. On such a morning ten thousand cloaks of life swirl between Ranginui and Papatuanuku. *Tihei mauriora ki a koutou*: I honour the breath of life in you all. I honour the darkness that holds the light, the silence that holds the sound, and the stillness that holds my thought.

The hens caw contentedly in the first warmth of the sun. The alpacas await me with mellow, token complaint. Beyond the glasshouse, sunlight drenches Siobhan's arbour, a recess in the bush, sheltered against almost every wind, a crude wooden seat and table in its centre. It was understood that when she meditated there, she could not be interrupted.

There's a commotion inside the glasshouse, just a few steps away. A trapped bird is trying to escape: a rifleman, the smallest of all bush birds, fluttering under the dirty glass apex where cobwebs conceal the air vent. It has forgotten how it got in.

So I lever myself out of the porch seat, and walk to the glasshouse. As I open the door wide, the fluttering becomes frantic and I duck low, crawling underneath, then standing at the far end, as a shepherd. The bird thrums away on wings draped in silk. Up in the glass where it came from, a funnel web spider scuttles, hiding its shiny black abdomen behind old webs. At my feet, the weeds are beginning a comeback, even against the carefully tended swan plants.

For the first time, I see movement in one of the swans. A thin, immature caterpillar with black, orange and white strips humps its way along a fragile branch. A quick check reveals another dozen amongst the leaves.

Siobhan!

Yes! Somewhere I see her arms thrust high in delight.

I hold my little finger in the path of the first caterpillar. It immediately halts and, anchored by its back end, waves its front about, looking for a more attractive path. I nudge it onto my finger, but it rejects the offer and falls off onto the glasshouse floor. I return it gently to the swan.

Then I return to the porch, settling onto the seat.

Now I hear the vehicle again, the sound waxing, waning, sometimes dipping below the threshold of hearing, but returning, then steadying and hardening. From the east porch, I can't see it emerge from the trees, but I follow it with my ears, across the pasture, past the reservoir and the blarney rock, up towards the barn. It sounds like a ute; an old one, the rattles competing with the blare from a holed muffler.

It stops. The driver's door slams, three times, each time more insistent. It seems odd that he has a vehicle. I wish he would just appear out of the mountains again, unencumbered by civilisation.

He will need me at my best, so I set to controlling my state of mind. Allow the nervousness, observe it, release it; direct anew. Calm... calmer... calm. This is how I defeated the beast, long ago.

He finds me quickly, clomping noisily around from the north porch, reversing the direction of his arrival on the first day. This time there is no limp. When he sees that my eyes are closed, he treads quietly and sits on the steps to wait.

I'm ready.

He's pale and drawn, but the unkempt beard is gone. His hair has been tamed, tied behind his head; his clothes are clean and more suitable for farm than mountain. The shorts are gone, replaced by jeans, and he's wearing a new weather jacket, with a silver flashing on the collar. Boa regards him from the porch rail, under the wisteria, a direct gaze.

He looks down at his feet, picks a splinter from the top step and inspects it, turning it over and over.

"How's Mikey?" he asks.

I nod towards the alpacas. "Back with Mama. The milk bar is back in business."

He ignores this invitation to relax. I pull myself out of the chair, stretch stiff limbs, and join him on the step, so that we both look outwards, over the vegetable garden and glasshouse. I doubt if either of us would easily sit face to face right now. The alpacas are lined up, to watch the new activity. Further down the valley, Sheba grazes in patches where the frost has melted away.

"Don't know what to say," he says.

I nod.

He shakes his head, eyes downcast. "I guess sorry isn't enough."

"It's enough. It's all part of the adventure."

"I got confused," he says. "I thought you were... a hallucination."

"I'm not. Not last time I pinched myself."

"I thought you were... him."

"You did make that clear at the time."

When I suggest that he'll be needing lunch, he lets his breath out in a relieved whoosh, screwing his eyes up momentarily against some intruding dust particles. He leaps up and ferries two large crates from his ute, pries them open and piles the contents on the kitchen bench. Groceries in brown paper bags, staples and luxuries. Frozen peas and beans and fresh *hapuka* steaks all wrapped in layers of newspaper. And string bags of vegetables: cabbages, onions and early spring carrots. Even in this micro-climate, it's still too early to be cropping most vegetables, and with no transport lately, supplies have been low. How did he achieve all this without getting arrested? But I know that on the West Coast there are many who would shelter anyone sought by the law.

He produces a kerosene can, brim-filled with fresh whitebait, gleefully lifting a handful of the tiny transparent fish. Then, with a magician's flourish, conjures half a dozen hothouse lemons from a brown paper bag. I applaud, while observing that he didn't need to do all this. He stops his act, just for a moment, and says, quietly, that yes he did.

We prepare the finest of all seafood treats: fresh West Coast whitebait patties with lemon juice. The secret to whitebait is in the batter. They're so delicately flavoured that it's a gastronomic atrocity to serve it in anything but the simplest and lightest of batters—only a hint of salt and pepper, served with slices of lemon. As we savour the feast, we don't talk much, just an occasional appreciation of the skills of the chefs. If Siobhan was here now, she would ask why it is that when men cook they must be told how wonderful they are. She told me once that when her mother first saw whitebait, she would have nothing to do with them until they were decently gutted and filleted. Since they are only two to three millimetres across, that was the end of the matter.

He is tolerating silences now.

He makes the tea, finding a real pot in the far back corner of a cupboard, along with a tea cosy. He finds the teabags, sniffs them to be sure, snips three of them open and drops the contents into the pot, one per person, one for the pot. Water added, he turns the pot three times clockwise—a charming anachronism in one so young—and the handle ends up precisely in its starting position.

"Tea's up," he says. Then, in exactly the same tone he adds, "The visions have stopped."

"The visions that put you in a psychiatric hospital?"

"Yep."

He doesn't elaborate, so I ask him, "Do you know why?"

"Nope."

"Do you know why you had them?"

He shakes his head.

Afterwards, he washes dishes and fetches firewood. He tweaks up his tent, which has drooped abjectly in his absence. He leans on the fence and talks conversationally to the alpacas, to Popper and Macchiavelli and Leibniz, who listen without moving nearer or further away. He enters the female enclosure, tickles Simone under the throat and drops to one knee to fondle Mikey, who is now a hand higher than when Matthew last saw him.

Now and then his eyes scan the farm perimeter.

There's a nor' wester due, so he moves his ute into the barn. It's a classic from the sixties, with it's original bile green paint showing through the rust and mud. If he was to clean the mud off, it would look worse than when he started. The seats are in tatters, the mirror on the passenger's side hangs by a metal thread; the whole thing is a moving prayer to be allowed to rust in peace.

He removes the rifle from the living room, asking if I want him to destroy it.

"You would do that?"

"Yes, I would," he says, looking me straight in the eye.

"Then there's no need."

In the early evening, I tell him we have unfinished business and he looks down at the floor and nods.

"But we can't do anything until we deal to your stowaway."

"Stowaway?"

"You brought guilt into my valley."

"Well, that's hardly a surprise. I pointed a loaded rifle at you."

"Regret it, fine. Feel guilty about it and you might as well pack up your gear and go back down the mountain. I can't work with it. Guilt condemns you to your core, regret helps you choose differently."

"I've done wrong, I feel guilty. It's natural."

"Guilt is a destroyer. It would eat you while we talk and you wouldn't hear anything."

"Then how the hell do I get rid of it?"

"You don't, not directly. When it feels unwanted, it will atrophy."

"Unwanted?" Annoyance flashes across his expression. "You're saying I *want* to feel guilty?"

"Didn't you just tell me that guilt is the natural choice when you've done wrong?"

He frowns. "But I don't want it now. You're not exactly impressed by it, are you?"

"So it was for my sake?"

He gives a short sharp laugh. "You haven't changed, have you? Right on my case."

"You want to get over feeling guilty?"

"Yes."

I fetch a box of matches from the candelabra. As I bring it over, his expression grows inscrutable. I pull out a match.

"What are you doing?" he says, eyes on the match.

"I told you, we're looking at how to get rid of guilt." I pause. "Is there anything you want to tell me first?"

"No, nothing. Get on with it. You're planning to set fire to my guilt?"

"That would be interesting, but no. Now. Watch my face, watch my eyes." I strike the match, closing my thumb and forefinger on the business end while the chemical reaction is still under way. He can see no hint of pain in me. He tries to remain inscrutable, but his brows gather slightly, betraying his interest.

"You didn't feel that?"

"Yes, I did. The pain was there, but I made sure it didn't matter. The trick is to move your mind to an external observation point from which you view the pain. Here's one way: say to yourself, 'I don't mind that it hurts.'" I hold out the matchbox, but he makes no move to take it.

"This is supposed to stop me feeling guilty?"

"It's a sneak preview of the mental state you'll need."

He gazes at the box, turns away, swings back, stares at it some more. Then he does it quickly, snatching the box, extracting a match, striking it, snuffing it out with his left thumb and forefinger, and dropping the matchbox to the floor. I can see no reaction in his eyes. He inspects the burned flesh, an emphatic white dot on each digit. Then he folds his arms and stares back at me.

I glance significantly at his left hand. "And?"

"Not bad," he says. "It's like watching the pain from a distance. Could be useful for the dentist. Or the Spanish Inquisition."

"More than that. What you just did was a party trick. Shall we move on to the real thing?"

"So what is it this time? A flame thrower?"

"I think not. Instead, it's time to master your own feelings. You are going to view the movie of you. When you learn to view the movie of you, you will rise above all pain, mental or physical, staying in control to direct the next scene as you wish. One more thing. Are you aware of your feeling of guilt right now?"

"Of course."

"Good. Because as you view the movie of you, you must not deny your unwelcome feeling, or pretend it does not exist. You must not fight it, resist it or judge it—or you will nourish it. Understand?"

"Yes," he says.

"Here it is, then. First, *Allow*. Allow yourself to feel the guilt. Accept its existence. Say to yourself, 'This part of me feels guilty.' Even in this first stage, you will notice a difference, because most suffering comes not from pain, but from resistance to pain. Resistance comes from fear, and fear is what makes pain hurt. Second, *Observe*. Close your eyes.

Strongly, vividly, imagine that you get up and stride a few paces away from your guilty-self then turn to look back at it as if it were playing on a screen. Say to yourself, 'That part of me feels guilty'. Notice the change from 'this' to 'that'. Third, *Release*. Release the guilt-ridden self on the screen, to dissipate in its own time. Don't push it away; it's not a rejection, just a letting go. Say to yourself, 'That too will pass.' Now you have freed your mind to control your next thought or action, consciously directing the new scene."

We go through it again. Allow, observe, release; direct anew.

Matthew puts both his hands on his chest, sliding them past each other until he is almost hugging himself. Then he drops them away, relaxed.

"And?" I demand.

He nods. "It's still there, but it's stopped twisting my gut."

"With practice you'll achieve all three steps and take control in less than the time it takes to breathe in and out. It's the equivalent of the martial art aikido, in which the master does not resist his opponent's offensive action. Instead he accepts it, sways to enfold it, moves with it, and allows it to progress until it can be exploited."

Later, as Matthew leaves, he stops abruptly in the doorway and turns around.

"You still think I'm insane?"

I chuckle. "Do you think *I* am? I'm the one telling you all the crazy stuff."

"Did you call the cops?"

"No."

He turns away, and I am tempted to call out and stop him, ask him for his real name. But I don't. He'll tell me when he wants to tell me.

Later, I see his tent lit from the inside. The lantern projects his shadow onto the fabric. He's on his back, a misshapen profile staring upwards. As I watch, he turns down the wick, the light shrivels and the black hush rears up and swallows the tent whole.

***

Towards midnight, a half moon vaults free of the ridge and climbs in search of its missing half. I leave the house, walk past the glasshouse and garden, through the pasture towards Siobhan's arbour. I am buoyant, but physically tired. My legs ache, my feet stumble. I come close to measuring my length in the grass and tell myself that in daylight it would not have happened. If I allowed the futile indulgence, I might yearn for youthful vitality, but I do not allow it. It would only accelerate my physical decline.

I had no reason to call for Siobhan beyond the desire to be with her. But as I push my boots through the ungrazed grass, I understand why it had to be tonight. The hard work is over. I have won Matthew's desire to master himself; success is inevitable and part of me is already relaxing. Now, more than ever, I can dream of crossing the Styxian warp for full reunion with Siobhan.

And there she is.

At this angle, it takes a moment to recognize what she's wearing, and when I do, I abruptly change my track across the grass. Grinning, I come out and around to face her from the opposite side of the glade so that I can bask in the full effect.

She's wearing her original ball gown, green satin with a sheen that prowls in the moonlight. Strapless, low-cut, the gold locket nestling in her cleavage. It doesn't matter that it rests on wrinkled skin, or that her hair is grey, because I remember the way it was when she first wore the gown, that night at the Westport miners' ball thirty years ago. I was so overcome with love and pride that when we left the car, I scooped her up in my arms to carry her into the ballroom. In my stag-like enthusiasm

I attempted to leap over a puddle. And dropped her in it, where she discovered that it contained more mud than water. Over the next few minutes our relationship came under a little strain.

In this grove, the gown has no stains.

A little madness seizes me. I bow, and extend my right hand, palm up. "May I have the pleasure of this dance?"

"Why, Sir, the pleasure would be mine. But let me consult my dance schedule. Oh, I'm sorry, but I'm only available for the last dance."

"Now," I growl huskily, discipline shucked off into the trees.

She frowns, standing slowly. She holds out her arms towards me, but her hands are up, palms forward, stopping me from touching her.

"Are you sure, Jack?" she asks softly. And before I can answer, she starts to change. Her waist begins to thin, her breasts to lift and swell, her silver hair to darken, and her face to lose its wrinkles. Then, in my own body, every cell begins to tingle, surging with new vitality. I look down at my hands; the dry skin is softening, the raised veins lowering. I clap my hands to my face; the flesh is firming. All it needs now is for me to step forward, and I will be through to the other side of the looking glass. Then she and I will finally touch, bringing an end to the long, lonely years. Half a step. Just half a step, and we will be truly together again.

Irreversibly.

I drop my arms and stumble back. Giddiness and panic make me stagger against the nearest tree trunk. My breathing is shallow and fast.

"It's not me doing this, Jack. It's you. You have to choose. Do you really want to be with me so soon? You have to be certain."

I raise my face to the night and howl a formless sound of distress. Then back to Siobhan, "I have to stay!"

In an instant her body is restored to the elderly state it was in the year before she began to waste away. And I am thrust, panting, back to my own normality, staring down at my hands, glad to see the return of wrinkled skin, liver spots and random hairs.

"And here's me thinking you were a consenting adult," she says gently.

To regain composure, I turn away from her. I stare at the broad-leafed grass, calf-high around us, bent over backwards and waving at the moon. I listen to the subdued ticks and squeaks of the night. I look out through the gap in the trees, down past the angular silhouettes of house and barn, towards the far sea, which wears its own satin gown, bejewelled by the lights of Hokitika.

I look around at her sharply, heart thumping again.

"Siobhan?"

"Jack?" If anything, her smile is deeper, her eyes more softened with love than I can ever remember. She is expecting this. And suddenly, I'm afraid that of all questions, this one is the first she might choose to answer.

"Sometimes I think you're not really…you're not…"

"Ask."

"Who are you, really?"

"Jack, I am Siobhan."

She speaks with the resonance of truth, except… except for that odd inflection, that slight upward hook at the end, as if the answer were true but somehow not complete. So it is not an answer after all; she has, yet again, answered a question with a question.

She leans close and speaks softly into my ear.

"Jack, me wonderful fine boyo, is it not the task of wisdom to know itself?"

Then she's gone. I listen a while to the pitiless bush, then wander back through the long grass. I must let the alpacas graze here tomorrow. Boa meets me half way and explores the pasture ahead, in small leaps, a panther in the dark, capturing and tormenting prey that is vivid in her imagination.

Sleep is mean and drawn out thin as spider silk.

***

The beast.

It stirs, far off over the horizon, a black hole sucking in the universe. My mind panics and flings itself above the surface of sleep, twisting and flailing away from danger. For a moment I forget to breathe. After three and a half decades? That cannot be possible. I defeated it. It atrophied and died with a whimper.

It's a dream. Only a dream.

My eyelid is puffy. Ah, that's what it was: a dream generated by a mosquito bite, the poison triggering a distant echo. Nothing but a trick of jumbled, ancient shadows. Not real.

Relief floods me, and I fall quickly into full, dreamless sleep.

TWO

I'm preparing breakfast when I hear him coming across the paddock. He's whistling an Irish tune I recognize because Siobhan was so fond of it she would sing it anywhere. I know it so well, I want to add the words to his whistle: *My young love said to me, My mother won't mind. And my father won't slight you for your lack of kind.* He appears in the doorway, towel over shoulder. He hesitates there, newly shy as if he can no longer take anything for granted.

"Morning, Matt."

"Mornin'."

As soon as he sees my face he laughs. "Wow. Looks like the romance is over. Was it something you said?"

"Mosquito," I growl. The eyelid is so swollen I can only see properly out one side. "It saved poison all its life just for me."

"And you the master of your own destiny," he says. I glare at him, but a one-eyed glare lacks credibility and he laughs again.

Boa winds around his legs, forcing him to bend down and briefly rouse her head. Then he stops doing that, which earns him a slash across the shin. Love me, but pay the price. He wrinkles his nose. "That cat has died up its own rear end. It needs a bath."

"Are you offering?" I ask hopefully. I'm thinking not so much of Boa's cleanliness as the entertainment involved in Matthew attempting to put her in the tub.

"I am," he says, and looks around. But she's gone.

"She knows," I say. "If you do catch her, you'll need the welding apron and mitts from the barn. Second drawer from the top, under the drill press."

"Really?" He looks seriously interested in the challenge, but decides to defer it until he has dealt with his own body. I nod my head in the direction of the bathroom. Ten minutes to breakfast.

While he's in there, I start cooking and I don't hold back on the homely kitchen noises; I scrape the kettle across the bench, clank the frypan onto the stove, pour water into a too-hot oatmeal pan. Knock the eggs, crack and sizzle. I didn't get the eggs from the henhouse. The hens don't do anything as convenient as laying in the henhouse straw; they hide them in the hay shed, under the porch, in snugs under the bushes—their ability to keep humans and eggs apart knows no bounds. Gertrude, for example, favours the ute, when it's here, laying in it, on it, or under it, preferably in the darkest and most inaccessible places, such as under the clutch pedal. Once, I found her creation in oily rags under the rear right wheel, and she tore strips off me for removing it. Or maybe it was because I asked if she was out of her tiny mind.

We eat outside as the sun clears the ridge; the food aromas rise clean and sharp.

He eyes my eye, and informs me that I look ridiculous.

"And you look as if you forgot to set the burglar alarm," I say, nodding towards his tent. One kea is dragging out his billy, the other tugs at a strap on his pack.

"Hey! Bugger off!" Matthew sprints downhill across the dew, in his socks, speeding up as he realizes that the birds have no intention of departing until they really have to. Even then, they don't bother to fly; they hop a few yards away and watch in lordly contempt to see what he does next. He throws everything inside the tent, ties it up and gives them the one-finger salute. Then he comes back uphill, to find me shaking with laughter. Which is infectious. For a while he's helpless with it, picking up his coffee and putting it down again to laugh some more. If anyone was to pass by, they would look around to see where we grow the green stuff.

The sun drops another filter. Steam wafts from Matthew's socks. I realize that in spite of the exertion, he hasn't coughed. Now that I think of it, I haven't heard his cough since he returned. Ridiculously, the thought tickles up a dry cough in my own throat and I'm struck by the absurd notion that our positions are momentarily reversed.

We finish eating and I catch him unawares.

"Matthew, you're already home."

He looks surprised and embarrassed, so I smile a little and hold up four fingers. He relaxes immediately.

"You are already home. Wherever you are on your path, that *is* your spiritual home. You are in heaven… now."

"Oh. Fine," he scoffs.

"It's your perception that prevents you from accepting immediate ownership of heaven and moving in. Your path is the perfect path for you, laid down by you and your field. Live now as if you were in heaven, and you will make it so. As Jesus of Nazareth said, 'Heaven is right here in the midst of you."

"Well," Matthew sits back. "I know this will amaze you, but I'm having a problem seeing my path as anything more than broken glass and barbed wire."

"I know, but looking elsewhere to find heaven is like going out to look for the horse."

"What horse?"

"The horse. There's only one. To look for it, you gallop to the top of the hill, and when you can't see it there you pull the reins and gallop to the next hill, and when you can't see it there, you-"

"Got it." Matthew says. He closes one eye, aping me. "You finding that mosquito bite heavenly?"

I grin ruefully, "No. But remember, pain does not mean suffering. You can know that you are in your spiritual home, in heaven, even in the midst of great pain.

Matthew's mouth twists with frustration. "So why *don't* I know that?"

"Because you are addicted to your own drama."

"What?!" He's on his feet before he knows it, ambushed by anger. Immediately he freezes, judges the anger and tries to evict it, desperate not to lose his temper in front of me. So I steer him back through the self-movie process. Allow, observe, release; direct anew.

It takes him ten minutes, then he grunts. "All right, all right. I'm okay. It's...over there." He waves his hand vaguely. But he's impatient now. "Look, how the hell do you get off saying I'm addicted to my drama?"

"If you can't be without your drama, that's addiction. But the good news is that we can nail the culprit."

"No kidding? That's a refreshing change from blaming me."

"Not so fast. The culprit is your ego."

Matthew emits a half groan, half laugh. "Wrong track, Jack; I don't think I'm better than anyone else."

"I didn't say so. The popular meaning of ego disguises its real potency. Your ego's job is not to raise you above others, but to maintain you as a separate entity, so you can go about your life with independent free will. That's its job description. It needs you to think that you are *not* in your spiritual home, so that you will then long for home and have adventures on the way. Remember the herd of horses? Remember the alpha male? Your ego."

"You said my ego must exist for me to be human."

"But it must be exposed if you would take control. Exposed, your ego is an excellent servant; hidden, it is a terrible master, responsible for most of your troubles. Your ego is fed by your thoughts that you are separate, and it doesn't know how to stop feeding. Not satisfied with the essential message, *You are distinct and unique,* it moves on to: *Anything that is not your mind and body is not you.* Then, unchecked, your ego discovers that it gets bigger results if it makes you afraid: *You are isolated and alone* and *Out there beyond your skin is stuff that can hurt you,* which means that you can live through entire incarnations blighted by anxiety, apprehension, disquiet and dread. And your bloated ego can even say—listen, listen to how cunning this is—*Your suffering makes you special.*

Matthew winces and shifts uncomfortably in his seat. "You don't take any prisoners, do you?"

"Listen to the message, not the medium."

"So my ego is the enemy."

"Only when it's in the shadows. But now let's expose its most cunning trick. This might be difficult for you."

"God, what now?"

"Before you came here, you believed that your current identity is all there is to you, yes?"

"Yes."

"And your current identity mostly suffers."

"Uh… yes, I guess."

"Then what do you risk if you choose to stop being one who suffers?"

He blinks. "I pretty much stop being."

"You just made an important discovery. If you believe you're a suffering victim, any attempt to change will be interpreted by your ego as a suggestion to kill your identity. To kill your self. So you resist. Of *course* you resist—you don't enjoy your drama and yet you'll fight hard to keep it because you fear extinction without it. Extinction. That's why you've been addicted to your life history, unwilling—not unable, but *unwilling*—to stop suffering. Do you hear me?"

"My God!' Matthew's eyes are wide.

"Until now, the last thing you wanted was to be rid of your drama. It was a subconscious choice to keep it, even to the point of death. And you have been close."

"Yes," he breathes, eyes flicking uphill towards the peaks.

"Now's the time to make a choice that will save the second half of your life."

There's a long silence. Matthew gets up, slowly, face haggard, moves around slowly, staring into space. He holds his hands to his head.

"Matthew, right now, your ego is shouting into every available microphone. This is a full security alert. It's about to be demoted to servant and it won't go quietly. It wants you to interpret this moment as an attack on you and your life."

He sits, lets his head drop forward until his forehead is on his knees, and he wraps his arms around his lower legs in an upright foetal position. For an instant he rocks, but catches himself in the act and stops. He looks up again and laughs, the sound a thin reed.

"Jack, you bastard, it's like you're reaching inside me and ripping out everything important. There's a fucking great hole in here. I hope you've got something to put in its place."

"I have. You spent decades feeding the troubled Matthew and starving the happy, in-charge Matthew. Do you think it might be time to control who gets to dine in your restaurant?"

"I do. But can you get a bloody move on?"

"I'm taking this as fast as possible."

His fist tightens and words tumble out. "Bloody hell! I made myself someone special with all my problems, always churning, and turning it over and over. I made up this special problem character, didn't I? I manufactured him and I didn't realize it was me doing it."

"Yes," I breathe.

Matthew shivers in disbelief. "When you first saw me, you could have just told me to get a grip, wake my ideas up."

"Would it have worked?"

"No."

"The idea that something external must be responsible for your unhappiness is compelling. But what compels you? It's your ego, which thrives on incompleteness. It wants, it craves, it wishes, it needs, it desires and it demands that you pursue the impossibility of completion through attachment to the passing forms of Earth. Here's a question for you. Ego's purpose is to maintain the illusion of separation from the field. The separation is felt throughout the human race and generates a great deal of fear. How do you think that fear might crop up in our mythology?"

"Satan," he says thoughtfully. "Ripping our soul away from God for a good turn on the spit."

"Satan is the symbol for ego. Mainstream religions do not suggest that it is desirable or even possible for God to rid the cosmos of Satan, because they intuitively understand that both separation and connection are fundamental to the adventures of the soul. Separation and connection are fission and fusion in equilibrium. The one has no meaning without the other. Together, they are the primary cause of all form, a dynamic dancing duo, exquisitely balanced."

"Cosmic tango."

"Indeed."

Soon he draws in a very deep breath as if savouring the oxygen. He slips his feet into boots, stands and walks away to talk to the alpacas.

***

We're in the top paddock, east side, planting *pittosporum* seedlings for a shelter belt: dig and lift, plant and press, move on with another seedling. We're working from the rear tray of my tractor Matilda, an ancient three-cylinder diesel that has never failed to start and never stopped without a direct order. Overhead, the skylarks stop trilling as a falcon sweeps downhill over the farm, crying out in flat, rapid tones. The skylarks start up again, the lower ones visible with their lolloping, roller-coaster flight.

When we stop for lunch, the sky is clouding over.

He informs me that my farm is three hundred and fifty-eight metres across at its widest, give or take seven metres. He tells me he learned how to make his pace one metre long, with a tested margin of error of two per cent. Tested. I thank him solemnly and promise to inform the Hokitika Guardian.

"Talk to me," he says, when the eating is done.

I look at the clouds. "We're not going to be here long."

"Start," he says.

"All right. How long have you allowed yesterday to eat today?"

"What's that supposed to mean?"

"I think you understand me. How long have you allowed your past to poison your present?"

"I don't like the way you put that." The laid back smile ebbs.

"You came here convinced that your parents crippled your life, still hauling those childhood visions like a cannon-ball attached to your ankle—those same visions you believe put you in a psychiatric hospital. When did they start?"

"I told you. When I was ten."

"So you've shackled yourself to this museum of misery and dragged it with you ever since. Admission free. Never closes."

Matthew straightens up furiously. "What are you doing? You actually want me to feel guilty? You're like my mother. I was ten. Ten! Do you seriously think I could have handled it better at that age?"

He stops abruptly, flushes red again, then waves his hand in front of him, clearing something away. This time he knows the drill and doesn't need me. He wraps his arms around himself, but soon releases them, and nods. Then he eyes the darkening sky. When he speaks his voice is completely back under control.

"We'd better get to shelter, unless the master wants to turn back the flood."

"I'm with King Canute," I say and we tickle up Matilda, bouncing her down the track that's about to become a stream.

The cloud unzips as we reach the barn doors.

Inside, conversation is impossible. Standing under a corrugated iron roof in a West Coast downpour is like living inside thunder. Outside, Sheba stops grazing and stands stoically, chewing cud, rain bouncing off her back. The alpacas clump together. Rivulets pour down the slopes.

We set up for the late spring shear, communicating by sign language, lip reading and yelling in each other's ears. We check supplies, oil clippers, test the press, and re-set a hinge on one of the shearing pen gates. Macchiavelli took a dim view of the gate last year and expressed his opinion with a hoof.

An hour later, the breeze shifts, the rain leans on the other foot and eases. We rest, sitting on the workbench, looking out the barn doors as the earth opens its pores and breathes again, sighing for its lover the sky.

Gertrude appears in the barn doorway. A fowl of easy virtue, her grief for my ute is over already and she spends her energies trying to lay eggs in, under and around Matthew's mobile wreck. But she spots me, drags a disapproving caw out of her throat and wanders away, whining.

Matthew looks at me, questioning, and we take up where we left off.

"All right," he says, "I've got it. You needed to shock me into understanding. So what happens now?"

"*Now* is what happens. To truly live in the present moment is to know heaven, regardless of time or circumstance. Whether you are naked or clothed, hungry or fed, poor or rich, in pain or in pleasure, each of those can transform, *right now*, so that it becomes merely part of the riches of heaven. But if you insist on projecting a painful past or fearful future into the present, you can only wait and wait in life's ante room. I am not talking about clock time, rather psycho-emotional time. Sustained intensely, it becomes an addiction—so strong in some that they subconsciously *seek* events that maintain their pain or fear. It withers and destroys lives. Listen…"

An old monk and a young monk journey through a forest and eventually come to a stream. There, waiting anxiously on the bank, is a beautiful woman. She tells them she is afraid to step into the water, which is swift and swollen by the rains. To the astonishment of the younger monk, the older immediately offers to take her across. She accepts the offer, climbs onto his back, and clings tightly to him as he steps carefully through the stream and safely out the other side. She thanks him and waves the two monks farewell as they continue their journey.

They walk in silence, until the younger monk can bear it no more; then, reproachful words pour from him. How is it, he demands, that the older monk could possibly have allowed himself to commit the sin of touching a woman?

The older monk looks at him in surprise and says, 'Are you still carrying that woman? I put her down back there by the stream.'

Matthew laughs appreciatively.

"It's your choice," I say, "whether to stagger on under the burdens of the past or to gently put them down. Imagine… that you're listening to a stirring piece of piano music. When it is half-way through, you believe that the music before and after this moment is fixed. But what if it turns out that the composer is you, and what you're listening to is coming from your own fingers on the keyboard? Now, you've just had an inspiration for a change to the melody. You try it out on the keyboard and realize that you will now need to adjust all the music before and after this point. From beginning to end. You are constantly writing past and future from the present moment and no other moment is real."

Matthew holds his hand out in front of him as if it had become a toad. He addresses the hand, slowly finding his words. "That would mean... Vesuvius did not bury Pompeii, Rome did not conquer the known world, and Christ did not die on the cross."

"Nothing is fixed," I say. "There is only perceived, subjective reality. Remember the discoveries of quantum physics? Past and future are man-made concepts projected out of now. The present carries past and future with it like a traveller with two chameleon bags that change colour and shape with every step. Your history is changeable."

"And yours," Matthew says. "You terminated your past."

"And you would have terminated your future."

He regards me shrewdly. "What about you, Jack? You must have a great aching hole in you too. Go on, admit it. With all this knowledge of yours, why haven't you filled it in? Why haven't you got your memory back? Why do you have no mirrors in your-"

"The rules, Matthew, the rules. No questions about me."

"How convenient. That leaves me as the only quarry." He glares at me. "You know, I once met a wolf that circled just like you, closing in, looking for a gap."

I look hurt. "I'm wounded by your defamatory accusation."

"Hmph. And Sheba will grow webbed feet and croak."

"If we get more rain, she might."

"I could tell you about the wolf," he says dryly, "but it's only my perceived history."

I grin. "Tell me anyway." I enjoy his Andes memories, probably because I have always felt drawn to that continent myself.

"I was walking across the altiplano," he says. "It was night time, miles from anywhere. I hadn't had anything to eat all day, it was hard to breathe at that altitude and I was exhausted. Next thing there's a wolf circling around me. It was so dark, I could barely see it, but I knew it was a wolf by the way it moved through the snow. It must have smelt my fear because it spiralled in, trying to get behind me, a little closer on every turn. I didn't know if I was going to live or die. Two things saved me; first, it was literally a lone wolf, no sign or sound of a pack. But also I threw a rock at it and hit it. I was snarling like an animal and I knew from before the rock left my hand that it was going to hit the centre of the forehead. In the dark. It was an almost impossible shot. I knew it wasn't a fluke and I've wondered about it ever since."

"So what happened?"

"Oh. The wolf dropped in the snow, forelegs splayed, like this... then got up and slunk away. I kept walking, holding a knife in my hand and trying to develop eyes right around my head, and chewing on coca leaves to stay awake. That accuracy; it was like something primitive in me stood up and took over. What was that about?"

"I don't know."

"Good," he says. "You don't know everything." He lifts callipers from the bench and examines the vernier scale. He moves his head about as if it needs a new position on his neck. Lays the callipers down.

"Look," he snaps. "We can talk about my Father, if you like. I'm not going to go off the deep end any more. But that doesn't mean I can instantly forgive him; this idea that he gave me some kind of spiritual gift... I know what he did to me. You probably worked it out already, but I *know* what he did..."

"The frog game."

He nods. Three times he opens his mouth, but can't force any words out.

I say, "You can't make it vanish from your memory, but you choose to stop being its victim. As victim you're not living, you are clutching a lifebuoy in the storm that you keep summoning from over the horizon. It's time to stop... time to choose to live every day as if you have never been hurt."

"Yes," he whispers. He looks up and smiles then, meeting my concern with shy, clear eyes. Some jagged crystalline structure within him has melted away. His shoulders lose their tension and hospitable silence enters the barn, hanging on the walls amongst tools and cobwebs and coils of eight-gauge wire. Outside, the first shaft of sunlight dazzles the reservoir, vanishes, then reappears on a patch of pasture, then again on the trees on the far hillside, then the hayshed and alpaca enclosure. The alpacas breathe puffs of vapour. Matthew and I just stand, watching, leaning against bench and wall.

He's smiling at some unexpected source of pleasure.

"I feel... I feel..." He pokes the wall beside him, as if he could prompt that blank space to cough up the missing words. He murmurs. "I feel... incredibly... light. Why is that?" The feeling takes possession of his body, which leaps playfully onto the workbench, swinging around the hand-tool panel and alighting on the barn stairs.

"What's up there?" he asks.

"The loft." I enclosed and lined it almost as soon as it was built, so that it could be used as a crash pad when the house was too full. Siobhan and I often didn't know when we would get visitors needing a place to put their heads.

"A loft with a door?" He bounds up to the door and pushes. It doesn't budge. "No handle!"

"Yes there is. Work it out."

Anticipating visitors with children, I built a spring-loaded door handle, disguised as a natural part of the frame. When nudged in the right direction, the door swings back. Nothing attracts the minds of children more surely than the whiff of a secret. With eager anticipation they would poke and prod around the edges before realizing that they had been looking at the solution all the time. Then they would rush triumphantly back to the house, announce scornfully that the secret was too simple, just for small kids, and could they have another scone with cream and jam?

It takes less than a minute for him to solve the secret of the loft entrance. He barely glances inside. Instead, he turns and bows to any audience that might have gathered below to applaud his achievement.

I take the hint.

He bounds back down the steps, along the workbench to the shearing-pen rail and walks along it, arms out, balancing. He grabs a corner post and turns to me as if a joke just occurred to him.

"Who the hell am I?" he says. "I've forgotten. I haven't the faintest idea. This is entirely your fault."

"Entirely," I say.

"Well, I just might have to make it up as I go along."

He jumps down to the floor, landing right next to Gertrude who is attempting another incursion. This time she bolts at speed, with an emphatic cluck. She has an abnormally large wattle under her chin; when she's in full flight, the wattle swings from side to side, obliging her head to join the rhythm.

Dear God, I feel an impulse to embrace him. How can that be, when I dislike him?

***

Twilight lends itself to dark. When he comes in, I'm playing the piano, so he leans on the dining room table and listens.

Immediately, my fingers struggle with the notes. Which is astonishing; this is a Beethoven sonata so simple that a third year student could do it in handcuffs. Yet, my hands and fingers are wading through molasses. It's baffling, because I have always been able to play in front of an audience as if no one was watching. I, who do not care a jot what people think of me. I falter, pick up the melody again, then grimly squeeze out every remaining note. Roll up, roll up, music is being murdered here.

Afterwards, Matthew says, "You know, you're human like anybody else."

"No question," I agree.

"You don't know as much as I thought."

"Undoubtedly," I agree, darkly. If there's any other answer to a statement like that, I don't know it.

"You're way smart, but you're kind of rigid, you know? Inflexible, like you've got blinkers on and you can't see anything but your own stuff. You miss things."

"You are certainly correct." I have to force my teeth to stop gritting.

After eating, I'm unusually tired and irritable. I tell Matthew we'll take a rest from all that is deep and meaningful. I turn on the radio and it pours out the pure balm of Barber's *Adagio for Strings*. Perfect. I settle into an armchair with a book and tell him to help himself to anything he needs.

He helps himself to a copy of *A brief history of time,* then chortles that of all books, this one has a typo in the publishing date. I'm reading and don't respond. He prowls the room, picking up ornaments and immediately putting them down. He stares into the painting of the clipper ship, eyeing the bellied sails. He attempts, again, to capture Boa for a bath, laying her meal on the floor to bring her in from outdoors, shutting the windows, sitting in wait behind the door, hand poised to slam it shut. Boa, who normally processes food like a vacuum cleaner, declines an appearance.

He finds the marble chess set in the cabinet, and tells me of his admiration for a 13-year-old boy, Bobby Fischer. Fischer played what became known to chess players as the match of the 20th century, astonishing the world by sacrificing his queen many moves ahead of the win. Do I want to play?

I don't.

Then do I want to play *Fox and the Geese*? It's a child's chessboard pastime of such coma-inducing simplicity that it can be mastered in a single match lasting sixty seconds.

I don't.

"Where's your TV?"

"I don't have one. I don't need a lobotomy."

"Well what do you do for recorded music round here? You don't even have a record player." I take this as a sly comment about my advanced age and point at the combination radio and solid-state pod. He looks at it admiringly and says, "Far out. Exotic. How do you change the station?"

"You don't. It's stuck for all time on the concert channel."

"Got a multi-meter? I might be able to-"

"Don't even think about it," I say.

He wanders into the corridor to the master bedroom, clearly intending to look around. So I suggest that he stays in the living area. As he returns, a thought occurs to him and he waves his hand around the room. "Look. All this stuff, and it says zip about your past. Anyone normal would have something personal from their past, even if they can't remember it. Where are you keeping it all?"

"I'm reading," I growl, exasperated. He's doing all this deliberately, of course; he *wants* to get under my skin.

"I bet your past is dodgy as hell," he ventures cheerfully. "Skeletons in that missing closet? Weird sexual proclivities, maybe?"

Then, before I can stop him, he's at the mantel and flipping the hourglass. I'm on my feet with horror, watching the sand running for the first time since Siobhan went. That was not for him to do.

"For God's sake, will you give it a rest?" I snap.

He's surprised. "What's the matter?"

"Nothing, nothing, just give me peace. I don't want more conversation tonight, all right?" So he has succeeded in getting under my skin. Again. It's one thing to be annoyed, it's quite another to lose control.

"Peace," he says, mimicking a stoned flower-power hippie. "Peace, brother. You've got it, no sweat. Everything's cool, man."

Later, I realize that he's not been bothering me for a while. When I look up, he's in front of the piano, studying Siobhan's photo. But when he knows I'm watching, he drops his eyes to the keyboard as if that was the real purpose of standing there. To strengthen this fiction he sits and plays a few notes. Then a few more.

"It's been years," he says.

"The radio," I groan. I can tolerate heavy metal, gangster rap and lift muzak, but I won't tolerate two simultaneous sources of music. He heads for the radio, finger poised. I think of asking him to turn the volume down slowly, but I am too late; he crashes out of Vivaldi in midsummer.

Then he returns to the piano, presses out a couple of minor chords and glances at me. Does this constitute a disturbance of my peace? I shrug non-committally. He comments favourably on the timbre of the piano. So he should; the crisp yet mellow tone outclasses most modern concert grands. I told the piano tuner so last time I paid him a fortune to come up to the valley, and he agreed.

Matthew massages a couple of arpeggios with the right hand, then starts releasing the first chords of Satie's *Gnossiennes One*. Stops, starts again. At first, his fingers hesitate as old synapses grumble and fire, but in a few minutes, the memory floods back. Then he forgets me and the house.

I lay the book down in my lap, close my eyes and let the

extraordinary chords wash back and forth on an unknown shore.

THREE

Matthew approaches Berkley with intent and a hypodermic needle.

Farm animals instinctively understand many of the very indignities they resist. Sheba gets testy at milking, yet walks to the stall of her own accord. Marmalade, a mare who lived here years ago, exhausted us before allowing saddle and reins, then had the gall to enjoy the outing. The alpacas obstruct the shearing that relieves summer temperatures, yet they'll avidly watch others take their turn. But when it comes to drenching with a needle, I can only imagine bafflement in the brain of an alpaca. The human closes in with a shiny device, feels around in the pit between leg and body, pulls the skin out, stabs it with the device, rubs the offended flesh, slaps a haunch, and promptly loses interest. Perhaps, somewhere in the infinity of parallel universes, there is one where this makes sense to an alpaca.

Now, they accept Matthew's presence. So when he asks to do the last one I agree. I give Berkley serious affection around the head to hold him. Matthew pulls skin, jabs, rubs and slaps and stands back to view the result. Not bad. Absent-minded Berkley whuffs and wanders away, looking back as if he suspects an event he would disapprove of if he knew what it was.

We sit on a knoll of bright green pasture, facing down the valley overlooking the reservoir. It's late afternoon and warm air eases over the ridge to nudge us with the promise of summer. For some time we say nothing at all. The sense of urgency seems to have left him, and I have not seen him so comfortable with silence.

Two paradise ducks beat in from the east, swishing to a halt on the reservoir near the south bank. They preen, then waddle into the reeds to fussle for food. I turn to look at the house and Matthew follows my gaze. Sure enough, Boa slides off the porch, slinks along the north wall, and disappears into the trees.

We take bets, loser to sweep the barn floor. I say she will get claw to feather, Matthew says she won't. There's a five minute wait. Then an orange projectile bursts out of the bushes, claws raking frantically, only to miss the nearest duck by the thickness of a quill. So Boa turns her back and nonchalantly cleans a paw while the ducks honk indignantly from the centre of the reservoir. But I refuse to concede. I suggest that the ducks' new heart condition will kill them shortly anyway, and Matthew suggests that I may have a weasel somewhere in my family tree.

Then he offers to tell me something I might not believe—an offer that's hard to refuse.

"I'm not making this up," he says. "I was in a remote town, all dust and mud walls, sombreros and ponchos, not a tree or shrub or even a blade of grass anywhere. Got the picture? Okay, I was looking for directions to a place: a secret kind of abbey hidden between the altiplano and the Amazon basin. I'm standing there on the street, wondering where to go next when this guy turns up, wearing a tailored pinstripe suit and a bowler hat, straight out of Savile Row. Like in a movie where people step out of a space portal into another planet. He was completely out of place. Immaculate clothes, ginger moustache, straight back, ex-army posture with stomach in and chin up; the only thing he didn't have was the umbrella. Well, he comes right up to me and tells me in English that I'm looking for the Abbey of the Seven Rays. Tells me. You like that? He *knows* why I'm in town. He tells me where to go next—a village called Yungacocha—then he ponces off round the corner, didn't even say goodbye. I was so stunned, by the time I thought to ask questions he'd gone."

I laugh with delight. "Good story."

"Yes, but do you believe it? I wasn't smoking anything at the time."

"I believe it."

"Would you count that as a message from my expanded self? My field?"

"Not at all. It's just a coincidence that a well informed, time-challenged, ex-army Englishman, wearing a pinstriped Savile Row suit and a bowler hat appears in a remote-"

"Yeah, right, and sarcasm is the lowest form of wit." He plucks a clump of spring growth and throws it at me.

He breaks off another broad blade of grass and arranges it between his two side-by-side thumbs, pulled taut. He lays his lips against it and blows it, producing a flatulent sound, barely recognizable as a note. As he straightens the thumbs, the blade tightens further and the crude note rises in pitch. "Quality grass," he opines with the tone of a connoisseur. "Just before I left school I did *God Save the Queen* right behind the school deputy principal. He actually started to get to his feet. This is the same guy who said it was all right to ride with the girls from Avonside High School, but please, boys, not more than two abreast."

He blows the grass gazoo out of his hand, leaving a green stain on one thumb, close to the burn scar.

Out to the west, velvet curtains open to catch the sun in the act of lowering itself into a golden bath. The coast stretches into the distance further than a fit man can paddle in a day. The bush starts tuning up for the evening concert and bellbirds come to the edge of the farm to chime the spring song.

"Something else happened in the Andes," he says.

"Another message?"

"You tell me. I screwed up. I mean I *really* screwed up. I

was getting closer to the abbey, still up on the altiplano, above
the headwaters of the Amazon. But I got the distances wrong
and I had no food left and almost no water. It was close to the
end of a day, and cold like I've never experienced—must have
been twenty below plus the wind chill. Ice built up in my
nostrils, my lungs burned, my fingers felt like they were in a
vice of ice, and my bones seemed to be radiating cold. I had to
reach shelter or I was in a heap of trouble. I wasn't afraid yet,
because I thought all I had to do was keep going along the
track. It was an old mining track, left over from when silver
mining turned the Andes into Roquefort cheese. I wasn't
expecting a problem because in the last village I went to a lot of
trouble to find someone who spoke Spanish: the mayor, *El Jefe*.
I asked him if there were any forks on the path ahead. This
helpful guy says, No problem, *Señor,* no fork, just one path."

"And there was a fork," I suggest.

"There was. I got to it just as the light was fading. By then
the altitude was getting me and I could hardly stand. Snow was
building up on the path and on my poncho. I was too far away
from the village to go back. So there were just these two paths
stretching away into the cloud. I knew if I chose the wrong one,
I'd be condor breakfast by dawn. One path to life, the other
path to death. The choice paralysed me. I just stood there in the
falling snow, weaving on one spot, wanting to lie down. And I
kept thinking: life or death. Life or death. Like Big Ben stuck
on two o'clock and bashing my mind with it. Life or death."

He frowns, seeing it all again. I feel a shift in the air, a pre-
evening chill.

"I went with logic. Logic said go to the right, because even
under the snow, that path was clearly the most used. The other
was harder to pick out. So I started along the path to the right,
but a few seconds later, a condor landed right in front of me.

"A condor?"

"A condor," he says impatiently. "Huge wings, had to be ten

feet across. A carrion eater, up close and way too personal, I'm not kidding. Right there on the path, just a few paces away. It stared at me and I stared back. It bobbed its head and neck and blinked at me sideways."

The chill is already raising goose bumps on my arms.

"So that was the end of logic; I went for superstition and turned back and took the other path. Which saved my life. Science would call it a coincidence."

"It would. It would talk of random events which appear related but are not."

"Christians would say that God sent the condor."

"They might, but it was no external deity. You were using your whole self without knowing it—your field. Which way to life? Which way to death? That's a passionately charged question, and your field sent the passionately charged answer."

He shrugs. "Everything dies."

He has instinctively closed in on the next session. Or he has guessed. I suggest we go inside to get out of the cold. He looks around, surprised, but shrugs, rises, and walks with me amiably up to the house. We settle into the chairs by the window, almost side-by-side so that we can look into the spectacular distance. This time, as I begin, he doesn't bother to arrange his facial muscles for spiritual poker. Instead, he holds up five fingers of one hand, and I nod.

"The fifth truth. There is no death. You will live forever. You cannot cease to be. Both life and death are a dream from which you wake, and when the time comes, you will look back at your body and know you are not your body, but that dreamtime being which used it and shaped it. All form dies, but that which made it passes on and creates new form again and again. *Ka ora mo ake tonu atu:* you live for ever and ever."

He looks wistful. "I wish I could believe that."

"Don't believe or disbelieve, just hear. I'll talk as if there is a past and future to make it easier to follow, but the reality—

before and after death—is that there is no time at all, only a vast, ever-expanding now."

He nods slowly.

"Your body has been part of you, its experiences have changed you, but you became attached to it, and when you discard it that attachment has to be broken. The chain of attachment hangs from all form—material, mental and spiritual. In life and in afterlife, attachment keeps you poor, while releasing attachment enriches you. Which brings me to the first principle of what remains unchanged when you die."

"*Un*changed?" Matthew's head tilts sideways. "Surely everything changes."

"Is that what you believe?"

"Something about my beliefs?"

"Yes."

"I still get what I believe?"

"Yes."

"Ah. The first truth."

"*All* five universal truths transcend what incarnate humans call death. But let's stay with the first. In the afterworld, you remain the director of your experience, the creator of every event, detail and nuance of your existence. How else could it be? The energy of ten thousand attitudes and beliefs does not vanish like a party balloon.

"In the past, there have been a multitude of different journeys through the afterworld. Chieftains routinely took weapons and armour, trappings of wealth, and slaves thoughtfully slaughtered for their post-life convenience. Viking warriors turned up at Valhalla on the horse buried with them. Many battled diabolical forces in order to reach the promised land. Some carried coins so the Ferryman would carry them across the Styx. Many, in the last two millennia, have waited by their graves for the day of judgement."

"What, no trumpets?" Matthew scoffs. "I was promised

trumpets. Get me a lawyer."

"You misunderstand me. What you most strongly believe *is* what you get."

"Noooo..."

"Yes. Depending on your deepest beliefs, angels might well sound trumpets for you. The field has an excellent props department. Expect to be judged and you will indeed go through what seems to be judgement."

"Seems?"

"No external being ever judges your actions, but your beliefs remain potent and creative. Millions now believe in the light at the end of the tunnel of death, so they must travel through a tunnel. Millions will not be convinced until they see Lord Krishna, or Jesus, or Mohammed and the virgins in paradise. If your beliefs demand a thin Buddha, a beardless Mohammed, or a blue-eyed, straight-nosed, pale-skinned Jesus for credibility, that's what you get. One way or the other, via your beliefs, your field will have meaningful and loving dialogue with you."

"You're telling me it's all smoke and mirrors!"

"You're not impressed by the perfection of the arrangement?"

"I'm not. Is it real or an illusion?"

"It's both, and it's not a contradiction. Form is always an illusion, yet form is our very human measure of reality. The law of attraction is also in action after death: what you think, you become; what you feel will follow; what you believe will be manifest around you. The only difference is that once you lose the illusion of time, what you think and feel and believe, *is*. Immediately."

"Then what happens to people who believe they deserve to be punished and go to hell?"

"There's no such fixed place; no hell, no angry god, no judgement, no condemnation, or punishment. But you can create a very convincing facsimile for yourself. And many do.

If you deeply believe in fire and brimstone, leg irons and red hot pincers, literal devils and horns, then that's what you get. The same applies at the other extreme—to notions of heaven. If you believe you deserve the great reward, then the admission tickets are already printed. If you want choirs of angels, buttercup meadows and babbling streams, figs and sweetmeats and virgins—then that's what you get. And if you believe that your church or religion has the only key to heaven, then you will only see others of your persuasion there."

"I see high walls with no windows," Matthew muses.

"But, if your idea of heaven is fixed, you will eventually pack your bags and leave. You will understand that nothing about the *form* of heaven or hell or any other part of the afterlife, is real or lasting. And so you will release it."

"Wait a minute." Matthew frowns. "Come back to hell."

"Certainly, though I've had better invitations."

"I can create my own hell? You said there would be no pain and suffering."

"I did. Now. Here is one fundamental difference between life before and life after death. After death, you will find yourself effortlessly observing your own Earth character from a distance. And that should sound familiar."

"Viewing the movie of me."

"Yes. In the afterlife, self-viewing becomes a fully conscious part of your existence. You will feel that you are watching your Earth personality the way you might watch your own hands at work. If that personality takes any belief in suffering through to the afterlife, you will see it going through pain and suffering—from a detached distance *without* pain or suffering—until you understand that it is no longer necessary."

"The small me, the watched me, is actually suffering?"

"No, there's no suffering at all. Think of it as an echo of suffering. Or imagine it like a hypnotist who knows that you can burn yourself with a cigarette with no suffering—which is an illusion created by your mind. And so in this stage of life after death you begin to release your attachment to the beliefs that made you suffer. Which means you detach from-"

"Oh no. From my mind." Matthew leans back and waves his hand, mimicking disgust.

"Oh yes. You literally lose your mind, your Earth-bound thoughts and personality. But still you cannot cease to be. When the time comes, you will look back at your mind and know you are not your mind, but that which dreamed it."

"But that would mean… that who I think I am right now..."

"You have it. Whoever you think you are now has no absolute existence. You are part of the essence that is dreaming you and is being changed by the dream."

His voice rises. "So I'm not real?"

"Understand the full extent of *I*. Your true *I am* is much deeper than your thoughts normally reach. Your thoughts create your personality; your personality evolves your *I am* like a wave that stirs the lake to its very floor, but has no separate existence in its own right."

Matthew mutters, "I have obviously been taking who I think I am too seriously."

"Exactly so!" I'm delighted with his insight.

"But what happens if I believe there's nothing on the other side but oblivion?"

"Ah, yes. What happens if you believe that dying will be the death of you? Then that's what you get, at first. But after the lights go out, you'll become aware that the lights are out, which will raise an interesting question mark floating right there in the dark."

"If I'm dead, who's this thinking I'm dead?"

"Almost worth an answer, don't you think?"

"I do. I think, therefore I am."

"More accurately, I feel, therefore I am. Descartes gave us the dessicated version, packaged for the age of reason."

Matthew glances out the window to the mountains. "What about suicide?"

"Suicide to escape, escapes nothing. How can it? You still take your self with you. And when the time comes to choose the next incarnation you will willingly and freely choose another that re-creates the same type of challenge."

"You say there's no hell. But what about someone like Adolf Hitler? Six million victims. Where's the divine justice? If you inflict suffering on others and can't be punished in this world, it's surely waiting for you in the next."

"No. There are no exceptions. It is not possible to do anything so terrible that it leads to external judgement and punishment in the afterlife. And yet you *can* expect perfect, divine justice."

"A contradiction."

"No contradiction, only a perfect balancing of the scales. You will go through a life review, in which the reviewer is your own greater being. It's like taking part in a documentary with prodigious production values. You will experience your life from the point of view of everyone who was involved: everyone's feelings, attitudes, motives and beliefs laid bare, including yours. You won't just observe through their eyes and ears, you will *experience* what they experienced. Did you steal from someone? You will *experience* his hurt and outrage. Did you give food to someone who was hungry? Then you will *experience* her relief and joy. Of course, your Earth personality could not cope with this review, because the emotional typhoon would sink the ship of your mind."

Matthew is open-mouthed, cynicism forgotten. "Then we literally experience..." he breaks off in wonder.

"Yes, say it."

"We literally experience being... one being."

"You have it. That is the ultimate meaning of empathy. Divine justice for all. What need is there for punishment?"

"That is… stunning!"

He surveys internal landscapes, shaking his head, then looks up. "All right, after the life-review, then what?"

"Then an infinity of possibilities. But here is one certainty: ultimately you will reach a place beyond body, mind and soul."

"Oh great," he says. You have disposed of my body and mind. Now you want my soul."

I realize, with a burst of pleasure, that for some time, I have not been thinking about my responses at all, rather I've been hearing them come from my mouth of their own accord. I'm watching both of us from a distance, observing the play. In this moment, I am once again strong in the field and the field is strong in me. This is the way it was, before Matthew brought his disturbance out of the storm and into my valley. He has worn me down, but now I know I can survive him and win. So I let the words continue to pour out of me.

"After many incarnations you will know that even your soul is not a separate entity. You'll see that all souls, combined, are like a great rock, which has a trillion moving atoms, yet is still and silent. Here, finally, is where you know yourself as the Field, the Source, the One. And once again, you long to know yourself in your own experience and so, once again, you ask the eternal question, *What Am I?*

"Created by the passion of that longing, galaxies wheel, stars wink in and out of existence. Dust clouds spiral inward, implode and are re-born as suns, with planets waltzing in the ballrooms of space. Suns blossom and turn themselves and their attendants to dust which gathers once more. On Earth, mountains spew fire and tumble to the sea, forests thrust high and die away, rivers flood and spill. Whales dive, dolphins weave, falcons sweep and soar, lions roar and hunt, and humans laugh and cry and project around them a billion adventures which are both the asking and the answering.

"For each incarnation, your soul says, *How shall I ask the question this time?* So in one country, one town, one street, and in one very special house, you eagerly burst forth in new form, to create another experience, another adventure. You look out of the eyes of a baby, locking onto the loving eyes of your mother. Once again, you are human and you are perfectly what you are."

Matthew breathes out slowly.

Over by the shelves, the grandfather clock ticks on. The fire is fading. The last flamelets flip-flop and embers fizz to remind us where we are. After a while, Matthew holds up thumb and finger and brings them so close they're almost touching.

"I feel about the size of an ant."

Then he muses, "I've just remembered something. When I was eight, Mother took me to the museum in Christchurch. She was making me learn all the Latin names. But when she put me in front of the giant moa, I was transfixed. It was like treading through dense bush, coming around a tree trunk and finding this enormous creature looking down at me, checking me out for a lunch date. *Dinornis giganteus.* More than twelve feet tall, three times my height and very hungry. So I screwed up my eyes tight and imagined I was the size of an ant, too small for a snack, too small to be noticed. I knew a lot about monsters. *Tyrannosaurus rex* was number one in the animal section, *carcharodon megalodon* headed up the fish, and *dinornis giganteus* pushed *pterodactyl* off the top perch for birds."

He bounds to his feet. "Got any writing paper?"

I find him a few sheets, but he wants more. He's not satisfied until I dust off a very old but unused student notebook: large, thick, high quality paper, with a hard black cover embossed with the imprint of an autumn leaf.

As the door closes behind him, the dartboard on the inside swings and steadies. I want to go after him, invite him to return for a darts match, a meal, a nightcap. Anything. We could play cards or chess. I would even consent to playing *Fox and the*

Geese and we wouldn't have to talk about serious matters. I would like that. But it would be ham-fisted and awkward to go after him now.

***

The light goes on in the barn loft. It's just like another moon, because the window is a brass porthole. It's one of the starboard portholes from James Cook's cabin in the *Endeavour*, acquired, with provenance, not long after I made my fortune. I built it into the loft side-wall as an amusement for visiting children once they had solved the secret entrance.

Now, moonlit clouds glide south behind the black bulk of the barn, creating the illusion that the barn is drifting north. With the porthole lit up, the barn is a ghost ship taking an eternity to pass by. Matthew moves once between light and porthole, carrying the notebook, the captain in his cabin. Down on the coast, the surf line shows up as a living doodle across the night, thickening and thinning and thickening again.

Just after midnight, the wind flings itself out of the northwest, flailing up the gorge and into the valley. It wallops the guttering and whines around the eaves and down-pipes and flexes the windows. A thigh-thick branch gives way on the elm tree out the back, hitting the ground with a thud that shakes the house. Something crashes directly above and tumbles down the roof. Outside, it proves to be a brick, torn from the old mortar holding the chimney together.

I help Matthew anchor his tent more securely, with cords to the campfire log and the nearest trees, and rocks weighing down the pegs. Once again I offer the sanctuary of the guest bedroom, once again he is not interested. He says that considering what just happened to my house, it's obviously safer in the tent.

"But if you feel unsafe tonight," he offers brightly, "you can sleep in the tent."

Cheeky sod.

***

In bed, I slide into a wafer space between waking and dreaming. The dreams are splinters in the dark, and waking just another shard.

Matthew is a baby, floating down the river in a basket of lilies. Each time I struggle through reeds and mud to grasp the basket, I miss. He floats by out of reach, calling, "It's missing."

Siobhan is under the bed, talking to someone hiding there. She's encouraging him to come out, but he refuses.

Then I'm in a prison cell, attempting to draw a geometry diagram on the wall. If I can succeed in trisecting an angle using only pencil, compass and ruler, then I will discover what's missing. But no matter how hard I try, nothing works. My fingers are clumsy. The pencil drops out of my hand. My maths report card will say, Has ability but does not apply himself.

I wake, face down, clinging to the bed.

Then the beast returns. Now there can be no mistake. It's on its way from the far mountains, hunting me again through the valleys and peaks, pushing against the wind, slinking around the roots of stately kahikatea and totara. With the pull of a thousand magnets, the black hole in the universe draws my attention. Each time I glance, it glides closer and reaches out towards me. I can hear the sound of a small boy screaming far off inside it. And it calls out to me in avuncular, reassuring tones, "Don't be afraid. Don't be afraid."

Cunning. Very cunning.

FOUR

We're mending fences.

The overnight gale came from an unusual angle, so branches that had grown wind-resistant sinews on one side snapped easily on another. When we toured the boundary, we found four breaches of the fence, and in two of them the branches had taken out every strand of wire but the lowest. Matthew was keen to begin repairs immediately. I couldn't see the urgency— the alpacas were safely in their enclosure—but his enthusiasm was infectious. So we loaded Matilda's tray with chainsaws, posts, ropes, pulleys, joiners, levers, strainers, a posthole digger, and every remaining coil of eight-gauge wire in the barn. On the way, I asked him to please refrain from turning any more of my fences into farm harps. He grinned, but I wondered if I sounded to him like a whingeing old man.

Now he passes his chainsaw through a branch as thick as his thigh, streaming red-brown chips around his waist and legs. I'm holding tension in the rope that will stop the cut branch destroying what remains of the fence. He's enjoying the physical demands of wielding the chainsaw, his muscles tight and toned. He has filled out since he arrived. I've not seen him looking so healthy and fit.

Suddenly his body goes still. The chainsaw jams, kicks once, and dies. He levers it out of the cut, and stands rooted to the spot.

"What's the matter?"

He lowers the chainsaw and turns to me, his face is full of wonder and he speaks so quietly he's almost bashful. "I know why I had those visions that put me in the nuthouse."

"Tell me."

"When I was a kid, I had to be bloody perfect. I had to be this bright-eyed little genius for my parents to become successful." He thrusts the chainsaw to the ground. "Don't you see? My father was a padre! What's the most obvious symbol of a perfect person?"

Yes. Yes.

"And when there was so much pain… so much…" He tapers off and wonder is replaced by incredulity. "Why has it taken me until now? I must be thick! Why didn't I see that way back when I was a kid?" He shakes his head, claps his hands to each side of his head and walks around in a circle. "Is it really that simple? It is, isn't it?"

Then he stands in front of me, grinning. I can feel him wanting some kind of physical contact, but neither of us move.

"I don't need to go back there, do I?" he says.

"Never," I answer.

He pulls the starter cord and the chainsaw roars back into life. The blade snarls into the cut with new vigour, tiny chunks of wood fly, and he whistles a tune I can only see on his lips. But I'm sure he can hear it and it will be pitch perfect.

***

When we return in late afternoon, my body is a symphony of aches.

Matthew stops on the porch and sprawls on the old sofa. I fetch beer and glasses, looking forward to saluting my raised feet. I will look at them through a friendly golden liquid in a glass that has condensation running down the outside. I use a bottle opener; Matthew uses his teeth, an expression of chest-thumping maleness which, he claims, once got him laid. No, it was not a lasting relationship. He tilts his glass in my direction, his mood more effervescent than the beer.

"Good health," I say.

"In your eye," he replies.

We each take a long swallow. There is no taste on earth quite as sublime as a sweat-earned cold beer, brewed in West Coast mountain water. As it slips down the throat of a worshipper, it can reduce strong men to tears of gratitude that they are in the presence of something greater than themselves.

He smiles at some private thought—a smile with no agenda, easy as a breeze in the grass. More often now, he asks a question and then tells me the answer himself. More often, he knows my intent and declares it. In the last few days especially, something subtle and strong has taken up residence in him. His tone has shifted, as if he is responding to much more than the face value of my words. I have an urge to reverse matters, to ask him questions just to hear him give the answers back to me.

"Jack," he says.

"Matthew."

"I'm ready."

"Not quite. One more thing has to happen."

"Like what?"

"Like taking control of your attitudes."

He laughs. "You already adjusted my attitude. Against great odds you applied a spanner to my head and tightened some loose nuts."

"Ah but the trick is for you to apply the spanner yourself." I sit forward. "Listen. If you take a thousand people through one event, you'll get a thousand different paths out the other side, depending on the attitude they adopt to the event. If you're going to master the quickening, you must learn to choose your attitudes to what happens around you. Attitudes shape your life as surely as a pen writing a travel itinerary."

"For example?"

"We'll discuss it after dinner." I gather up the bottles and give him an order. "We're short of firewood. Start chopping."

He's disconcerted by the shift in my tone. "There's plenty for tonight. I'll do it in the morning."

"I said do it now."

He blinks. "Huh? You're putting me on."

"Stop when it gets dark."

"Hey. What's got into you?" His jaw flaps for a moment. "I don't mind chopping the bloody wood, but how about a bit of please?"

I take my beer inside and his voice rises in exasperation.

"Hey, Jack. I'm talking to you. I can choose not to do this, you know!"

Eventually, I hear him move off the porch. At the wood pile he stares back at the house, baffled. Then he hefts the axe and splits the first round of macracarpa with such force that the axe buries itself in the block underneath and he has to place a foot on the block to lever the axe out. His mouth moves now and then and it's a safe bet the words are not fit for sensitive ears such as mine.

Normally, chopping wood is one of his pleasures.

I prepare bean stroganoff. It's best made with wild mushrooms, but at this time of year I settle for the limp commercial cousins Matthew brought with him when he returned. Outside, furious chopping continues, the thump of an axe swung too hard and the clatter of wood landing at world-record distances. He'll be raising blisters bigger than the mushrooms.

In half an hour, the sound stops. He appears in the doorway, glares at me, heads for the first aid cabinet. Cuts off a generous hunk of plaster, glares at me, applies it to his left palm. Starts out the door, glares at me, stops when I speak.

"How's it going?"

"How the hell do you think it's going?"

"What's the matter? You normally enjoy chopping wood."

"I don't go for being ordered around. Why did you speak to

me like that?"

"It was something *I* did?"

"Maybe I owe you plenty, Jack, but I don't appreciate being treated like some kind of servant, all right?"

"Let me get this right. Chopping wood is usually an enjoyable experience, but this time it's a bad one, including blisters, and the difference is something I said?"

"Well of course. You made me feel b-" The coin drops through the slot and registers with a clang. He struggles with a new burst of anger. Then he sighs, and slumps sideways, leaning against the doorway with folded arms.

"You devious bastard."

"Never mind the endearments. Are you going to tell me, or shall I tell you?"

What he tells me is how much my personality could be improved by a brain transplant, and offers a poetic description of all of my ancestors back to Adam, favouring those with receding foreheads. Then he shakes his head mournfully.

"It was about my control of my attitudes. You warned me. Good God, you told me directly and I still missed it!"

"True."

"I was stupid."

"True, but take it easy with the self-abuse. You'll go blind."

He laughs. It's a rich, open laugh, filled with delight. Then he makes me wait, token vengeance for my shameless manipulation. He takes his boots off, hauls another beer from the fridge without asking, and puts his feet up. His socks smell worse than Boa.

"All right, here it is. I chose to chop the wood, but the real choice was my state of mind. I let *you* choose *my* state of mind. I chose to suffer, and I blamed you for my choice. I've got the point."

"Yes, yes, you have." I cannot prevent a smile. "Now, make yourself useful. Chop the carrots."

"What's the magic word, Methuselah?"
"Please chop the carrots."
"Certainly, decrepit one. Pass the knife."

***

We continue after the meal.

"It's time to stop drifting and take conscious command of your own mind. Ask yourself, Does this attitude hurt me or help me? Does it express who I want to be? Stand back, view the movie of you, and direct it to embrace attitudes of mastery that automatically bring you spiritual and temporal wealth."

"For example?" Matthew asks.

"Courage. Contentment. Optimism. Abundance. You can choose the life-creating attitude of abundance even when you start out penniless. Choose to see the glass half full, not half empty. See the flower, not the thorn. See your life as so overflowing with good and pleasurable things that you give of yourself as naturally as a stream gives to a river. When you simply can't contain all of your joy, laughter and appreciation of life and it must spill out around you, then you have abundance."

"This is another take on how existence works, isn't it?" Matthew points out. "The only reality is perceived reality. Control our thoughts and feelings and attitudes about reality and we control reality."

"Yes! You understand."

"I hope that's not an attitude of false encouragement."

"Heresy. Try this one. You can choose the life-creating attitude of happiness."

"Hah!" He shakes his head, bemused. "Just like that."

"Just like that you can do away with the destructive belief that your happiness is dependant on other people."

"Just like that I could also choose to be the village idiot."

"But who is better off? A fool who chooses happiness, or an intelligent man who knows better?"

Our smiles fade. We exchange glances which say, Will you? Or will I? So, he can see it coming. He sighs, smiling sadly, looking out the window as if an old and disreputable acquaintance is hoving into view on crutches, wearing an eye patch and intent on delivering a black spot. It will, then, be him who raises it, and that's as it should be. Soon, he will not need me.

"You left out forgiveness," he says.

***

It takes him two days to get to it.

I'm attacking the mould and moss that crept out of the bush under the cover of winter and climbed my south and east walls in the spring. In places it's thick as my thumb. That's not the worst of it; the real problem is the rotten state of the weatherboards. So many are crumbling that the entire south wall could do with replacing. There must have been something wrong with the original treatment of the timber. I will not be around to replace it, so the temporary fix will have to do. I fetch a scraper from the barn and begin, peeling long, intact strips of mould and moss away from each board, letting them drop to the porch.

Matthew appears beside me on the porch and joins in with another scraper. In the way of young men, he likes the productive nature of the operation: lots of spectacular result for minimal effort.

We finish the south wall, then move around to the east. Boa is already there, in the sunshine at the other end, occupying the top of a barrel. She lifts her head, and keeps it up, her attention never wavering from Matthew and the threat of bath.

I glance casually at the glasshouse, then pause, because I

can't immediately see the swan plants. I walk over to check. The plants are there, but talking to them has just become redundant. Most of the leaves have been stripped away; in their place scores of cocoons hang from branches and stalks, light green, almost translucent, spaceships from a miniature galaxy. Inside each cocoon, in the body of the caterpillar are cells which hold the image of butterfly. Now, a most necessary battle is under way; the caterpillar's immune system attacks the butterfly cells as foreign bodies, a meltdown assault that must always be launched and must always fail so that the butterfly cells multiply. In some cocoons, the battle is already lost and won, and I can see the muted colours of the new adult waiting to break free.

When the east wall is clean, Matthew drops his scraper and looks at me, a little pale, with the air of one who has made a weighty decision. We sit on the edge of the porch, surrounded by mould and moss. He wraps his arms tightly round himself, turns his face to the strong sun and screws his eyes shut.

"It's too late for the forgiving," he says.

"Tell me."

"I told you I never saw my parents again, but it isn't true. I saw Father again. I went to his house a few days before I turned up here. I heard he was in a bad way and I wanted to help him. How about that? I actually wanted to help him." He laughs softly.

"Why?"

"Don't really know. I did and I didn't. When I left home the Progenesis Project collapsed and he and Mother had to sell the house. He resigned his job at the home for delinquent boys, and rumours started about why. Then some people got to wondering why he left the priesthood in Australia, and after a few international phone calls, the rumours were more than rumours. Mother walked out on him and died of a bone-marrow disease two years later, and I heard he was drunk at her funeral.

But, you know, I still wanted to support him, maybe it's because you only ever get one birth father. I found myself in churches, on my knees—can you believe that?—trying to get some kind of guidance. I'm telling you, I prayed to a God I hated, to forgive a father I hated even more. How's that for scrambled brains on toast?"

I say nothing, so he continues.

"I went to see him, mid-morning to make sure he was sober. Even before I walked up the path I could hear him playing *Greensleeves* on his trumpet. Did you know Henry the Eighth composed that? How does a melody like that come out of a psychotic tyrant? I nearly turned around and went back, but he saw me through the window… so I kept going and knocked on the door. When he opened it, I could see all sorts of discarded clothing behind him, and junk food wrappers on the settee and over the chairs. The place stank. But the piano was there with the metronome still ticking."

My stomach twists with apprehension.

"I hardly recognized him," Matthew says. "And he didn't recognize me at all. I must have looked pretty rough, beard and mountain clothes and all; I was 18 when he last saw me in the nuthouse and I'd been living the mountain life since then. I had to say 'Father' before he knew who I was. He just stared. Then he looked like I had a bad smell and asked if I was there to apologize or to put the boot in. I pretended he hadn't said that and I told him I wanted to get over the past and get back to being father and son; maybe we could have a beer and a chat.

"And his face lit right up. He said, yes we could chat. We could chat about how I had betrayed him and Mother and thrown all their sacrifices for me back in their faces, and how it had killed Mother just as surely as if I had put a knife in her. I backed away down the steps and he said I disgusted him. In my wickedness I had tempted him and he had fallen from grace, but the Lord in his infinite mercy would forgive him. But not me. Not me. "Don't come back, genius,' he says. 'Don't ever come back.'"

As I listen to Matthew, a hot flush passes through me, followed immediately by a chill. I clamp down against his emotions; they're like an invasion. Overblown sensitivity on my part is not going to do him or me any good.

"I walked back through the rain to the ute and sat in it for a while. I couldn't seem to breathe properly and had to keep my mouth well open to get enough air. I walked to the nearest garage and bought some cigarettes and brought them back to the ute. I never smoked before and I didn't like it, so I didn't even finish the first one. I threw the pack out the window and just sat there all day until it got dark."

My heart is beating faster than it should, surging. I deliberately slow it while Matthew continues.

"My head was humming like an electric generator; everything was in a red fog which was beating in on me like... like being inside blood with a heartbeat pushing it around." He looks up at me, puzzled. "I really wasn't angry. You have to understand that. It didn't feel anything like anger. I mean, when I threw the cigarette packet out into the gutter and it floated away, I even noticed how the rain bounced on it straight up. I wouldn't notice that if I was angry, would I?"

As I listen to him, I watch my left hand do something of its own accord; it lifts up and moves sideways to cover Matthew's hand. Astonishing, because I gave the hand no such order, and the intimate physical contact seems out of place. But now I'm stuck; my hand is there on his and I don't know what to do with it. Matthew doesn't withdraw and we stay like that, staring down at coarse hairs and wrinkles and liver spots on one hand, and young, firm flesh on the other. Joined.

"Anything can be forgiven, Matthew."

"You don't understand," he says.

"Forgiveness is about you, not about him. He doesn't have to hear it or even know about it."

"No you *don't* understand. Listen to me, will you? It's not him who needs forgiving."

Suddenly, my apprehension tightens into a bolus of nausea. I don't want to hear what comes next. But I must, so I surround my stomach with steel.

"If I wasn't angry then it was in cold blood, really," Matthew muses. After a moment, he sucks in air and continues. "I had matches now, and a full can of spare petrol in the tray, so I took them back and stood in front of his place. Under a streetlight and the rain was pissing down, rattling on the can. There was a flash of yellow light from a neighbouring house, and someone looking out, probably wondering what kind of idiot would stand out in the rain.

"I went up the path and I could hear Father's television set on. I just opened the door and walked in like I lived there. He looked at me with his mouth a bit open and his expression didn't change, not even when he saw what I was carrying. He had an empty bag of salted peanuts in front of him, with skins and bits of salt all over the coffee table. The television was showing something about kids who could delay gratification— how if they ignored one available marshmallow and held on for two they would end up with happier lives. I watched the TV screen for a few seconds, and he watched it too."

Matthew's face is in the sun, eyes closed against the rays which penetrate the flesh of the lids. "It was just like this," he muses, "Red everywhere and pulsing. Only back then my eyes were open."

Boa studies him, head between paws.

"I turned off his TV and turned to face him and I could tell he was afraid. I told him to get up and he did. I told him to go into his bedroom and he did. I told him to lie on the bed and he did that too and he didn't say a word. I told him this time *I* wanted to play the frog game, but the rules were going to be different. You know what he said then? He didn't talk about my wickedness. He told me my mother was a cold woman who never loved him, and all he ever wanted was a little love and affection. How about that?

"I went out and got his trumpet and brought it back and put it on his crotch and told him that would do for the handsome prince. His legs were shaking so much the trumpet fell over, but I jammed the wide bit under his thighs so it stood up fine. I told him that this time we would have a princess in the game and opened up the wardrobe, and Mother's best floral dress was still there after all that time. And her velvet hat with the peacock feather was still in the hatbox.

"I laid the dress over him and the trumpet, and put the hat on his head, and opened Mother's top drawer and found an old lipstick and put it on his lips. He made a sound like wet clicks in his throat and his eyes went all yellow around the edges and he was gasping. I kept thinking, This is my father, this is my mother. I poured the petrol over where the trumpet pushed the dress up, and I kept pouring until it was all over his clothes and in a pool around him. He could have got up, you know. He could have fought back, but he didn't.

"When I pulled a match out of the matchbox, and struck it, he started a little babbling whisper, 'Lord I commend my soul to Your infinite mercy...', and when he got to the word mercy, he shuddered and his body sort of arched upwards, then he collapsed and he was... dead, even before his body stopped moving up and down. And I thought: Just like that, mercy, right when he called for it. God must be listening to him. The match burnt out in my fingers."

He looks at the scar between his left thumb and forefinger, then up at me, puzzled. "It didn't hurt. There was no pain at all."

FIVE

He pauses while passing the piano. Without sitting, he leans over and plays a phrase with one hand, defiant, upbeat, cocky. And unfinished. The last note hangs, looking about for consummation. Then, with an impudent grin, he walks away out to the porch.

A challenge. A dare.

And a great relief. For a day after revealing his father's death, he stayed in his tent and didn't eat, saying only, 'I'm okay' when I checked. For the following week he hardly opened his mouth, and then only to manage the necessities of food and farm work. In that week he has often been absent for hours at a time; once overnight, without warning or explanation. Not that I need one, it's clear enough.

I've been glad of the respite, because his torment has thrown a grappling iron at me, and is attempting to board, wielding *his* pain, affecting *me* far beyond what is reasonable or helpful to either of us. I am afraid that, in spite of everything I have achieved, in spite of knowing the need for professional distance between teacher and pupil, I might have become emotionally attached to the boy.

Fortunately, not so. Last night, even as I opened my mouth to complain to Siobhan, I realised the error in my thinking. It *is* emotional attachment, but not to Matthew—I have become attached to the goal itself, one of the great barriers to the quickening. Bequeathing my knowledge began as a healthy desire but has obviously became a need, a liability, about as helpful as a cannon ball shackled to my ankles, and to Matthew's. It is unprofessional.

Siobhan was less than sympathetic. "Jack, do you remember telling Matthew how we walk our paths with scales over our eyes?"

"Yes."

"Are you a human being?" she demanded.

"That's a tough one. Do I have to answer now?"

"Are you on your own path?"

"That doesn't deserve an answer either."

"Do you think it might be time to remove your own scales?"

"This again… You drop hints, but no clues."

She said something I didn't quite catch. In the last few days I had developed an intermittent tinnitus in the right ear— chirruping like a tree full of cicadas demanding mates and not getting any. Irritated, I asked her to speak up.

"What are you missing, Jack? Even as it dances in front of you and you look directly at it with your own two eyes?"

I didn't beg for the answer. I wouldn't lower myself that way any more, and she knew it. She just smiled and vanished. I sent a thought into the empty space she left behind. *Who are you really, Siobhan? And what use are you, if you won't tell me what I need to know?* Yes, childish petulance for which I was ashamed. I flicked the thought away, though it still left a residue of anxiety. Another weakness to undermine me.

Now, the piano still hums with Matthew's musical taunt. The cicadas beat on my ear drum.

I look at him through the window, where he leans contentedly against the wisteria. We should really maintain a distance. But then I remember how he told me he had been taking himself too seriously, and how enthusiastically I agreed with him at the time.

I go to the piano, repeat his impudent phrase, then add another of my own. Challenge accepted. It will be pianos at zero paces.

He weaves in through the door, grinning hugely, flexes

maestro fingers over the keyboard, and reapplies himself; his phrase, then mine, then another of his own.

So, the contest is on. Back and forth, longer each time and more demanding on memory. This is most enjoyable. He sits and provides a left hand to support the right, extending the tune further. I muscle him aside and go further, fluffing the notes only once. Next he is beside me, playing the lower keyboard while I play the upper, so for five minutes we circle each other, improvising in the key of G. The pace steps up until our fingers fly beyond their normal limits, then it becomes impossible and I crash out a single discord. We fall away from the piano stool laughing.

Now would be a good time to restore the teacher pupil relationship to a more appropriate reserve. While wondering how to do that, I find myself opening the very last McWilliams Cabernet '65.

Within seconds he produces a joint, asserting that the finest devil's lettuce has always come from West Coast mountain water and always will. He offers me the joint, I hold it for a moment and smell it; it's been so long since I smoked it, marijuana has become a distant memory. I hand it back, because it might undermine control of my faculties. He takes a series of tiny drags, holding it deeply in his lungs before breathing out. He does not seem the least concerned what I might think of him.

I return to my priceless cabernet.

When we're both mellow, he tells me he once worked a teenage holiday job as a rousie in a high-country shearing shed, where poker-faced humour is an art form. The shearers persuaded two innocent Australian rousies, students on a working holiday, that it was an important and responsible job to sort sheep manure pellets according to size.

So I tell him of another farm favourite: sending a newbie to find the mythical crimp machine. Everyone on the farm knew the joke, except the victim.

Hey Tua, go get me the crimp machine.

Crimp machine? What's that when it's at home?

Well, son, it's a machine for adding crimp to the fleece.

Where is it then?

Ask up at the kitchen.

Joe sent me. Got the crimp machine?

No, ask them over at the tool shed.

Hey, Joe wants the crimp machine. You seen it?

Ask Api. He's down the south paddock.

And so on. On a big property it could take two hours for the victim to catch on.

I tell Matthew about the time I climbed a ladder to fix loose iron on the barn roof. I was just squaring my hammer up to a leadhead nail when I felt a raking blow on my left ear. When I turned around, there was Boa, still only half grown. She was so keen to ambush me she'd climbed the tree next to the barn and was hanging from a branch—I'm not exaggerating—by one paw and swinging viciously with the other. My ear dripped blood.

Matthew swings his head to study Boa and her head rises instantly. Since bath time became an inter-species issue, her sleep has been shallower, her mood testier. They consider each other's position. He knows that in this state he can't move fast enough. So does she. Her head sinks back on her paw and she closes her eyes to the narrowest of slits.

He embarks on a string of limericks describing the unlikely sexual adventures of a young man from Taiwan. This renders us both stupid with laughter and I beg him to stop. No one should have a dirty limerick repertoire of this magnitude.

"Haven't heard you laugh like that," he says.

"Me?" I'm surprised.

"Good to see you relaxing. And look at the way you're sitting. You never sit square on to me like this."

"All right, we begin. You'll use the quickening to implement the law of attraction, and pluck what you desire out of the field of consciousness. You have something you want to create?"

"I have."

"You must be certain you can live with the result. Attaining what you desire can be worse than not attaining it. Do you understand? If you're not certain, find another desire."

"I know what I want." He looks me directly in the eye, and on the piano, Siobhan smiles her Mona Lisa smile. I no longer know what the smile means, but I think da Vinci painted the wrong woman.

"Before we start, do you have any doubts?"

"No. Let's get to it." But his eyes flick away and back.

"The quickening is not a quick fix," I snap and his eyes narrow at my harsh tone. He exhales, a sharp huff that pushes his lips out.

"All right. I do have a doubt. My goal depends on someone else. Can this quickening really influence someone I've never met and who doesn't know who I am? I haven't forgotten what you said, but if I-"

"Yes. The but. How are you going to disarm the but?"

"Viewing the movie of me."

"Do it."

After a hesitation, he closes his eyes, speaks aloud. "Allow the doubt… observe it… release it… direct anew."

"Completely useless."

His eyes pop open, startled. "What? Why?"

"You recited it like a recipe, inserting the word doubt as if it were a dessert ingredient. You mouthed symbols like dried husks, without getting anywhere near the negative belief. Do it again, take all the time you need and this time focus *vividly* on the shift in perspective."

He resumes the process, taking his time, intensely focused. Then he returns to me and there's a long silence while we

"Pot calling the kettle," I reply indignantly. His imagination was overactive even from the first day.

"A coin," he demands, casting about. "My kingdom for a coin."

I find him a fifty, which he inspects, shaking his head.

"No. No good. This has two heads. I need a normal one."

"What?" I reach for it, but he demonstrates its two-headedness by holding the coin, heads up, in the palm of his hand, then flipping that hand over, landing the coin in his other palm. Heads again. He says, "See, this thing's dodgy, it's a two-headed monster."

"Wait just a cotton-picking minute, there…" I take it from him and check. It has only one head of course. But I think I can see how he must have done it. "The hand didn't turn the coin over, the hand turned over the coin. I'll see if I can do it." He watches me practise, the trick being to drop the hand, just before it rolls over the coin. In other words, the coin must be momentarily weightless before one head can become two. After a few tosses, not so hard.

He strolls over to the kitchen drawers, pulls out a ball of string and cuts off a piece about the length of his forearm. He sits in front of me pushing one end into his left ear and pulling it out of his right. Then he grasps both ends and pulls it side to side, apparently through his head, via his ears—a stomach-turning party trick.

"That's truly disgusting," I say with sincerity. Then, as proof that I have over-imbibed, I find myself practising the ridiculous act. He watches and advises me, slurring his words, on how important it is to keep the two hands precisely the same distance apart. It occurs to me that I should go to bed shortly; it would not do to be obviously tipsy in his company.

"Who are you?" he demands suddenly.

"What do you mean?" I stop moving the string.

He giggles. "I mean who the hell are you, really?"

"I'll tell you that when you've worked out who you are. Do we have a deal?"

"Well fuck you too," he says blearily. Then, "You know what?"

"No, what?"

"I've got this all figured out."

"Thass very good. Congratulations. I'm going to bed."

"No, really, I've got it sussed. S'all a dream. I'm gonna wake up in the morning and you won' be there. You and the farm. House of cards. All it needs is a puff of wind. Poof. Gone." He giggles. "You'll be an ex-Jack, Jack... Hey, I've got the munchies." He walks to the breadbin, hacks off a slab, and pours honey onto it directly from the pot.

Out in the bush, the black hole beast drifts through the trees.

SIX

Siobhan sits on top of the piano, next to the photo candelabra. Her hands are down on the polished sur over the end. I send her the thought that parking her b there is disrespectful to the memory of my wife. In she turns her earth clock back sixty years and be schoolgirl again, her shoes black leather pumps, he pigtails, and her tongue poking out at me. Then she lo at her legs and claps them together idly, like a b waiting for a friend. On this earth, she was a memb Greymouth Dramatic Society.

"You okay?" Matthew asks me.

"Completely," I reply sternly. The laxity of last e behind me.

Every morsel of the meal has been consumed, t washed and dried and put away, the bench wipe steams in front of both of us. It occurs to me that it while since I saw evidence of his compulsive obs haven't seen him arrange his mug, or any object, i alignment with other objects like the table. I have regaled with useless information, such as how many human takes per minute compared to a cat, or if y every strand of the farm's wool clip end-to-end how stretch twenty-three and a half times the length of the c

He sits on his hands, his shoulders open to me, expe

"So, you think you're ready," I say.

"I am ready. You made me wait forever. So this h be good," he adds with a hint of humour. His gaze is directly focused on my eyes.

appraise each other. In a matter of weeks his strength has grown prodigiously. Of course with the arrogance of youth, he now sees himself as my equal. Perhaps, in his eyes, I am becoming merely useful, like a text book.

"Make the decision," I say.

He looks blank. "And?"

"Make the decision—to have, do, or be what you desire."

"I've done it. That's how you start? It seems kind of obvious."

"Ah. You want a procedure that's more deep and meaningful and carries punch?"

"Well, yes, what's wrong with that?"

"You want an incantation so power-packed that you need only start with a whim, or a vague wish? Maybe all you need is a fuzzy image of your desire? Maybe all you have to do is mumble the correct ritual?"

"Hey, hey, easy with the whip," Matthew protests. "I'm a dead horse already."

"Then get the point. The quickening is not a reality by-pass. Most goals never arrive because the clear decision—to have, do, or be what's desired—was never made. Your decision must be a trumpet call announcing *in advance* the certainty of fulfilment, or it is nothing."

"Why are you getting so worked up about this?"

"Because to make the quickening happen, *you* must be worked up. You must push yourself into that state where everything—not just the immediate goal—falls into place and you know you are living a charmed life. Did you think this was going to be a list of dry bullet points?"

"No," he says.

"You've made the decision?"

"Yes," he says.

"So you're already feeling the excitement and pleasure that your creation is about to be part of your life?"

"Take it easy, we've just start-"
"Are you hard of hearing?"
"No!"
"Get out."
"What?"
"Have you turned your ears off? Don't waste my time. Get out."
"What?!"
"Take a walk. Reach inside yourself to find out what it really means to create out of the *present*, not out of the future. Don't come back until you've made the decision that the goal *is* yours."
"Bloody hell! You're pushing my buttons!" Amazed, wide-eyed, Matthew walks out.
He spends an hour sitting cross-legged, back to the house, in the exact centre of the female alpaca enclosure, surrounded by baffled animals. Popper approaches with the intent of nuzzling, but changes her mind and retreats back into the circle. Then Matthew stands, vaults the fence, and strides back to the house. He walks in with a gleam in his eye.
"Let's do it," he snaps. "And don't stuff me around."
"You have made the decision. Now you will imagine your goal."
A twitch around the eyes betrays his impatience. Once again, I seem to be giving him something mundane. He wants the secret and he wants it now. So I pick up my cold coffee mug, place it next to his and point to both.
"Choose which one you're going to touch *without* first imagining the touching."
He contemplates this for five seconds.
"That's impossible."
"Of course it's impossible. Nothing happens without imagination. Every creation is consciousness imagining itself into being. Thoughts become things, events and states of being.

Imagination is reality about to be born, it is intelligence with an erection, it is everything."

"All right, all right. I've got that. Can-"

"It is the way you focus your imagination that counts. Look around the room... yes, around this room... and remember every red thing you see."

"Red," he mutters, and does so.

"Done it? All right. Now tell me what blue objects you observed."

"Blue? You moved the goal posts."

"You were wearing a red filter, so only red could materialize for you. The same goes for sound, taste, touch and smell. Most of your life your focus has bounced here and there like a wild cat in a yard full of dogs. But as you discipline your focus, the cat walks in a straight line and the dogs slink away. Your imagination develops purity and potency."

I lean forward. "*Now* imagine your goal. *Now* focus that imagination. *Now* enter the world of your goal achieved. Unlock the tunnel between you and the field, which sees no difference between imagined and real."

Matthew blinks. "That's it? That's the whole thing?"

"No it isn't. Go away. And when you've tamed the cat, come back."

He rises. "Can I draw a picture of what I'm going to create? It'll help me focus."

"Yes, it will. But remember that it's only a prop. Don't hand your power to props and rituals. The real power to conjure from the field is in you."

***

He returns two hours later, with a folded sheet of paper, and we resume. His intense focus is now clear in his eyes, waiting on my next words.

"Here is the heart of the quickening."

"At last," he murmurs. On the piano, Siobhan's impenetrable smile tucks in a little deeper.

"You have made the decision, you've focused your imagination. Now you'll focus your passion. This step, above all, compels the field to produce. Picture the classic wizard casting a spell. He thrusts his staff to the skies, and cries out in commanding tones, calling upon the powers of darkness to bring down a plague of locusts upon the king's enemies. If this is a movie you're watching, especially a cartoon, the spell will be accompanied by thunder and lightning and great wind and rain. That's no casual detail. It represents a mass intuitive understanding that direct manifestation involves extreme passion, conducting and directing power that, to most, is not of this Earth."

Matthew is bewildered. "Wait a minute. Passion? *Passion* is the essence of the quickening?"

"It is."

"You can't be serious. That's hardly a magic ingredient."

"No? Why not?"

"Everyone knows about passion. How can that be the essence?"

"Ah, but that's the best part. That's the cosmic joke. Merlin's magic ingredient has been under our noses all the time and few have realized its potency. That's because most people, out of fear, deliberately avoid passion, and they laugh half their laughter and cry half their tears. Fewer still have known how to focus their passion. And for masters, focused passion does not use up energy, it creates a portal that pulls energy directly out of the field. Passion is Merlin's wand, with or without words— so focused, so intense, so powerful, that legend calls it a spell. *That* is the secret of the sorcerers."

Shortly, Matthew rises and paces, clutching his folded paper. "And I focus it how?"

"Pot calling the kettle," I reply indignantly. His imagination was overactive even from the first day.

"A coin," he demands, casting about. "My kingdom for a coin."

I find him a fifty, which he inspects, shaking his head.

"No. No good. This has two heads. I need a normal one."

"What?" I reach for it, but he demonstrates its two-headedness by holding the coin, heads up, in the palm of his hand, then flipping that hand over, landing the coin in his other palm. Heads again. He says, "See, this thing's dodgy, it's a two-headed monster."

"Wait just a cotton-picking minute, there…" I take it from him and check. It has only one head of course. But I think I can see how he must have done it. "The hand didn't turn the coin over, the hand turned over the coin. I'll see if I can do it." He watches me practise, the trick being to drop the hand, just before it rolls over the coin. In other words, the coin must be momentarily weightless before one head can become two. After a few tosses, not so hard.

He strolls over to the kitchen drawers, pulls out a ball of string and cuts off a piece about the length of his forearm. He sits in front of me pushing one end into his left ear and pulling it out of his right. Then he grasps both ends and pulls it side to side, apparently through his head, via his ears—a stomach-turning party trick.

"That's truly disgusting," I say with sincerity. Then, as proof that I have over-imbibed, I find myself practising the ridiculous act. He watches and advises me, slurring his words, on how important it is to keep the two hands precisely the same distance apart. It occurs to me that I should go to bed shortly; it would not do to be obviously tipsy in his company.

"Who are you?" he demands suddenly.

"What do you mean?" I stop moving the string.

He giggles. "I mean who the hell are you, really?"

"I'll tell you that when you've worked out who you are. Do we have a deal?"

"Well fuck you too," he says blearily. Then, "You know what?"

"No, what?"

"I've got this all figured out."

"Thass very good. Congratulations. I'm going to bed."

"No, really, I've got it sussed. S'all a dream. I'm gonna wake up in the morning and you won' be there. You and the farm. House of cards. All it needs is a puff of wind. Poof. Gone." He giggles. "You'll be an ex-Jack, Jack... Hey, I've got the munchies." He walks to the breadbin, hacks off a slab, and pours honey onto it directly from the pot.

Out in the bush, the black hole beast drifts through the trees.

SIX

Siobhan sits on top of the piano, next to the photo and the candelabra. Her hands are down on the polished surface, legs over the end. I send her the thought that parking her bottom up there is disrespectful to the memory of my wife. In response she turns her earth clock back sixty years and becomes a schoolgirl again, her shoes black leather pumps, her hair in pigtails, and her tongue poking out at me. Then she looks down at her legs and claps them together idly, like a bored teen waiting for a friend. On this earth, she was a member of the Greymouth Dramatic Society.

"You okay?" Matthew asks me.

"Completely," I reply sternly. The laxity of last evening is behind me.

Every morsel of the meal has been consumed, the plates washed and dried and put away, the bench wiped. Coffee steams in front of both of us. It occurs to me that it's been a while since I saw evidence of his compulsive obsessions. I haven't seen him arrange his mug, or any object, in precise alignment with other objects like the table. I haven't been regaled with useless information, such as how many breaths a human takes per minute compared to a cat, or if you joined every strand of the farm's wool clip end-to-end how it would stretch twenty-three and a half times the length of the country.

He sits on his hands, his shoulders open to me, expectant.

"So, you think you're ready," I say.

"I am ready. You made me wait forever. So this had better be good," he adds with a hint of humour. His gaze is open and directly focused on my eyes.

"All right, we begin. You'll use the quickening to implement the law of attraction, and pluck what you desire out of the field of consciousness. You have something you want to create?"

"I have."

"You must be certain you can live with the result. Attaining what you desire can be worse than not attaining it. Do you understand? If you're not certain, find another desire."

"I know what I want." He looks me directly in the eye, and on the piano, Siobhan smiles her Mona Lisa smile. I no longer know what the smile means, but I think da Vinci painted the wrong woman.

"Before we start, do you have any doubts?"

"No. Let's get to it." But his eyes flick away and back.

"The quickening is not a quick fix," I snap and his eyes narrow at my harsh tone. He exhales, a sharp huff that pushes his lips out.

"All right. I do have a doubt. My goal depends on someone else. Can this quickening really influence someone I've never met and who doesn't know who I am? I haven't forgotten what you said, but if I-"

"Yes. The but. How are you going to disarm the but?"

"Viewing the movie of me."

"Do it."

After a hesitation, he closes his eyes, speaks aloud. "Allow the doubt... observe it... release it... direct anew."

"Completely useless."

His eyes pop open, startled. "What? Why?"

"You recited it like a recipe, inserting the word doubt as if it were a dessert ingredient. You mouthed symbols like dried husks, without getting anywhere near the negative belief. Do it again, take all the time you need and this time focus *vividly* on the shift in perspective."

He resumes the process, taking his time, intensely focused. Then he returns to me and there's a long silence while we appraise each other. In a matter of weeks his strength has grown prodigiously. Of course with the arrogance of youth, he now sees himself as my equal. Perhaps, in his eyes, I am becoming merely useful, like a text book.

"Make the decision," I say.

He looks blank. "And?"

"Make the decision—to have, do, or be what you desire."

"I've done it. That's how you start? It seems kind of obvious."

"Ah. You want a procedure that's more deep and meaningful and carries punch?"

"Well, yes, what's wrong with that?"

"You want an incantation so power-packed that you need only start with a whim, or a vague wish? Maybe all you need is a fuzzy image of your desire? Maybe all you have to do is mumble the correct ritual?"

"Hey, hey, easy with the whip," Matthew protests. "I'm a dead horse already."

"Then get the point. The quickening is not a reality by-pass. Most goals never arrive because the clear decision—to have, do, or be what's desired—was never made. Your decision must be a trumpet call announcing *in advance* the certainty of fulfilment, or it is nothing."

"Why are you getting so worked up about this?"

"Because to make the quickening happen, *you* must be worked up. You must push yourself into that state where everything—not just the immediate goal—falls into place and you know you are living a charmed life. Did you think this was going to be a list of dry bullet points?"

"No," he says.

"You've made the decision?"

"Yes," he says.

"So you're already feeling the excitement and pleasure that your creation is about to be part of your life?"

"Take it easy, we've just start-"

"Are you hard of hearing?"

"No!"

"Get out."

"What?"

"Have you turned your ears off? Don't waste my time. Get out."

"What?!"

"Take a walk. Reach inside yourself to find out what it really means to create out of the *present*, not out of the future. Don't come back until you've made the decision that the goal *is* yours."

"Bloody hell! You're pushing my buttons!" Amazed, wide-eyed, Matthew walks out.

He spends an hour sitting cross-legged, back to the house, in the exact centre of the female alpaca enclosure, surrounded by baffled animals. Popper approaches with the intent of nuzzling, but changes her mind and retreats back into the circle. Then Matthew stands, vaults the fence, and strides back to the house. He walks in with a gleam in his eye.

"Let's do it," he snaps. "And don't stuff me around."

"You have made the decision. Now you will imagine your goal."

A twitch around the eyes betrays his impatience. Once again, I seem to be giving him something mundane. He wants the secret and he wants it now. So I pick up my cold coffee mug, place it next to his and point to both.

"Choose which one you're going to touch *without* first imagining the touching."

He contemplates this for five seconds.

"That's impossible."

"Of course it's impossible. Nothing happens without imagination. Every creation is consciousness imagining itself into being. Thoughts become things, events and states of being.

"As an apprentice, you will focus passion by cultivating a combination of three specific feelings—certainty, exhilaration and triumph. As you vividly imagine your goal, you will infuse those three feelings, blended as one, until you feel an inner shift, as if your axis has tilted. You will open a tunnel to the field and experience a quality of life that compares with the old the way a rainbow compares to a single colour. And don't be humble about it. Ultimately you *are* the field, not its needy offspring. It's not ask, believe, receive; it's command, assume, receive."

Matthew's excitement is returning. He mutters to himself, "Certainty, exhilaration, triumph," glancing now and then to his folded piece of paper.

"Wait. Hear this. Make sure that your passion is applied to what you want, not what you don't want."

"Obvious," he retorts.

"Is it? Let's take an example. How was it you described your vehicle this morning?"

"Uh… a flatulent heap of shit."

"If you were to defame your ute again and shout petulantly, 'I want a new ute!' what message would the field hear?"

"Seems clear enough. I'm after a new ute."

"That's what your words said. What did your passion say?"

"Ah."

"Name it."

"Frustration. That I don't have one."

"So the passion is not in the new ute, but in the lack of one."

"My God. The field has to supply the lack of a new ute. And I'm already well supplied in that department."

"That is why countless millions of goals are never realized: belief in scarcity, in *I am unfulfilled,* is stronger in most than belief in *my goal is on the way.* The field always says, Yes. Do you understand? Always, Yes! Not to your words, but to your most vivid passions. So… " My eyes flick to his folded paper.

"… whatever goal you have there, take care what passion you attach to it."

Matthew turns, struck by a new thought. "You said the quickening was for an apprentice. Why was that?"

"I meant that the quickening is the safe way for an apprentice to begin."

His eyebrows draw together. "Safe? Are you still holding out on me?"

Suddenly I'm apprehensive. I had not anticipated this. What is it about this extraordinary young man that so regularly wrong-foots me? *Siobhan?* Still on the piano, Siobhan has lost the schoolgirl appearance, and her expression has shifted. There's a knowingness to it now, her smile no longer looks like a smile. And it gives me nothing at all.

"What are you looking at?" Matthew asks.

"Nothing. Very well. I will tell you the rest. But understand this. Do not attempt what I'm about to tell you until you are experienced and confident with what I have already said. This is a safety warning. Clear?"

"Yes."

"No it isn't, so I'll change the warning. If you try what I'm going to tell you and become frightened or even anxious, you must stop. Immediately. If you do not, your current life will be in danger."

Matthew is startled. "You're not kidding, are you?"

"I am not. Are you reading me? I want your word that you will take the warning very seriously."

He hesitates. "All right. You have my word."

"Then here is the hidden core of the quickening. There is no limit to the power of passion. None. The quickening I described—that blend of certainty, exhilaration, triumph— works well for an apprentice using indirect creation. But the masters go on to a far greater passion. They use the quickening merely to get started, as if they were striking a match in order to build the full fire. Soul fire. *Fuego del alma*. From *el fuego* comes direct manifestation. It snatches physical reality directly out of the great field of consciousness. Believe me, you do not want to play with this particular fire until you can play confidently with the match."

Matthew frowns. "It's hard to imagine any passion stronger than certainty, exhilaration and triumph."

"*El fuego* harnesses and directly uses the life force. In other cultures it's known as ch'i, ki, tao, mauri, prana, kundalini, serpent power. It's that essence which flows through and sustains all physical things, and some individuals have spent lifetimes trying to invoke it or harness it in their own way. There is no word to adequately describe the intensity of the passion involved."

"How would I generate such a passion?"

"For now, you can't. But one day, when you are practising the quickening, perhaps when you least expect it, there it will be; the first ember of *el fuego*, pulsating, glowing, waiting for you to breathe on it."

"I will see it?"

"*All* of your senses will be involved. Colours will be richer, sounds sharper, smell more subtle, tastes more diverse. You will feel a tingling at the base of your spine, then an intense heat rising up through your vertebrae—and your body will feel as if a force field emanates from it and can be directed. You will feel powerful and invulnerable, which, ultimately, you are. But be warned, the first time is the most dangerous."

"And if I rouse *el fuego* too soon?"

"It would consume you. You would end this incarnation quickly or you would be institutionalized. A small few, pre-disposed to fear, anger and aggression, have become megalomaniacs, generating suffering on a wide scale. Others have called them evil."

"But you do not."

"No.

After a long silence, Matthew changes tack. "This is the occult we're talking about, isn't it?"

"Yes. It's the essence used by practitioners of the occult."

"So you're turning me into the sorcerer's apprentice. I was raised as a Christian. The Bible says sorcerers, witches, wizards should be killed."

"The Old Testament God was very offended."

"Maybe, but whoever dreamed it up didn't see this as hogwash."

"No question. Early Christianity knew it was dealing with a serious competitor. Some of those burned at the stake really did invoke power in the forbidden ways."

"Such as the quickening."

"Yes. The quickening by many other names. Zealous religious leaders have been so blinded by outer form, they could not see that the essence of prayer is precisely the same as the essence of quickening.

"How's that?" Matthew asks.

"Let's take the simplest example. Imagine... A little boy comes to his mother in the middle of the night, upset by a nightmare. He says, 'The giant is coming to eat me again.' So the mother tells the boy to draw a picture of the giant, then helps him set it alight in the fireplace while chanting: *Bad dreams with me do not belong. With this fire, bad dreams be gone.* The drawing goes up in smoke as the child—with unwavering faith in the process—claps three times and cheers, triumphant that the nightmare is been banished. It's good psychology, it's prayer, it's witchcraft, it's the essence of the quickening."

"It could be used to harm people."

"Of course. So can Christianity and Islam."

Matthew stares down at the folded paper in his hands. He opens it facing him, but the paper is thin and the outline of a human figure is obvious. Abruptly, he refolds the sheet, thrusts it in his breast pocket, then heads for the door.

"Wait." I go to him, stand in front of him. "You still think we are bound by a fixed external reality?"

"No," he says.

"Is what you desire on the way?"

"Yes," he says softly. "It is." His eyes glitter with anticipation. I spread the fingers of my right hand so that the tips describe a circle, place them on his lower belly over the pubic bone and give it a sharp push. He expels a rush of air.

"From there," I say.

Light spills out of the loft porthole until late. Captain Matthew Smith paces, plotting the course, navigating the winds of passion. Just after midnight, I hear a muffled, prolonged shout. Then nothing.

***

The following morning, I hear him before I see him. Or rather, I hear the piano. The generator has been running roughly and I have the parts laid out on the barn workbench, timing mechanism exposed, spacer poised for tinkering.

When the first notes of Beethoven's *Appassionata* reach me, I stop moving. During the next dozen bars I straighten slowly and stare into the wall. Matthew is no longer aware of the house or the farm, or me; he may no longer be aware of the piano. He has fully entered the music, which now carries him, sending a current through his spine, pouring out through his fingers and hands, through the piano, out into the air of the farm.

I have never played the way he is playing now.

SEVEN

He has been waiting three days.

He exudes imminent success. He talks in tones of certainty, walks as if all about him is as it should be and in its natural place. I'm sure it's not a veneer for my benefit, nor even for his; he has grown a presence I might have envied at his age. Not that we speak of it, because now only he can see the process through to the end. Instead we talk about the practicalities of farm and food, and the extra-ordinary, unpredictable weather this year and what might be causing it.

One thing becomes all too clear. He has used the quickening to summon a woman. A woman! How outrageously, astonishingly ambitious for a rank beginner.

He lies in his tent for hours at a time. In my more fanciful moments, I imagine I am him, lying there, content in the assumption of success, watching the japara fabric waft in and out to the vagaries of a breeze, skin registering the shifts in air pressure.

Or he talks to the alpacas, feeding them lucerne and nuts with such unwavering devotion that if anyone passed by they would hesitate to interrupt. Or he walks the circumference of the farm, touching leaves, twigs, stones and mosses, dipping fingers in the rushing stream, picking bluebells and inhaling their aroma, and plucking parachute seeds from soft air.

So he is now a young man in love with the woman of his imagination—behaviour fitting of a Greek god. Anticipated love has become new love, so he is suddenly a sightseer in his own land and must go about staring at all that is familiar as if it is new and wondrous. I would not be surprised if he was penning poetry to her. He delights me, in the way that young lovers have always delighted the world. I find that when I get out of bed in the morning, I look forward to seeing him. My day does not feel completely under way until we have breakfasted together.

But I am also appalled.

A woman? It's not that it can't be done, but my judgement is in question because I did not warn him to start with the small things. To conjure a woman out of the field is hardly the same as conjuring a mug of mulled wine.

I am caught. It's too late to get him to change the goal. So I must now contemplate the possibility that I have set him up to fail. His cup brims with confidence, my stomach churns with anxiety.

There, I confess what must now be all too obvious. I have been blind. I have not only become emotionally attached to the boy, I am also fastened to his success like a leech to flesh. That I have developed such weakness disturbs me intensely, but I cannot say anything to him lest I endanger his quest. I am becoming a doubt-ridden old man on the inside, while parading on the outside as a source of wisdom.

Which is pretence. Deceit.

I wish Siobhan was here, if only to nag me yet again about my inability to see what is missing even though it is supposedly glued to my eyeballs. I have called for her by playing *The Swan*, and I have called for her using the painting of her great-great grandfather's ship, but she does not come. In the lonely nights, I sometimes talk as if she were there, but she is not taking the hint.

I work the coin trick, conjuring two heads out of one so often that the subtle movement has become a meditation. I can now do it without thinking about it.

A woman. He wants the love of his lifetime and he wants it now. I do understand why Matthew chose such a goal. When he first limped in out of the winter snowstorm, there was something deeply starved in him that bread and wisdom would never satisfy. So why did I not see this coming? *Is that what I was missing, Siobhan? Is it that?* I am afraid for him, yet I was the one who presumed to teach him how to render fear powerless. I persuaded him to stay, I encouraged him, then I pushed him out onto a path that hangs over a precipice.

But that is a destructive thought. I will not entertain it.

Allow, observe, release. Direct anew.

It's gone.

***

Three days becomes five.

He sits on the main post of the alpaca gate for hours. The animals nuzzle him, he tickles and strokes and talks to them. He sprawls on the hillside opposite the house, watching the breeze billow the grass on the way to the trees. Or he goes to Siobhan's arbour and lies flat on her seat, looking at the clouds. He doesn't think to ask if he can go there, but that's all right. I even wish she would appear for him there and speak to him directly. She could encourage him and not leave all responsibility to me.

Sometimes he pushes his body to exhaustion, jogging up the valley and along the ridges on either side of the farm; when the sun is behind him he's a black exclamation mark drawing a slow demarcation line between land and sky. Sometimes he disappears from the skyline and ranges into other valleys only to return many hours later.

After one such excursion, he says with amusement, "There's a clump of apple trees in the middle of the bush, miles from the track, growing fruit." He turns a knowing gaze through the window towards Siobhan's photo on the piano.

"Vonny Appleseed," I admit, with a theatrical sigh.

He begins to turn away, when there's a flash of colour near his upper arm. I reach out urgently to stop him.

"Wait! Don't move."

A juvenile monarch butterfly has touched down on his upper arm. It flexes its tapestry slowly back and forth; gleaming, bright orange interlaced with black veins, and a black trim sprinkled with white dots.

"It's a sign," Matthew jokes, but he's not really joking. The butterfly flips away, giddy on the breeze.

I rush to the glasshouse like an eager schoolboy, finding it well-seasoned with monarchs which have not yet found the ventilation vane. I yank open the door, throw it wide, and they emerge almost accidentally, each wing stroke thrusting them to some random check-point in the air. *They've come. Siobhan, they've come. Where are you? Come and see.* The new orange and black inhabitants of the valley are so eager for freedom, none of them linger to land on me. Some alight on the elm, clustering on the same branch, lending it a new season. Then, they too disperse, spreading their random brilliance across the pasture.

But still, Siobhan does not come.

The same night, Boa loses the battle of the bath. Matthew walks into the lounge and finds her carelessly asleep on top of her pile of books. She wakes, eyes popping, toppling the pile, streaking for the safety of outdoors, but it's too late. He slams the door, beats her to the window and sings, as if it were the climax of an Italian aria, 'Boa, it's bath time!' She emits a low-throated yowl, backs under the table and prepares to debate the issue. I sink lower in my seat and Matthew accuses me of cowardice. He runs the bath himself while Boa pads in circles, rumbling and moaning; then he fetches the welding apron and mitts and a thick blanket to get her into the bathroom, where he slams the door. Prolonged human, cat and water sounds emerge from the bathroom, penetrating the cushions over my ears.

Soon, Boa creeps out of the bathroom like a skinned water rat, slinking along the wall and out the door which I open for her. Matthew appears, rubbing his hands with satisfaction and announcing that he has created a cat of great purity, whose body odour will no longer strip wallpaper. I would go after Boa and offer comfort, but she would take it out of my flesh.

Matthew takes the sextant off the shelf, fetches brass cleaner and rags, and sets to work. He rubs furiously, with more energy than needed for polishing.

"Why has your memory not returned?" he demands to know while he polishes. And when I don't answer, "Maybe you don't *want* to remember."

"Are you trying to analyse me?"

"What is it? What are you afraid of? The dark? Guilt? Grief?"

"I have no idea," I snap.

He looks at me for long seconds, holding my gaze, then he returns to polishing. An hour later one side of the sextant is gleaming, so he takes it down to the tent with him to finish the other side, lighting the fire so that he can see the orange gold shine in the dark light of the flames.

And late every night, he goes to the barn loft to write. I imagine that his writing is lyrical, filled with the dreams of a young man anticipating all that love and life can offer. Does he also write about me and all the words that have passed between us? Does he speculate about my missing years?

***

Seven days. Now, he too is counting. Uncertainty circles him, looking to land. It lands briefly when he asks me the question, "How long should it take?" But he immediately regrets asking and says, "No. No, don't answer. I'll handle it."

He strides off to the barn, where he will use the self-movie process to rid himself of the uncertainty. While he does that I go quietly to my room and conduct my own quickening, even though it feels like cheating. In my universe he will succeed, the woman will come to him. She'll be his own Siobhan, to fill the hole in his own heart.

I find him next to the hole in my lounge wall, the one his desperate fist left weeks ago. He's looking at the ragged edges of the plaster, vaguely surprised. He reaches in and down, and pulls out the missing piece which had dropped down onto the framing. He knocks it with his knuckles, testing its soundness, then offers to plaster it back in place and repaint the wall.

"No, not necessary. I'll do it myself." But I'm not sure I will—it doesn't seem to matter.

He wanders away, tense and distracted.

One morning, when the sun falls on his tent, he begins a frenzy of cleaning and tidying. He hauls out every last item, including the groundsheet, and heaps it on the dry moss by the fireplace. He borrows an old pair of my corduroys and a shirt to wear, then runs all his clothes through the house washing machine and dryer; except for the merino mountain shirt, which, if subjected to a hot wash and tumble, would only fit a dwarf. That gets careful treatment in cold water, and he hangs it up with the sleeping bag on a rope slung between two trees. He offers to wash *my* clothes, and I can't allow that. He resets the tent ropes, tightening them, taking out all the sags and folds, and hangs his reading light from the pole behind his sleeping position. He uses my hearth brush and pan to attack every surface and corner, purging all leaves, twigs and dirt.

When all his gear goes back in a few hours later, it is arranged, folded, in order. The rifle has its allotted place, on a square section of fence post he uses as a shelf. He has shown no more interest in hunting, so I don't know why he doesn't store it in the barn.

When I come by, his tent is, for the first time, aroma-free

and a pleasant place to dwell amongst the trees. I say so, adding dryly, "I suppose this isn't a good time to remind you how comfortable my guest bedroom is."

"Right," he agrees. "It isn't."

Later, while I'm sitting at the kitchen table, the phone rings. It's the same policewoman as last time.

"About that young fella we want to talk to. Just want to warn you, we've had a call from a party of hikers who say they saw him in Harper valley, just over from you. That was yesterday. Any sign of him?"

"No. Not a thing."

"Nothing disturbed or out of place?"

"No. Nothing."

"We'll be sending an armed search party into Harpers first thing tomorrow. Give us a call if you see anything untoward. Please be very careful. Keep any firearms securely locked up, remove the bolts and hide them, okay?"

Okay.

"Check your extinguishers and hook up your fire hoses."

Okay.

I no sooner put the phone down than it thrums again.

"Good morning sir, please hold for Brett Kowalski."

After a pause and a click, "Good day to you sir, am I talking to Jack?"

"You are."

"A.k.a. Conrad Fleming?"

"I don't give interviews. Goodb-"

"I'm not the press. I'm a senior physician with the Jensen Medical Institute in Chicago. I'm a neurosurgeon. It's a real pleasure to finally talk to you, sir, you're a hard man to track down."

This is new. It's been more than three decades since the medical world tried to make me live in a goldfish bowl.

"You're a little late Mr Kowalski. I was discharged thirty-seven years ago, and-"

"Well, let me get right to the point, Jack. I have some very good news for you. I don't know how to put this to you slowly, so here it is. We've seen a digital copy of the original x-rays and we know we can safely remove that bullet."

I let that rattle around in my head for a moment.

"You still there, Jack?"

"Yes. I'm here."

"I understand this will be coming as something of a shock after all this time."

"I was told it would never happen. It's impossible."

"Never is a long time, my friend, medicine has moved on. These days we can mosey around in your IQ factory pretty much anyplace takes our fancy."

"Really."

"Sure. Of course there are some hoops to jump through. We'll need to find out where the bullet is parked up right now. We'll need to check out your general health. And you'll want to check us out—I appreciate that I'm just a voice on the phone."

"Wait."

I hold the receiver away from me. Questions and their answers chase each other around the dance floor. In particular, can I see myself existing without my little lead time bomb? The answer surprises me. I bring the receiver back.

"Thank you for the offer, but I'm going to decline."

"I... uh, you are?"

"I am."

"Oh, look, I'm sorry, Jack. I didn't make myself clear back there. You understand you wouldn't have to pay a solitary dime? Travel, accommodation, surgery, everything... we'd take care of all that."

"I heard you. But I don't want to lose the bullet."

"You don't?! Uh... you don't. Well, I'm truly sorry to hear

that. Uh… I'm curious. You mind if I ask why?"

"It's a long story."

"Tell you what I'll do, Jack. I realize that this news is very sudden. Why don't I give you a couple of weeks to think it over, and-"

"No, don't call back. I have made-"

"This is a little hasty, don't you think?"

"All right, here's the short story. In a couple of weeks, I won't be around to benefit from your offer."

"You mean… You mean that you…"

"I do."

"Say, are you putting me on?"

"No I'm not. I'm making my answer clear, so you won't be in any doubt. I'm not up for divorcing my bullet. I would be a serious alimony defaulter."

"Well, I'm truly sorry to hear that." There's a pause while he wrestles with a parting shot. "For the record, Jack, I believe you really do need some professional help with that head of yours."

Shortly, Matthew walks in, helps himself to a slice of bread and a slab of cheese and takes an enormous bite. On the way out, mouth still full, he jokes in passing. "God helps those who help themselves, right? Maybe I should help the field out by heading into town for a bit of socialising. Give her a chance to…"

But he stops then, and looks at me, and swallows.

"Your decision," I say.

"I was joking." His smile is thin.

A few minutes later, I see him walking past the reservoir. And this is interesting because he has two distinctly different ways of passing the deep water. If his mind is on love, he forgets that he is near it and his subconscious takes over; his feet automatically take him well clear—by as much as a dozen paces.

Today, he remembers. So he forces himself to walk near the edge, this time within a single pace, closer than I have seen. He walks with studied nonchalance, deliberately slower than his normal pace. But even from the house I can see the sweat shining on his forehead and the tension in his body. The child in him still does not know the end of fear and waits for deep water to rear up once again and drag him under.

Is this what's holding back his quickening?

***

I'm crawling along a wharf towards a clipper ship moored at the far end. She is straining at the mooring lines, eager to depart, white canvas already spread, right to the uppermost tops'l. The skipper, in white uniform and bold-braided cap, is consulting charts and pacing impatiently in the wheelhouse, looking at a chronometer, stabbing furious glances in my direction.

A voice crackles out of the marine radio. "The devil made me do it."

Frantically, I search my pockets for the fare, a penny. Not this pocket, nor this one, nor this. Then I realize that I have been holding it in my hand all the time, and in that moment the penny drops, through my fingers, down through a gap in the wharf sleepers, down into blue-green sunlit water. It flips on the way down, flashing heads, heads, heads, heads, through water, down towards a plastic doll with hair wafting in the current and a single green eye staring up at me. The penny settles directly on the eye.

I wake gasping and twisting on the bed. I stare at the ceiling. Something vital is slipping away. I listen for a sound, as if this could tell me, but all I hear is a warm breeze whispering to the bush, and the insistent comeback of a bush owl. *I... am... I... am...*

Siobhan? Where are you?

No answer.

*Siobhan, help me. I don't know how much longer I can stay
strong for him.*

No answer.

An insane, impossible longing drops onto me from the
ceiling. I must have the real Siobhan—not the impostor—the
Siobhan of long ago, who knew how to hold me and talk to me
and tell me what I needed to be told. I want to curl up like a
baby and be enveloped in her physical arms and lay my head
against her physical breast, so that I can close my eyes forever
and think no more and feel her loss no more. Grief returns
against my will and I sob in the half-dark like a baby.

Weakness.

Matthew must not see this. Matthew must never know.

EIGHT

For just an hour on any day in December, sunlight sleeks deep into the shadows of Ringa Gorge. The beam passes down between stands of massive kahikatea that were proud before humans came, down between ranks of branches that point to each other across the river. Then it stands square on the Ringa Falls. Caught in the beam, the river hesitates, then shrugs over the lip and plummets ten times the height of a man, raising foam and mist as it thunders into the pool below.

Matthew stands above the falls on one bank, I on the other, both of us in shadow. For the purpose, I climbed to an easier crossing and came down the other side, only to be roundly mocked for cheating. For now, he stands back, where he can't see the deep water below, and where the cavernous thundering is muted by jutting edge and foliage. The moment he steps forward, his fear will be upon him.

"I need my head read," he calls, a tremor carrying across the water.

"You tried that years back. It wasn't a good read."

"Old goat!"

"Impudent pup!"

He looks long and hard at the fifteen paces that separate us. The sun penetrates the water as easily as glass, lighting up emerald green weed. The flat, greywacke lip would be an easy path, if it were not for the slippery weed and the force of knee-high water. The air shifts back and forth, listless in the narrow confines of the gorge.

This was my idea. It came from one of those moments when two people open their mouths simultaneously and find themselves talking about the same thing. Yesterday, at the end of the seventh day of waiting, he asked if the reason for the delay could be his lifelong fear of deep water. I agreed immediately, proposing the self-movie process as the cure and Ringa Falls as the clinic.

Yes, you're right. I am now playing God with his life.

And yes, it's a risk. But it's surely a far greater risk to allow him to fail his first quickening; he has far too much to lose. I know; I have made significant errors in judgement in the saving of Matthew. This may be the final error, but I cannot do nothing; I will not allow his mind to return to the abyss, so he and I are both past the point of no return.

A piwakawaka tumbles over my head, this one glistening-black with white feathers in the fan. It flips out over the water, and then upriver. Matthew looks at me sharply; is the fantail a good sign or a bad one?

"You want me to talk you through it?"

"No,' he snaps, then tunes me out. He holds still, fists clenched. He's trying to stack the odds by lecturing himself with logic: the worst that can happen is that he'll slip, go over the falls, pick up a few bruises, then scramble out of the pool and survive. But more sweat beads pop onto his brow—so much for logic. He sucks in a deep breath and steps down into the cold water, which swirls around his calves, puckering his flesh.

"My left bum is twitching," he says, trying to maintain humour. It's an understatement; the entire muscle mass of his upper leg and buttock are jiving around the bone.

He begins to take control and I can feel his thoughts as if they were my own. *Allow; this part of me is afraid, and that's okay. Observe; I'm away into the trees and looking back at my shaking body—which is afraid, and that's okay. Release; that fear too will pass... will pass... will pass... Now direct anew and that version of me chooses to take the first step forward.*

And he takes the first step, eyes wide, legs wide and arms spread for balance. Another step. Another.

"He's starting to relax," Matthew whispers about himself. "His bum has stopped shaking."

He feels out each foothold, shifting weight only when firm, more confident with each step. Once, the foot closest to the lip goes deeper than he expected, over the knee, and he gasps as he is sucked back into the terror. It takes him five seconds to restore the status quo: allow the fear, get out and observe himself again, release the fear, choose again. He pushes forward.

And reaches the bank, where he staggers against a boulder, closes his eyes and breathes deeply. Then he sits up abruptly and lets out a whoop of triumph.

"Yes!"

He charges to his feet, sets his state of mind and forges out back across the river, faster, more certain with his feet. Then returns, this time stopping deliberately in the middle of the river at the very edge of the falls, looking directly down through the mist into the pool. He raises his fist.

"Yeeeee haaaaah!"

When he reaches the bank the second time, he runs around pointing his finger to the sky as if he has scored the winning championship goal. Our grins can barely be contained on our faces. And yet, even now, something holds us back. We grip right arms fiercely, hand to elbow, in the style of the soldiers of ancient Rome, clapping left hands to each other's shoulder.

We walk a few paces upriver.

The fantail returns with opportunist companions, feasting on insects stirred into the air by our movement. Matthew now runs his mouth on autopilot, while I am the quiet one. As he chatters on, he collects bone-white twigs that have been carried on past floods and deposited amongst high rocks and fissures. He stops and sets light to them inside his thermette, a simple but brilliantly conceived device that folds a jacket of water around the flames like an upside down megaphone.

The beam of sunlight has tilted and thinned, invaded by branches, standing to one side of the gorge floor like a ragged slice of cheese. Unexpectedly, the air has warmed and the breeze has died altogether, rendering the conditions seductively pleasant. I don't trust them for a moment; the people with the shortest lives in the alps are those who think a blue sky is a promissory note for good weather. We'll have to be under way shortly. I'm not looking forward to it; we were up before dawn, it took five hours to hike here, and I am aching as I have never ached. I will need to conserve my energy.

The thermette spews a geyser of boiling water, which puts out most of the fire that started it, which turns down the heat— we have the technology. We sip scalding tea, watching the icy water slide by. Matthew chatters on, relating his river-crossing to me as if viewing the movie was his own discovery. "It was so clear, viewing my fearful self in the river. I could have strolled over and had a chat with him."

"And the place you observed from?"

"Peaceful and powerful," he says. "It was like being on the border of an exotic country I've not seen before. You know, in that state of mind I would still have been calm if I had gone over the edge. I could have chosen any course of action. Everything seemed to be all right, the way it was meant to be. Like viewing my own dreams."

"You were," I say.

"What do you mean?"

"It was the dream that you were afraid of deep water. That's all it ever was. You woke up."

"I did," he says in wonder.

There's a lump of driftwood alongside the rock, weather-worn into the unlikely shape of a wheelbarrow tray, the stumps of old branches as handles. It's iron-hard and must have been making its clumsy way down the gorge for decades. Matthew places it in the water so that it floats with the inside surface dry. He puts in a small rock as a token load, glancing up at me to see if I have caught the significance. Then he gives the barrow a gentle shove and it turns downriver, heading for the edge of the falls. It wedges between two rocks, but he throws a hefty stone and the splash breaks it free. "Good riddance," he says. Barrow and burden tip over the edge and are gone, wiped from the universe.

"It's very quiet," Matthew says, looking around again.

It's too quiet. All birds have put their calls on hold. Except for the river, there's no sound at all; the trees have ceased all movement and hang, breathless. Skinks twitch their tails once, blink once, then scuttle off the sun-warmed rocks into the shelter below. The quality of the light has shifted. Then, so fast that we can see the change as it happens, Ringa Mountain grows a bracelet of cloud around its fingers. Something out of nothing. Two peaks further back, a low line of bruised blue-grey cloud thickens.

Time to move, and quickly.

Douse the fire, dunk the thermette, dump everything into the packs.

We cross upstream and stride up the track, through beech and undergrowth so thick that shortcuts are out of the question. The track winds back and forth up the eastern side of the valley, a snake side-winding towards Ringa Pass. The air pushes down like a stifling blanket. But as we climb, the temperature drops swiftly. Black-backed gulls come soaring in from the coast, skirling overhead, seeking shelter in advance.

When we emerge from the tree line, it's early afternoon but dark as twilight. There's no wind, but we can hear it howling somewhere. The mountain has vanished, swallowed by a boiling wall of grey shot with purple. A few fat snowflakes drop lazily, straight down.

Then *Tawhiri,* the storm god, smites us.

Wind first: a brutally cold punch that snatches our breath away and tosses debris up and over the bush behind us. Then, in seconds, a mixture of snow and shotgun sleet blasts our faces. The snow is horizontal, sleet almost so, the two angled to each other like scissor blades; and watching this mid-air criss-cross makes me giddy. For this storm, the entire Coast from Haast to Karamea will be battening down. We can't retreat to the gorge, because there are no tracks out below and if the snow is thick, we could be trapped in there. We can only go forward, which means climbing over Ringa Pass into the teeth of the tempest.

We'll need speed and we won't stopping to admire the view.

We un-sling the packs and pounce on them, pulling out weather jackets with hands already numbing with cold. As I thrust my second arm securely into my jacket, Matthew cries out. His oilskin has been ripped out of his hand, instantly airborne. It becomes a black crow tossed high and ugly over the bush. As it drops out of sight, beyond any hope of recovery, he screams obscenities after it.

He turns to me, sleet slicing at his face, furious with himself. And afraid. He thinks he's in serious trouble—a thought which will already be weakening his ability to survive.

I unzip my jacket and start to remove it.

Matthew bounds up close and shouts into my ear. "What do you think you're doing? I'm not taking your jacket!"

"I don't need it, you do. It's five hours to the farm. Take it."

"What are you talking about? Put the fucking thing back on. I couldn't live with myself. You got that? I'm warning you, Jack, if you don't put that back on, I'll leave it here."

Suddenly, a shock runs through me.

Of course.

Clarity. This is how it ends.

"Put it on!" he demands.

I put my arm back in the sleeve and pull the zip right to the top. Frantically, Matthew rips a pullover out of his pack, snatches up the pack and dashes behind the shelter of a rock.

A voice speaks behind me. "Hello Jack." The sound is low-pitched, viscous, easily penetrating the wind. Just two words, but they convey the book of us, Siobhan and me, spanning the decades. Her tone tells what has been and promises what is to come. Something ending, something beginning.

When I turn, she's sitting in the tussock like Bo Peep. Her skirt and hair answer only to her movements, not to the wind, which wraps her and the tussock near her in a bubble of still air. She's wearing her all-time favourite denim skirt, the one she spent hours decorating with languid yin yang waves around the bottom edge.

She rises and walks over until we are close, almost touching.

Something ending. I want to lie down and sleep. Every cell in my body yearns to rest now.

Something beginning.

Where have you been?

Then she shows me the real Siobhan, the Siobhan I once knew. She lifts up two hands to almost touch my face. Tears spill over and slip down her cheeks, twin rivulets that know nothing of the howling wind. On her face there's all the love and longing I know is also on my own. The surface of the looking-glass has never been as close as this. So close, so easy, just half a step to the end of pain. I could do it swiftly, right now, before she has a chance to change back.

Of all times, why do you tempt me now?

I stumble back, half a step.

Immediately, she changes to the other Siobhan, that impostor, who now drops her hands to her sides and beams at me. "And what will you be doing now, Jack?"

"Still questions, Vonnie? Still no answers?" Neither of us has to shout. The wind already knows what is happening, the cloud knows, and the bush and the earth.

"You're still missing something, Jack. It's the last piece of the jigsaw. When you've found it, I'll give you the answer."

"The answer? Only one?"

"Just one. It will be the answer for all seasons."

"Will it tell me who you really are?"

"Yes!" she laughs. "Yes, it will." Then she is gone on a gust, and the tussock that was upright around her feet beats the ground in frantic search of her.

I am back into the forty furies. A falcon, caught out over the mountain, swoops low overhead, buffeted savagely, individual feathers at odd angles. It dives, then, a plunging U-turn, regaining partial control, rocking down to shelter.

Matthew emerges from behind the rock, wearing his spare pullover. The weave is about as wind resistant as a wire fence and snow is already collecting on the strands. The Coast hasn't seen a summer storm like this in a generation.

He shouts, "Freaky wind—sounded like a woman talking."

He dances on the spot, teeth chattering and when he speaks again his voice is high and harsh. "Let's go! Let's go!' He shrugs the pack around to the side between him and the wind; it's flat now, emptied of every possible scrap of weight. Loose strap ends flog the canvas; one end flails at his face and he ties it off angrily.

Something ending. Something quickening.

"Wait." I have to shout close to his face to be heard above the rushing elements. "You have a decision to make, Matthew."

"What?"

"You're going to decide to be warm."

That gets his full attention; briefly, he stops shivering. He understands exactly what I have just said, and wastes no time with stupid questions. He just nods, eyes eager.

"Walk," I shout. "I'll start you, then you're going to take it over."

He whirls and sets off. I fall in just a pace behind him, both of us leaning into the wind. He begins at a furious pace, well beyond mine, so I yell at him to slow down. He does so, glancing back, and with marvellous intuition settles his rhythm so as to effortlessly lift my own. The wind levers itself up another notch, shrieking, trying to tear even our thoughts from our minds. Now I have to yell, straining throat and lungs.

"Ready?"

"Yes!" He glances back to give me the benefit of his intensity. His eyes are glittering with intent.

"Is a warm body yours or is it not? Yes or no? Is it waiting for you? Yes or no? Don't rush it. When you're ready, make the decision! Do you hear me?" The effort saps my energy as if a tap had been opened.

He steps on, uphill, head hunched, arms between himself and the pack. The temperature is still dropping, wind-chill rising fast. Sleet is thinning, snow thickening and building up on one side of his clothes, from hunter's hat down to trouser cuff. In the near dark, he looks like a walking black and white stripe. His boots flick back and forth, crunch, crunch, crunch, crunch, like a metronome, so regular it's hypnotic. If the terrain forces a delay or advance on the rhythm, he makes up for it.

He takes his time about the decision. But finally he glances back and snarls.

"It's *on*! Warmth is *mine*!" This is not a man expecting to die anytime soon. His feet are deliberately robotic: crunch, crunch, crunch, crunch in the whitening shale.

I step even closer until my right foot is falling by his left, and my left by his right.

"Link to the field! Imagine, imagine. Dive into your belly. Imagine a single body cell. It starts to radiate warmth. Then the next cell starts to glow. And the next and the next and the next until there's a whole chunk of your belly starting to glow red. You can't feel the warmth yet, don't rush it, just imagine that the glow is spreading, slowly reaching out towards your limbs. Imagine, imagine, imagine."

My throat is raw. The effort has been so costly, hot moisture springs into my eyes and starts to freeze.

The slope sits up as we begin the last climb to the pass. To keep the rhythm, we take shorter steps. We're in muffled lockstep now, the snow already ankle-deep. My muscles wrench on every swing of the leg, but I remove myself from their complaints until they whimper in empty spaces. The snow muffles the beat, but the metronome clicks on, crunch, crunch, crunch, crunch, whack, tock, tick, tock, whack, tock, tick, tock. *Thank you Mother, for this act of love.*

The temperature drops again. No more sleet now, just the snow taking over, rushing devils, carving out a white, malicious universe with their horns. Ahead of me, Matthew hesitates. I hear an exclamation and scream at him not to rush into the crucial next step. "Delay the passion, hold it back a little longer. Strengthen the link. Just imagine the glow, spreading, spreading, spreading out through your limbs and outwards towards the surface of your skin. Don't rush it. Imagine, imagine, imagine!"

The slope starts to flatten. The pass is only quarter of an hour away, and when we reach the top we'll be fully exposed.

Matthew pulls fists out of his pockets and punches the air, then glances back, eyes glittering. Time, Rumplestiltskin. Let sleepers awake and spinning wheels spin and wands work their magic.

I grasp his arm and haul him round to me, then slap him hard across the face.

He gasps, stumbles backwards against the wind, shocked, staring. I leap forward until our faces are separated by no more than a hand's width, so close that I can drop my voice below a scream.

"It's time to grow up, boyo. Time to reach into the core.

Focus the passion! You know what to do. Now, get back into your belly and light the goddamn fire!"

Immediately, he's striding ahead, outpacing me once again. In less than a minute I hear a long drawn-out howl of triumph, which tracks across my chest, tingling on the back of my head and neck and down my spine.

It's done.

But I'm cold, so cold. There is ice in my chest. I no longer have the will to do what Matthew has done. My calves and thighs are trembling. Fatigue has cast a cilice of hooks into my flesh, dragging every body cell down. But it's more than fatigue; it's uneasiness. It grows in my stomach, until it seems that I *am* the unease, held in the stomach of the beast—which is very, very close now. I look behind without altering my pace. Nothing but the streaming white curtain.

I'm near the top, where the blizzard funnels its greatest fury through the throat of the pass. My march is reduced to a stumble and I'm pushing hard to move forward at all. Somewhere in a far meadow, alpacas are alarmed, heads up, looking in my direction. They know. My thoughts are running wild, like unbroken horses, bucking after I have been thrown from their backs. My mind wants to run and hide from itself, but I must use it to keep my body moving forward. Keep moving. This foot, this foot, this foot, this foot, glance behind. This foot, this foot, this foot, this foot, glance behind.

Then I know that the beast is not behind me at all. It's ahead.

And there it is, a few steps away, the hole in the universe is waiting for me on the edge of the track. Now there can be no escape. *It's not fair. It's too soon. I need more time.* I'm gasping for breath. My heart is racing, surging in my chest, booming and rushing so loudly in my ears that the beast can't hear me. *I must have more time.*

As we close, the black beast takes definite shape. It develops four legs and a head and becomes a wolf with lolling tongue and grinning teeth. I'm not fooled for one moment, I know what this is. This is Matthew's wolf from the Andes, the one that was discouraged by a meal that throws stones in the dark with stunning accuracy. Now, it lopes up close and speaks to me, urging me.

"Remember," it pants.

"I will," I reply.

The wolf stands on its hind legs and turns into Mother... no, I am confused, it is Matthew's mother... in her smartest floral dress and her velvet hat with the peacock feather. And now I am taking my very first steps, charged with certainty and exhilaration and triumph. This step, and this one, counting, shouting the numbers out loud.

"Un, two, tree, faw..."

Mother puts her hands on her hips, smiling approval and satisfaction.

"Herbert? Herbert! Come here. Look at this boy." She pulls open a notebook, extracting a sharp lead pencil from the spine. She makes a note, then looks at me, drills me with her eyes.

"Remember," she says.

"I will," I promise.

Un, two, tree, faw...

Now she has turned into Father, who drops to one knee and spreads his arms. "Oh you dear, clever boy. I'm so proud of you, son. Walk to me, that's it, you walk right over here to Father for a great big hug."

Un, two, tree, faw...

But I pass by him and his eyes fill with sorrow.

"Remember," he says.

"I will," I assure him, though he is already behind me.

Then I'm alone again, but to my amazement, against the escalating assault of wind from the front, I'm speeding up. I look down at my legs. My knees are bending more vigorously, my feet lifting and falling of their own accord.

A blurred figure appears, straight ahead, like a pencil-rubbing on streaky paper, moving about erratically.

Matthew has made it. He's reached the top of the pass.

Here, high on a mountain pass in a full blizzard, he is deliriously happy. Feet planted wide, square on to the elemental gods and he's laughing, inviting them to do their worst. Which they are, and he is loving every moment. He spreads his arms and roars into the wind, a drawn out bellow of accomplishment. He is steaming, his bare hands and fingers pink, face glowing, his aura brilliant around him. He radiates a lightness of being, as if some fool had switched off gravity and made him float. He breaks into scraps of songs, *Black Matai* and *Henry Martin*, musical phrases snatching erratically at my ears. He is like an irrepressible boy, dashing here and there in the storm, leaping from rock to rock, laughing, shouting. He throws stones upwind, he unzips and urinates downwind. A gust knocks him over and he farts so loudly I can hear it. He gets up, but is rendered helpless by laughter and the wind fells him again.

I'm not sure where I am, geographically, in relation to this performance. Am I in front of him? Behind? North or south of him? It seems important to know where I am before he sees me.

He sees me, turns to face me.

I can't say who moves first. One moment we are still, the next we're walking towards each other and when we meet, we embrace fiercely, competing to reach each other's ears, shouting and listening, shouting and listening, exchanging scraps of thought and word that make us laugh and sob with relief.

Then we're observing us from a distance, from somewhere back in the blizzard, almost as if we were watching a movie of us.

NINE

If I open the eyes, I will have to own the rest of the body, which promises to be a sheath of pain. It would be easy to remain afloat here in this netherworld, where nothing needs anything, where there is nothing to achieve or control, nothing to run from, no void to fill. And yet I do feel drawn back to the fleshly prison. No, I *want* to go back, one more time, though I cannot think why; the field has, after all, already had its way, having used me just as much as I have used it.

But perhaps there is a detail I have overlooked.

Eyes open.

I'm on top of the bed. The body feels both familiar and strange. The pain, it turns out, is surprisingly tolerable, but the flesh is leaden and the limbs warn that they will resist.

Weak sunlight loiters on the wall, a rhombus the colour of blended whisky. It nudges a corner in the ceiling, pushing at spider lace which stretches out perfect hyperbolae in three dimensions, speckled by husks of spiders and spider meals past. The wallpaper is peppered with fly spots, and has curled back from the seams like crusted lilies, leaving triangles of grimy plaster. This is my room, yet it feels like that of a stranger I used to know.

Except for boots, my body is fully clothed, dressed for the great outdoors.

My joints protest like rusty gates. By who's permission do I order them about? I force my legs out onto the floor and sit up. I'm breathing hard, steadying myself with hands to the bed.

My knees are strangely elevated. I lean forward for the cause and discover that my feet are not on the floor after all; they're resting on a tiny suitcase, old, with high-quality leather and metal studs on the corners. The label says *Conrad Fleming*, and the name is no longer empty, of course. *The vacancy is filled.*

I lift my feet away to one side.

There are my boots. This same pair has taken me around the farm and the mountains and valleys for years. Every wrinkle is moulded to my feet, texture and weight and smell as familiar as my own skin; but in putting them on, I feel like a thief in the night. I push the right foot in and rest, panting; now the left, with more panting, then I do up the laces. I recall one of Father's better jokes, that you know you're old when you do up your shoes and while you're down there you look around to see what else you can usefully do. I snort with amusement and the air from my nostrils blows fluff from my knee and down onto the suitcase. All around, there's dust, thick as cardboard.

While I'm down there, it seems useful to lift the suitcase up onto the bed beside me. I'm not sure why I bother, because the only surprises inside will be in the detail.

It takes forever to open it because my fingers are clumsy, also because the straps have been shaped by the buckles and dried in place for more than thirty years. The tarnished catches resist briefly, then snap back, one of them breaking off and falling into the deep dust with almost no noise.

Photographs and newspaper articles—all of them loose as if they had been collected hurriedly and thrown in. Almost all are black-and-white. There I am, perhaps only hours after my birth, with a new baby's old-man wrinkles; only my face is visible, the rest of me wrapped in enough swaddling to suffocate a horse. And here, in this one, I'm little more than a dot in a pram that's all wheels and springs. And here, yawning hugely at Mother, who looks as if someone placed me in her arm by mistake. Here, I'm a toddler, hand in hand with pin-striped Father. Here I'm in front of the school gates, first day, socks high and wrinkle-free, hair creamed and parted in the centre.

Here, smiling stiffly in front of a cabinet stuffed with silver cups, ribbons and certificates. Here, I'm shaking the hand of a black-gowned headmaster. Here, I'm playing the original home piano, with blank face and perfect posture. Mother is behind me in her best floral dress, chin up, competent, in charge. The metronome is frozen between vertical and horizontal and Mr Whippy is the thinnest of shadows between piano and wall.

And here are breathless Christian periodicals, always with a photograph. *Herbert and May Fleming, with their genius son Conrad, talking to thrilled audiences about the Progenesis Project, the Creation of Genius.* Most of the shots were taken on a stage or platform, with me at the piano or the microphone.

Then, at the bottom of the suitcase, I find a large envelope. Inside, there's a bundle of articles cut from daily newspapers, all dated in the winter of '74. The paper is stiff and yellowed, the printing faded, and the rubber band that once held it all together has become sepia-coloured crumbs in the corner of the envelope.

Every article talks about the boy wonder now wanted for questioning about his father's death. One weekend scandal rag, Truth, had unearthed a photograph taken a decade and a half earlier: in it, I'm graduating, with mortar board and gown, my teenage visage filling half the front page. At the foot of the photograph, the article repeats the original legend from 1957. *Christchurch teenage genius achieves physics-biochemistry double degree at 16.* Over the top, in lettering suitable for the outbreak of war, is the banner headline *Is this the face of a killer?* The writer was one Max Skinner.

Did child prodigy kill his father?

Armed police are hunting the Southern Alps east of Hokitika for Conrad Fleming, 33. He is wanted for questioning in connection with the death of his father, who was found lying on his bed, clothes soaked in unlit petrol, with a matchbox and a spent match close by. On the evening before the discovery of the body, Fleming was seen standing outside his father's house, holding a petrol can.

He is armed with a high powered rifle and is an experienced hunter. Police say he is mentally unstable, and should be treated as highly dangerous. Anyone seeing him should keep well clear and call the authorities immediately.

By any measure, Fleming's history is remarkable.

His parents, Herbert and May, were national figures, celebrated for their theories on raising babies to be super intelligent. His mother's book, The Creation of Genius: how to turn your child into a prodigy, *became an international best-seller when Conrad's academic brilliance became obvious.*

At 12, he passed university entrance exams, a national record which has not been equalled since. However, no university would enrol him at that age, an outcome his parents fought bitterly and publicly for the next three years. He remained at Christchurch Boys' High School, where, in his thirteenth year, he was encouraged to sit the senior scholarship exams and stunned the school community by winning every available prize.

But it was his unofficial activities that turned his fame into notoriety.

Ex-pupils have told me that at the age of 13, Fleming engineered a school riot. He picked the lock of the glass-fronted school notice board and posted five large photographs. Each showed a different boy's bottom after a brutal caning, each with blood running down the buttocks and legs. A mob of boys formed in front of the notice board then ran through the school smashing furniture and destroying equipment.

Fleming sent copies to the education authorities.

The city's photographic development labs emphatically denied printing the shots, pointing out that it was against the law for them to print 'indecent' photographs. Fleming was known to have amateur developing equipment at home, but nothing was ever proved. It was considered impractical to identify the caned boys by inspecting their buttocks, so there was no one to interrogate about the identity of the photographer.

Nationwide outrage over the savagery depicted by the photos led to a commission of inquiry, and within a year the legal limit for the number of strokes of the cane was lowered to six, with restrictions placed on cane thickness.

Sources tell us that Fleming was also responsible for the public humiliation of a school physical education instructor. The instructor, known particularly to the junior forms as 'Fingers', found a crowd of pupils around his vehicle, laughing at photographs glued to every available surface. The shots were all of small boys, many of them known to the pupils around the car. No photo was indecent, but en masse, the implication was clearly something that cannot be spelled out by a responsible newspaper. The teacher drove away and never returned. Again, Fleming's involvement was never proved.

At 15 he enrolled at Canterbury University.

His double degree followed within two years. At nineteen he was well into doctoral studies, researching the bio-chemistry of the brain and experimenting with electroencephalography. When he also excelled at rugby and cricket, commentators began tipping him to become the nation's youngest ever Rhodes Scholar.

However, at 20, he suffered a severe mental breakdown, extinguishing a career with glittering promise.

He ran amok driving on the highway between Christchurch and the West Coast, crashing into and destroying a police car, and forcing all other vehicles off the road. He was apprehended on a one-way bridge near Arthur's Pass, then committed to a secure unit in Christchurch's Sunnyside Hospital.

Even there, he soon showed an extraordinary talent for disrupting the established order.

Ex-patients say that in spite of his youth, Fleming successfully posed as a psychiatrist. He introduced himself to new patients as Dr Matthew Smith, and conducted interviews with them in unoccupied offices. The offices were always locked, but Fleming had somehow obtained keys and used them as if the offices were his own. Subsequently, those patients would ask for him again, some refusing to speak to genuine psychiatrists. His reputation spread swiftly amongst patients and even after he was exposed as a fraud, patients were asking to speak to the 'new young doctor'.

Hospital spokesman Dr Robert Schneidemann told me the story was apocryphal—an amusing fabrication that has grown with each telling. He also told me it would be the height of irresponsibility to publish it because it would undermine confidence in the mental health system and jeopardise the care of future patients.'

When I suggested that Fleming's departure was embarrassingly swift for a committed patient—more like an eviction than a discharge—Dr Schneidemann became impatient. When I requested the original records, he answered that they had gone missing some years earlier. When I commented on how convenient that must be, he accused me of muck-raking, suggested I consider an antonym as a new name for this publication, and disconnected the call.

Truth magazine will bring the truth to its readers no matter how inconvenient it might be to those who would hide it.

On your feet boyo.

I stand, swaying, then steady. The pain is lifting, but the muscles are reluctant. This bag of sinew and bones seems to have forgotten how to walk and must be coaxed along.

I leave the suitcase open and shuffle into the corridor. I pass the guest bedroom, where the quilt is still undisturbed, the towel and facecloth still placed diagonally on the end, all now under dust. The thick grey carpet has smothered the colours in the room and the still life on the wall has faded into its own background.

I glance back towards my bedroom, but beyond that doorway there is only a fog-like haze. I rub my eyes, almost falling over with the effort, but the fog remains and I can't even see the bed, let alone the suitcase. Fog, in which nothing moves, from which nothing comes.

So I move through to the living room, past the shelves and the grandfather clock. The fog treads on my heels and spreads, hiding things. I can't see the piano, or the fireplace, or the clipper ship painting. The phone rings, just once, but I can't see where it is.

A black fantail flips and cavorts in front of me. Inside.
I know, I know. I'm coming.
All I can see now is the doorway, dazzlingly bright.
Boa? Where are you? I can't see you. Boa.

As I walk towards the door, I can't hear the familiar creak of floorboards, but I don't look down.

On the porch, it's much easier to see things. There's no fog anywhere. Ringa Pass is solid white, the peak above it caught with the evidence—a hand dipped in vanilla ice cream. The storm has left see-forever skies and white pasture. The alpacas mill by the nearest fences. On the snow just in front of me, Rangi and Papa are quarrelling, each using wings to buffet the other's head, then hopping sideways under the return assault.

Boa occupies my deck chair, waiting for me. *Mine,* she says. *Back off or suffer the consequences.*

I rock the chair, so she stands on the canvas, hissing and lunging. I hiss and lunge in return, but so feebly, she thinks she has won. I summon energy and lift the chair from behind and turn it into a vessel on a choppy sea. After one poorly aimed slash over the back rest, she concedes. She scrambles off and stalks away past the wisteria and around the corner, her back eloquent: *Don't think this is the end of the matter, buster.*

As I tread out onto the snow, Rangi and Papa accommodate me by skipping sideways, immediately resuming their tiff. I watch them fondly, but keep on towards the alpacas. The air is invigorating. The very last pain in my muscles drops away. An electricity replaces it, a current which runs through me, pulling at me, wanting me.

I know, I know. I'm coming, Siobhan, I'm coming. And I feel very, very good.

The alpacas crowd the fence frantically to say goodbye. I call Mikey and he is brave enough now to leave his mother's side and approach me on his own. I lean over and tickle him under the chin, until his front knees buckle. But when I stand to give them all a final farewell, they're not there any more. I'm only waving at snow. No fence, no hayshed. No house or henhouse or barn, or glasshouse or garden. All of it gone.

So I turn, finally, towards the reservoir. The snow is lumpy now, made so by all the tussock beneath. But I don't stumble, or sink in. I am exquisitely light as I leave the snow and cross the reservoir and come to the sun-drenched blarney rock.

Effortlessly, I reach the top and sit next to the being who once went by the name of Siobhan.

I reach out to her hand and she doesn't move it away. I touch it, I press it, I hold it and stare at it with inexpressible pleasure. I raise it to my lips and kiss it. I remark that it is a very fine hand and I believe it must belong to someone supremely beautiful; would she happen to know the owner? She replies that she knows the owner very well. And furthermore the owner has always held my opinions in the highest regard and her pa has completely changed his mind about me.

We marvel at how the valley looks, like a too-perfect chocolate box, sparkling, unspoiled. From the highest ridge all the way down to the rock, it's a clean white sweep, cleft only by the stream, bounded on both sides by virgin bush. On all of the snow there is not so much as a single footprint. It is as it was on the first day I came here, thirty-seven years ago.

Ah, there's Matthew—over by the trees above the stream. He's beside his tent, sitting on a log by the campfire. When the billy boils, steam billowing, lid clattering, he crouches forward, pulls down his sleeve to hold the handle and pours water into a mug to make tea. He stirs in milk powder and sugar, then sits back, watching Rangi and Papa dispute ownership of a nest of huhu grubs.

I speak to Siobhan. "About that answer you promised."

"And here's me thinking you would never ask," she says. "But here's the thing, Jack; the answer is another question.

I roll my eyes at the infinite sky. "Why am I not surprised?"

"It's the first question and the last," she says. "It's the only question. It gave birth to the stars and the planets and the earth and to every human being. Here it is: the answer to life, the universe and everything is the question *What am I?*"

A random bubble rises in the reservoir water. It's deep down, a smidgeon of silver, pulsating upwards, growing larger near the surface.

"I want another divorce," I say.

"I'll be sure to look into it," she replies.

A large party of hikers comes off the track on the north side of the valley. All are in oil skins, japara overtrousers and puttees, all looking the worse for wear, caught out and delayed by the unheralded storm. A map appears from one of the packs, generates a bad-tempered argument, then disappears. The group heads across the valley towards Matthew. When he sees them he moves abruptly towards his tent, but hesitates, then returns to his log seat. He doesn't stand to greet them, but when the hikers thrust their map in front of him he jerks his head downhill and says something that causes them to shout with relief and punch the air with their fists.

Though he has not made them welcome, they lower their canvas packs and rest. A few pull out what little food they have left, crackers, sugar, tea leaves, most of it in aluminium screw cap containers.

A woman with glossy, black hair asks Matthew if they can top up his hot water to make their own tea. He shrugs, indifferently. They gather wood and build the flames. The group, out of politeness, address comments or questions to him now and then, but he is unresponsive, so their attempts tail off.

Suddenly, he pulls food out of the tent—bags, tins, and several packets of dried meat stew—and hands it around, ignoring their protests. Some of them exchange glances, registering that there is something odd about this character. Even so, they accept the gift gladly and one of them quickly empties all of the stew packets into one of their own billies. In half an hour the aromas have them groaning, then they eat with the worshipful appreciation so well known to exhausted hikers. They have cooked far too much, but it doesn't matter now; they will be back in civilization before nightfall.

The black haired woman is nearest Matthew on the log. When she refills her mug, she does the same with his, and he accepts it without a word. His face is expressionless, but when she glimpses his eyes, she imagines a hurt animal dragging itself through the bush, wounded but dangerous. She is intrigued by him. She would like to engage him in conversation, but doesn't know how.

Then she spots the rifle in the tent and asks about it.

He shakes his head, but she persists. He turns to rebuke her, but no words emerge. Instead, he shrugs, brings out his rifle and hands it to her. She hands it back and asks more, so he works a round into the chamber, explains quickly, then lays the weapon aside, across a tree root in the moss behind the fire.

Still she does not let him go and asks about the terrain, because she suspects he knows it well.

So he warms a little, pointing out various features on and below the skyline, from Ringa Mountain to the north, around to other peaks south and south-west. Now and then he volunteers information before she asks anything. She listens closely, following his gaze, occasionally stealing a sideways glance.

He steals his own glances, but they never coincide.

The group prepares to leave. They clank containers, wash plates and mugs in the stream, work liniment into limbs, tighten bootlaces and puttees, close packs, doing as much as possible while sitting.

They sling packs with theatrical moans of dismay. The woman is slower than the others, last to swing her pack, last to snug the straps. She isn't talking or clowning like the others, just frowning at the snow around her feet.

One more push, the hikers say to each other. One more push, then it's home-cooked meals, hot baths, real beds with soft pillows, sleeping in until the sun is high, calling bosses to say they were delayed by bad weather. As they imagine these delights, their bodies warm with pleasure and the complaints die away. There's a chorus of polite thanks to Matthew and two men extend their hands to him. He looks at the hands, then, slowly, allows his own to be shaken. Between shakes he glances at the woman, and this time their glances coincide.

The hikers walk away, down towards the stream, the woman last to leave. Matthew rises and moves a couple of steps after them, hand bent at the wrist as if he would like to raise it. As the first in the group splash through the bustling water, the woman lags behind, walking more and more slowly until she stops in her own tracks on the near bank. She looks into the water as if searching for something in the submerged pebbles, then turns and stares at Matthew who is already staring at her.

She returns, plants herself squarely in front of him, hands on hips, head tilted to one side. She's trembling slightly and so is he. They gaze at each other in silent appraisal.

One by one, the other hikers realize that something significant is happening behind them. They turn and gape, from the opposite bank, while a fresh breeze rolls up the valley from the plains, raising goose-bumps, stirring clothes, attempting to lift hats from heads.

On the far side of the farm, four armed men stand in the shadows of the trees, intent on Matthew. They're in plain clothes, but their rifles, boots and haircuts are standard issue. Three look to the leader for orders, one of them pointing to the radio on his belt. But the leader motions them to stay still and quiet and all four focus intently on the scene unfolding before them. Before they can act, they must understand.

In front of Matthew, the woman moves abruptly. She drops her pack, takes two paces and turns to stand beside him. Then she waves regally, radiantly to the others. They're astonished, open-mouthed, then grinning. They return the waves vigorously, and walk away, hooting with delighted laughter and shouting back to her with ribald comments and gratuitous advice her mother never offered. So the young woman with the black hair and the gold locket and the *pounamu* jade eyes also laughs, with pleasure and with anticipation of whatever may lie ahead.

Rangi and Papa take full advantage of the unattended campsite, scratching and scraping for morsels. Papa tries to drag away a plate. Rangi pecks at the lid of the stew billy. Papa abandons the plate, stands on the rifle, walks up the stock, steps on the telescopic sight, and hops, finally, onto the trigger.

The bullet passes out of the barrel, through the billy and its remaining contents, and travels on, its velocity greatly reduced. The sound of the shot echoes back and forth, crisp and sharp off the smooth surfaces of the valley. The woman gasps and spins around, shocked. Matthew stumbles slightly, half a step sideways, and stands, puzzled, raising his hand to the side of his head. The woman spins again, to look at him. As the last echoes die, he studies his hand, drops to his knees, then tips to one side. Fresh, bright blood flows out of a hole behind his right ear, down onto his neck, off his Adam's apple, and pools on the white snow.

Somewhere, a grandfather clock ticks on.

Afterword

The astronomer Arthur Eddington once said, 'The universe is not only stranger than we imagine, it is stranger than we can imagine.'

A central theme of *Finding the Field* is that we create our own reality, that what we think most frequently and most passionately is what the universe arranges around us. So for the last four years, I have written and thought exactly that, frequently and passionately. I have expressed my imaginings through two characters: a young man who comes down out of the mountains, and an old man, more than twice his age, who has discovered the ultimate Truth about life and the universe. The old man assumes, in the three months they are together, that the flow of Truth will be one-way, that he has nothing to learn from the young man.

He is wrong.

What I'm going to tell you now is not fiction. When I'm not writing, I work for a training and consultancy company in Christchurch, New Zealand. I was sitting at my office desk— this book almost complete— when the phone rang. A young male voice greeted me.

"Good morning, Michael. My name is Björn Hofmann. I am calling from Nepal."

I had no relatives in Nepal and had never received a call from that country. So the conversation advanced like this.

"You're calling from where?"

"Nepal."

"You mean Nepal with all the mountains?"

"Yes, with the mountains. And I want to work in your company."

At the time, I thought it no more than an amusing fluke. But then this remarkable young man did persuade our chief executive to take him on, and he did come to work with us. For three months. As it turned out, he was assigned mostly to me, to learn from my teaching experience in presentation and media skills. And since I was more than twice his age, I assumed that the flow of knowledge would be one-way, that I would have little to learn from him, especially with regard to what I teach.

I was wrong.

All of which tells me that the universe is *precisely* as strange as we imagine. No more, no less.

Thank you, Björn.

M.B.

Acknowledgements

I cannot express enough appreciation to my wife Sue, who edits my obsessions, not only with a sharp eye for consistency and detail, but also with an instinct for writing that works or does not work. She also keeps me anchored with variations on the question, "Yes, but what does that mean in practice?" If *Finding the Field* counts as accessible philosophy, then Sue deserves much of the credit.

And thank you to my wonderful sons Andrew and Sam, whose ears have been bent by "Dad's stuff" for most of their lives. Not that they just stood there and suffered it—they gave as good as they got and made me defend it. They're both streetwise, and they too have forced me to make my ideas more practical and relevant. Andrew, where would this book be without your knowledge and instinct for the web and the new publishing mind-set? Sam, thank you particularly for three words you said to me at the perfect time: "Dad, just understand." So I did, and now I do—which I know will only make sense to you and me.

Thank you to Sugu Pillay, first for her cultural perspective on the universal truths, but especially for her penetrating—and sometimes hair-raising—insights into the construction of the story. With one comment in particular, she made an extraordinary difference to this tale. Sugu, you know what I'm talking about. And yes, I do still want to talk to you.

Thank you to my brother Ralph for editing my first draft without mercy. To give this book to a card-carrying atheist is surely an act of faith, but then Ralph plays an accomplished devil's advocate. The debate continues.

My thanks to Linda Watts who was on the path when we met and already living many of the ideas. She brought a perspective that often gave me new ways to make the ideas understandable and relevant.

Many people have helped me, often more than they realize. I want to specially mention Shirley Watkins, Cynthia Spittal, Charles Shaw, Daffyd James, Ian Gill, Philippa Burns, and to Mary-Ann Robertson, who also told me to stop messing with her head.

Thank you also to Jason King from the Maori Studies department of Auckland University of Technology.

Thank you to David Graham of Vino Fino Wines, to Matthew Tipple of Gun City, to Dr Kai Fu of Christchurch Hospital. And to Greg and Rachael of Valley of Peace Alpaca stud farm, who took time to make sure that what I wrote about these beautiful creatures didn't stray too far from the facts.

Made in the USA
Columbia, SC
17 August 2018